Y0-DYF-916

our
used
book

local
author

GHOST RAIN

Best wishes —

Rebecca L. Durocco

The Last Coffin
the first Attorney General Kate Guesswine mystery!
ISBN: 0-595-19622-5

Mysteries by Rebecca Duckro:
The Last Coffin
Ghost Rain

Look for the third Attorney General Kate Guesswine mystery in which
Kate becomes embroiled within the chaotic world of looting and
smuggling antiquities! Murder, mayhem and romance are all around her!

duckro.com
rduckro@wcnet.org

GHOST RAIN

Rebecca S. Duckro

Experience an Authentic Psychic Connection!

iUniverse, Inc.
New York Lincoln Shanghai

GHOST RAIN
Experience an Authentic Psychic Connection!

Copyright © 2005 by Rebecca S. Duckro

All rights reserved. No part of this book may be used or reproduced by any means, graphic, electronic, or mechanical, including photocopying, recording, taping or by any information storage retrieval system without the written permission of the publisher except in the case of brief quotations embodied in critical articles and reviews.

iUniverse books may be ordered through booksellers or by contacting:

iUniverse
2021 Pine Lake Road, Suite 100
Lincoln, NE 68512
www.iuniverse.com
1-800-Authors (1-800-288-4677)

This book is a work of fiction. Names, characters, places, and incidents are products of the author's imagination or are used fictitiously. Any resemblance to actual events, locales, or persons, living or dead (unless otherwise stated), is coincidental.

ISBN-13: 978-0-595-37245-4 (pbk)
ISBN-13: 978-0-595-81642-2 (ebk)
ISBN-10: 0-595-37245-7 (pbk)
ISBN-10: 0-595-81642-8 (ebk)

Printed in the United States of America

Acknowledgments

Author's Notes:

Although this is a work of fiction, some of the events in *Ghost Rain* are based on a recorded conversation with internationally renowned intuitive specialist, Nancy P.Vann, Ph.D. A psychic with extraordinary intuitive skills, Vann is the Executive Director of Multi-Sensory, LLC, and a member of the Edgar Cayce Association for Research and Enlightenment, Inc. She holds a Life Guide Certification from SERCO. She has presented helpful information regarding a murder case to the Tampa, Florida Police Department, is an expert on channeling, energy systems and is a gifted medium who, because of this novel, has now become the first psychic literary consultant.

I also wish to thank the following for their encouragement and expertise: Sally Whalen, Joy Kantner, Judy Wical and Jan Woodend. Source of pertinent information: Judge James Bachman, Aromatherapist Jane Frye, Artist Joan McKee, Kerr Health House & Spa, Grand Rapids, Ohio, Special Agent Robert Hawk (Cleveland FBI), Bowling Green University Flight Instructor John Mexicott, and Mike Hodges, Airport Manager of Wood County Regional Airport Authority. Grounds for Thought coffee house, Tommy Perkins, manager of Shelter Cover Marina Ships Store and Santiago Heyo, owner of Java Joes, Hilton Head Island. Special thanks to Dr. Lucy Goodenday and Dr. Mary Ellen Clifford.

Posthumously, I say thank you to my dear cousin, Jay Springer, for his wonderful true tale about his personal encounter with Tennessee Williams, most of which I have adapted here.

Foreword

Clearwater, Florida, February 2003: Psychic Reading and *Ghost Rain*

As a testament to her skills, Dr. Vann held in her hand the pen that I was using to write my initial draft of *Ghost Rain,* and this became a symbol of a tibia and other victims' bones that are found off Dragon's Point in my novel. Astonishingly, her psychic reading of the killer and his activities presented much of the text that I had previously written, including data from my notes and what was yet to be put down on paper from my subconscious. It was completely accurate! Although in my novel there is no physical resemblance to Nancy Vann, and the inclusion of my own literary characters in the chapter focusing on Dr. Vann's reading is purely for fictional enhancement, the rest of the account as written in *Ghost Rain* is exactly as we recorded it and is presented with her permission.

Prologue

Ritual: any customary or formal repeated act or series of acts

At the stroke of midnight, the priest looks both alive and dead. His body like a puff of black smoke skirts the altar that someone once carved from a large boulder set between the sacred remains of two great cypresses. Spirits pour into his body. He speaks strange words learned long ago from other members of his South Carolina voodoo community.

The priest lights candles. To cleanse the nude body of a woman, he removes sheets the way one peels gauze from a wound and begins to pour 'kleren', the favorite rum of the spirits, rhythmically across her cool skin. Over and over he undulates above her, wondering when her life no longer was a sacred place, her destiny assured by the dubious choices made late at night while lingering in bars and on street corners.

Although it is common in death to hold a celebration of sort—to chant, to drink, to eat—the priest knows that no one will do so. To prevent anyone from ever practicing black magic on her bones long after life has ceased, he removes snippets of her hair and nails to burn.

The time is near. He takes his rattle, a large pod of dried seeds. Clattering resonates above the dying woman. Amid the chants, her body shakes violently. She struggles upward, hesitates and collapses. Then he reaches for the knife with the handle like a long black viper. Death begins to flow. By now he knows what parts of her body he will share with the living to redeem the misdeeds of the woman. He smiles for he knows that there will be others.

CHAPTER I

As I crossed the intracoastal and onto Hilton Head Island, I watched the last of the late afternoon fog drag upward and dissipate above the yaupon holly that lay like scattered warts across the marshes. Slabs of rain shifted over my windshield, making taillights nearly invisible and almost bringing traffic to a halt, so it was no surprise when the meteorologist on my satellite radio declared that the October storm, which had been forecast to pass to the east, was clipping the coast instead. I was sure that the tourists, who had been squatting against the cool sand earlier in the day, were scurrying for the embrace of the many restaurateurs along Route 278 to get out of the bad weather.

The past months and a week without sunshine had left me sullen and dispirited. Under ordinary circumstances I wouldn't have regretted accepting Judge Allison Thomason's invitation to vacation at her family's inn on Renaurd Island, but already the social interaction to be required by such an acceptance was beginning to depress me. At any rate, catching the last ferry wasn't the only thing that was on my mind.

As the attorney general of South Carolina, it had more to do with the eleven unsolved Beaufort County police files on the seat next to me, cases which contained a compilation of notes and grisly pictures of bones found off Singleton Beach Road near Dragon's Point.

My cell phone rang. I slid on my earphones.

"Hey Katie Guesswine? That you?"

"None other," I said to Detective Justin McCreary. An obvious advantage of knowing a cop who happened many years before to have been my husband was that there was a bit of insider trading which sometimes went on between my office and his world of police work. If

I needed information, he dug it up. Yet, mostly he was like an arthritic knuckle that flared when you least expected it to. "So what's up?" I asked impatiently.

"Hey, are you on the island?" he asked, his words mingling with his police scanner.

"I'm headed to Renaurd Dock," I said. It was located at Folly Creek, an ocean inlet on Hilton Head's eastern shoreline.

"Hey listen, I got news that'll set you on your ass!"

"Mmm hmm. I'm already there, thank you."

"I'll catch up with you."

"Better hurry. I'm going over to the inn."

"Don't you leave until I've talked to you!" he ordered and hung up.

But by the time I reached the dock, Justin hadn't arrived, and I parked my Explorer in a gated holding area. From the distance I saw no one except a man sprinting near the bow of the leftover Chesapeake sailing craft, which had been converted into a sixty-five foot ferry. When he saw me, he made no gesture for me to come aboard, no thrust of hand, any turn of head, his attention elsewhere. I stumbled up a narrow plank with only one rail-rope to the deck.

"Look out!" he yelled.

I hadn't seen the rogue wave coming. I slid onto my knees, my eyes drifting up to a blue skullcap that captured nearly all but a gray banner of hair over the shelf of forehead that I suspected had been leathered by years of Atlantic wind. Teeth looked like tiny stalactites between his mustache and beard. He reached down, locked powerful arms around my waist and yanked me up, his trim body still towering above me.

"Whew. Thanks!" I said, thinking about the barnacles on the retaining wall that would have torn me to shreds had I gone into the sea. I proffered my hand.

"I'm Captain Coneras," he murmured. "I've seen you on the news. You look 'bout the same."

Intermittent rain lashed me. I wiped my face with my sleeve. "Well, these past months have added a few strands of white to the ole' auburn," I said and smiled, remembering that I had become somewhat of a celebrity because of serial killer Cole Barnett. "Say, aren't there craft warnings?"

Coneras's right hand knuckled against the wind. "I've taken this ole' sturgeon across this end of Port Royal Sound in far worse weather, if that's what you're askin'!"

Although I reminded myself that I had lived all my life near the water and learned to trust those who made a living by it, there was one childhood tale that still brought doubt about the safety of the sea. First, a nor'easter would sneak into the night and scoop up the water into vast clouds. There would be calm. And then the storm would strike over and over like a dagger, dragging nearby vessels into the graves of hell. *Ghost Rain*, that's what the old sailors called it, its credence proved by the dozens of sunken derelicts off the coast of South Carolina. And I remembered hearing that like the Ghost Rain, life could pluck you up and smash you to the bottom if you didn't heed its warnings, too.

"Ever since the Judge found out you were finally coming for a visit," Coneras continued, under what I thought was a touch of whiskey breath, "well, she's been a fussing up the inn; Holden and Barclay Renaurd, too! Warning us to make you feel like you was one of the family! For days now, know what I mean?"

Remarkable friendships have a way of presenting as if no lapse in time has occurred. It had been years since I worked on Allison's campaign when she was running as the first Black woman judge in South Carolina; yet, at an impromptu lunch or coffee, we could drone about the public interest, newspaper editorials, the legislature—and because of the recent attacks on judges—the lack of protection for public officials. In some ways, Judge Allison Thomason was my mentor, and I respected her more than anyone I knew.

Suddenly, the rain ceased, but the wind picked up. Coneras told me to hold on to a tightened down rope that was playing a tug of war between the stanchions and iron post connected to the deck ridge, and then he mechanically busied himself with other ropes and pulleys. But I longed for the security of the dock and a time when there had been calmer mornings in the sound, and currents sliding parallel to the coast sculpted tidal pools that trapped tiny marine life, their delicate bodies a cache of food for seabirds, the sun and the brine bleaching their skeletons to wash them back into the sea.

Before long a trim woman coated in dark green tweed to her ankles, and whose face was away from me, swept by and disappeared inside the deck cabin. Then I turned to see Justin McCreary's new truck shredding the gravel in the parking lot. Two gulls landed in front of his bumper, and an updraft of wind sucked their tail feathers like a vacuum cleaner. By the time they moved, Justin was sprinting three planks at a time, his over six-foot frame coming to a halt in front of me. He wasn't soap opera handsome. But his dark hair, charging eyes, and straight nose gave him that rugged outdoor look. A man's man, as they say, although he sometimes behaved more like an adolescent. And I was sure that the perfect cleft in his chin was the one feature that still turned a woman's head. *It had once turned mine.* Now I felt a rush of resentment whenever Detective Justin McCreary commandeered my time.

"Hey, Katie, how goes it?" he asked. In a bold move, he kissed my cheek, something he no longer had a right to do. I had learned to choose my battles. I simply moved inches away.

"So why are you here?" I demanded.

He hesitated and took me by the shoulders. "Bad news…" he began, "we think we've found Jennifer Renaurd's remains…" and then he paused and put his hand on my shoulder, "…over at Dragon's Point!"

As if on cue, as if bad news had some great power over the weather, the rain began to sprinkle again, and the wind gusted so hard that we gripped the rail ropes to keep from being swept off balance. The news was almost too much for me to hear, and after clearing my thoughts, I blurted out, "No—you can't be serious!"

Justin let go of the rope with his other hand, and drew me briefly into his arms. "I'm sorry," he whispered. "You know the case, of course. Jennifer was wearing an ankle bracelet when she disappeared. So yesterday, well off the beach beyond the tree line, this guy with a metal detector pulls up a tibia with links of 14 carat gold embedded in it. You can bet your ass he wishes he'd stuck to pop tabs!"

"You haven't told Allison? Or Holden and Barclay?" I asked. I thought of the newspapers, and when the news broke how they would dig up every bit of information possible about this Southern aristocratic family.

He shook his head. "Not yet. We're still looking for the rest of the bones. It's a case that's always bothered me,"—he pointed to his head— "her being a rich teen from prominent white family. And those so-called brothers of hers. One a prick US senator. The other with a rap sheet long enough to paper all of Hilton Head. Your buddy Allison's the only one worth her salt."

I looked him straight in the eye. Sometimes I was curious about his need to put others down. A salacious comment here, a raucous laugh there. It was worse since our divorce and often aimed at those I cared about. "Holden has a long and distinguished career in the Senate," I said with a reprimanding tone. "And Barclay's been in no trouble for years and you know it! He manages the inn. Does a good job at it."

"Shit Katie, you know what I mean," he said.

He was too late to exercise tact, and I thought but didn't say: Allison had lived and worked at the inn since she was twelve, (although she now owned a condo at Port Royal Plantation on Hilton Head Island, a place she sometimes stayed when she had to catch up on judicial work or the weather was too bad for the ferry to go over to the inn). The Renaurd family was to be commended for having years before paid her way through law school, and no one was surprised when she inherited a third of the inn and island from Leighton Renaurd when he died…not even his sons, Holden or Barclay. They were pleased to call her 'sister'; it was never an issue that she was black and not 'blood' related.

I decided not to fan Justin's nasty diatribe about the Renaurds—it was like arguing with a brick—so I pointed out that, "Something about this case simply doesn't play right. I haven't read the details in awhile, so correct me if I'm wrong, but wasn't Jennifer almost fifteen when she disappeared eighteen years ago? Yet, the other victims were killed within the last few years. And they were much older, too."

"It's like lancing a goddamn boil," he said swabbing his dark hair with cupped hands. His eyes were intense. "All these years the Renaurds believing that their sister was abducted. And you know that Jennifer's been in the database at NCMEC for years."

"National Center for Missing and Exploited Children…"

"Yep. In fact, a few months ago, just out of curiosity, I consulted that Model Age Progression site you set up at the state crime bureau."

"Who did your work?"

"Helene Troutman, the specialist who came over to you from the Louisiana MAP," he said. "The chub hub with pecks like a guy."

"Don't start!" I growled. As I held his gaze with my scorn, he knew that I meant it. Helen was a tall, large-boned woman whose daily work-outs at the gym, along with her black, bushy brows and mat of black hair made her look like a hippie body builder. But to know her fine smile and fine eyes was to appreciate her lightheartedness and humor.

The wind came back hard again. It was difficult to tell the direction. Briefly Coneras disappeared into the cabin, and I watched as the water pushed, pulled, rose up and down like mini tornados, and then died as it skipped across the skin of the deck. I gathered my ruana shawl tightly around my neck, burying my hair against my shoulders. A van passed by, backed up, and went forward before disappearing down the road. It was strange, I thought, but then I reasoned that someone was simply lost.

"But here's the wrap," Justin said. "I always believed that Jennifer split with some dude, pumped his well dry, and then came back here to live. He followed her. For whatever reason doused her light and dumped her at Dragon's Point all those years ago."

Quickly, I referred to a list of mental notes and said, "Near the groin that the Office of Ocean and Coastal Resource Management gave a permit for a few years ago. The one which many people now want demolished." I recalled litigation that had come across my desk in Columbia from several groups who had opposed its construction, a pile of stone running perpendicular to the coast that allows sand to get trapped and replenish a beach. People living to the south of the groin often complain of the erosion to their beaches because the sand trapped to the north wouldn't reach them.

Justin clicked his fingers. "Maybe the digging dislodged her. No trail mix to find."

"Do I need the embellished graphics?" I asked. "But other than where she was found, what possibly could connect her remains with those belonging to the other women?"

He used his sleeve to pat rain off his face. "That's what I've been trying to tell you. They all have the same striation cuts on them!"

"I'd like to see the forensic reports myself," I said sternly.

He cleared his throat. "Okay Attorney General, you'll get them tomorrow."

"That wasn't an official order."

"I'm never sure about that," he said, raising his brows. "You'll tell Allison and the Renaurds then? And I'll come over to the inn tomorrow so they can positively identify the bracelet?"

We were both grave. "Mmm hmm. Yes. All right." And then with a sigh, I remembered that I was supposed to be on vacation, but as the bearer of bad news, I didn't want to go to Renaurd Inn. The concept of death and even those who had died or even those who were dying had never been alien to me until now, and the nagging loneliness of the last months made me want to avoid the isolation that death—real or perceived—brings. And now there was Jennifer…and selfishly, I wanted to be somewhere warm and to hear the peal of laughter.

I looked around. Everything bad about the weather had come back. There was an unrelenting rain, and overhead the black clouds hung like a sheath from which lightening serrated over and over.

"Listen Katie, I'm soaked through," Justin said. "I'm taking off."

"Yes, it feels colder. Go home," I said sympathetically. "Get some rest."

He shook my hand, held it too long. "Say, why Renaurd Inn? While your cottage is being renovated, why aren't you staying at your motorhome at Anchor Resorts?" he asked.

"Allison has been trying to get me to spend time with her at the inn for as long as I can remember. And I haven't had a vacation for a long time. Opportunity knocked."

"And knocked me off your doorstep," he said grinning.

He had given up his apartment and was living two streets from my Pace Arrow. "Go home to your Winnebago!" I said.

He turned away and bounded down the ramp to his truck. How vulnerable he seemed as he stood by the door and waved, his clothes soaked and disheveled, how alone. Even while I had been with David Smithe these past few years, Justin sometimes presented a playful, subtle hope about reconciliation. But I knew that it never would happen. While I thought that I had changed completely, I knew that little had changed about him since those days before our divorce. Professionally he was a good cop, one who went by the book, one who meticulously filled out forms and reports, his motivation to be the best, to be liked, propelling him quickly to detective on the Beaufort County police force. But off duty he still drank heavily; I knew that, too. Smoked cigars. And quarter to three in the morning was usually the clock he either went to bed by or got up to.

As he drove away, a sense of dread returned, and rather ashamedly, I was more miserable than I could recently remember. Suddenly Coneras swept by me and went ashore. He paced nervously about. In due time, he trotted behind a slowly moving van that took a long time coming to a stop. Was it the same one that I had seen earlier? Then he flipped open the back doors, and I saw a large metal drum like the ones that hold industrial solvents, but this one was riddled as if someone had used it for target practice. Quickly, the driver came around the side. Although his back was to me, he shifted his position, and I heard the remnants of what appeared to be an antagonistic conversation. Then the driver slammed the doors, crawled back into the front seat and wasted no time exiting the parking lot.

Coneras sprinted by me again, and I thought it very strange that he reeled abruptly—pausing as if he had forgotten something before saying with a little nervous twist at the corner of his mouth, "That was nothing! Nothing you need know about!" And then drawing back, he shielded his mouth with his hand to stifle further speech, turned on his heel and busied himself with the boat. As I headed to the cabin, I felt as if somehow I had been taken to the woodshed. Little did I know that my visit at Renaurd Inn would bring the emotional beating of my life.

CHAPTER 2

Cursing the wind, Coneras threw the lines ashore and folded away the ramp. I watched as the jerk into reverse presented a slight swag to leeward, and then we were away from the dock and quickly between stone jetties that like two fat arms embraced the sea.

Already I could feel the waves chafing the bottom as we skidded across their crests, and I thought of the catboat David Smithe and I had once owned. We would sail it along the coast on mild mornings, when only the shrimp boats were out and all was silent except for the high pitched kak-kak of the royal tern cruising at great heights above us. The boat had no rig and had a very used single cylinder engine that often died. He would say, 'All I have to do is turn her over once and she'll run,' and after a dozen or more tries and a little spitting on it, we'd laugh and then all he had to do was turn me over under the canvass. He could do that in an instant. My thinking about David was beginning to put me into a two-martini dinner mood.

The wind was increasing. "Please get inside," Coneras yelled to me. "It's too dangerous out here!"

"Mmm hmm. You're the captain!"

The pocket door slid easily. The cabin looked to be narrow and cramped, and with the touch of my finger, any wood, any trim that had not been dusted in a long time gave off puffs of gray. The linoleum floor was peppered with scraps of paper, petrified gum and dirt, and I had the urge to sanitize the area before I sat on one of the benches that lined the perimeter, but instead someone in the corner immediately distracted me. I thought it to be the woman I had seen come aboard earlier, a striking young woman, and I was to learn quickly that she was called Bina and that her family was descended from the first generation of slaves whom the Spanish had brought to America in 1680, a slave society that resembled the Caribbean culture of Jamaica, Barbados, Haiti and the Bahamas and whose drudgery was to clear most of the cypress swamps around the Lowcountry. She was Allison's secretary.

"You must be Kate Guesswine. I heard you were coming," she said in a soft voice. She tapped my arm. "The judge said that you're a VIP."

"Well, I'm simply a guest in need of some rest," I said. I couldn't imagine what PR job Allison had given everyone.

She looked at me long and hard. In spite of her quick smile and large black eyes that reminded me of a newborn calf, there was a dispirited way, and I had a sudden fear for her. Then I realized that my fear might be due to the figure looming beyond the door, someone who must have lingered unseen before I had arrived, a man whose body seemed to synchronize with the pitching of the boat. He came into our space and said nothing. He was a tall man whose skin stretched thinly across his bones, the back of his chicken-like neck fused with hair the color of old silvered wood, and with strands braided with slivers of starfish bones and shafts of crow feathers.

Her eyes widened after she saw him. "Dragon touchez-nous!" Bina said.

'Dragon touch us' was an easy French translation. "Mmm? Why did you say that?"

She shook her head. "Oh, but that's Zaccheas Bird," Bina whispered. She explained that his reputation was part of folklore that seemed to amuse the guests who came to Renaurd Inn for massages, facials and pitchers of sweet tea. Whenever he came fleetingly close to the veranda, everyone would set down his glass and race to snap his picture, its image seemingly eluding the film like the ghost deer does the hunter in the dense marshes of the north end of the island.

"Hello," I said to him. He didn't answer. As if to underline his mystique, there jingled unnaturally on his chest a large cache of small beads, animal incisors and what looked to be the dried eyes of long dead fish. And although the commotion of the sea was unbearable at times and the vessel rolled like an old fashioned crib hanging from a violent limb of wind, he didn't flex a muscle.

"Hello," I said again. Several waves shook the boat. I fell unintentionally into his arm, his skin like wet leather. That I should touch him brought no response either, but then I shuddered and fell quickly away from him almost as if he had commanded me to.

Mechanically, he retreated outside again, his eyes staring straight into the stinging rain without a blink as if they had the power of an umbrella. "Oh! You really mustn't speak to him," Bina insisted as she sucked in some air. "He considers it an insult."

I frowned.

"It's just the way it is," she continued. "He is highly revered!"

"By whom, may I ask?"

"A community that practices voodoo near here. The members are the Lakous."

"Oh? The Lakous?"

"Yes. Several families who support each other's needs," she said. "As the eldest, Zaccheas Bird sometimes visits them and they sit at his feet. Often, he doesn't eat for days. He sings. Rarely speaks. It seems that his extraordinary age—why, he could be more than a hundred—lets him walk in and out of the spiritual world as he pleases!"

"He's a voodoo priest then?" I asked.

"Goodness no! That person would be the 'oungan'. The current one is a very autonomous person," she explained. "And it's a bit of a problem, so I'm told. Only those closest to him know who he is. I've heard—and mind you, it's only hearsay—that he keeps his face covered during rituals and rarely shows up at social functions, often sending initiates instead. You know, beginners."

"Why would the 'oungan' do that?"

"Some believe he is quite prominent. Perhaps he only attends critical functions in order to keep his identity secret so as not to jeopardize his career. Like the rest of us, priests live in houses, eat and pay bills, too!"

Who are these people? I wondered. *Who are these millions of people who practice this strange religion of secrets?* As attorney general, I knew then that I needed to know more. I added it to my mental list of things to do.

As we crossed the open water between Gaskin and Joiner Banks, swells kept battering the boat, and I was worried that a rogue wave might capsize us, but to my relief, we soon careened by the calmer waters of the South Channel, into a brief expanse of the Atlantic toward the southeast approach to Renaurd Island. There it wound sharply through a marsh of waterlogged pine and oak whose roots were exposed by the ebbing tide, roots that were tangled together among vast spreading grape vines like the tentacles of a hundred octopi.

It seemed ominous that the only way to Renaurd Inn was this uninviting channel where the reeds and rushes hid the snakes and alligators, and osprey—or fish hawks as the locals call them—who on better days sunned themselves high above the cooter turtles who were doing the same on logs below. There were places that we passed, places that ambushed the senses and had the stench of too long settled water inside undisturbed tidal debris. For me the mud had always been an inoffensive odor, I supposed, one that instead had been bred from the familiarity of long gone storms and simmering days followed by bone chilling nights and more simmering days.

Soon the canal eased into a clover shaped lagoon divided by mudflats and limbs burdened with too much moss that swept the water like a street cleaner, and it was hard to believe that when the sun came out, the landscape could look inviting again, but it would, I knew, its legacy lingering in its soul the way mountains or valleys do—have a soul that is—for the people who are native to those areas.

"Have you ever seen anything like it?" Bina asked excitedly. "It's like a scary movie. And yet, I find this place so peaceful, like it might run right up to the Lord. See? A path to the Lord?"

"But I think Coneras simply has slowed down, and that's the wake from the boat," I answered. "Don't you think?"

"Now Holden wants to sell off parts of the island for a golf course and fancy condos," she explained.

Bina's words yanked the cord to my thoughts, and I repeated what Allison had told me when he had first mentioned it: 'Nonsense. It would take an earthquake, a hurricane *and* a volcano to get me to agree. I'd better be dead if he tries that…,' she said.

Bina and I went onto the outer deck and stood just beyond Zaccheas Bird. "Ever smoke mullet in wet leaves and drink ginger beer," she asked. "Did you ever chew tobacco?"

I laughed. "Not guilty! Did you?"

"Oh yes. And I ate a ton of raw oysters, too."

Half-consciously, other images languished in my mind, of how the oysters grew in Broad Creek on Hilton Head Island above the low water mark where there wasn't much salinity, where the tide gently forced the seawater through the oyster's gills. Bina's talk of oysters? I thought of the recent quagmire I had been in. Of a better day, a flame of a day, when David Smithe and I took the long three-pronged fork and picked dozens of oysters from their beds.

I remember:

…at the cottage where we sat on the reclaimed church pew on the front porch, and he whimsically told me, "Jonathan Swift said, 'He was a bold man that first eat an oyster,' so Kate, if you're going to shuck them, then you should know their history."

I remember:

…a glint in his eye, a soft whistle and his playful words, "In early spring the water turns to about seventy. A young oyster is called 'spat,' Kate. And spawning happens—ooh, boy does it happen. And no, I didn't say *spooning*! And the little critter, that spat, throws out a sticky substance that cements itself to some clean place. Sound familiar? That sticky substance? (Winks) A place for the shell to grow, which is called 'culch'. Others follow and soon there are clusters of oysters. Ooh, the taste of them all!"

I remember:

…that I marveled at what David Smithe knew, his mind like a lantern waving in the darkest of nights.

I remember:

…my life being in limbo ever since he had gone away. I wanted nothing more than to put the pain behind me, nothing so much as a good night's sleep and the relief of a clear mind.

Right then I wanted to stop thinking about it all, so I welcomed the slight bend of the land as the boat yawed right. Every so often we passed wooden pole lights, and if I shielded my eyes from the rain, I could see the remains of a road that ran along the shore, uneven and made of discarded mounds of shellfish and thousands of oyster shells that I suspected dated to before the Civil War. I wondered if the Indians or slaves had put them there. I had heard that Hurricane Hugo in 1998 had skirted the island and had carried a whole corner of a nearby graveyard into the shallow black water along the canal, the tides moving the bones back and forth across the sand like wandering ghosts.

Overcome with fatigue, the unpleasant pictures in my mind suddenly gave way to lightheartedness as we approached the far end of the lagoon, the wind hard now, the rain, too, and then just as suddenly as it had begun, the squall coasted into a soft intermittent shower. I had no other desire now except to get on land, happy when I looked beyond the mooring of two other boats to see Renaurd Inn, stately and somber under a thick brow of black clouds.

I had heard that the timber for the inn had been chosen long ago from black cypress that was now extinct, the planks having been carved with the songs of slaves filling the spring air, when wisteria and dogwood were in bloom, when the mansion sheltered the tyranny of a master. Even though it had been thrashed by hurricanes and war, I imagined that the inn hadn't changed much. In the wind I could almost hear the voices of the small boys and girls playing near its foundation of shell and limestone, the color of black and white meaningless as it often is to children not yet acquainted with the prejudices of the world.

As we glided under the large, low slung branches of a live oak, I was impressed by the wooden verandas that fronted the main house, its two stories flanked by Doric porticos and covered by a gable-roof. Noticeably, too, were the corner towers Allison had told me about, ones with thin narrow trapdoors that once had been used for powder magazines during the Civil War, and whether you liked old mansions or not, there was something comforting in their permanence, in fact, about the inn itself. I could imagine myself having lived in such a place, my body swaying to the spinet piano while I wore those wonderfully long gowns that ballooned similar to the ones worn by Scarlett O'Hara in *Gone with the Wind.*

My eyes were so filled with awe that I was startled when we hit the dock that jutted several feet from the riprap, a sloped seawall of stacked stones, probably old ship ballasts built to protect the bank from the eroding channel tides. Coneras jumped off and was tying the huge rope around a pole while Bina shot up nearby steps and out of sight. When I finally got my balance, Zaccheas Bird was no where to be found, and I could only think that this particular crossing from Hilton Head had been most unusual and unsettling, and I wished to remain not one instant longer near water.

"Hello Kate!" Judge Allison Thomason skidded off the last of very steep steps, the hem of her yellow rain slicker sweeping the mud next to a metal railing. Seeing her soothed my frayed nerves. "God I'm glad you're here! There are gale warnings out!" she said.

The boat groaned. I disembarked and fell into a big hug. "I'm so happy to see you, Allison!"

Her frame was stately; in fact, statuesque and authoritative, a woman with electrifying dark eyes and beaded corn rows that had sprouted from the short curly hair that I remembered from months before. There was nothing cold or hard about her, nor even judicial, I supposed, but as a judge she was tough and fair.

"You're soaked!" she said pulling me up the stairs and onto flag stones that wound toward Renaud Inn.

"Only an idiot would have left her raincoat at a restaurant," I said, thinking about a very combative lunch with one of the young lawyers on my staff, "and not remember I left it there until it poured again!"

Allison smiled and looked over her shoulder. "Coneras, see me later. You know better than to bring the trawler over in such horrible weather! Why you might have capsized!"

The wind pasted his parka against his body, and I saw how really frail he was. "Tweren't bad when I left, Judge. Tweren't." Without looking down, his eyes seemed to die away. "We got here, didn't we?"

"Nevertheless!" she reprimanded. "We'll talk about it!"

We passed an old horse trough on our left, and Coneras went around us. "Whatever you say, Judge."

Her lips skirted my ear, "I do believe his brain is going!"

"I can sympathize," I said. "But don't be too hard on him."

"Oh you can bet I will," she said winking as he walked out of our sight. "We've been bantering since I was a child. He thinks he runs the place, I suppose, but I have to sit him down now and then and remind him that the Renaurds and I pay the bills."

My senses were bombarded as we wandered through a vined pergola that marked the entrance to terra cotta terraces off to our left and right, seemingly secretive places where dense flowerbeds had the symmetry of circled plantings, most of which had died in an early October frost. Still I thought the grounds didn't look unkempt and were much like a landscape still trapped in slow motion between fall and winter. In the South, winter did that, obscured the once manicured gardens of spring and fall, preventing the tourist from capturing them on camera.

Near the grand steps that led to the veranda was a magnificent joggling board, one about eighteen feet long and a foot wide, a piece of yellow pine that was a couple of feet from the ground and hooked between wooden posts with slots in them. I couldn't deny a quick stop.

"I think it was the first trampoline," Allison said when I bent down to touch it. "Barclay told me that his mother used to say that those who bounced on the board were doomed to be married, like it or not!"

Strangely, I wanted to go on standing there, imagining the ripples of affection between young lovers, but water running down the spouting onto a stone gutter caught my attention. I swung around to see someone walking toward us.

"Hello Gabe," Allison said. "Meet Attorney General Kate Guesswine. She'll be with us for awhile."

"Hello," I extended my hand into a grip of self-assurance.

"Nice to meet you," he said with a slight drawl. He looked carefully at Allison and then me, his eyes noticeably green, his hair black and his skin the color of a sparrow. The brim of a large safari hat with leather strings hanging untied across his unshaven cheeks rocked in the wind, and he was the first man that I had ever seen who wore a ponytail that didn't make him look like a cast off from the sixties.

"I'll be here for only a week or two," I said. "Then perhaps back and forth for a few weekends while my cottage is being renovated."

Gabe flipped the wet ends of my hair. "Didn't Grandfather give you some rain gear?"

"Allendro Coneras is Gabe's grandfather," Allison said. "We've always called him by his last name. I'm not sure why. But this is Gabriel Coneras. Gabe. And we've always called him by his first name, and I don't know why!"

We climbed the stairs and paused in front of the mirror-like double doors that were crowned by a narrow transom. I looked as if I had just tumbled out of the washing machine.

"I'm a sight!" I said.

Gabe pivoted in front of me. I caught his eyes scanning my body. "You'll do," he said, flashing an insolent grin that both annoyed and intrigued me.

"He's our caretaker," Allison said. "In more ways than one. He'll flatter you a dozen times a day. Don't pay any attention."

"I'll consider myself forewarned," I said wryly.

He took my hand. "I'm afraid I've been caught!"

I pulled away and gave a playful wink. "Mmm hmm. Yes, you certainly *have*," I said.

"So I'll say good evening," he said. "I hope your stay with us will be a pleasant one." Then in the half-light of an old porch sconce that seemed to have come on automatically, he grinned, flipped a wave, and with the spring of a teenager, bounded down the steps.

"How old is that one Allie?" I asked.

"Thirty seven. Old enough to know better," she said. "And so are you!"

"Nonsense. I wasn't…oh, don't be ridiculous," I said blushing.

But then she whispered, "He does have a disastrous amount of sex appeal, doesn't he?"

"Eyes that could kidnap a woman's libido," I noted.

We both giggled like two teenagers. Before I could say anything else, Holden Renaurd opened the doors, and there, as if springing from the pages of a history book, were the great rooms of Renaurd Inn.

CHAPTER 3

There are first impressions that leave you quickly and first impressions that are preserved forever in the formaldehyde of memory. I realized that there would be moments in the future when I might be some place else, and I would see and smell Renaurd Inn, its spacious central hall cutting through rooms that once held the grace of grand parties and probably the soiled boots of the pre-Civil War planters.

Had he lived back in the seventeen hundreds, I believe that Senator Holden Renaurd would have been one of those planters, for it was said by many who knew him intimately that he was a patrician by taste, and a gourmet of fine things: silver, linen, furniture, art and Gregorian chants. At sixty-two his back and shoulders were still as straight as newly split lumber, his gray hair and facial features cut the same, too, every line and curve a measure of his years. Yes, he was striking, I thought, but more because his wizened hazel eyes when riveted on yours, made you believe that you were the only person in his presence. Still, his demeanor could be stiff and commanding, and I was sure that in the olden days, he would have wielded a big black riding whip at any-one who disobeyed him. In fact, because I likened him to my father, Holden's unintentional intimidation of me—either imagined or real—was so strong that I sometimes avoided him when we were both at the statehouse on business.

But upon seeing him, his full body squeeze stole my breath, and I realized that at the moment my fears were unfounded. "Kate. My, oh my! How great to see you my dear," he said.

I stepped out of his grasp. "It's has been awhile," I said.

"Well now, you look lovelier every time I see you," he said with the gaiety of a schoolboy. "Say—your hair...why now, I like it down like that. Attractive!"

"Oh stop flirting," Allison laughed.

"Well now, you just indulge me, Kate," he said kindly, "and tell me all about David Smithe." His words ambushed me, and I was not prepared to answer.

"I don't think so," I said meekly. Indeed, David's decision to leave fell under the guise of personal business which I struggled to keep unemotionally from others. He wasn't dead, although I sometimes wish he had died. It would have been easier. He wasn't abducted and held for ransom. He wasn't off having a hot romance. No, I recall that he simply got up one day and told me that he had resigned his position as English professor. For personal reasons he was leaving the country. *Personal? Wasn't I part of his 'personal reasons'? Didn't I have a right to know?* Then after he presented me the deed to the cottage and the key to his Land Rover—explaining that he wanted me to have them because I had contributed more money than he had to our lifestyle—he fended off my near hysteria with his brusque repose, swiftly kissed me goodbye, climbed into the airport shuttle and left without further explanation.

For the next few months, real or imagined, I was sure that everyone was saying, 'Poor Kate. She looks ill, doesn't she? No color in those generally rosy cheeks. Too much food and booze. After five years, David dumped her...didn't you know?'

Those unforgettable moments.

"Senator, that subject is a 'no-no' for now," Allison scolded. I was surprised that she addressed him by his title, and I decided that I had better, too.

"Well now, Kate, you just flash those pretty little lashes if you need me," he said with a slight smirk. "I'm told that I have a gentle 'ear' for these things!"

Quite the contrary, I thought. In the Senate he was said to be stubbornly opinionated and could be punitive when sidetracked from a well-planned agenda, anything that perhaps might forward his political career. He was known to cement the members of his inner circle into his own mold, and I had heard that you'd better never cross him.

I touched his sleeve. "I'll keep that in mind," I said.

"Well now, where's that Barclay?" Holden abruptly asked. "I am reminded that he's to be a third to my fourth at bridge with two of our other guests, Mr. Stephan Atchison and Mrs. Trudie Peabody. How about you, Kate? Do you play?"

I shook my head. "Not lately. Not with my work schedule."

"Don't worry," Allison said, steering us down the long hall, her arms entwined in ours, "Barclay will be along! Poor dear. He's been sleeping most of the afternoon. That dreadful business with Mrs. Trample-St. Synge last night!"

Holden turned to me. He straddled my shoulder with his arm. "Well now, Kate, I'm afraid that our sleep around here is much too animated these days! I hear my dear brother skedaddle from his room most nights; a most miserable sleeper, you know. And sometimes Allison gets up and makes tea. I, myself, rarely doze off until after three! Do you suppose it's those goddamn low pressures from Florida?"

We all stopped at the bottom of the back stairwell. "Meanwhile Kate, your luggage is in your room! The most private at the inn," Allison said. Before I could say anything, she had proffered to take me there, adding, "Why, it's a sieve for the glorious East sun!"

"Well then, I have some calls to make. Dinner at seven?" Holden whispered. He planted his lips on both of our cheeks.

"Mmm hmm. Yes, Senator, 'til dinner then," I said, half wishing I could simply dive into bed and be left alone, although it was in the back of my mind that I needed to find the right moment to tell everyone about Jennifer.

He went through a side door, his footsteps diminishing on the wide planked floor, while the two of us, our arms still locked, ascended the stairs, the bare threads of the deep green carpet leading me to believe that it had been heavily traveled for a century or more.

"I'm so glad you're here, Kate," she said. "I've missed you!"

"I've missed you, too! And do forgive me if I'm off limits," I said, "but what's happened to Barclay?"

"Oh now you just put away your attorney general role while you're here and don't trouble your mind," she said with a completely carefree tone. "It was nothing. Nothing at all. Just a little 'Soldier of Fortuning' by Barclay Renaurd, I suspect, to spark the adventuresome spirit of our guests!"

We reached the upper landing and then entered a long, narrow hall. At once there seemed to be cold air exhaling from the walls, walls with turn-of-the-century yellowed paper that had the roughness of an old woman's skin, the second floor apparently never having been renovated, as I had thought.

"The ole wandering ghosts legend, huh?" I asked.

She waved a hand. "Why yes. It lends character to our brochures, doesn't it? You'll want a relaxing soak now, won't you..." she continued in a tone that was more of a command than a request. "We've put some lovely oils in some bath salts for you. Chamomile and sweet fennel, too. Do you like jasmine? Mack, our masseur, has taken courses in aromatherapy, and now he thinks he's the godfather of oils! Well, he is, I suppose. Oh, and while you're here, he'll give you a rub most women can only dream of."

"Sounds sensuous!" I sighed. I thought of how little attention I had paid to myself lately. Manicures and pedicures were scheduled after appointments with detectives and sheriffs. Shopping for new clothes was unheard of. Soon my shoes would unravel at the seams. Yet, I had enough reserve in my closet to still present myself professionally and socially so that no one thought I possibly was about to live with the bag ladies over in Savannah.

Next to an alcove, we stopped abruptly before two amber and green oval windows with shadows from giant oak limbs dancing only inches beyond their panes. Through the clearer upper glass, I got my first glimpse of the back of the inn and its unadorned lawn. Along the side, a narrow gravel boulevard that was dimly lighted by coach lamps strangely configured like old men dangling from gallows, stretched far into a horizon of pines.

"The estate seems to go on forever," I said. "How do you get around?"

"By the strength of your ankles. And a little fortitude! You know, there never have been cars on the island. No roads to speak of. Only planked and dirt paths," Allison said.

As I stood there, my mind wandered back in time again. I could imagine finely garbed men disembarking from the ferry ahead of their porcelain-skinned women, their purpose solely to be pampered and plucked for a long weekend, while beyond all this perceived civility, and cut like a huge scar, were the ground houses—long abandoned slave houses that were like West African coastal houses—where clay was mixed with sticks and sandwiched between more clay and shells beneath wooden floors so that the night air-cooled the mixture and kept the temperature bearable during the hottest of Carolinian afternoons. But however grim I thought that the past might have been, the gale warning had finally caught up with us, and wind and rain were beginning to play the attic rafters like a kettledrum resounding a requiem.

"How *is* Barclay? Really?" I asked. We continued along a section of the hall that had the stylish appointment of fine antique side tables.

"If you mean has he given up motorcycles and women," she cautioned, her tone one of protection, "well, yes he has. Women? I don't know of any. But I do wonder sometimes. Why, I mean I think life is sometimes a looking glass for Barclay. I confess that I wish I could find the courage to tell him that someday he'll reach into it for something important, something he really needs"—she pursed her lips—"and the glass will shatter!"

"Or perhaps he'll become the man you've always hoped he'd be, Allison," I added quickly.

She paused and then laughed, "Yes. I suppose. Well, never mind. He does so love our guests," she said, pursuing a different thread of conversation. "He does so love to tell stories about the early days of his travel long ago. Long before we opened this place to the public. Unlike the Senator, he's got the gift of gab, you know. Why, once Tennessee

Williams was sitting on the porch of an old inn in Abington, Virginia after one of his plays had been at the playhouse there. And Barclay...I tell you Kate, Barclay, well he said—of course, I can't do it in Barclay's deep southern drawl—but he said, 'Mr. Williams, I have a brand new bottle of Gentlemen's Bourbon. I'd be honored if you would share it with me, sir.' And didn't you know, Mr. Williams said, 'And I sir, would be happy if you shared your fine liquor with me.' Why, they sat there in that refined culture of literature and politics for nearly two hours until Mr. William's secretary came down and reminded him that it was time to retire. A little later, the secretary shared a drink with Barclay and told him that Mr. Williams would spend the next hour writing letters. He did that faithfully every night at nine o'clock before retiring for the night. Yes, it certainly was a fine moment for my dear brother. Barclay Renaurd can be so charming, so loving, and so jocular. Why, not at all like the Senator who can be down right mean-spirited when things don't go his way."

At the end of the hall, Allison opened the door to my room. I immediately settled, the way someone does when you see charming things, warm and inviting things: pale pink walls with small stenciled roses, pictures of seabirds framed in small white shells, and beautiful fluffy pillows on a light mauve comforter that skirted the dark green carpet. And yes, I don't know why, but I wasn't surprised to learn that Gabe had placed the fresh flowers on the nightstand beside the four poster bed with the white islet canopy. Instinctively, I brought them to my nose, and for some reason, I suddenly felt a rush of anxiety.

CHAPTER 4

What everyone had said about Renty being a terrific chef was true, and after a fabulous dinner, Allison, Barclay, Holden and I moved to the large formal living area, while the other guests went into the adjoining game room, their boisterous voices rising and falling like the whirl of an electric can opener. Someone had a headache so there was to be no bridge after all. Allison served coffee and tea. I tried to conjure up my courage to tell the family about Jennifer.

There seemed to be a tremor in Barclay's eye while Holden appeared better bred than anyone; near the andirons, he stood staunchly with an unlighted pipe, his deep chest thrust out enough that I thought he might pop the buttons on his starched white shirt. "It's these weekends that I enjoy here," he said.

"And not particularly with the family, heh?" Barclay said cynically.

"Oh now dear, why it's quite nice, I do think, that we're all here tonight," said Allison as if there were an understanding among them—a silly consolation—as if they had invented the virtues of family together-ness. "Why I do believe…"

Barclay interrupted playfully, "Now that Kate's here, I feel like I could turn summersaults. Let's do it! Let's you and I steal away and go turn summersaults on the lawn by the gazebo!"

"Do be serious," Allison pleaded.

"Mmm hmm. I can see the tabloids now, can't you?" I said when no one said anything. "Attorney General Guesswine goes berserk!"

"Why, Barclay, did Mack give you a shot of B-12 today?" Allison asked.

"He's had something," Holden said, setting his jaw. "I suppose it's not what we think!"

Barclay poured bourbon into his coffee and waved his cup. He fluttered his eyelids. "He's had *something! Something! Something!*" he mocked.

I was puzzled. It must have shown.

"Oh, all this jabber is *really* nothing," Allison said turning away from me. "Let's do change the subject."

I got up and added sugar to my tea. Everyone seemed on edge, and I wondered if it were the storm with its resounding thunder and rain lashing the windows or that we were all tired, or I was tired and needed to get on with the news about Jennifer.

"Kate, do you sail?" Holden asked.

I moved next to him. "Senator, it takes everything I have to keep from falling off the deck," I said. "We'll go?"

"Love to! But I've got to be away," he said. "After that?"

Allison flicked on the stereo; a Viennese waltz graced the room. "Oh?" she said, "Oh? And where to this time, Senator?"

"No doubt at the taxpayer's expense," Barclay uttered with disgust. He turned to his brother.

"No doubt? That's bull," Holden exclaimed. "As a ranking member of the agricultural committee, I often have official government business in the Bahamas."

"Oh? And will you be stopping by our Careco Industries offices while you're there?" Barclay asked.

Allison smiled at me. "The boys are always worried about our businesses!"

"Well now, I've been damn good at it!" Holden said. "This time I'll be with a delegation. But I'll get over there sometime soon. Unless you want to go, Barclay?"

Allison looked surprised. "Why *no—no he doesn't*, Senator! His job is to run the inn and see to our guest. And you know what I mean, sir!" She turned to me then, "Would you like more tea, dear?"

I could have bottled the tension. I pretended to ignore what seemed to be an escalating war, one of those on-going family spats, I think, between Holden and Barclay, for beneath their bickering, I detected a deep hostility, a slow festering sore. It seemed more than brotherly sparring.

Should I excuse myself? Would it embarrass them if I did? Instead, I wandered around, looking at porcelain figurines and delicately hand-crafted bisque flowers. I was curious about a shelf of old books and soon realized that they were first editions that were probably put there to protect them from the guests who borrowed books from the inn's library.

Barclay drummed the knuckle of his right index finger on the table. "Holden needs to pay more attention to the purse strings of *this* place! Pay attention to all our interests! Not just his own!"

While deciding how far to let them go in front of me, I observed their eyes darting to each other. Their talk made me uncomfortable. I was fidgeting. It's true that I was a dear friend; yet, it was generally true of everyone, wasn't it? One's worth…bank accounts, checkbooks, credit cards…any discussion of finance was generally off limits to anyone but immediate family. But ironically, the most intimate details of one's personal relationships often were not.

"Now gentlemen," Allison said firmly, "we don't need to discuss any more business in front of our guest."

"It's unfortunate that it was even brought up," Holden said, his lips as stiff as steel.

Barclay turned. "Hiss, hiss," he snarled, "I tell you, brother's pissed."

"Don't be a skulking ass!" Holden retorted.

Allison jumped up and put her arms around me. "Gentlemen! I mean for you to cease this conversation immediately!" she said over my shoulder. "You are stressing our guest! Do forgive us, Kate!"

At last everyone relaxed. "Let's all have some port," Holden said lightly before reeling to the cupboard behind him that held liquor. Then he poured into fine crystal. It was curious that Barclay smiled so, then laughed like a nervous child, and after a short hum, shook his head and laughed a more cunning laugh. I wanted the evening to be over. Was he about to get into something else?

My impulse was to wait until morning to tell them about Jennifer, to wait until Justin came with his report. I swallowed hard, and then a kind of guttural climbed up to clear my throat. Still hesitating, I set my goblet on a side table where light languished across a genuine Lladro vase.

It was after ten. It was *time* to speak the unspeakable. Around me, *time* was everywhere. The small French mantle clock, the faces of our wristwatches, even the wind outside oddly *timing* its creaking through the joists in the walls. And Jennifer had lain buried in the wet, dark earth until it was *time* for her name to be added to the list of other Dragon's Point victims. So was it my *time* to speak about it? Should I hint? Come right out?

As if I were at a podium, I positioned myself in the center of the room, an outrageous thing to do, I supposed, standing uncomfortably straight and silent while anticipating their possible reactions. But their eyes spotlighting me only made me more resolute!

"I have news about Jennifer!" I finally said.

No one moved. No one said anything. Their expressions blank, Holden finally muttered, "She's been found!"

"Off Dragon's Point, I'm afraid," I said. I felt a sense of dread, and immediately, I regretted having not told them earlier.

Holden propelled back. Barclay took his place. Allison's shoulders slightly stiffened. I didn't need to read her mind. I knew that she was wondering how I could have participated in the merriment of dinner and wine and shared their conversation while harboring such horrible news. Her eyes fixed on mine. "Then you've known since you arrived, haven't you! And you said nothing?"

"I'm sorry, but I was trying to find the right time," I stammered. "I've only made it worse, I'm afraid."

"It might have been better not to have waited," Allison said tersely.

"There was an ankle bracelet…" I said.

Holden rigidly poured another glass of port, gulped it with a coolness that belied any grief he might feel and said, "Well now, we all know about that!"

"After all these years," Barclay said. "Hard to believe, isn't it? To die that young! Then again, dying doesn't belong to any particular generation does it? How did she die? You say she was found at the Point. Did she die there?"

"She could have been killed somewhere else and taken there. It's probably been too long to establish an exact cause of death. Detective McCreary's coming tomorrow with the report," I explained, my voice sounding hollow when I resisted an impulse to talk about the similar striations found on all of the victims.

With every passing minute the room seemed grotesquely dark and silent. I searched each face for some sign of sadness, but I only saw lingering disbelief. And then it seemed inappropriate that Holden took a hand-made chocolate from a box, then passed the rest around, each of us in his own way shoveling out a piece from the foil with our fingers, for it seemed incredulous to me that someone had died, and we were eating chocolates that cost twenty dollars a pound.

I looked at the door. I assumed that the other guests must have gone up the back stairs to their rooms, the inn void of sounds except for someone overhead who was walking across uneven floor boards. I could picture the women in front of their mirrors as they creamed their faces, floating in their flannels to bed, their romance paperbacks settling firmly in their open hands. And after removing his false teeth, Mr. Atchinson probably slept in his long underwear and dreamed of taming mythical sirens, beautiful bird-like creatures with the gorgeous breasts and arms of women who lured sailors to their death.

Allison stood up. "In the meantime, let's leave it at that," she said lightly.

"Yes, well then," Holden said, "that's that. Goodnight ladies." His lips brushed our foreheads, and with Barclay at arm's length and humming a tune, they headed into the hall.

Allison seemed reluctant to go to bed. I helped her take the teapot, cups and saucers to a small holding area off the dining room, one that had a dumbwaiter to the kitchen beneath the main rooms. Except for hall lights, one by one we shut off table lamps as we wound our way through the maze of rooms and headed to our own on the second floor.

She put her arm around me and said, "There's something not right, my friend. After all of these years, you find our Jennifer? The others? The same area?"

"I hoped that it simply might be a coincidence, Allison," I said rather unconvincingly.

"Anything dishonest from you," she said, "and I'll be disappointed. It would have to be an extraordinary coincidence and you know it! But I'm too overwhelmed tonight. So you'll tell me what you know tomorrow, won't you?"

I never had to answer her though. She kissed my cheek and said goodnight. As she disappeared into the room across from mine, I could feel a strange draft. Immediately, the leaves of the magnolias on the wallpaper seemed to shimmer while I observed that the empty hall, hollow and dark, drew me in as if I were falling down the throat of a corpse.

CHAPTER 5

It was late afternoon a week later as I headed from my office in Columbia to my motorhome. I was feeling bewildered because my administrative assistant, Fran Dunlap had suffered a serious heart attack; she'd be all right, but I didn't know what I would do without her while she took a month to recuperate. Since I had become attorney general, she never let me forget my pledge to the people of South Carolina to be an advocate of individual rights. Of course, I was lucky to have Paul Hanes, my deputy DA, and after I had spent a grueling morning pouring over cases that were about to come to trial, he assured me that he had everything under control and then kicked me out of my office and ordered me to continue my vacation.

The traffic along the 278 approach to Hilton Head Island was bumper to bumper. My cell phone rang.

"I'm ready to pull out my hair," Justin McCreary said in a rage into my earphones.

"I wouldn't do that. Your hair is beginning to thin," I said chuckling.

"I tell you Katie, I never liked working with a partner."

I had heard that Sheriff Sparkman put that new 'two on patrol' regulation in motion. "It's safer, you know Justin," I said. "Too many weirdoes out there ready to take you out if you're alone."

"Yeah, well, I don't suppose this new rule came from your office? Sounds like something on your menu, Katie."

"I had nothing to do with it. Besides, you don't like any kind of partner," I said trying to relax my grip on the steering wheel. "It's like you've had a lobotomy when it comes to couples."

He didn't laugh. "Ah, don't barb at me Katie. I'm fried. Ever since my partner parked her thunder thighs in my truck, I've had no control of my life. I can't even get a good night's sleep."

"You seldom slept when we were married," I said, "so that's not unusual, is it?" I bit my lip. I sensed I had said something I'd regret.

He laughed. "Yeah, well I wasn't awake because I was having sex with you."

There it was. The same old story. The deprived husband. "No," I said firmly, "because you were getting it from that cute little police officer over in Savannah."

"Shit! I fucked up one time! You never let me forget it!"

"No Justin, you fucked—period! And it wasn't with me. *That's* why we weren't having sex," I said. I recalled that at that time, we both were unhappy, buried in our work, lacking communication, and after a year of having my nerves frayed by his infidelity, I didn't want to go to a therapist in order for us to find more stimulating positions to thwart *his* boredom. "And now why don't we change the subject so we can keep a semblance of civility in this phone discussion," I added, curtailing my anger. "In fact, why don't you tell me about your new partner? Who is she?"

I could hear him breathing heavily. I had rattled his rancor, but he wasn't up for a full-blown argument. I'd win, close my cell phone and he knew it. His voice immediately transformed. "Isabella Marinchino. We call her *The Cherry*," he blurted out. "A transfer from Charleston."

"Why isn't she with you now?"

"Cause she's in the 'mart getting us some java," he said. "And no cracks about the female getting coffee, you hear?"

"No argument there," I said slowly. "What else?"

"Huh?"

"There must be something else you wanted to tell me about her. Otherwise you wouldn't have made such a big to do."

"She's one of those go-by-the-book twats. I can't even sneak off to my motorhome for a fifteen-minute snoozeola. She grinds the shit out of me!" He was getting more agitated. "Opens her big drawer when she shouldn't. Says, 'Where were ya? What's ya been doin'?' She screws up paper work, too, even when I dictate the shit to her. How in the hell am I supposed to testify in court when she screws up what I tell her to write? Huh? You know what else?"

"I can't imagine," I said half listening, my mind thinking about FBI agent Drew Greer and her fax, which said that she was being assigned to the Dragon's Point investigations. We had a history. We were room-mates in college and briefly shared an apartment afterward. She stood up for me at my wedding and cried with me after my divorce. After David left, her phone calls kept me sober. And we forever reminded each other of our vulnerability and that our friendship brought power to that vulnerability.

"She talks on our police radio like some goddamn crab in the sand," Justin said, trying to suppress his anger.

Although it sounded as if he needed an emotional rescuing, I said firmly, "Live with it."

"Yeah? Well, it's not your ulcer that's kicking up!"

"That only happens to you when it's convenient and you know it." I explained. I was becoming increasingly desensitized about his problems. Sometimes I was abhorred that Justin might be like some of the police officers I had come to know in my years as attorney general. Officers who were generally skeptical about women being part of the police force, officers who were part of a macho brotherhood where women officers, especially detectives, were the butt of sexual jokes or comments and often ostracized into a world where their complaining about it might even put them in physical danger.

I remembered a case in Chicago where a young female rookie complained far too much about her assignments...even suggesting harassment, and during a robbery her backup was slow to arrive at the scene, some said intentionally. She was killed. Not that Justin would ever do anything like that. He loved women. All women. That was his problem.

We were divorced before I was elected attorney general so he knew me in my roles as wife, lawyer, prosecutor and DA. After I moved in with

David, I suspect that he believed that I was neither qualified nor deserved to be the chief law officer of the state, that the position needed 'cop' experience, someone who had been out working the beat. He told me that it frightened him because I carried a Beretta, but what he didn't realize is that most cops won't ever pull their gun but once in twenty years on the force.

"So did you only want to tell me about Detective Marinchino?" I asked impatiently.

"Nah. I'm headed to Dragon's Point," he said. "Thought you'd want to come along this time."

"Not another set of bones!"

"The real gizmo. A gal who's got skin and the rest of her trimmings."

"How long dead?"

"Don't have any details yet," he said.

"You're fading out," I said quickly.

"Then I'm going to hang up," he said. "Anyhow, here comes The Cherry."

"What?"

"The 'Spanish Coffee' who's about to get into the car."

Even with no one to see me, I blushed. "Really Justin, that's enough!"

"Yeah, well, I'll catch you at the Point."

"Mmm hmm." I said abruptly. I knew that Detective Justin McCreary's mind was on more than the store bought coffee he had sent his partner in for. I knew that *Spanish Coffee* was a derogatory term that referred to 'getting laid.' Detective Isabela Marinchino had my sympathy.

CHAPTER 6

Already yellow police tape had cordoned off the crime scene that spanned from beyond the tree line to the beach at Dragon's Point. A police photographer took video, and then after a lengthy discussion with a couple of detectives, he moved rapidly to other areas that needed to be photographed in greater detail. Everything that might be connected to the crime would be documented. There would be photos of tree limbs, disturbances in leaves, and even what appeared to be barren soil or sand. I parked my Explorer, passed the evidence van and started around the tape.

A murmur of recognition rose up from forensic pathologist Dr. Bree Packer, her tee shirt, 'Don't Bug Me', reflecting her sense of humor. She heaved her hand in the air and wandered over to me, her sharp cheekbones and blue eyes catching a shaft of sun. "Well, Kate Guesswine, this is an unexpected surprise!"

Often when a forensic anthropologist was needed, Bree Packer was summoned to the scene, mostly for tough—what seemed like unsolvable cases—and I was curious how she was going to forensically relate this murder to the previous victims. I quickly saw that she was wearing gloves, booties and a hairnet, which she had retrieved from a sterile box. She motioned for me to do the same while reiterating how much trace evidence was lost in the Nicole-O.J. Simpson investigation when photographs showed the lead detectives had not worn protective covering. She was a stickler for procedure, pointing out that the first couple of hours at the scene were the most crucial, the time when a perimeter must be established so that the detectives, criminalists, medical examiner (in very small towns, the coroner) local police and sometimes the DA can protect the evidence and its chain of custody.

"It's been awhile," I said. "At that forensics meeting in Chicago last summer."

She was chomping on gum. Breathing heavily, too, and I assumed that she was still a pack-a-day smoker—the gum a sort of tranquilizer while she was working.

"Something, isn't it? Finally, something more than bones. Although unfortunately, our poor victim's facial features mostly have deteriorated," she said, "but there's enough for our forensic artist to sculpt a three-dimensional reconstruction."

"By the way, Sheriff Sparkman called and asked me to come on board," Bree said. "Something about this being victim *thirteen*," she said under a chuckle. "Say, is our sheriff superstitious?"

"Does walking around an open ladder count?" I asked. "Why isn't he here?"

She shook her head. "At a conference in Charleston. Detective McClenahan's in charge. Say…where's Justin?"

I looked around. "That's strange," I said, tilting my head so that I could search all the approaches to the crime scene. "I just got off the phone with him. He was heading here."

Dr. Packer looked at her watch and motioned for me to follow. We skirted part of the crime site that was zoned by stakes and more yellow tape and walked carefully past two wooden barricades to an area near the beach where there had been violent horizontal movement of water that had breached the groin, probably from the last nor'easter, water that had flooded land to carve an inlet about twenty feet long and four feet wide back into the palmetto scrub.

From here came the stench of rotting flesh, the horrific odor ten times worse than that which might catch you when you've forgotten to set the garbage out on pickup day and it accumulates for another week in the plastic container in a hot garage. It might have caused other investigators to wear a special mask. Instead, Dr. Packer handed me a cream that had the aroma of wintergreen oil, and as I rubbed it under my nose,

I could tell by the rush of pleasure in her eyes that she was pleased that it was all that I needed. We watched while the criminalist collected trace evidence and various soil and water samples before vacuuming near the tree roots where the body was partially wedged.

"A Jane Doe?" I asked.

"Yes, but I'll call her 'Anastasia'. Did you know that Anastasia is Greek for 'resurrection'? As I told Justin, I think this lady's going to resurrect what seems to be a somewhat stalled investigation! Our lady's suffered quite a blow, you know," Dr. Packer said. She straddled on bent knees at the edge of the washout and peered over the side. She used a magnetic sketchbook, one like kids draw on and then made corrections as she transferred her notes to a paper pad. "See that?" she continued. "The left frontal area slightly above the forehead shows a distinct circle about the size of a golf ball."

I looked down. The victim's head was all that rested upon any solid ground. There were clumps of light colored hair on the left side but nothing on the other. "Yes. Yes, I see it," I said.

Her upper torso was at a sitting angle, her back and buttocks partially wedged under oak roots. Swaying outwardly in murky water were her bloated legs, the circumference of her ankles reminding me of the two hawsers, the five-inch heavy cables on Coneras's boat that were used for towing or mooring. I remembered how they sometimes drifted freely, too.

Dr. Packer tugged at the latex on her glove. "The rest of the skull looks very much like a windshield that has been fractured. See those spider threads going out from the wound? I'd guess that a round object was used to separate the skull. There are pieces barely attached and some are missing."

"That's how she was killed then?" I asked, peering again at the head.

"Not necessarily," she said standing up. "It's possible that her head was smashed to attract the sharks. And I imagine like the other women found in this area"—she paused—"that she was taken out beyond the jetty *after* she was dead."

"And yet, the killer didn't use enough weights to keep them down," I suggested.

Dr. Packer looked hard at me. "That's curious, I think. Perhaps eventually he wanted them to be dislodged. To be discovered."

"Unlike Jennifer Renaurd whose body wasn't found for years."

"Only to be exposed by wind and water eroding her grave," she explained. "Now poor Anastasia is speaking for Jennifer and all of the other victims."

"Speaking? In what way?" I asked solemnly.

Dr. Packer's eyes shot open, and then poured into a squint as she furrowed her eyebrows. "Remember Melville's Captain Ahab? Remember his arm beckoning after he became entangled in the lines of the harpoons that killed Moby Dick? See our lady's arm across her chest? The other one straight out? She's asking for our help. I tell you, it's a 'sign'! Our lady is saying, 'Give me my name back! Give me justice!' Yes she is!"

Then I was distracted by a tourist at the water line who was snapping pictures, his macabre fascination with death not unlike someone who comes upon a ghoulish car crash. In his exhilaration, was he hoping for a closer look at the victim? But then I was relieved when he turned and left.

"How long has she been here?" I asked Bree Packer.

"It's hard to say exactly. As I'm sure you know, the body deteriorates more slowly when left in water," she explained. "No one's bothered her. But she'll be difficult to autopsy. So much of her is badly decomposed. The deep blisters on her thighs are from gases escaping when bacteria takes over. Some of her internal organs probably have liquefied by now. Her nails and most of her skin are gone. But there's still muscle. And see that substance that looks like cottage cheese?"

"Mmm hmm. Adipocere."

"That's right. It forms when the fatty tissue hardens, and it acts like a preservative. You sometimes see it when rotting fish wash up and lay on the shore. There'll be mushy threads shredding out like tentacles."

"Yes. It happens frequently in the marshes around my cottage when fish get trapped in tidal debris."

Bree Packer looked about and motioned for one of her assistants. "Oh? I heard you were selling?"

"At this point, renovating," I said slowly.

She smiled, reassuring me. "Well, it's terrible, I know. I was at an international forensics conference in Europe when I heard about you and David. I remember that I liked him when you brought him to that lecture of mine a couple of years ago. And the reception afterwards."

I choked up.

"And you aren't doing too well?" she continued.

"Oh, perhaps one glass of wine too many just about every day," I said.

"Then I'm sure I can't imagine," she said touching her elbow to my shoulder, in a gesture of kind familiarity. "I'll tell you this. If my Karl did that, I'd flip out, I'm afraid! I'd track him down and stuff his beautiful body in a meat grinder!"

I wondered if I should laugh. "It wasn't another woman, if that's what you mean," I said. "But isn't it something? As smart as I thought we women were, I can't figure out why some us are so vulnerable that we can only attract men who are willing to stay in a relationship until their own cup runs over. The hell with ours!"

"So he needed a middle aged fix of some kind?"

"Only he didn't have the courtesy to let me know."

She shook her head. "You're strong, my friend. Your work will keep you that way."

"But a bed can be very cold," I said, grimacing. "Anyhow, I've cut my losses. Still getting rid of the leftovers…his clothes and furniture and much of what we bought together. Why…a few days ago I even went on a shopping spree and bought a couple of thousand dollars worth of new clothes!"

"Spending money always revs up my spirit, too! Hey Roy!" she yelled, as she guided me over to one of her assistants. "Our Anastasia has shifted a bit. Dam up that area immediately around her. Siphon the water away and strain the muck again. Make sure we haven't missed anything that may have fallen off her body. Get in the water if you have to. And tell Glenn to get more pictures. I want all angles. Then let's pull her out, take her to the morgue and autopsy her. Our lady has been soaking far too long!"

An hour later the officers put the body onto a white piece of polyvinyl chloride, and after that, I didn't hang around. I went to the motorhome to pick up an overnight bag. It was Allison's birthday and there was to be a family dinner. As I drove to the ferry, the wind was picking up and dying down like a fickle woman who couldn't make up her mind. The phone rang. Bree Packer's voice was abrupt and disturbing. I had not expected her to say, "Kate. It's curious. The autopsy on Anastasia? Those internal organs? Not much there, of course. But I guess I almost missed the obvious. I see signs of excision and evidence that skin was peeled. There are very deep striations on her ribs, too. And the teeth were deliberately extracted. I think she was killed during some kind of ritual! In fact she may have been alive!"

All rational thinking seemed to go from me, and I could only imagine the horror that Anastasia might have gone through. Bree Packer hung up, and within seconds Justin called and said that he and his partner were over by Beaufort checking out a possible Amber alert. It made me sick to think that some deviate might have stolen an innocent child, the worst of all crimes, as far as I was concerned.

As for the deviate who had murdered thirteen women? As I parked the Explorer and boarded the ferry, I vowed that his luck was about to run out.

CHAPTER 7

The four o'clock crossing to the island with Coneras was as soft as cream. Inside the cabin my feet kicked up a swirl of dust every time I changed position, but I was delighted to be the only passenger, as it gave me the solace I needed to mull over Anastasia and the other victims. Excluding Jennifer Renaurd, five had been identified and confirmed to be prostitutes who had frequented truck stops or brothels in the Southeast. Seven remained unidentified now. All had knife-induced striations on their bones. In fact, to my disgust it appeared that Anastasia had been picked over like a gull savaging shore rot.

After we arrived, I went to Allison's party and returned to my room late. The brochure on my nightstand said, 'Renaurd Inn: One of the world's most exclusive health retreats.' Although occasionally there had been celebrity guests, it was usually word of mouth that gave the inn its impeccable reputation. At no time had the Renaurds accommodated more than ten visitors, their goal to bring to capacity the mind and spirit within an all-inclusive atmosphere of personal attention.

Finally, after a cup of decaffeinated chamomile tea, I slept well for the first times in weeks, and at first notice of a screen of subdued light across the bedroom carpet, I dressed in an orange Gabanna shift and brown fringed shaw and went down the hall, my eyes shifting to a noise behind me and then to a dark figure that seemed to have been standing within the shadow of a large fichus tree. Whoever it was didn't answer my inquiry, but instead disappeared quickly, I was sure, into one of the unoccupied guest rooms. I had misgivings about knocking on the door, and an uneasiness swept over me so I headed down the stairs to the dining room. I needed a hit of caffeine.

Thinking of the recent days of cool rain, I said, "Good morning! It's nice to see the sun today!" Mrs. Trudie Peabody and Mr. Stephen Atchinson nodded while Mrs. Constance Trample-St.Synge, whose eyes were focused on a plate of bagels and eggs, returned a very broad smile. As usual, I chuckled because her voracious appetite seemed to match her big stomach.

"Kate. That yo' darlin'," she said, her heavily penciled brows furrowing through half glasses. "Sit yo' little ole self down here and eat somethin', hear now?"

I was compelled to stare at what I believed was the stereotypical ill-bred Southern lady who is often contrasted with the gentile belle of the country club cotillion. From a small purse she took out lipstick and mirror and swathed on two false bumps above lips that had thinned with age. Then with spittle on her thumb and forefinger, she twirled wisps of yellowed hair onto a forehead marked noticeably with folds of thick skin. "I 'spect yo' haven't made it ta' the beach yet?" she said while clearing her throat.

"I think you would agree that it hasn't exactly been good 'walking' weather," I said. I was aware of others passing through the hall behind, their footsteps interminable, but no one else came into the room.

Mrs. Trample-St.Synge politely nodded and took out rouge. Her cheeks seemed to jump until she toned them with a beige powder that also diminished the shiny tip of a bulbous nose. The ritual finished, I marveled at the diamonds that drenched several fingers up to her slightly arthritic knuckles, but her pierced ears had gaping holes that were grotesquely empty.

Her shoulders melding into heavy cleavage, Mrs. Trample-St.Synge grasped a muffin, after which she propped her elbows on the table and fed herself while holding it in one hand and pinching the crust with the other. "Ma' I accompany yo' ta' the glorious Atlantic?"

"It is such a lovely day," I said light heartedly with no intention of including her on my walk. Her uninvited chattering, her inability to say more than a couple of sentences without inflecting 'darlin' would be a constant abrasion to my mind which needed to be fed only the welcomed monotony of the surf. I poured coffee into fine vitreous china with the letter 'R' boldly rimming the cup, noting that the Renaurd insignia was everywhere: napkins, tablecloth, plates and candleholders and even in gold on the large oval mirror above the long cherry buffet.

Next, Trudie Peabody stood up. Everything about her was petite except for a cavernous smile, her fillings catching the light of the crystal chandelier. "We could all go together," she said. "A kind of outing. The way they do up in Charleston. Like those people who belong to the Nature Conservancy. Yes, let's have an outing to the beach to look for shorebirds! But first Constance, why don't you tell Kate the *story*?"

"If you go to the beach, it's far too chilly for shorts, ladies," Mr. Atchinson said craning over an old copy of *The Poems of Keats*. A stout, partially bald librarian from Terre Haute, Indiana, he had gone on and on at dinner the evening before about how he had retracted a marriage proposal to devote his life to wayward animals and eradicating illiteracy among the poor. An African Safari had almost done him in, his suffering from chronic malaria now an albatross around his traveling plans. "If you could see the veins in my legs…"

Mrs. Trample-St.Synge frowned. "We don't care ta' Stephen."

I lowered my eyes and hid a chuckle.

"Oh, but look," he said hiking up the right leg of his khakis, "even though I had them stripped, my veins still look like shriveled eggplant!"

"The *story*, Constance!" Mrs. Peabody goaded.

"In due time, dear. It's true Stephen that last year when yo' were here, yo' were warned not ta' go through that surgery by Mack himself, who by the wa', had two years of medical training before he went into the Army," Mrs. Trample-St.Synge noted while piling more eggs onto her plate.

Mrs. Peabody's hand on mine drew my attention. "Mack knows everything about all that. About herbs, medicines. Those shots he gives us are heaven sent!"

"Humph! Humph." Stephen Atchinson pursed his lips. "B-12 injections, dear hearts, you know."

"Over ma' dead body!" said Mrs. Trample-St. Synge, winking.

"Now Constance, why are you putting off telling Kate about what you saw at the motel? Do tell the *story*!" Trudie said.

"That Mack's like a doctor, yo' know," Constance Trample-St.Synge added quickly. "Just ask him 'bout blood pressure, gout and eczema. Yo' mention liposuction…"

"Or bring up breast enhancement," Trudie said poking her own breasts. "Why he knows all about facelifts, too!"

"It took a forklift of Botox ta' get rid of ma' jowls! Had the treatments right here, as yo' remember. And that Barclay? Why he seems ta' be a walkin' pharmacy, too. Can get any pill."

"Mmm hmm. Well, not without a prescription, I hope," I said raising my brows.

"Well, I certainly haven't seen *that* as a problem," Stephen Atchinson said. "He got me sleeping pills last year! Knows a very good doctor on the mainland, I am told."

"A hem! Don't yo' go tellin' the attorney general anything that'll get Mack or any of the Renaurds in trouble, Stephen! After all, we are going ta' be their guests for weeks!"

Weeks? Allison deserved a medal. I shook my head. She was right. And while on vacation, I wasn't going to nose into things that didn't concern me.

Trudie Peabody stood up. On another day she had told us that she was perilously close to eighty-five. Now I thought that a noticeable dowager's hump probably confirmed her age. "Do tell Kate the *story* before she gets away Constance!"

"Perhaps yo' right. My dear, please sit down," Mrs. Trample-St. Synge said to me again. "But have a muffin, please!"

"No thank you," I said folding my napkin in half. I rose and poured a fresh coffee from a carafe on a narrow oak table that held other breakfast liquids. "Now what's on your mind?"

"I 'spect the cinnamon-raisin ones are quite exceptional," she said, "although if I eat ta' many, why it puts ma' insulin levels out of sight and I become quite light headed!"

"What's the *story*?" I coaxed.

"Something quite strange has happened," she said, "Yo' ever been ta' Tybee Island in Georgia, Kate?"

"A friend and I fished the surf there," I said sadly. Suddenly recalling a pleasant June morning with David made me grab a plain bagel and lather it with pure butter and peach brandy jam. What's another pound in the scheme of things? I nibbled around the edge and then put it aside, covering it with my napkin. Out of sight, out of mouth.

"Why, only days before I arrived here, I was over at a motel on that luscious island," she said excitedly. "I da' believe I had a touch of fluid in ma' lungs and was about ta' come down with a full-blown case of pleurisy! I went there for the purity of the sea air. Not knowin' who else was stayin' at the motel…well, it simply drained my sinuses when I saw *him*!"

"Finally! The *story!*" Stephen Atchinson sighed.

"I travel, yo' see," she said. She patted her mouth with the back of her hand. "Why I intend ta' sleep in all fifty states. It was a goal of ma' husband's, God rest his soul. Sta' at a motel as soon as we cross each state line. I 'spect we did so at seventeen before he fell dead on the toilet in a Holiday Inn in Lubbock, Texas. It was a nightmare, mind yo'. Oh ma'! A genuine nightmare. There was an autopsy for sure. His heart, they told me. But I swear it was a full blown assault of hemorrhoids!"

I politely said, "Now why didn't the coroner think of that?"

Mrs. Trample-St. Synge continued, "Now 'bout Tybee Island and that motel. I had ma' crock pot in ma' room. Restaurant food can be most disagreeable on the hiatal hernia! My husband was English yo' know, God rest his soul. But I was born and bred in Savannah. If yo' all didn't notice, like all gentile Southern women, I got a very distinct Lowcountry accent. In fact, ma' voice has been compared ta' the enigmatic Julia Child's!"

"I would never have guessed!" I said forcing a civil tone.

"Of course you wouldn't! Vanity certainly is not one of ma' faults!" she said as a chunk of muffin that hung in the corner of her mouth fell into her lap. She ignored it. "Anyhow, I made Yorkshire Puddin' for an early dinner. But yo' know, I don't like ta' eat alone. Do you? I took a batch out ba' the pool. Roast beef, gravy and those biscuits made with flower, egg and milk. There were some pretty shady characters there. Toot, Scooter and Chalks from New York City. Would ya' believe I heard that they were bookies on a holiday?" She rolled her eyes. "Why, only minutes before they had come from one of those nearba' beach bars, and mind yo', to no end they had been siphonin' the whiskers off the brew and who knows what else!"

"Really Mrs. Trample-St. Synge," I protested, "I don't see the point!"

Trudie Peabody squeezed her eyes. "Do go on Constance."

"My point is Kate darlin', that later, this stranger, who in fact, generally always had his body away from us, came out with this quite voluptuous young lady. They sat a spell ba' the pool. Neither one of them said a word. And they wouldn't try ma' puddin' either. But see, later they hurried back to *her* room, which was next ta' mine. I 'spect they were there a good five minutes, mind ya', no doubt havin' a shake and bake in the sack. Then the fellow left!"

I loathed gossip. Suddenly I was irritated. "It isn't our business!" I snapped.

Mrs. Trample-St.Synge glared at me, her hand slicing the air. "Why it most certainly is! Yo' the attorney general and all! A woman of impeccable references! Yo' should be interested in this!"

"Trust me, Mrs. Trample-St. Synge. Although I work at my job like most everyone else, I *hopefully* am taking a vacation from it."

"Well, yes, yo' misunderstand, but I must tell yo' that immediately after this fellow got outta there, the belle left in a taxi. In spite of ma' cataracts, which have not come ta' the middle of ma' eyes yet so they can be operated on, I saw it all. The young lady didn't come back that night. Or the next day. Her cosmetics, a blue lacy nightgown and a flowered dress with a disgraceful plunge ta' the naval were left behind. And she didn't take her toothbrush. Now I ask yo', who would leave for the night and not take a toothbrush?"

"Or dental floss for that matter," Trudie Peabody said.

"Her name?" I asked.

"According ta' the motel register, a Barbara Jones. But the police checked. *Jones*. There are millions in the U.S. Can yo' just imagin' going though life knowin' that all those people had the same name as yo' did?"

"Wouldn't you think that the Social Security Administration *and* Visa would get everybody's accounts mixed up?" Stephen Atchinson pointed out.

Mrs. Trample-St. Synge blinked excessively and then got up. "No doubt," she said, "but I overheard a very nice detective tell the manager that there was no Barbara Jones who had been reported missin'. I heard him in spite of ma' permanent loss of hearin' due ta' a devastatin' middle ear infection years ago which has left me with tintinitus!"

"Perhaps it was an alias," I said finishing my coffee.

Mrs. Trample-St.Synge gave a polite burp into her napkin. "Why, do pardon me. Acid reflux, of course! The strange thing is that I can't be positive. I mean I couldn't swear on ma' mother's King James what I'm 'bout ta' tell yo'."

In preparation for a possible long drawn out speech, I sat down. "Well, go on!" I said, my patience coming unraveled.

"I told Judge Thomason that even though I only got a glimpse of the man that this belle had been with earlier, he looked very much like Senator Holden Renaurd."

"Can you be serious?" I asked, suddenly intrigued.

Mrs. Trample-St. Synge's fingers pattered the edge of her plate. "The judge asked me the same thing. Why she told me that her brother had been in Washington that very day and night! That I was sufferin' from an incurable case of mistaken identity. Of course, I did concede that hallucinations might be a possibility, perhaps from raw fish I had eaten the day before, but unlikely, as I didn't have Montezuma's Revenge. She told me that I should forget about it. There was such a thing as being sued for slander."

Mrs. Peabody waved her napkin in the air. "My goodness, Constance, you wouldn't want that!"

"Let me remind you that one's reputation is the Holy Grail!" Mr. Atchinson warned.

"But I *know* what I saw!" she said measuring her frustration with a smack of her hand against the table. "Yo' can bet yo' britches that it was Holden!"

Recalling my first hours at Renaurd Inn, I wanted to pry about something else. I began, "Mrs. Trample-St.Synge, the evening that I arrived here, I heard Judge Thomason and the senator talking about an incident. One, which apparently caused you to be quite upset? Can you tell me about that?"

She curled her fat ring-laden fingers around another muffin, and after a small bite, said, "Oh ma', that business was about *dreamin'*," she said. Her voice was becoming more high-pitched. "It happened when Barcla' failed to sho' for bridge the night before. Dedicated to the game, he was. Why, he once played opposite Omar Sharif in the Grand Masters tournament in Lubbock, Texas."

Stephen Atchinson's nose quivered into a wad of old Kleenex. "Say, that man has the patience of a priest to sit there all those hours!"

"Well, comparin' him to a priest certainly doesn't hold water anymo'," Mrs. Trample-St.Synge sneered.

I wandered around the table and slid into the chair beside her. Offering a smile, I simply hoped to get to the bottom of this. "About the dreaming?" I paused. "What exactly did you see?"

Mrs. Trample-St.Synge didn't hesitate. It was evident that she loved an audience. Her eyes knitted together as she explained, "Yes. Renty's spaghetti sauce was brutal! Stewed up ma' esophageal spasm. Well, it was close to one in the mornin'. I went down ta' that dreadful kitchen ta' get a glass of milk…with a shot of brandy, too. I take pills so that I am no longer lactate intolerant. That place is like one of those eighteenth century dungeons, I must sa'. When I came back up the stairs, the door ta' the back veranda was ajar."

She leaned into my face and continued. "I looked outside. No actually, I stepped out and there was Barcla', his body stiff and his eyes vacant like in those old black and white Boris Karloff TV movies. Why, seeing him immediately Osterized ma' nerves!"

"You told us that he was a walking zombie!" exclaimed Trudie Peabody.

"Yo' got it," she said.

"Did he speak to you?" I asked. "Did you let him know that you saw him?"

"No, but I watched him glide down the path into the fog and disappear."

I was becoming more and more curious. "He came back soon?"

"Abruptly. Ba' a different way," Mrs. Trample-St.Synge said, getting up from the table.

"I don't understand," I said.

She smacked her lips. "Yes, well, he suddenly was ba' the steps, as if he had floated there on a feather."

I persisted. "Did *you* say anything to him?"

"I did not," she said defensively. "He nearly scared ma' nightgown off when he came up those porch stairs. I was afraid that I might get a fatal heart beat and die! He was droolin' and sweatin', his skin white as fresh cut onions! Why, I thought he might be possessed! Even though I was shiverin' down to my ingrown's, I flung the door completely open! He swept past like I was invisible!"

"Why the idea sends chills right through my root canals," Trudie Peabody said.

That comment brought laughter from everyone. "You spoke to him about it? Later?" I asked.

"Goodness no. And the Judge dismissed it as a prank. That Barcla' was pretendin' in order ta' make Renaurd Inn have a sense of mystery. People especially love haunted inns with ghosts! When they spin in third floor ballrooms or creep down dark halls and scare the livin' daylights out of everyone!"

"Is that what you think happened?" I asked.

She paused, drumming the side of her cup with her forefinger. Her eyes rolled. "Nah. I think the po' guy's got a bad case of the night terrors. Ma' cousin did when she was only five. She'd be at ma' place for a sleep-over. Run down the stairs and out the door as fast as a chicken chased ba' a fox. Ma' daddy grabbed her. And when we'd wake her up, she didn't know she'd even gotten out of bed!"

"What utterly strange business, don't cha' think?" Trudie Peabody asked, a sigh hanging in her throat.

"Sure is," Stephen Atchinson agreed, stuffing one of those menthol sticks up his skinny nostril before running to the window. "I, for one, don't know what to make of it. But I do believe the sun is going to stay."

Mrs. Trample-St. Synge's stories about Holden and Barclay disturbed me, and I wanted to be alone. I went toward the door, wondering if I could sneak away to the beach.

"Well, excuse me, but I have something to do," I said, my announcement unacknowledged, and they paid no attention to my leaving because Mrs. Trample-St.Synge was vehemently chattering about an Irishman who long ago had haunted the remains of an old cave near her hometown.

CHAPTER 8

There was a lot about the 'ground' floor beneath the porches at Renaurd Inn that made me uncomfortable. By night it was dark and bleak, by day, too, a catacomb of massive stone walls carved into smaller rooms where slaves once slept on straw mats, and where in drafty mornings they organized supplies that supported the household through the long humid summers and gray cool winters of South Carolina.

Beneath planked ceilings, I could hear creaking from footsteps above, and after pausing near a niche with its very revealing bronze of a man and woman in a somewhat compromising position, I continued down a narrow corridor where it appeared that nothing else had changed much over the years, not even the sauna, massage, manicure and informal snack areas. Then I entered a twelve by fourteen kitchen that in spite of health department regulations still seemed fused irrevocably to the eighteen hundreds. I stood still. There on flashing behind a six-burner iron stove above which hung grand iron skillets and pots, my eyes focused on hand crafted tiles of mariners and shipwrecks. An old chop block in the middle of the room was covered with roots, weeds, and bottles of powders. I saw strange labels: *Dong quai, uva ursi, calendula.* Others more familiar: *comfrey, mugwort and cayenne*, familiar because cooking had been one of David's hobbies.

For a moment sunrays flickering through the glass block behind the cast iron sink, caused a prism of iridescence in Renty's blue eyes as he came toward me. And despite the noticeable yellowing of his collar and his frayed pant cuffs, his chef's apron was partially clean, although I hoped that he would sanitize both his body and his clothes before putting his nail bitten hands into any more of my Caesar salads.

With a soft voice, he said that he had been to Hilton Head to get herbs, which often he mixed into a special concoction that gave food at the inn its supreme cuisine reputation.

Once again the light came through the glass blocks, and Renty poured coffee into a stone mug next to a can overflowing with cigarette butts. I had the impression that he didn't feel that I belonged there, for it seemed that he stared at me curiously when I asked, "Is there bottled water?"

He crossed in front of me, his hips straddling the door of a stainless steel commercial refrigerator. He folded his arms. "In here," he gestured with the tilt of his head.

"Thank you," I said, moving toward him. He didn't budge. My first instinct was to bolt from the room to get away from him, but on second thought, I didn't care to get into any Olympian altercation, so I said simply, "The water…"

"Top shelf," he said, momentarily turning his back on me.

Allison had told me that Renty ran the inn at the 'labor' level and often gave Barclay's instructions to Bina who then relayed them to the housekeeper and assistant cook, two people of foreign descent who rarely spoke to anyone and who seemed to stay to themselves. Of the help, Renty was the least respected socially because he drank too much and was after all, as Holden pointed out one evening at dinner, 'simply an uneducated worker who Allison dragged from the shore because he needed a place to hang his hat', and although I found his mannerisms irritating, I reminded myself that Allison must have seen something in him that no one else had.

His Adams Apple worked silver beads around his neck. He ripped off the bottle cap. "Here," he said, shoving the water into my hand. With loping strides he was quickly at the door. "That all, Ms. Guesswine?"

I wanted to ask him questions about Jennifer Renaurd. I followed him into the adjoining room, one with a player piano and wicker chairs and a table with neatly stacked health magazines. Wooden brackets holding brightly hand-painted dishes adorned the gray stone walls. I weighed my words. "Renty, can you tell me anything about Jennifer that might help with our investigation?"

At first with the corners of his mouth drawn downward, I expected him to tell me to mind my own business. Instead, he jerked his head toward the archway and folded a piece of gum before putting it into his mouth, his eyes returning coldly to me. "She was a lonely child," he said mournfully, "I wasn't surprised at what happened to her."

I sat on the piano bench, the energy in my fingers softly tapping out a very poor Chopin. I needed to show caution. "Did you see her the day she disappeared?" I asked.

He frowned for a moment, grinding his teeth and twisting his earlobe with his fingers. When he didn't answer, I suspected that it was because he didn't want to tell me anything else. In a bizarre way, it empowered him. And what he remembered was his secret and his alone—stray threads of no significance, of little consequence in the spool of an investigation—nothing more than the girlish things that teenagers talk about, of long drawn treatises about boys, of clothes and music. But in my suspicion, I was determined to learn more. I took a chance. "Well, Renty, have you told me everything?"

As if provoked, he strode toward me, and for an instant I saw in his eyes a fear that wild things have when they are trapped in unfamiliar territory, but then he regained his composure and without throttling a muscle in his face said calmly, "She was killed by someone here on the island." Then he bowed and backed away.

It wasn't what I had expected. I jerked up and followed him into the kitchen. His whinnying could have been drawn from the belly of a nervous stallion, and it caused me to step away. Fearful of traveling down more uncharted roads, I remained still until he regained his composure and his laughter melded into a slight smile.

"The apple never falls far from the tree," he finally said.

"Please, I need to know more!" I said.

"Miss Jenny, she was a beaut'! Raven hair. Why she gave you the feeling that she was going to bust out of her blouse the way a flower comes out of its bud in the spring. The day she ran off," he said, "she was over there at Gabe's the whole day."

"Ran off? Who told you that?"

"Coneras took her to Hilton Head," he said. "That's who said it."

"Did anyone else see her leave? The others?"

"All I know is that Miss Allison was at her office that day. Holden in Washington. Barclay on his boat. A stiff wind made for a good sail."

"Renty, what about you and Bina? You told the police that you both were here at the inn, didn't you?"

He swiped his hand definitively through the air. "You're forgetting, that was years ago! Now if that's all, I've got work to do."

At no time had I heard Bina coming down the stairs or through the hall. Had she been listening?

"Don't stop on my account," she insisted, her mouth gaping, and not before she had set her eyes on Renty who was motionless, looking hard at me, and with a look that pled for me not to betray his confidence. My voice broke, "Oh well, we were sharing tales about how quickly the weather can turn this time of year."

She pulled aside her lips into a little smirk. "Sometimes soak the land to its gills," she said. "I suppose that's what he was telling you, wasn't it?"

I kept wondering how to gracefully get away. "Speaking of water," I finally said. "I'm off to the beach. We'll chat again Renty." But before I had shut the door, I heard swearing and Jennifer Renaurd's name, and suddenly I was glad to give in to an overwhelming need to jog. One more piece of the puzzle had been added, but I had no idea where it belonged.

CHAPTER 9

"Careful now!"

"Mmm? What?" I tuned my eyes to a ruggedly handsome man in a loosely fitted blue sleeveless shirt and dark jeans with ragged gray socks bordering brown sea-boots. His charismatic smile diminished any caution Allison had warned me about Gabe Coneras.

"The wind brought the tide in a little higher last night," he said. He stood so close that I could feel his breath. "The trail to the beach might be flooded."

"If it is, I'll turn around," I told him.

"Sometimes a snake will take refuge on the wood. For the sun."

"I'm not afraid of snakes," I said, slouching back so I could see him better. "But a run in with a spider will put me in a dead faint!"

"You shouldn't walk any place on the island unless you've had the nickel tour," he warned.

"Oh? I assume you are talking about the north end?"

"That's right. Lots of gators. There's muck that could swallow up a full grown person! Like quicksand."

"Well, I've already been warned by Bina that it's a pretty dreadful place. I suppose that it is simply more of island folklore, isn't it?" I asked, remembering Mrs. Trample-St. Synge's reference to ghosts, as well.

He took my arm. "Just be careful. Let me walk with you to the beach."

"I don't think…"

"To the stairs."

"I really don't think," I said, "I mean, I'm not at all afraid. You forget that I grew up around marshes."

"So you did," he said, relaxing his fingers.

His broad smile coaxed one from me. "For your information, I'm partially a mud puppy!" I said lightly. He followed me past sea-oat covered dunes until we came to a portion of the boardwalk breached by a quarter inch of water, and we were forced to stick our shoes under our arms and wade to drier boards. Nearby were nettle and ivy, their tendrils floating like parts of a water garden under the atrium of a giant banyan tree. Then after awhile the wood became dry. Above me, the furrows of white clouds all but blocked the sun, but it seemed warm.

"Air's great, here, huh?" he said, taking several deep breaths.

When we came down two wooden stairs, I paused at built-in benches to take in the clear view of the surf raking the beach with shells and seaweed. "Have you been the caretaker for the Renaurds long?"

"I go way back. Why?"

His heavily lashed eyes made me uncomfortable. I was instantly flushed. "Please don't do that!" I asked awkwardly.

"What?"

"You know what I mean. That thing you do with your eyes."

"You're a pleasure to look at," he said, pointing a finger at me. "I won't apologize."

Still barefoot, we stepped upon the warm sand, where all night a steady east wind had strung seaweed near the tide line, where Gabe walked backward so that he was facing me.

"And before that?" I asked.

"What?"

"Before the caretaker job?"

He sighed. "Oh a year at New York State. Liberal arts. I wanted to be an artist. Instead, I actually did a stint on *Guiding Light*. Got killed off after five appearances."

"Mmm hmm. You were a starving actor then?"

"Nah. But I wore one of those, 'Will work for food' signs," he said winking.

"People everywhere must have wanted to hire you, you so charming and all?" I teased.

"Every minute of every day!"

And then he moved beside me and it was a while before I said, "Mmm hmm. With a line like that, well, I'm absolutely not surprised!"

He stopped, got in front of me again, and straddled his foot upon a piece of driftwood. "May I say something to you Kate?"

"Is there much likelihood that you won't?" I asked grinning.

He didn't grin back, and a look passed between us that indicated that he was dead serious. "When I was in Spain," he said, lowering his voice, "a few years ago to visit relatives…"

"Oh, that's the connection, then."

"Connection?"

"You're from Spain?"

"Indirectly," he said. "My ancestors were from there. They helped erect Fort San Felipe on nearby Parris Island. They were master carpenters."

"So that explains why Allison says that you're good with your hands. A genetic predisposition," I said, turning over his palm as if I were about to read his fortune. It was calloused and large, and I blushed when I thought of all it might be able to do. Perhaps toying with the idea himself, he gripped my fingers and held them too long, looking as pleased as a child. I pulled free and darted into the surf where a surprising gust of air seemed to lift the waves, soaking my shift up to my knees. As accustomed as I was to getting drenched on long beach walks, my wet legs brought a chill and I bolted from the water. "Damn!"

"You asked about the Spanish connection…" he began. "Well, some of my family came from the Asturias region on the north central coast of Spain. They were *adelantados*."

"And what might that be?" I went a few yards ahead of him.

"Well, they came to the New World to inhabit the Appalachian area. It was supposed to be as fertile as the Andalusia Plain, you know. Instead they ended up around St. Helena Island."

"Near Beaufort."

"Yes. Very sturdy stock. My great-great-great grandmother was one of several women left with about twenty soldiers to defend the Spanish fort against over 500 Indians. Well…"

I kicked up sand and then he was beside me. We both squinted because of the sudden appearance of the sun that turned the sea into shimmering platinum. "Well?" I asked.

"Huh?"

"You said, "Well…""

He caught his breath and rolled the cuffs of his pants, his lower leg hair glistening with a sheath of salt water. "Well…they—the women— begged to be taken away," he continued, "but General Hernando Miraudo refused. So you know what?"

"Not a clue!" I said.

"Those women seized him!"

"Oh my, don't tell me! The first instance of women's lib?"

"Couldn't say. But they expected another attack by the Indians. So they forced the general to abandon Fort San Felipe. Board his ship and move to the mouth of Port Royal Sound while the Indians destroyed the fort. Those women saved a lot of lives!"

He stopped, coming around to face me, pulling my shawl around my neck as if he knew that I was still having a chill, and I too, reached up and secured the ends. "What happened to her?" I asked. "What happened to your triple 'g' grandmother?"

"Rumor had it that she was sent to Cuba. But a cousin of hers returned in 1577 to help build Fort San Marcos about fifty yards away from San Felipe."

"I've seen that fort," I said. "I've watched the Marines train nearby. You were raised in Cuba then?"

As if he were part of the blue of the sea, he stared off to the south, taking it all to be his—all of it, the light and dark of the blue sea and the sun carved patches of light and dark that appeared when the clouds moved. "My father was an American businessman in free Cuba," he said with finality. But then he said more. "After Castro took over, my parents moved to Miami. Others followed."

"Coneras, too?"

"Actually, he came here long before my mother left Cuba."

"And the connection to Allison and the Renauds?"

He cleared his throat a couple of times. "I guess I would respond like this. Leighton Renaurd and the Mrs. were on a vacation in Havana. Americans used to do that before Castro, you know. They offered my grandfather work. He took the job."

I tried to wring out some of the water still dripping from the hem of my shift. I walked ahead...up the beach, my feet thumping around old stones that might have crossed the Atlantic in the worst of storms. "And what about your mother?" I asked over my shoulder.

"Heart attack after she returned to Cuba to visit a sister. My father died there after a visit, too. His body was never found. So my grandfather sent for me. It seems I've always been here. First as a small child. Then as a young boy playing in the hidden corners of the island. You know, like in stories...like one of those jungle boys raised by wolves. All that playing. All that exploring until I left. Sometimes I came back for holidays. Then I came back permanently a few years ago. I'm here to stay, I suppose."

"I think you're a bit of an enigma, Gabe Coneras." I said unsteadily.

He jumped in front of me and laughed. "Intriguing enough to make you interested?"

I went around him. "Why, I don't mean that at all," I stammered.

For a short time, I thought that he had grown sullen, but it didn't matter. I just had spent five years in the grip of a man who without provocation could transform into the most ghastly mood, and although I would attempt to figure out his every unreadable gesture or word, he had fascinated me beyond reason by his very sullenness.

"Hey, well, in Spain I went to this museum," Gabe finally said, bringing back a smile. "There was this painting of a woman. Eyes the color of topaz! I thought I'd never see those eyes again. And then you came here. You're a dead ringer for the woman on the canvass."

His studying me again was embarrassing, and I could not consciously look at him. I tried humor. "Oh you *really* don't get anywhere with a line like that, do you?"

"You'd be surprised!"

"Mmm hmm. I can see that they made a mistake throwing you off the soap operas, and you a devoted Thespian! My my!"

"Now I suppose you'll take me to the gallows for saying you're knock out gorgeous!" he said.

"Allison did warn me about you!"

"Strike three, huh?" he complained. His forefinger lifted my chin.

At once I sensed that he wanted to continue to touch me, but I gauged my distance, for something about him was familiar, something which I had seen in 'moves' that other men had made on me in my life. "I suppose that most young Galahads paying a compliment to an older woman is like sending a downpour to a desert? Mmm?" I asked.

"Not at all. Age has nothing to do with it," he said, his softening voice compelling me to look at him.

I coughed. "Oh, it has everything to do with it!"

"Boy, you're tough! Someone must have creamed your self-esteem! And I suspect that you're anything but a desert!"

"Mmm hmm. Well, it might be better if you don't say things like that!"

"What's a guy to do?" he said whimsically.

His roving eyes attempted to be subtle. I looked hard at him, and with my forefinger admonished him with a strong, "Aah…no!"

"Now, that's a 'no!'" he said kicking a shell into the water.

I dropped to me knees, determined to change the subject. "When I was a child, my sister Courtney and I could sit for hours and build castles surrounded by motes. Do you think all children do that?"

"Your sister's the late night talk show hostess over in Savannah, isn't she?"

"Midnight to three," I said proudly. "Have you listened to her?"

He crouched, his knee nearly touching mine. "I've heard her once or twice. Her guests talking about their 'out of body experiences' and voodoo," he said.

"She has almost fifteen million steady listeners," I pointed out.

"Then don't give it a thought that I'm not one! Other things interest me, though. Look over there," he observed, gesturing with his arm extended toward the mainland.

He stood up, his knuckles foraging hard into his denim pockets. "You can barely see it. Dragon's Point," he continued. "I've sailed my boat parallel to it dozens of times. Oh yes, I know. That's where Jennifer Renaurd's body was found. Close to a sandbar. Where sharks hang around."

"You've no doubt heard about the other bones that were found there then?" I said slowly.

"Lives get altered don't they? But I've no interest in violent things," he said.

"Well, that's a relief," I said jokingly. "Then hockey won't replace Rachmaninoff, huh?"

He gave me a serious look and then broke into laughter. "Never replace it," he mumbled. "Say, there's a concert at the Self Arts Center next weekend. Will you go with me?"

"Oh, but I was only joking," I said awkwardly. "Listen, Gabe…"

"Un huh, I understand," he interrupted. "No fraternizing with the help?"

"Look, it's nothing like that. I'm simply here for a rest. And nothing—and I mean nothing—more!"

His chin sagged. He slipped on his shoes and bolted toward the stairs, pausing to say, "Well, I've got work to do! Oh, and Kate, I really do like Rachmaninoff, especially his second piano concerto in C# minor."

I strained to watch him until he disappeared into the curve of the boardwalk. *Nice buns. Gabe has damn nice buns*, I thought afterward, my eyes focusing for the longest time on a piece of driftwood next to the steps. It was the first time I'd dared think of anyone but David, but then I put away such thoughts and collapsed upon the warm sand, my arms under my head to make a pillow, my mind dreamily traversing the clouds above, my body nearly asleep until a robust figure bounding down the boardwalk began to sing in a soprano voice, 'Yo' ho, Kate! I thought yo' might want company!' And I wondered what the penalty for drowning someone was. 'Life' or lethal injection?

CHAPTER 10

The first weekend in November, I had come down with a terrible case of bronchitis, and for three days, armed with chicken soup and a bottle of Coastal Mondavi, I put myself in self-imposed exile at the motorhome. After that, I still wasn't my old self. But without too much discussion I promised Allison that I would use additional 'comp' time and return to the inn for more rest and relaxation as soon as I could. In the meantime, official business prevailed, and I spent a few days at my satellite offices in Greenville and Charleston. Although the attorney general's domain was divided into subdivisions, it was mostly my forty assistant attorneys general and the other 100 employees who kept the divisions running smoothly while I dealt with criminal appeals and unusual cases such as the Dragon's Point murders. I also worked amicably with legislators, prosecutors, sheriffs and the police.

Amicability was generally true of my relationship with the FBI, too, especially agent Drew Greer who, while her Cessna was in the hanger for repairs, had driven her Hummer from Washington to Charleston on business and then the fifty miles to Hilton Head.

Except for my appointment with psychic Bernadine Tynbrock late Saturday morning, I had cleared my schedule, and after breakfast Drew and I met Digger Martin, the Beaufort County District Attorney, at Java Joes off Coligny Circle. This small Hilton Head restaurant had many colorful beach locals who some said had stretched their minds in the wrong direction, but that's what I liked about the place—people who didn't play the same tune as the rest of the world. We went in. It was a warm and welcoming room with a counter at the west end. People were lined up all the way to the door, but Digger had commandeered two flowered settees that faced each other near the front window. We got coffee from one of those pump carafes, and I thanked God that I was being spared Digger's infamous 'put the hair on the chest' mud water that he kept in a grungy pot in his office.

In many ways the DA was what I might call an endangered species: tousled hair and very thin, and the way his arms dangled over the back cushion—a scarecrow of a man. His trademark attire of a wrinkled plaid shirt, gray pants and white socks might have been in the Maytag for days. Conspicuously, the silver gun emblem he wore on his belt buckle was missing, and I wondered if he still kept the big picture of Charleton Heston in his office now that the actor was no longer the president of the NRA.

Digger turned and he didn't get up. "Hey Lady! You dropped a little flab there," he said jamming his finger into my thigh, a familiar gesture we all knew about but ignored because it was just one of Digger's 'ways'. Without a word I followed Drew around the coffee table and slipped onto the opposite settee.

"And you there," he said leaning forward with an intense frown that was nearly always there when he addressed Drew, "How's the Auntie Mame of the FBI? You lookin' little milky 'round the gills." He was partly right. Her hair was a drab brown frizzle and cropped high above her ears. She was noticeably frail.

"Yeah, well don't go there, Digger, or I'll have to talk about that tire under your damn belly button," Drew said sarcastically. Ever since they had worked together during a sting, there had been friction between them, and often in private he had made reference to her old ways of cavorting with men and doubted that she had given up her excessive drinking. I knew better, of course; I knew she had been seriously ill and was doing all she could to hold on to her job as one of the FBI's lead serial killer investigators.

Digger tussled with papers and magazines on the coffee table between us, splitting his tongue between a wad of Skoal and a gulp of coffee. "So what...'er...we got here? More of your pit bull bureau shit,

Drew?" He frowned. "And don't wheelie your fuckin' eyes at Kate either!"

Drew balanced her thin buttocks on the edge of a cushion while carefully removing the elastic from an accordion folder, gripping it as if it might take off from her knee like a heavy transport plane. She cleared her throat, took a sip of latte and scattered the papers in front of us—an emergency landing of sorts because it was done with much deliberation. "I think you'll both want to see this!" she said.

I recognized the title at the top of page one. "*Lazarus?*" A short while before, Paul Hanes, who always arrived at sunup at my office in Columbia, had faxed the file to my car machine. "I haven't had a chance to read it yet," I said.

Digger emptied brown spittle into a napkin. He chased it with coffee. "Yeah, that's the FBI"s code name for the bone cases. M'dear, it don't mean shit. Sheriff Sparkmen's had that info' for days now...er...I already read it."

I was puzzled. I usually received FBI reports before local law enforcement.

Drew swung her legs back to the floor. Her body bristled. "Not this one! You both were the benefactor of this within the last hour. Now do you want to hear about it or not?"

"Only if you *both* lower your voices and quit acting like of couple of children," I said. Suddenly, I was aware of their lips freezing on the brims of their cups. Neither of them liked to be reprimanded. I reached for one of the pages. "Lazarus? Mmm hmm. Like when someone dies and then sits straight up?" I asked.

"That's right," Drew said. "What do you two know about the body parts business?"

"I don't think I'm gonna like *any* of this," Digger said.

"It's a big enterprise," I said. "I know that there's hundreds of millions of dollars being made from harvesting cadaver parts."

Drew tilted her head forward. "Well my friends, not just from the dead ones. How about people who aren't so dead?"

"Say, didn't someone auction a human kidney on eBay back in 2000?" Digger asked. "'member that?"

"Yeah," Drew said. "There was a bid of $100,000 before the transaction was shut down. But organ trafficking has become an international smorgasbord! Lungs, kidneys, corneas, bones, skin. Why, one cadaver can provide over a hundred people with parts!"

Digger raked his bushy brows with the palm of his hands and said, "Well, I'll be a son-of-a-bitch!"

"I've recently had several memorandums come across my desk in Columbia about it," I said. "Even famous models have used cadaver skin to build up their lips."

"...at a thousand bucks or more per treatment," Drew said, "and skin and bone to enlarge penises. Get rid of old lady's wrinkles."

Remembering my last root canal, I said, "You probably know that dentists buy ground up human bone to repair a couple hundred thousand jaws each year!"

Digger cupped his chin in his palm. His mouth hung open. "I was thinkin' about getting...er...teeth implants. Screw that!" he said. "Or that business with the 'dicks'."

"Yeah? Well, I wouldn't rule that out," Drew said.

Everybody laughed. "But there are strict federal laws," I said more seriously.

"That's right," Drew answered. "The National Organ Transplant Act of 1984 federally regulates the sale and distribution of procured organs. But the problem is that trading and trafficking goes on in other countries, too—in Brazil, Turkey, Philippines, Bahamas and regions like the Balkans just to name a few places. In fact, let me read you something." Her voice stilled. We waited.

Digger extended his size thirteens under the table. "Awe shit, what's this gotta do with the bone cases?"

"Indulge me," Drew said perusing papers.

I kept thinking that Digger might get up and leave. It was his way, his fidgeting, being abrupt and then dismissing everyone as if they had no consequence, but then he suddenly seemed more distracted by a cavalcade of people outside, especially a young couple standing near the window, a man and woman who were pleasantly caught up in one another, and I thought how strange that we kept going on and on about the dead when everyone around us seemed so alive. It had always interested me about how we could sail in and out of a moment with our minds. How when we are younger, we don't give a damn about the moment because we believe that there will be so many more. And when we are older, we watch life like a voyeur because we know there will be so very few.

"Mmm hmm. I think I know where you're going with this," I said quickly.

"Yeah, get on with it," Digger said anxiously. "My ass gets like an over ripe plum if I sit too long."

It occurred to me that he probably wished that he had gone shopping with his wife after all.

"That's what I'm trying to do," Drew said. "For the most part, there were over a million tissue transplants this year in an industry worth over a billion dollars. And while it's illegal to profit from the sale of body parts, it's perfectly all right to make money from procuring and processing human beings. In fact, anyone could make a hundred thou' or more from one body."

Digger sat straight up. "It's the gold rush of the new century, eh?"

"That's putting it mildly," Drew said. "The FDA routinely inspects tissue banks, but there could be as many as 350 that aren't registered. They're like illegal chop shops for cars. No pun intended!"

"None taken," I said.

"And that's where the FBI comes in," she continued. "We're after these body brokers. The guys who harvest the organs and ferry them illegally to hospitals where they're sold to the wealthy or VIP's who privately will pay as much as a hundred and fifty thousand for a kidney. Do you know that there are actual catalogues with a price list for the body parts?"

I looked gravely at Digger. It seemed Frankensteinish that more and more of the boomer population wished to deny the quintessential reality of death. Supposedly religion and the taboo custom of body mutilation had gone down the tubes, while kidnapping, murder and body tampering seemed to be the new Draconian custom. "If you remember," I said, "when Dr. Packer did an autopsy on Anastasia she found heparin in her tissue."

"That shit prevents blood clottin'!" Digger said.

"That's right," I said. "She also found traces of a tranquilizer. And remember, Dr. Packard believes that someone extracted most of her skin from her chest and back. Her kidneys, pancreas and liver were probably taken, too."

Drew crossed her legs. Her eyes trailed Java Joes memorabilia near a wall.

"Christ!" Digger said. "That means she could have been alive when that skin…oh shit, I'm going to the toilet!" His face was red. He jumped up to his right, wove around tables and disappeared behind a door across from us.

"But unconscious," I said. "The excision has to be done quickly. Parts shipped immediately to preserve the organs. Keep them fresh!"

"In dry ice generally. But some organs—corneas, bone and tendons and skin don't need to be handled in the same way as some of the major organs."

Digger returned and said, "Well, damn it, look at that!" He stretched his arms. Twisted them like a pretzel before he sat down, commenting about a man outside with a parrot on his shoulder before he added, "So you're sayin' that we've got some asshole around here who's kidnappin' women, cuttin' out their innards and sellin' 'em to some fat cat with a big purse—maybe a doctor or his patient—before thrownin' the rest of 'em to the sharks off Dragon's Point. That what you sayin' Drew?" he asked.

"Something like that," she replied.

It was still unclear. I was thinking about Jennifer Renaurd. Drew could see it coming from me. She frowned, her fingers dancing and clicking in the air the way they often did in the old days when we were young lawyers and I disagreed with her about a case.

"Serial killer? Probably," I said. "But Jennifer Renaurd's remains? What's the connection? She was young; the others older. She was a budding artist; the others prostitutes. She came from a good family; the others from poor, broken homes. And we really can't prove that anyone but this last victim had her organs excised."

"It's a matter of time," Drew said, her voice constrained.

I glared at Drew. "What haven't you told us?"

"Later," she said.

"I feel like I'm listening to mambo jambo," Digger said, as it started to rain. "It's why I hate working with you FBI'ers. Now look at that doggone weather out there!"

Drew stood up. She was so thin that I suddenly remembered that I had been worried about the unknown illness that had kept her in bed so many days during the months before. "Tell you what, guys," she said. "I'll give you this: We know that most of the women may have had connections to either illegal gambling, drugs or prostitution. And there may be a connection to the Bahamas and possibly the Philippines and Cuba."

I pushed my body up. The joint in my knee cracked. "I want to know *now* what the FBI knows," I said angrily. "I'm the damn attorney general!"

"That doesn't make you ordained!" she said as she shoved her fist playfully into my arm. "You know the rules."

Leaning into her face, I warned, "Don't make the mistake of making them your personal rules."

"So what's…er…the plan of action right now?" Digger asked with a more upbeat tone now that the meeting was over.

"I'll have an official briefing in a few days!" she said.

And I knew her word was good, that any prodding on my part would only make her more resolute and Digger anxious. Minutes later, my emotions drained, the three of us went in different directions to our cars. Justin's big truck pulled in next to me. He looked disagreeable. His eyes were dark and he hadn't shaved, believing that weekends freed him from the razor, and I suspected that he hadn't had his coffee. I glanced at my watch. We had a good half hour before our meeting with psychic Dr. Bernadine Tynbrock.

"And the 'top of the morning' to you, Justin," I said saccharinely.

"Case solved yet?" he asked smiling.

I pointed to a picture of a coffee cup on Java Joe's window. "Oh shut up. I'll buy you a 'fix'."

He kissed me on the forehead. "I did *not* say with cream and sugar!"

CHAPTER 11

Later, Justin and I arrived early for our appointment with Dr. Bernadine Tynbrock, a well-known psychic, an intuitive sensory specialist, who had done casework for police divisions all over the nation. Her one story office building was a benchmark for the small bedroom community of Bluffton, a flagship for craftsmanship in the development of coastal towns. We strolled the wrap-around-porch, admiring the ship's railing and fascia around the fish-scaled cedar siding and scalloped rafter tails protruding like a ship's bow at each corner of the building.

"Hey Katie, I wanted to tell you," Justin said, taking off his left shoe and rubbing a bunion that had bothered him for years. "You know that scarf we found during our investigation over at Tybee? That purple one covered with little lady bugs?"

"What about it?"

"Do you think it might help if I stick a photo of it in the papers? Maybe somebody will recognize it?"

"Never know. Now put your shoe back on before your foot swells and you can't."

He grinned. "Then no one will ever refer to me as a 'flatfoot' cop!"

I always had believed that if you kept at something long enough, you'd prevail, so I knew that it was partly Justin's perseverance that made him exceptional at his job, although he hated those years when he had been a uniformed officer, his having to adjust his hat, his shirt, and his jacket according to regulations about as bad as having a fungus to put salve on. He never was a 'regulation man'. No, Justin didn't like any kind of ceremony or restrictions. When he made detective, he donned jeans and a basketball cap, didn't shave a lot of days, fitting in perfectly with the street battles that went along with working undercover. Unfortunately, the day he made chief of detectives, he seemed out of sorts again, maybe because he had to put on a coat, shirt and tie again. I never knew if his becoming so disagreeable in our marriage was because of the change in wardrobe or the change in his job status.

A small bell chimed from a stainless-steel clock hanging near the glass door at the front of the building. We went in. There was no secretary. After shaking my hand and to my surprise, Dr. Tynbrock greeted Justin by his first name. I could only imagine how he must have known her, but then she cleared it up by saying to him, "I hope that session I did last month on that rape victim from Hilton Head helped you and your division."

"Yeah, well, it did, Bernadine," he said. "We got the son-of-a-bitch. Those fancy T-bar skivvies he left behind are only sold at a few places around here. I went through the list like a chainsaw. One of the owners dug out a credit card slip. That was that! We caught the bastard. Didn't I get his sorry ass in jail?"

They smiled hard at each other. Why did I suddenly think that perhaps they had shared a drink together, and then I chided myself for caring that Justin would have noted that the fortyish Dr. Tynbrock was long on looks, built like a brick shit house—as guys would say—with abundant breast poured into a huge green organza blouse that hung to the knees over buttock revealing leotards. With dark round eyes, sleek black braids twining along the side of her long neck, and skin of an Indian princess, she was unusually striking to men and women, her appearance very sculpturesque. Her reputation was long on looks, too. Several degrees adorned her pale blue office wall, including one in cultural anthropology from Ohio State and another in psychiatry from University of Michigan.

"Dr. Tynbrock, you've heard about the bone cases?" I asked.

"Oh yes," she said, quickly motioning for us to sit on one of two green corduroy sofas. I felt as if I were in someone's comfortable living room. There were vines twirling from wicker baskets and ceramic and clay pots filled with begonias. Gullah paintings by local artists adorned the walls, their subjects rich in hues of yellow and brown, the colors of scorched summer yards. "Coffee?"

"Thank you," I said.

Justin shifted in his seat. "Real stuff?" he asked, even though I was hoping that it was decaffeinated.

"Pure granite," she said.

After she poured into salt glaze mugs that looked like ones I once had purchased at the pottery in Williamsburg, Va., Dr. Tynbrock sat opposite us so that she was near a small recorder that was connected to a microphone attached to her lapel. She ceremoniously put on dark glasses and began moving her hands through the air as if she were conducting a symphony. I knew Justin would be chuckling to himself while I totally believed she had been blessed with some unique power. In fact, my skepticism about such abilities had disappeared after I had been involved in a case in which a Colorado psychic, an acquaintance of mine, helped the police find the exact location of a child's body by using a pendulum dangling over a map. "Are we ready?" she asked.

"Mmm hmm. As ready as we can be," I said.

Justin crossed his arms and leaned back in his chair as if he were at a movie theater.

"You have an object for me?" Dr. Tynbrock asked.

I opened a brown sack. "A tibia," I said, while in my mind I apologized to Anastasia (who was still at the morgue) for temporarily borrowing a leg bone. There was still a reverence about the bone, I thought, for it had been part of a walking, talking, human being that had been attached to a name, a Ms. or Mrs. or Miss perhaps? I saw Justin grimace. He didn't view it the same way that I did.

"I see. Yes. That will do nicely," she said casually. "Let me *feel* the bone. I am going to tap into its energy." She stroked it but never looked once at it. "It is a female we are talking about. White. Blonde hair. Long skirt. Perhaps flowers. She's wearing a peasant's blouse. Near a bar at the beach. I don't know where."

"Is she alone?" I asked being careful not to shift too frequently in my chair.

Dr. Tynbrock held the bone to her chest. "At last I'm tapping into where she is. Ah, she's being flirtatious. Outside a café. An island bar. An outside patio. Not where the average tourist would go. No. A shady beach bar. Called…sounds like Eddies. Teddies. I can't be sure," she said.

"Say! That could be Headlies!" Justin said, "That half-assed motel-diner down near Coligny Circle, that joint where the Palmetto bugs are known to shit in the soup!"

The veins in my temples were pounding. "Do be quiet!" I said. I couldn't go into it right then, but supposedly under new management, Headlies had cleaned up and no longer had cheap rates and dinners that required a bicarbonate chaser, although the motel office still had a condom machine that was usually depleted by the end of a weekend.

Dr. Tynbrock continued. "She's at a table. A four top."

I knew that was restaurant lingo for four chairs at a table.

"There's a young couple. And a male that she's picked up. I can retrace her steps. Yes. It looks as if…okay now…everyone's getting kind of chummy. He's getting friskier with her. The other two, the couple, want to leave. And she wants to go to the lady's room. I'm seeing a clock, a fake metallic one that's peeling around the edges, strung over the bar. It's a quarter 'til one in the morning."

"Maybe we should just get to when he punches her ticket," Justin said.

"Shush!" I said.

Dr. Tynbrock's expression remained impassive. "There are two men at the bar. They don't notice as she passes by. Wait a minute. I'm getting into the energy of one of them. Actually, he's very well—better dressed than he should be for a beach club. Uh, he's looking at his watch. She's paused near him. In spite of following her with his eyes, he's being discreet. Moving on, she stays in the lady's room for a while, close to a half an hour. By that time, the guy who she earlier has picked up realizes that she is not returning. And I'll go back to see where he is in the picture. Oh, I see. He's decided, 'okay, I'm being dumped.' He is leaving."

"He'll probably sue," Justin laughed.

In frustration I slugged his knee with my knuckles. "Oh do be serious!" I whispered into the canal of his ear.

"She stays in the bathroom until one forty. Now she's coming back. She seems to know the bartender. He's the owner. Okay, I see that they chit chat."

I listened for clues. I knew that there could be an element of coincidence and that Dr. Tynbrock might simply guess about some piece of information that we already knew. Cold cases were always more difficult, not only for us, but especially for psychics, and even Dr. Tynbrock wasn't sure which victim she was talking about. I hadn't told her that the bone belonged to Anastasia. Yet, I somehow felt that she sensed that the energy locked within the porous bone might belong to all the women and they are reaching out collectively for some small piece of revenge.

"It appears that she is leaving," she continued. "In her mind she was going to go home. The bartender—what happens is that the bartender turns around. He's talking to someone and doesn't pay any attention to the well-dressed man who is getting up from the end stool."

I kept thinking of the bartender in the wee hours of the morning, his brain a shaft for alcohol induced verbiage from the vermin who are one shot away from puking all over the bar, a head-rest for a wife beater, child molester or murderer. And this, too, for the bartender. No matter what he sees or hears, his own survival depends on his indifference, his letting all that verbiage slide in and out of his mind the way a man does while he is having intercourse with a stranger.

"Once outside everything happens quickly for the woman," Dr. Tynbrock continued. "She doesn't get into the cab. She doesn't have any money left. So she's decided that she's going to walk. Before she notices him, the well-dressed man is beside her. He is distinguished. The man I'm seeing has brown hair with graying at the temples, and when he turns around, well, I'll tell you what color his eyes are. Uh, I see that they are not blue. Not brown. Isn't that strange? They are mixed. I can't be sure."

"He's probably a goddamn transvestite, Bernadine!" Justin said.

"You must be still!" I warned.

Dr. Tynbrock's eyes blinked. "Uh, I can't tell his ethnicity for sure either."

Justin stood up. "Hold the thought. Gotta go to the can," he said before disappearing behind a door with a rather large cartouche, an ornamental framed painting of a 'throne', a symbol for 'toilet'.

Dr. Tynbrock finally collapsed against the pillows and smiled. "Well, then it's break time, isn't it?" Carefully she laid the bone on a tiled side table and reached for her coffee. "More?"

I shook my head. "I notice you use only your left hand and run it continuously across the tibia," I said.

"Exactly. There's strong energy in that hand. A special 'light'. I'm told by my colleagues not to lose it. You know, in an accident or something? My right hand doesn't seem to have the sensitivity, although I'm told it can be trained, also."

A short time later Justin returned and helped himself to several chocolate truffles that were neatly placed on a square blue plate. Regaining her serious posture, Dr. Tynbrock politely pretended not to notice and began again. She picked up the bone. "This man? I see high cheekbones. His lips are not big but they're bigger than normal for a man. They're out of proportion for his face. He has an unbuttoned dress shirt on. It is of a cream color, and he has brownish tan slacks on. Uh, yes…oh my, his shoes are brown loafers with tassels, and are very, very expensive. He's out of place. I'm surprised that he's even there. That's how different he is. That's how much he stands out! He has a gold watch on his left arm and a ring on his finger, but it's not a wedding ring. It's more of a college insignia. It has an initial on it, but I can't read it."

I was baffled about that. Why would a killer wear something that might draw attention? I ventured a suggestion. "Dr. Tynbrock, is the man clear enough to you to have one of our police artist draw a picture from your description?"

"Perhaps. Yeah, he *really* is in my mind. He's really there!" she said, pulling her left leg under her.

"Please go on," I said. "You're incredible!"

"Yeah. Better than those TV psychics," Justin said, fluttering his eyelids.

"Uh, that, well…that ring? It means something to the killer," she said, her eyes firmly closed again. "It's some kind of an ego ring. He's proud of it, the way someone harbors old coins and fine paintings, but he stops looking at it. No longer twists it. He speaks to her. Uses her name. He had heard the bartender say it. She turns around, and uh, wait…the *light is very strong now*. I see it. I feel the energy from this. She sees that he is a man of class, and she thinks, 'Oh, wait a minute. This looks like money. I'd better check this out.' And she's had too many drinks and goes to him easily. He's talking to her now. He's saying, 'It's late and you don't know what's out there. It could be dangerous. Why don't I just drive you home?'"

Sadly, I couldn't help but think that it was the same old story. Sips of wine, a wiggle and jiggle 'come on', a cold kiss, the lure into the backseat with the prospect of a good pay off, and sadly, many prostitutes end up slaughtered and dumped at similar Dragon's Points. Didn't they know that every day in America there are at least five thousand predators waiting to snare their victims? Didn't they know?

Dr. Tynbrock became expressionless. She took a drink of water and began again. "Now they are walking. He has his hand on her wrist, but he's barely touching it. She tells him that she lives nearby. But he tells her, 'Let me drive you home, please. You seem to have a lot of spirit. I'd like to know you a little better.' So he's very friendly. He's very approachable. Their interaction is non-threatening to her."

"It fries my mind," Justin said. "These women are so damn lonely that they'd pick up The Wolf Man himself just to have the prick curl up in some flea bag motel next to their already used-up bodies so they can get some meth' money!"

He was referring to Methadone. Shut up Justin. You are interfering with Dr. Tynbrock's energy!

Patiently she went on. "Uh, so now his expensive car is parked behind the bar. It looks out of place because there are mostly revved-up trucks and junky cars, all beach kind of vehicles. Ah. It…oh my…I see that it is a very shiny black. Very sterling. Now she definitely believes he has money."

"This gouging-the-guy for his bread pisses me off," Justin said.

I put my finger to my lips.

"But when she closes her door, he doesn't approach her sexually. No, not at all. He doesn't want to do anything to take advantage of her. Yet, he finds her attractive in a strange sort of way. Is there something that he doesn't understand? He studies his watch as if he is on some kind of a schedule. Oh well, he's looked at it several times and she comments about it. 'Hey, do you have someone waiting for you? Am, I keeping you?' That kind of thing. And he says, 'Ah, no. I'm here on business, and I need to get back to my motel because I have an early meeting tomorrow. But I'll drop you at your place.' So she buys that story. Oh my. I can tell you that the energy is *very* strong now! The energy is here in this bone!"

"That's why I hate bones," Justin interrupted. "All this talk gives me the creeps."

"Really Justin," I said with only threads of patience left, "You must refrain…"

"It's really all right," Dr. Tynbrock said, opening her eyes again. "He has a point. I do understand. But let's go on." She pursed her lips and her eyes focused on the bone again. "Anyhow, as they drive toward the motel, she doesn't object, but when they arrive, she says, 'What are we going to do?' She's starting to get a little fidgety. 'Oh, just a minute,' he tells her. And he says, 'There's a conference tomorrow. A friend took the 'red eye' from California and should be arriving by taxi at any minute. He needs these papers so that he can look at them first thing in the morning. I won't be long.' And then she tells him, 'Okay. I guess it's okay.' Then he invites her in."

I changed my position on the sofa. I thought, *don't go! Any idiot can see there's danger!*

"At first she tells him 'no', but then she agrees and says, 'Well, I have to go to the bathroom anyhow.' He says, 'Yes. That's perfect.' And she looks at him curiously. They go in. No wait! She goes in first. He lingers a minute outside. Then follows. There's no lock on the bathroom door, and she notices that. But doesn't think much about it.

She asks, 'Where's your friend?' She is looking hard at him now. She is looking at the door. After he pulls a piece of paper from the drawer, he tells her, 'Here's a note from him. He was here and left. He'll be back soon.' But after about ten minutes, she is getting concerned."

"Can you see the room Doc?" Justin asked, finally interested. "The motel? Any clues as to location?"

"It isn't far. They didn't drive far. The room is nondescript. Walls the color and texture of a sponge. Finally, the woman glances at the clock radio. It is two-thirty. As she looks around, she realizes that there are no clothes. And nothing is setting around. No luggage. The coffee pot is unused. No sign of occupancy. Styrofoam cups are stacked. She realizes that there is no evidence that anyone has been staying here. She's concerned. She begins to sweat. She wonders what he is doing. He sits on the bed and folds his hands and looks at her. 'He'll be here,' he tells her. 'My business partner will be here.' At this time he finds her quite beautiful. For a prostitute, that is. He notes that her flesh is clear and soft, that her hair is clean, but her red nails are garishly tattooed and long. He notes that her waist is trim and that she is heavily breasted, and he is beginning to feel aroused."

"Oh yeah, I knew he'd get around to screwing her," Justin said sarcastically. "It doesn't take a psychic to figure that out!"

Dr. Tynbrock wasn't amused and shot a look of disbelief at him. "But she doesn't like what she sees in his eyes. Warmth that has turned hollow and cold. She stands up and goes toward the door. And now he has to make his move. He knows that. Her palm is on the handle and her back is to him. He quickly has his hands around her throat! She is so startled that she doesn't attempt to scream. And then it is too late. He presses his fingers on her carotid arteries, massages them, and she falls unconscious to the floor. He drags her to the bed.

He doesn't want her dead yet. He needs her. Uh, he has something in the closet. A bag. It looks like it might belong to a doctor. I'm not sure. I see that there is strong energy around it, a very bright luminosity. Quickly, he pulls out a candle and lights it, moving it slowly across her body until a small bead of wax falls on her forehead. After several minutes, he realizes that it's no longer a sexual thing. And now he's opening up the kit. It's got a…actually he's taking out a vile of liquid. Let me see, he's giving her a shot of something, putting it in her left arm. Soon she's in a deep state of unconsciousness. But there is body movement. Her body jerks as if she might wake up. But then it calms. It really isn't his intention to kill her yet. Then he takes…uh he takes…oh wait. No, he's looking at his watch. He's timing something.

Then he wraps her in the bedspread and carries her to the car. He places her in some kind of a container. I can't see it. But I sense that it is lightweight though. I don't know. He takes the container across water!"

Dr. Tynbrock fell back against the cushion.

"Are you all right?" I asked, touching her hand.

"I can feel or see nothing else," she said blandly. "It is dark now. All I see is darkness."

"Could you look a little deeper in the darkness and see if you can get a make on the license plate?" Justin asked.

"No! I can see nothing," Dr.Tynbrock sighed. She stood up and removed her glasses, her eyes having lost their brightness. "So, was I of help?"

I took the tibia and placed it back in the bag. I thought it unusually warm. "Oh my, you were. Thank you!"

"My secretary will make a copy of the tape," she said.

"Yeah, great going Doc. We'll be in touch," Justin said. "Of course, you'll probably be able to 'see' when!"

Dr. Tynbrock shook her head. "Policemen are my worse customers. They want evidence carved in steel! I've helped solve a dozen cases across the nation, and the blue boys still look at me as if I'm one of those wizards floating in the middle of a glass globe."

"Nah, listen Doc," he answered. "It's just that if we can't book the evidence, it's hard to accept."

As we went out the door, I winked at Dr. Tynbrock. Meanwhile, I heard a clap of thunder somewhere to the west, and I was thinking what a pain in the ass Justin had been. Later as we approached my Explorer, he gave me a pat on the back. "I'm kind of hungry. How 'bout we grab a bite together?"

"Oh, I suppose so," I said reluctantly.

"I can take hamburgers, chicken nuggets, even a piece of fish. But don't order anything with bones in it, Katie."

CHAPTER 12

After a restless few days at the motorhome, I left behind unreturned phone messages and went over to Renaurd Island. The light frost and brisk air kept most everyone inside again. I slept well, although a bleak overcast coaxed me to stay in bed an extra hour while I read briefs that Paul Hanes had faxed to me. I reluctantly rose a little after eight, bathed in an herbal aphrodisiac, and took coffee in my room, preferring the clatter of the rain outside my window to the clatter of Mrs. Trample-St.Synge's deplorable gossiping at breakfast.

I was exhausted and plagued with excuses about why I shouldn't go through the small box of files that David's department chairman had sent earlier and which Allison had kept for me. David's image rode like an uninvited warrior through my room, while I imagined his fingers rummaging through papers, his notes hastily written in margins, his broad sweeping signature like a 'case closed' stamp. Yet, I hadn't gone near the box. After all, the files were his. One thing for certain…it was hard to believe that he wouldn't want them at some point in his life. Wasn't it all that he had salvaged from his career as an English professor?

With coffee in hand, I whistled as I swept around the room. I often did that when I was thinking. Finally, I crouched, and then sat on the floor, tucked my legs under and pulled the box close. As I popped the lid with no effort, I wasn't surprised that I burst into tears when I saw a picture of David and me in the dingy near our cottage, his arm slung cavalierly over my shoulder. He could be the most restful man I had ever been with, and it startled me how painful it was remembering that we could be together in ways that I could never be with anyone else, deriving hours of pleasure from hiking or snorkeling or simply being physically close. I ached for the smell of his dark hair and olive skin, the slow peeling of his strong thighs after foraging my body after we had been engrossed in some fascinating discussion about the eclectic ways of life. Yet, I kept thinking of the times of his disassociation, when our being together wasn't going well. When it happened, it could cause the temporary destruction of me emotionally, and I simply continued to live within his life and wait…and wait for his duplicity to return to normal. Now I wondered if life were always to be so empty without him. At least it was this particular day.

From where I sat, I could see beyond the corner window. Oppressive black clouds slugged ominously at each other. It was a bad sign, I decided. But I took several files, spread them across the floor in front of me and perused pages that were mostly drafts of poetry and speeches. Strangely, unlike his personal things at the cottage, the files seemed so ominously unorganized.

My finger flicked through what appeared to be mostly insignificant data. Then I saw a red legal folder. Red? Call it a premonition, call it 'seeing red'—the long folder—like the flag on a beach that warns that there's dangerous surf. Stay out of the water. Perhaps it would tell another story. The fear grew stronger. I carefully pulled back a red tab. Something fell to the floor. It was a plastic card similar to the ones that fit hotel doors, and it looked as if someone had taken a hole punch to its edges. Maybe there was to be more. But I had been to his safety deposit box containing gold coins, the deed to the cottage, the Land Rover title, an old revolver and his last will and testament. Had he only thrown me scraps?

I shifted my legs and took a deep breath. Several pieces of notebook paper and a calendar emptied onto my lap. Each page listed different weapons assigned to the U.S. Special Forces. In small print there appeared to be significant data, much of which had been redacted; yet, charts containing details of guerrilla warfare—booby traps, mines, ambushes—details about a mission in which eight men had gone behind Iraqi lines, were no longer stamped 'top secret mission'. On eight by eleven maps someone had highlighted specific places in California,

Ohio, New York, Denver and Seattle. Something was jumping out at me and I didn't know what! And then I stared at the calendar.

The darkened dates rattled my thoughts. I sucked air. Scrambling up from the floor, I was enraged that I was visiting a place in David's life that he had deliberately kept from me, and I felt resentment so strong that I fell immediately ill. As if the files had taken on human form and slugged me in the stomach, I threw them back into the box and began to sob, shedding the kind of tears that made the line, 'I'm going to wash that man right out of my hair,' take on a new meaning.

'Crying jag' also had a new meaning, and I spent the rest of the day sleeping and reading and generally feeling sorry for myself, not necessarily in that order. After dinner and two glasses of Coastal, with all but the air bags under my eyes having recovered, Allison would be late returning from court, later inviting me to have dessert while she picked over a tray of club sandwiches in her private quarters, a bedroom with an adjoining sitting and dining area.

I thought I would mention Barclay's possible sleeping disorder, which Mrs. Trample-St.Synge had alluded to, but before I had the chance, Allison reached into her black briefcase and removed a leather bound book. I can still see her bending over to proudly present to me *The History of South Carolina Revisited*, her other hand holding a bottle of wine from her private selection.

"Finally! Your family's history was included then..." I said, recalling that she had told me months before that there was a good chance that it could be. "How exciting!" As part of my professional responsibility, I have had to write and publish articles related to criminal justice, but for many, writing anything of worth, then alone getting it published is an unfulfilled dream.

"Yep! Our version of '*Roots*,' Allison said. The *Isham* family is only one chapter, of course."

She invited me to join her on the settee and poured me a glass of wine. "Do you realize that I never knew your *real* name?" I said.

"But why would you? And it made it easier when I was going through law school. Everyone's always known me as Allison Thomason. I was christened Alika Isham! Many times I've thought about changing it back!"

I tapped the pages with my forefinger. "Mmm hmm, read some to me!"

"Oh goodness no," she said with hearty laughter.

"A little, please. I insist!"

"Oh, but I thought you said you wanted to talk with me about something."

"Yes, yes, I do," I said. "In a bit! But first, read!"

Allison sighed. "Let's see, the interview was about a year ago. Let me summarize it. I have a good memory about what I said."

She definitely had that, I thought. "Then go on!"

"Well, you know that my family came from Sierra Leone in Africa," she continued. "They had spent a year in Haiti and then the Bahamas before being brought to St. Helena Island. Like most slaves, they knew how to grow cotton. Remember? The Sea Island kind known around here as long staple, the beautiful cotton of the Southern states."

"Mmm hmm. And it wasn't sent away in bales," I said, remembering my mother's own stories.

"That's right," Allison said proudly, "It was packed loosely so that its fine strands weren't damaged. But what a vile time, however! I'm afraid that in those dreadful days the slaves who gathered cotton from the fields of gold, lived with both a frailty and stamina branded on their muscles like none other before and none other after! The poor women would sit on the cold floors with that long staple in their laps and take 'de yeller from de' whi'…the slightly soiled from the pure!"

"You must have heard incredible stories from your parents and grandparents," I said.

"Oh yes, and as children," she replied. "Why, you have read the Brer Rabbit tales, haven't you, Kate? Did you know that the slaves passed those stories down to the white people?"

"No I didn't. And isn't it a shame that we're such a mobile society. Many of the family traditions that make us care about each other are going by the wayside, Allison. You know, I remember fried frog legs jumping above the heat of a big iron skillet at my Grandmother Ashley's kitchen. When my father made me eat one, I threw up because I thought the poor creature was still alive! And who on earth gigs frogs today!"

"Oh that Barclay does," she said raising her brows. "I suppose that surprises you. Why I mean, he likes so much to hunt at the north end of the island that I sometimes think he'll build a house there someday and go off and live like a hermit!"

I said subtly, "No condos or golf course to be built there then?"

"Why, whatever gave you that idea? Renaurd Island is far too vestigial!"

"Then Holden has no intentions…"

"The senator would need Barclay and me to sell our shares in Careco and probably the inn…"

So that was their understanding.

"…and we wouldn't do that," Allison continued. "Why no, just so that the Yankees could rip out more of our Southern heritage with their golf carts and hot tubs?" She flapped a cloth napkin hard against her knee. "Not on your life!"

One thing I knew right then, was that even though I wanted to understand more about the family corporation, Allison Thomason would never allow herself to be manipulated into telling anything about the Renaurds that she didn't want me to know. Even though she had a different name, she was one of them. Besides, Justin had already launched his own inquiry into Careco, and it was a matter of time until I knew all about their finances. I didn't feel good about that. About playing Miss Marple behind Allison's back. "Finish then," I said. "Finish telling me about the book and your family."

Although her face was as animated as a child's, it was awhile before she continued, preferring instead to point to pictures and the captions beneath them. Then she stood within the bathroom doorjamb and methodically removed her shoes and nylons before exchanging her black linen suit for a maroon kaftan that swept the floor like muffled broomcorn when she moved.

"Not all was well, however," she said. "After the Civil War and during Reconstruction, freed slaves tried to move to the North. Of course, that was creating a problem. So the Union housed many in barracks. Not a very pleasant way for free men and women to live, do you think? But with the economic help of the Union, our people became blacksmiths and carpenters among other jobs, and Mitchellville became the first Freeman's Village for former slaves in Beaufort County."

"After that, how did your family end up on Renaurd Island?"

"Well, in some ways that was a stroke of extraordinary luck. Doesn't it happen? Luck. Haven't I had my share? During the Civil War, Planter Daniel Renaurd on the sly had helped the Yankees. He was given this island in payment. Don't ask me what he did for those Northerners. I don't know. But when the war was over, he brought my relatives here to work. They were starving."

"But they were *free!*" I exclaimed. *Didn't I know better than to have said that?*

Allison grimaced, and without breaking a syllable, the creases in her forehead multiplied when she spoke again. "Why, of course, they *wanted* to be, but they didn't know *how* to. You see, the Renaurds worked a small plantation. Small compared to most; they grew indigo. When the railroad opened up the West, the Renaurds, like so many other owners, decided to abandon the island. They sent my family back to the mainland. That was right after my great-grandfather got his toes cut off for stepping inside a house near Beaufort just to tell the white Mrs. that her prized rooster had gotten out and had been eaten by a gator."

"I didn't know!" I said.

She shut her eyes. "Sometimes I hear him scream. Oh, not a blood curdling scream, but more like a hurt animal, you know? When it's writhing in such pain that you could snap its neck with your bare hands to put it out of its misery? I hear the scream when it breaks up, too, breaks into a whole bunch of screams, little screams, long and pitiful like the ones coming from the ghosts of tortured slaves. But say, Kate, doesn't justice have a way of rearing its head? Many years later, when the island wasn't even fit for those damn gators, my grandfather bought it from the Renaurd heirs for pennies on the dollar."

"*Your* family owned this island!" I said, with such rude incredulousness that I was beginning to wonder if I were suddenly stricken with foot and mouth disease.

Allison didn't react, instead busying her hands with a nail file. "Well anyhow, after the Civil War, it was quite common for black people to own land. Of course, every White on the mainland turned away his head when my relatives went for supplies. I don't know, did times get hard? I suppose. My daddy couldn't pay the taxes, which kept getting higher and higher. Eventually, the Renaurds returned from the West and at auction bought the land back. My relatives were allowed to live where Gabe does now. Years later, when my own family was mostly gone—most of them dead—I moved in here and took care of Mrs. Leighton Renaurd until her heart gave out. As you know, her husband was very good to me."

Whether I thought it was ironic that Allison should end up owning part of the Renaurd Island after all, didn't matter, so I wouldn't mention it, but I thought of my own heritage, my connection to the big sea island planters, but in a different way. I remembered living at my Grandfather Ashley's mansion on Hilton Head Island and the occasional trip to Charleston, the grandiosity of his plantation home there making it appear isolated among smaller ones near the sea, its great piazza wrapping like pulled taffy around the entire house. Inside there were fine crystal chandeliers, great sconces and curved stairways that went on forever with spindle rails for peeking at my father and mother who would join my grandparents while the most important people of South Carolina danced across the pine floors after the imported Italian carpets had been taken up.

Now here we were, Allison and I, whose heritage in another time and another place would not have allowed us to be friends. I, the great-granddaughter of pioneer planters. She the descendant of slaves. But I never thought of Allison Thomason with that concern. No I didn't. To me she simply had the skin of a woman.

"Goodness, Kate" she said pointing to her watch. She yawned heavily. "It's after midnight. Why, enough of 'this is my life'! Now what did you want to tell me?"

"You're exhausted," I said. "Tomorrow?"

She placed the dishes onto a tray and started for the door.

"Let me take those," I said putting my veneration of her away. "My legs could use a little deep vein thrombosis prevention! Thank you for the lovely dessert, fine wine and a little more of 'you.'"

"Nonsense. But the rest of the 'literary me' belongs in the bookstores," she said tapping the book spine. "Goodnight then."

Her arm hovered around my waist before she shut the door, and then I moved swiftly into the hall and down the back stairs where I deposited the tray onto a dumbwaiter, a platform attached to pulleys that lifted and lowered objects to the kitchen. Afterward I entered the hall off the main living quarters. Along the way the lights were either dimmed or off, the shadows of drapery, furniture and fine chandeliers crawling in such a grotesque distortion across the walls that I had a sudden attack of anxiety and imagined that someone else was present. At once I considered turning around. But I wanted something to read, so I continued into a small alcove near the front of the inn, a place where my eyes gravitated to a door with a small brass sign that said, "Librus."

The door was ajar. A shaft of dull yellow from a wall sconce made me uneasy, and after a few seconds, I went in and found the switch to table lamps. Although I knew of no one at the inn who smoked, odor from a cigar seemed to waft near a tufted sofa by a stone fireplace where wood had long ceased to smolder. Books filled massive cases, but never having been in this room, the fourth wall with its gray speckled paper jumped alive with framed landscapes that appeared to change grotesquely before my eyes as if they were suspended in some deep holographic grip, while in others, the scenery blurred from black to crimson.

The paintings were disturbing, of course. What poor, misguided soul had no beauty in his life and had taken the green of fields and trees and burned them black with bristles of acrylic while becoming trapped within conjured-up images of self-destruction? For nearly an hour I perused their details, my senses bedraggled until I needed to abandon the sense of dread they caused me. I turned to the books, my eyes ensnared by subdued covers and eclectic titles; that is, until fatigue finally overwhelmed me, until I tucked a copy of *The Prophet* under my arm and set off for my room.

However late it was, I found myself unsettled and careful so as not to disturb anyone above. I was on the landing at the back staircase when I heard shuffling from the corridor below to my right. My intuition rooted in a sense of strong foreboding, I was wise enough to recognize fear, but curiosity stole my caution, and I stopped, turned and went back down two more stairs.

At first glimpse I could see someone silently at ease, as if his body were floating free of the floor beneath him. His colorless lips did not move as he glided slowly beneath me, and it was only when I recognized Barclay that I came down one more step and stammered, "Are you all right?" He revolved mechanically, the lines of his face set as if in death, his eyes the color of dirty glass. "Barclay?" I said again. Then he lingered motionless, and I wondered what he was thinking or if he were thinking at all. I wondered if he knew where he had been or where he was going.

The cold demeanor of his body did not encourage me to speak again, for I thought that he had not heard me say his name, and although he appeared to stare at me, I believed him not even remotely to be aware of my presence. Afraid to further draw his attention, I backed cautiously up the stairs. At the creak of the top step, he turned abruptly, paused and swept by me as if I were not standing there.

For the moment I didn't know what to make of it. It was unnerving, and minutes passed before I headed toward my room, my arm bracing dizzily against the shadowed dampness of the hall wall, my eyes not quite believing it when I saw Allison slipping away from Barclay's room with a large brass key in her hand.

CHAPTER 13

For November it was an unusually fresh morning, one with the sun pat-
terning the leaves of a tree as if they were old lace draped over the door
of Allison's private office at Renaurd Inn. Justin's left hand was wrapped
around the latest Dragon's Point files, his right grabbing fresh potato
donuts and glass after glass of orange juice. After a short while, he told
us about one of the locals on St. Helena's Island who had a strong
proclivity for practicing a bizarre form of voodoo and therefore was no
longer accepted by most members of the regular voodoo 'Sosyete'.
Allison said little. She seemed listless and distant, and when her small
desk clock chimed ten, she left without a word. When I noted that he
hadn't brought much new information, Justin fell into one of his
disagreeable moods, yanked himself from the chair and made a fuss
about having come at all, and then he said goodbye and had Coneras
take him back to the mainland.

The wind had picked up, and even though sailing was not something
I was in the mood for, I returned to my room, changed into a green
jumpsuit and put on Sperry Topsiders. As I went down the path toward
the dock, I turned and caught the lethargy of eyes from a familiar face,
one that looked strained and gray. It was Barclay whom I saw at that
second floor window, his lips puckering downward, and then I thought
it peculiar that when he realized that I had seen him, he stepped aside,
his body profile becoming lost in the curtains.

"Good afternoon," Gabe yelled as he drew elbows back before
jumping from his skiff to the dock. He had already pulled the sails from
their bags.

I knew little about the mechanics of sailing. David had always taken charge. Mostly, I thought of how he had attached the jib to the headstay, always with the same methodical way, the purpose of the boom and mast to have a place to string out the mainsail. "I haven't done this in awhile, Gabe," I said.

He cradled my hand in his and winked. "You haven't done a lot of things in a good while, I suspect. Come aboard." His white cargo pants, teal shirt and sockless canvass shoes presented a handsome figure. He continued, "Didn't think you were coming."

"Am I really that late?"

"By mariner's time?" he asked.

"There are two times?"

"Land and sea time," he said. "So I say, let's be off!"

I pointed to a picnic basket that I had brought. "Where can we keep this?" I asked.

"To your left. There's the fridge. And thanks, Kate!"

"I confess that Renty's responsible." I opened the door and saw a bottle of Coastal Mondavi, some Brie and a bag of vegetables next to a small bowl of strawberries. "And thank you," I said wondering how he knew my favorite wine.

He nodded. Then as if he were giving me a lesson said, "Headstay has the jib attached. Ah, well, yes, you know that much, don't you?"

"That much," I said. We laughed.

Very little sound came from the hum of the motor as he maneuvered the sleek boat from the channel into the open sea, and I immediately recognized the smell of the salt air, and for a long time, except for my hair blowing wildly in the wind, I was motionless and I was still. He was still, too, his eyes seldom leaving me until he set the sail. At once we were into a lively wind that brought an occasional splash over the hull, unnerving to a novice, but invigorating to any seasoned sailor, I was sure.

"Exhilarating!" I said, wheeling around.

He nudged my thigh with his. "Grandfather Coneras can feel the direction of the wind as soon as it hits his skin!"

"And you?"

"It must be in the genes."

We came around Renaurd Island, and I turned my eyes on the Eastern horizon where the clouds looked like old factories with puffs of black smoke billowing from their stacks. There was a blast of wind and the boat skimmed across the water into the Atlantic, the spindrift lashing our bodies.

"I love visiting Renaurd Inn," I yelled above the roar.

"Yes, well, a day here. A weekend there. Don't you ever think you could stay a full week?"

"Hard to with my job," I said.

"I met your ex-husband," Gabe said.

"I'm not surprised."

"Damned nice," he said.

"So I'm told," I said.

"What?"

"I said he has his moments!"

"Anyone since him? Are you with someone now?"

"I'd rather not go there," I replied.

Gabe shrugged, gathering up some rigging before easing the sails. "I'm taking her 'off' the wind. 'Reaching', as we say. She'll soar like an eagle now." He pulled me in front of him. My lower body was between his thighs, the muscles of his arms closing around my waist. His hands moved up. "Here," he said quickly drawing my fingers under his so that we were both steering. "Feel her push and pull!"

His chin pressed into my shoulder. My throat closed. I thought I couldn't breathe. "She's a fine boat!" I finally said.

"As she slides through the water, she vibrates a little too much," he said steadily. Then we eased off the crest of a wave, met a trough obliquely and lifted with the sea. "But you learn to touch her like you touch a woman. Gently." He whispered into my ear. "*Always gently. And she'll move the way you want.*"

It was the first time in months that I was aware of my need for closeness, like food and water and sleep. My spirits soared. Instinctively, I pressed into him. "Have you sailed long?" I asked trying to get my mind off his touch.

"I can't remember when ! haven't, Kate," he said. "Say, he told me that he was working on those Dragon Point murders."

I was startled. "Mmm? Who?"

"Detective McCreary."

"And what with all the press lately, you were curious?"

"Don't give a rat's damn," he said leaning into me. Then he let go and moved in front. He lifted his head, cupped his eyes as if he were looking down a telescope and stared east. "*You* steer her a bit!"

I took the wheel. Minutes passed. "Justin will probably talk to you about it," I said. "Or did he?"

He came behind and straddled his legs around mine again. "No, we had a casual meeting on the dock, that's all."

"Mmm hmm. Well, he's a good detective, and he's begun to interview anyone who knew Jennifer Renaurd," I said gravely, "Her death may be connected to the other victims."

He bent his face over mine. His breath was warm. "You didn't come along just to grill me about my relationship with her, now did you?"

"Should I?"

"Well, right now I'd better worry about this sudden change in the wind!" The pitch of his voice was higher. He looked at the nautical chart. "Grab that rope! Hold on! We're going to turn downwind and run with it!"

I could feel the air rushing over the stern. After we had gone a few miles, the wind died back, and he said, "Let's drop anchor here. There are plenty of rocks and clay. A good place for grouper and flounder."

David had taught me how to make the unslippable knot, the fisherman's bend that held the anchor, and as one of the sharp flukes grabbed the bottom, I could feel its tug. "How deep?" I asked.

"See the markers along the rode? The lead line? It's about ten fathoms. I'm cleating the rode now so that it is secure. Then I'll wrap the upper part with this."

"What's that?"

"Chafing gear, a piece of neoprene hose. Keeps the rope from being cut when it brushes the bow. Let's take a break after we throw the bait in," he said.

I put live shrimp on my hooks while Gabe poured wine. Then we ate crackers and Brie, too, and with a different kind of hunger, took in each other, bantering like would be lovers, and after awhile all parts of us were immersed in the fishermen's silence that comes with being part of a rocking boat—the waves and wind falling into the melodic chords of a cantata, and the absence of land, the depth below, the line of the horizon creating an esoteric place of its own.

At the strike of a fish, I had meant to keep my line tight, and judging by Gabe's posturing, he had, too, but we were misled by a rogue wave, both of us losing our footing and falling hard into each other. Our lines tangled. The fish escaped. We laid the rods down. It wasn't something that we wanted to do right then, untangling those lines.

He kissed me lightly. I shrank back. Then he did it again. I let him. There was a long smile before he leaned to the side, looking pensively before saying, "I remember my grandfather at stroke oar before he had the newer boat to take passengers to Renaurd Island. He had nautical intuition comparable to none. His oar would bite the water at breakneck speed. That damn boat took on a life of its own! I was no more than six, but I remember that there were three oarsmen who would sing, 'Halleluiah.' And when I was tall enough to reach the wheel, I got to be an oarsman, too. Did you know I could sing just like them? Do you know, I could sing 'Halleluiah' right now just being here with you?"

Our bodies drifted together like seaweed again, and he kissed me repeatedly, but then I thought that if I stayed in his arms much longer that there would be no turning back. All the energy which I had worked up caused me to pull away. "Do you bring all of your women out here?" I asked.

His neck and shoulders stiffened. He stood, his shoes resounding heavily over the deck as he moved about and restored the fishing rods to a thin box attached to the side. "You know, it's an incredible place, the ocean. It can be sullen or soft. It can swallow an ocean liner with a blink or scuttle a boat like this without so much as one. So what you're finally asking about is Jennifer, aren't you. The answer's yes, I brought her here to fish." His eyes crept away.

I was thinking *what things did you do with Jennifer? Young and vulnerable as she was, even though you were only two years older, I was sure that you, Gabe, could have persuaded a wild cat to chase its own tail.* I had many questions. Still, even though he had read my mind, I knew that this wasn't the time or place.

"Well, you do have the right to remain silent, Mr. Coneras," I said playfully.

"And anything you might do in the present situation could give you the edge in my court of law," he said, attempting to kiss me again.

I put up my hand, suddenly having second thoughts about the whole trip. "Ah, no! I plead the fifth," I said smiling. I stepped back.

"So this captain's grounded?"

"Mmm hmm, I'm afraid so," I said, forcing a smile.

We were quiet, and he put away the food and wine, and after awhile, I could see that the deck was covered with a fine mist that tried to rise in wind that seemed to come from many directions. Far away and above the horizon, lightening shot its warning signals like a flare gun. Gabe looked stern. "A front's barreling down!" he said, his eyes straining under fingers over his brow. "Suppose we'd better head in! I'll up the lines!" He tucked wine glasses into a small net pocket and jumped ahead of me. With no effort the anchor came out of the water.

I made an effort not to look totally terrified at the suddenly changing weather. "What can I do?"

"Put your sweater on," he said sternly. "It's going to get wet real fast!"

As the boat challenged the waves, Gabe needed no compass or navigational equipment, instead relying on his own directional skills and knowledge of tides and an aversion to ever visiting Davy Jone's Locker. But without warning I was surprised when we slowed, made a full turn and stopped, the boat freely challenging the waves while we dropped anchor again. He waved his arms to the sound of a large cigar boat that was speeding in from the south. Finally, it maneuvered beside us. I didn't like the situation or the man who loomed across from me.

Gabe seemed defensive. "Listen Kate, this is Stacks Sandover. A tired old cuss who can smell the Atlantic fives miles inland. He's a true Neptune! What you doing here, Stacks?"

The man dipped his neck and rubbed his chin with big hands that reminded me of inflated latex gloves. "Ain't she a looker," he told Gabe.

He certainly wasn't a looker, and it was his unbuttoned shirt that drew attention, revealing the V of his hairy chest and a belly button the size of a half dollar. Like a partially crumbling waterfall, his gut cascaded over a tight pair of duck pants. He scratched his pale, Bratwurst-like arms, while I wondered what cave he might have crawled from.

"Stack's daddy was once a captain of a 60 ton schooner," Gabe said. "His great-great granddaddy was one brave SOB, too. During the Civil War, he would run down to Cuba and get a load of salt. Sell it to the Confederacy. They used it for meat preservation. Isn't that something?"

I didn't answer.

"Yeah. Back in 1862," Stacks said, his lips and nostrils widening. Thick sweat filled lines that ran deep from the sides of dark eyes to the middle of puffy cheeks. "Back then when the South was about to get its butt kicked, the old geezer dumped a shit load of the stuff off Charleston. But before the Union got him, he burned his boat and jumped overboard. The cuss drowned! Imagine that! Escape only to drown!"

I checked my watch. It was close to four. I had briefs to read, and I didn't like the situation that was unfolding before my eyes. "I think it's time to go," I said.

"Soon, Kate," Gabe said, dismissing me.

"Say," Stacks said, scratching his chin, his eyes studying my face, "you look as familiar as a baboon's ass."

I chose not to answer.

"You don't know her," Gabe said quickly.

"Yeah. Okay. Yeah. But when do you want the *goods*?" Stacks asked.

"Not today," Gabe said sternly.

Stacks turned the ignition key. The rage of the big motor made him have to shout. "It's your call, then!"

"I'm not comfortable with any of this," I whispered. "What does he mean? The *goods*?"

Gabe stood motionless with his hands on his hips. "Stacks has been in bed with the Cubans for years," he finally said. "Once in awhile he brings a few cigars for Holden and the guests at the inn."

"I never forget a lady's mug," Stacks sneered. "And what a mug you got lady. She's hot, man. Hold on to her. And shit, it'll come to me some day. It'll come to me where I've seen you lady."

"Better head in, Stacks," Gabe warned. "That storm's not going to hold off much longer. I'll be in touch!"

"Peace be with you bro." His eyes came back to me. He pulled at his chin again and said, "You ain't a model are you lady?" And then he sped away.

"I'm bothered by all this," I said, thinking about the possible consequences for both of us. I was annoyed. After all, even an innocent package of cigars was contraband. Coast Guard arrests attorney general? It wouldn't have looked good on my resume, I thought. I caught his eye. "Had you planned to meet him out here?"

"No. He must have picked me up on radar," he said. "Ah relax, he's harmless."

"I didn't mean that. But there's no such thing as a little illegal, Gabe. You can see why I would be concerned, can't you?"

"You're overreacting."

"Who pays him? For the contraband?"

"Damn it! It's only a few stogies!" he said angrily.

His harshness startled me. Stack's boat disappeared into a wave, and I knew that Gabe was watching me. "Please, let's go," I said softly.

"I'm sorry. He left nothing and took nothing,"—Gabe paused—"and it never occurred to me that you'd get so upset. You are, aren't you? Please don't be." He flicked me another kiss and then handed me a rain parka and pants. He took my hands. Fastening my wrist snaps, he pulled the drawstring on my hood and secured my ankle straps before doing the same to his own. The rain and wind were coming hard against my face.

"I think we should hurry!" I said. "This turn about in the weather reminds me of the Ghost Rain!"

"Yes, it's going to get rough soon," he said. "Here, let me help you with these boots. They're skid proof."

He slid a safety harness over both our shoulders. Large clips at our waists secured a lifeline. He moved away from me and quickly furled the mainsail. And then not ten minutes later it was as if someone had picked us up and dropped us in the middle of a violent storm. I feared I was in for the ride of my life!

"I hope I took enough Dramamine!" I shouted.

"You're in good company. A little *mal de mer?* Seasickness? Even Admiral Chester Nimitz suffered from it. Sit tight. Hold on to the rope!"

"Tell me when I'm about to drown!" I said obeying until my knuckles turned white.

It was a long time before he said, "I'm putting a working jib forward and jigger aft. This will balance the sails. I'll keep the bow headed into the waves. Steady as she goes!"

Within minutes, the weather had turned so violent that I could barely hear Gabe's shouts. Water was booming over the boat, across my boots, dancing around my ankles like little green tornadoes. Then the boat heaved dangerously left and right while I hung from my harness, everything around me dipping in and out of the frothy wave tips…a great take for the Weather Channel's Storm Stories.

But then the sails furled and I only could see bare poles. I yelled, "Gabe, I'm frightened! Call the coastguard!"

"Nah. I'm lashing the tiller to leeward. She'll be fine!"

I looked up. The rising of the sea into enormous mounds of water was ratcheting my heartbeat, making me gasp for air—every wave a granite wall cascading over the top of us before we would disappear into a valley only to be covered by the wall again and again. The running rigging, in danger of being torn off, compelled me to scream, "She's going to break apart!"

"She's as sturdy as steel! But I'll trim her," Gabe shouted cavalierly. "We're going to heave to and ride through this shit head on! Heave to, you son-of-a-bitch!"

It was the wildness in his face that frightened me the most, and I found myself thinking that women and men had another difference I hadn't thought about. Oh, I don't mean physically, of course, but for men, their fear, their fearlessness is like a knife carving out a good adventure. Call it the Indianapolis 500, the Super Bowl, the World Series or a simple day of scuba diving. It was about challenging and winning. That was a man's world. That's how they got their adrenaline fix.

"What's all that foam around us?" I shouted. "I can't see!"

"The wave crests create it when they fall," he shouted. "It's like taking a bath in a tub of Heineken!"

"More like having drunk a tub full!" I sighed wearily, hoping that my stomach contents would remain where they belonged.

"Whoa! I can see Renaurd Island! Hang on, Kate! Just a bit longer!" Gabe said. His eyes were wide with excitement. "Now brace yourself! The tidal flow's strong; why…probably close to 10 knots. We're coming upon the channel. I'm going to ram her down its throat! In we go! We'll beat windward so we don't heel over! What a ride!"

Plowing through the last of a squall, the boat emerged unscathed, its hull creaking as it dipped a few more times. Gabe was as calm as the placid water near the inn, but my nerves had seen the wrecking ball. At the moment drenched hair and a rain-chafed face underlined my viewpoint of camaraderie with nature. To hell with sailing!

CHAPTER 14

A week later on a clear Saturday morning, we drove in Drew Greer's Hummer for a seminar to the new 155 million dollar FBI lab in Quantico, Virginia. Its old cramped quarters were now spacious, pure air labs where DNA and fingerprint analysis would be the latest. The Director, Robert Mueller, told us at the dedication that the lab was to help the FBI and its "partners solve more cases, prevent more crimes and save more lives." Standard speech. Standard bull. Quick trip.

Afterwards, I needed to get back to Hilton Head for a long planned dinner with my sister. While she was investigating Lazarus cases, Drew was staying with me at the motorhome. She was in an unusual feisty mood—telling offensive jokes, lodging an unlighted cigarette at the corner of her mouth and saying 'fuck this, fuck that.' She constantly went over the speed limit to irritate me and argued about a bill that Holden Thomason had co-introduced in the Senate that would require states to collect DNA from people who were arrested for misdemeanors, his aim eventually to have a sample from these Americans, something the Civil Liberties Union and Drew, with her liberal attitude, both abhorred and opposed.

I reminded her that the FBI already had a million and a half DNA profiles of convicted criminals and that the new state crime lab, for which I had cut the ribbon the previous year, was part of the FBI's CODIS, too,—the Combined DNA Index System—and through federal funds, we already were providing DNA samples from our own state felons. But she didn't want to hear that perhaps our bone killer may have been picked up on a misdemeanor at some point in his life, and had his DNA been catalogued, we would have been ready for him if he left his fingerprint, semen, saliva, or something like that at the scene.

We bantered some more, and then with her photographic mind, she summed-up what the FBI knew about all but two of the bone victims at Dragon's Point (excluding Jennifer Renaurd, who in my opinion, still didn't fit some of the categories). She said that they probably were in their teens to mid-thirties, and were drug addicts or prostitutes who had possibly worked in the Bahamas before coming to the States. Within the folder on the dash, she had pictures of missing persons, too.

'Friends, Romans, Countrymen, lend me your ears…' I thought. Someday, when the killer was caught, the whole world would know about these poor women. Their names, family history, pathologist's post-mortem report, all of it in newspapers and on TV. And once the killer's trial was over, the liberals would refer to him as poor, disadvantaged, morally wayward while the conservatives would brand his victims as immoral women who deserved a Scarlet P on their tombstones. Ah, so much for the political pundits!

"There's something else that'll tickle your tits," Drew said, reaching into a small cubbyhole and pulling out a match.

"Is that the vernacular for 'rattle your balls'"? I asked.

"Just old husband talk," she said as she finally slowed down to sixty-five. "That jerk who I was married to for six weeks? The one who paid for my perfect size C's? He always said that! Now what *was* his name?"

"You're incorrigible!"

Predictably, she lit her cigarette, dragged incessantly on it until I told her that I might possibly throw up from the odor. Like a fussy child, she complained that I had forgotten what it feels like to have a nicotine fit. *If she knew how much money that I had spent on Benson & Hedges only to throw them away after just one deep inhalation.*

"What doesn't jell, Kate," she began, "is that witnesses said they saw an older gray haired man with three of the victims, a young dude with another and a scruffy guy with one of the others."

Three killers? Were we dealing with some Satanic Cult? Some rogue religious group? What about the theory of the excised body parts?

Generally, in voodoo, mutilation was unheard. Even in the 1800's, when it was thought to happen, it was well known that the practice of human sacrifice had merely been a rumor propagated by English officials in order to control the so-called 'barbaric Haitians', who first practiced voodoo, and convert them to Christianity.

"Well, whoever our killer is," I said adamantly, "we're getting closer, and I intend to be at his execution!" Drew came to a quick stop. She had driven past the entrance to Anchor Resorts, so she backed up the Hummer, sped down the narrow boulevard, used my gate card and circled the streets to the motorhome. As I transferred to my Explorer, I yelled, "There's baked chicken in the 'fridge'. Salad, too." It was useless to worry about her being so thin, and I hoped that she wouldn't drink herself to sleep.

Ten minutes later I rang the bell at the Palmetto Dunes, Ward Alston-designed home which had appeared in *Architectural Digest*. I was unsettled and not in the mood to deal with family problems, but I was always glad to see my sister, although we had disagreed many times about how Courtney had wasted most of her adult life on an emotionally abusive husband who had indulged in compulsive gambling and indiscretions. In fact, had she not been tantalized by the suave demeanor of Jeremy St. James, a well known multi-million dollar real estate agent, she would have remained in Europe after college and painted seriously; she was an excellent artist. Over the years she survived, I believe, because of the financial patronage of other artistic types, who in recent years, helped lead her to a successful radio talk show in Savannah.

When she answered the door, I smiled and said, "Say sis, I heard that the popularity of your talk show has gone through the roof!"

"Especially the national ratings!" she told me. In front of the foyer mirrors, she finished putting on a big leather belt. As usual everything matched…the camel sweater and pencil skirt, Italian leather shoes and filigreed gold necklace and bracelet, all perfectly coordinated and com-plementing her long blonde hair and recently manicured nails.

We went directly to a small dining room that had the warmth and coziness of a magazine picture during the holidays. A fire was in the hearth and three-tiered candles glowed on a nearby dining table. She shoved a glass of red wine into my hand, and with some surprised easiness said, "Now that I have a new contract with the station, every weekend's free! Why don't we spend more time together? Take some trips."

"Mmm hmm. That's temporary, and you know it. Those associations and clubs you belong to have most of your time corralled!"

She giggled. "Oh, I only joined those because the list would look good in my obituary!"

"Mmm hmm. What about your new contract with the station? And no more paying off Jeremy's gambling debts, I hope!"

"Four fold salary increase," she said proudly. "And I'm giving Jeremy an allowance of sorts. I know. But I don't want a lecture. In fact, let's not talk about him."

"All right. You're in charge of *all* the menus tonight," I said. "Verbal and culinary! Have they changed the format of your show?"

"Does that question mean you haven't been listening?"

"Do good intentions count?" I said, thinking of my erratic sleeping habits.

"The program's the same, but paced differently. Open lines the first hour. You know, I think the night freaks have come of age? Baby boomers? An audience that's more political, more educated and more women! In fact, one called the station and said that you, dear Kate, needed to dig deeper into the gambling industry."

I laughed. "Me personally? Or my office?" I thought about how many investigations a good attorney general might be involved in. Hundreds. Gambling, prostitution, money laundering, identity deception to name a few.

"What's it been? How long since the video poker was outlawed?" she asked.

"I don't think that the gambling industry in South Carolina can be touched," I answered. "At least not right now! They have unlimited access to lawyers and money. And the illegal gaming devices keep popping up all over the state. SLED has its hands full shutting them down."

"What's that?"

"State Law Enforcement Division," I said. "The problem is that there are a bunch of new games out there. For example, the Lucky Shamrock? It's mostly in bars and 'carry outs.' Finally the state circuit court agreed with my office and said the machines are illegal. So we win some and lose some. And recently our lawyers won a case in Spartanburg County Magistrate Court over the game, Jungle King. But it's the tip of the iceberg."

"Well, be careful, my dear sister…"

"If I have to, I'll confiscate every machine in the state," I interrupted, "and take every establishment to court!"

"Oh well, I suppose that's what I love about you, Kate. You mean what you say. You mean to do that!"

We served ourselves a spinach quiche and fresh fruit from a small buffet. "It's only impossible as long as more games keep cropping up," I said, "including the latest, Pot O' Gold, a pull-tab-er that throws out horoscopes. Doesn't everyone want to know the future?"

"I wouldn't mind pulling that tab," she said laughing.

"Mmm? What?"

"Forget the money. I mean choose a winning horoscope! One about me and maybe one about our family?"

"Ah, la familia!" I said, exaggerating my Spanish.

"Speaking of families! A Doctor Diamond appeared on the show last week," she said, her voice teeming with animation. "Quite a character. A Lowcountry farmer who says his family goes back to the first slaves. Scary kind of guy though. He wore purple tinted aviator glasses and had braids down his back."

"That's funny," I said. "I've heard of him. In fact, he's someone I'm interested in interviewing myself! What did you find out?"

Courtney looked surprised. She put her fork down. "Oh I don't know. He's self-educated in theology and philosophy. Rather flamboyant. Referred to his vocation as the art of conjure. Personal magical power. Uses voodoo dolls. Mojo talismen."

Those images sent a cold shiver through my body. "Well, I call it sorcery," I said.

"Not according to Dr. Diamond. In addition to the dolls, he uses roots, herbs, potions, and black magic to supposedly gain health and prosperity."

"Did he sound convincing?"

She shrugged and looked down. "Justin told me yesterday that voodoo somehow might be involved in the Dragon's Point cases."

I snapped my finger against the plate. "He's not supposed to discuss that! Were you at your motorhome? I expect you know that he lives at Anchor Resorts full time now?"

"Yes. I was putting fresh roach traps in our Prevo. Even million dollar coaches get visits from the palmetto bugs, you know."

"Still, it would be best if he didn't talk about police business," I said.

Courtney cut fresh apple pie. "Honestly Kate! After *Midnight in the Garden of Good and Evil*, the whole world knows that voodoo is practiced in the back woods of South Carolina. Why it's colorful press. Past movies have been cloaked in myth and mysticism, too, dealing with zombies and sorcerers with magic, and spirits and a pilgrimage into the unknown. No wonder those old Boris Karloff flicks brought in the money!"

Yet, for some reason thinking about voodoo made me cringe. I changed the subject to Jeremy St. James, my sister's soon to be ex-husband and the biggest blowhard I had ever known. I remembered that under false pretenses, he had agreed to go to counseling for his on-line gambling addiction and instead had gone off with some bimbo he had met while trying to sell her real estate.

"I've finally filed," Courtney told me when I asked about the divorce. "But now he doesn't want one, even though he's living with that woman from his office," she said. "He told me that he will get her out of his system and come home."

"But that wouldn't be good for you, Court," I said. I remembered that Jeremy had almost wiped out their personal accounts with his gambling. "Financially? Can I do anything?"

"Nah. With my new contract I can afford to keep this place. But I'll sell the motorhome," she said with a twinge of disappointment.

"Then let me at least pay for your trips to Charleston," I said. "You stay at that hotel next to the sanitarium, don't you?"

Courtney flicked a piece of lint off my shoulder. Her eyes drifted to me. "Why don't you go with me? Dad does sometimes."

"Good for him. And good for you that you're having a relationship with him. I don't care to," I said. I hesitated. "As for our sister…she looks at me as if I'm a stranger. I seem to frighten her. When I hug her, she doesn't respond. It's as if I have come uninvited into her safe world of nurses and doctors. Sometimes she bolts from the room. Unlike you, I have failed to gain her trust!"

"Spend more time with her. She'll come to love you the way I do!" Courtney exclaimed.

I started to clear the table. "I seriously doubt that." Although my conscience sometimes picked an argument with me, a relationship with Leah was not something I could work on at this point in my life.

"I hope to bring her back here again some day."

"Have you forgotten that the doctors told us that she may never get well enough to leave the sanitarium? That business at mother's estate when she was a child did more damage than we thought."

Courtney followed me into the kitchen. "Look, I know that. Having her live with me at first was a mistake. Jeremy only made her worse. But I'm convinced she's going to get better!"

The stove clock said nearly midnight. "Then she's lucky to have you in her corner," I said, plunging one last fork-full of pie into my mouth before heading toward the door. Spending a few hours with Courtney usually left me feeling happy and relaxed. Not this time. I felt like a Python had coiled around my body.

When I arrived at the motorhome, I had expected to find Drew Greer asleep, but instead she was slumped back against the pillows on the sofa. She had polished off a half bottle of *Absolut*. When she heard me, she giggled a little too forcefully and then let out a long slow burp. I was reminded of our college and apartment sharing days when she came home loaded, and I would have to pour her into bed after she crawled out of the arms of some stranger she had met in a bar.

"Old roomie, I must tell you something," she stammered. She fell on her side and then rolled over on her back.

"Tomorrow, darling. You're soused. Why, you're going to choke on your own words if you don't go to sleep!"

She smacked her lips. "Kate, don't you want to know my secret?"

"Now be quiet and close your eyes!"

I retrieved one of my pillows and took her a blanket. I kissed her forehead. Even her skin reeked of alcohol. Sometimes friendship was put to the test.

After chugging a glass of milk, I slipped into a blue silk gown, creamed my face, and brushed my teeth and collapsed into bed. With the hand crank, I opened the window and brought in both fresh air and the sound of rustling leaves. Deer perhaps? At night they roamed unnoticed all over Hilton Head Island. And then with my eyes half closed, I read a fax from Paul Hanes with the directions to Dr. Diamond's trailer on Lady's Island near Beaufort, and I thought it uncanny that he had just been on Courtney's late night show.

I drifted in and out of sleep and dreamed of David, his lips moving bizarrely like a street cleaner across my body until finally I was awakened by the sound of Drew straggling around the bathroom, her mouth open, her forehead mottled by perspiration reflecting from a small nightlight. Then she sat down on the edge of my bed. In a flash, she dragged her finger across her mouth and wiped away spittle. She looked long and hard at me. "Kate. I thought you should know," she said without the clutter of emotion. "I have aids."

CHAPTER 15

Crying always made my eyes feel like a split of toasted bagel with a glob of cream cheese in the middle, but if I could get a handle on my anger with the government for not funding more aid's research to eradicate the virus, maybe I would stop bursting into tears when I thought about the hell that Drew Greer was going to go through in the next few months. After checking on renovations at the cottage, I stopped on Carteret Street in Beaufort for coffee and a chicken salad sandwich at a small restaurant that was known for its mud pie—triple chocolate with a river of mint julep, decadence guaranteed to chase away the doldrums from even the suicidal or your money back. My mouth jack-hammered through one slice and I bought another 'to go.'

There was a lashing rain and unexpected construction as I went over the drawbridge onto Lady's Island along Sea Island Parkway. Eventually, I found Dow Road, but by then the sunset had flaked away like old rust, making road markers almost impossible to read without crawling to a stop. I could only imagine the remote area where Dr. Diamond lived. *Should I go back?* Resigning myself that I didn't want to get lost, I turned around and passed an old peach stand, which had collapsed into a pile of rubble, and it was then that I realized that there had been no other traffic, and I was completely alone in an isolated area. *I really should have brought Justin!* Darkness was now all around me, but my headlights scoured loblolly and slosh pine and caught groves of palmetto scrub dissecting a narrow gravel road to my right. There, hanging precariously on what looked like a shepherd's staff, was a narrow rudimentary sign with a King of Diamonds carved on it.

No more than thirty feet into furrows of mud, my tires threaded an even narrower road not unlike the right-a-way used by rangers to check for fire in the national forests. Darker and more menacing than anything that I had ever driven on, my headlights were of no more help than a dim flashlight among the thick stand of pines that stood along the marsh. Did Dr. Diamond practice his voodoo in such a place? With the edge of my hand I cleaned the vapor from the inside of the window and kicked up the defrosters. My skin crawled with anxiety.

Eventually, the road gave way to the gray from a pole light that sprayed over a long single-wide mobile home sentried by a sphinx-like cat appearing to guard the ramped entrance. Near a small graveyard fenced in by railroad ties and about an acre to the north, several smaller mobile trailers were in a semi-circle. The surrounding area was a pitiless place with its beat-up tires, stoves, refrigerators, and sofas, and it looked as if it needed the wrecking ball of a junkyard. Did the sun or moon ever shine on Dr. Diamond's place, I wondered?

I got out of the car, my feet disappearing into the uncut grass. If what I remembered about Courtney's interview were true, then supposedly this strange man had gotten his name during card reading. And then he himself had become a card reader, although during the winter he told her that he no longer put himself in a trance and practiced that ritual, his having made tons of money during the tourist season. But according to Paul Hanes's fax, Dr. Diamond's 'winter' forte was voodoo.

Was I about to get an earful of something I didn't want? Little by little I edged toward the trailer. Stealthily, the cat stole away as I approached the front door, and when I realized that I had come this far unscathed, I took a deep breath, adjusted my shoulder harness and told myself that it was times like these that my Beretta—not diamonds—really was a girl's best friend. I knocked softly.

Dr. Diamond wasn't wearing those aviator glasses Courtney had mentioned, but immediately, eyes that looked like polished onyx and features so sharp that they could have been metamorphic rock mesmerized me. His chest was hairless and above each step-like cleavage was a 'gad', a tattoo—in this case, a hand with the 'first and forth fingers' straight up, its position averting anyone who tried to give him the plague of the evil eye. More gads were on his biceps, but I would need to consult *The Complete Idiot's Guide to Voodoo* for their meaning.

"I've been waiting for you," Dr. Diamond said with a deeply quiet voice. He looked behind me, as if he had not expected me to be alone.

"I apologize for being late," I said. "I had difficulty finding the turn-off."

When I was finally inside the door, the fear I was feeling fell away…mostly because I had jumped the first hurdle on an unknown track. I stopped in the middle of newspapers, rattles, conch shells, stones, ribbons, beads, and what looked like human hair that I assumed were simply wigs. Then, too, there were crates of small apothecary jars marked with the names of various herbs. Surrounding a large barrel and standing at attention like soldiers were bottles of raw rum.

He beckoned me to another room, one with two metal chairs and a metal small table, and he wrenched open the door of a metal cabinet where he retrieved and lighted at least a dozen candles before turning off a metal floor lamp. I had the feeling of being smack in the middle of a ritual where there seemed to be nothing but metal and wax. I didn't like it. But I wasn't going to be afraid. I stood until he told me to sit, and even then I waited until he had sat down.

"I'll get to the point," he began, his voice vapid. "I don't like outsiders. I don't like cops. I don't like attorneys general. So be brief."

Unlike Courtney's viewpoint of Dr. Diamond, I found nothing flamboyant about him. To counter his threatening posture, I sat as straight as he did and uncrossed my ankles, too. *Thinking, here goes. Stay strong, Kate!*

"Then I'll not take up a lot of your time," I said firmly. "I will get to the point, as well. I am here on official business and as attorney general of the state of South Carolina. My questions will be to the point, too. First of all, I would like to know who the main voodoo priest is in this area. Where does he practice? Where is his temple? I want to meet with him." I looked back through the door, and realizing how isolated I was, I unfolded my arms so that I could reach my gun if I needed it.

His head swayed his dreadlocks, the interwoven beads clicking like someone fanning chips in a poker game. "I no longer am part of that group," he said slowly.

"Mmm hmm, so I understand," I said, remaining steadfast. "That's why I am asking for your cooperation. I want to know everything about the high priest!"

He ran the back of his hand over his lips. "The *oungan* is everywhere. Those who follow him gather where and when he chooses."

I tried not to react. "Then he has that kind of power?" I asked.

"I will get a message to him," he said. "He'll contact you if he wishes to meet with you. Is that all?"

I didn't move. "No, it isn't. I've been told about the makeshift temple where objects used in rituals are stored. Isn't that where your *oungan* sometimes practices?"

Dr. Diamond continued to sit rigidly. "Oh, but are you referring to that small, empty house close to the Hilton Head airport that is well known among law enforcement?"

I nodded. "There have been rumors filtering down from the back-woods community…snippets of gossip. Perhaps while sipping beer, a whisper about the rituals there. A graphic story at a picnic about the sacrifice of goats. Secretly made CD's of melodious chanting, and yet, no one willing to go on the record for fear that his life might be in jeopardy. And I suspect that you know, Dr. Diamond, that because activity has been slow at the house recently, the police nearly have ceased surveillance."

"That is true. The *oungan* seldom goes there anymore," he continued, "preferring the more natural settings of the marshes and woodlands. However, his assistants, who are called *laplas* and *oungenikon,* do meet occasionally at the house with some of the rest of the initiates. Of course, there are others of less importance. And each dreams that he will become an *oungan* within his lifetime."

I was startled when he jumped up and extinguished the candles, instead returning the light from the metal lamp to the room with a click of a switch. It was the first time that I noticed that the walls were of gray cement, the floor, too, with gaping cracks shielding spider sacks among thick webs. My eyes followed the beam from the lamp up to Dr. Diamond's fixed smile. "The others you mentioned…those of less importance? What do they do?" I asked.

Dr. Diamond hesitated, his eyes widening. "Certain worshipers welcome the Iwa, the spirits, sometimes becoming a welcoming repository when the Iwa choose to possess them," he said more lively. "They perform chants and prepare items and animals for sacrifice."

"I beg your pardon?" *Animal sacrifices?*

"You heard me correctly," he said. He blinked and said nothing then, as if our conversation was finished, and I should make the next move.

I needed to think what I wanted to say next. Time after time, animal rights advocates touting anti-cruelty laws had stormed my office in Columbia. It was the one time that my job put me in the middle of the proverbial divided frying pan, on the one hand prosecuting animal cruelty laws and on the other defending the US Constitution and the right to practice sacrifice as part of a religion.

"I hear about it all the time," I said with loathing, "and hope I personally never see it."

"You look pale," Dr. Diamond said. "Would you like a glass of water?" He stood and put his hand on the knob of the door, clicked it, and through the opening I could see a kitchen filled with bottles and jars and piles of weeds and grasses. And sprawled across the floor were the carcasses of chickens and rabbits, some appearing mummified as if they had been there a long while.

All at once I had the strange sensation of floating and having my breath stolen. *Ridiculous. Get a grip!* "I'm all right now, thank you," I stammered. "Then you will arrange for me to meet with the priest?" Slowly I stood up.

"I want you to understand that those who practice voodoo are not mysterious barbarians," Dr. Diamond said, touching my arm. "Death must always have a purpose, or there can be no purpose to death! All animals used in the rituals die humanely. Most enter the body of those who need nourishing and as food for the Iwa, the spirits. And Mrs.

Guesswine, perhaps you *will* meet the *oungan*. When? Where? Only he'll know."

"I see. Then I'll be expecting to hear from him soon," I said.

Without words, I knew to follow Dr. Diamond through the door. He mentioned one more thing. "What I've told you is all that anyone will tell you. Any attempt to find out more could prove a problem for you."

I moved away inches, stopped and turned. "Did you say a *problem* for me? If that's a half-veiled threat, I don't scare easily," I told him, when actually, I kept my visibly shaking fingers loosely over my holster, my right hand ready to jerk out my Beretta.

His eyes and lips released no response. To my surprise he opened the door for me, stood very still and watched as I crossed the lawn. I started the car and drove away with the impression that at least Dr. Diamond was a gentleman.

CHAPTER 16

When I stayed too long at the cottage, the thought of more gray days brought anguish, so I decided to squeeze in more weekends at Renaurd Inn. But I would never get used to Mrs. Trample-St. Synge, who like a horse out of the gate, charged toward me at breakfast with inappropriate prying about the bone case victims. This particular morning was no different.

"Absolutely no comment!" I told her.

I excused myself and set off for a jog down the trail beyond the back of the inn. There was little weather. Yet, nature seemed put upon by steely clouds and sixty-degree temperature. At least I wouldn't sweat if I paced myself. At least I wouldn't draw the no-seeums.

When I came to a fork where one boardwalk headed east to the beach and the other north, I remembered that there had been talk at dinner the evening before that the island harbored the 'trickster', a guardian angel who was mischievous but harmless, a spirit often referred to by many Blacks on the outer sea islands as the devil. Not the same evil entity that the Judeo-Christians abhor, but one who instead was a teacher of sorts, whose antics could enlighten both the intellect of anyone who listened and one whom I hoped I wouldn't encounter. But then, I don't know, didn't my curiosity sometimes cut at my common sense? So instead, I headed away from the Atlantic and into the so-called forbidden North end.

Renty on another occasion had told me that an old black woman, Tapest, who looked after Coneras, often wandered the area where she caught the fish that sometimes got trapped in the inlet pools after a high tide. He said that she spoke Gullah and didn't have any education but read and wrote well enough to keep track of the money she earned. She, too, had lived the history of the Renaurd Island. And I had heard that she openly practiced voodoo. Would I come upon her unexpectedly?

I scarcely knew where I was going, had not gone far when there was an abrupt turn to the left. Ahead, a fogbank blocked a path that was as worn as old shoes. There was a noise here, a voice there—the hog-like snort of a gator, its fourteen foot body appearing like boiling froth in front of me only to slither with astonishing swiftness beneath a solitary palmetto. But my theory of survival was simple. I quickened my pace, conscious of my every move, of going forward, of not sliding off the planks that went around slight inclines and through strong rivulets that suddenly disappeared into debris-clogged tree roots. Soon a dull wind broke, and there was the sense that from every dismal shadow a solitary eye raked my every move. But I saw no one. Yet, with my perception razor keen, I was sure that something forded the path a fraction behind me. Again and again I stopped to dare a look, each time, anxiety seeming to zap my energy.

I suspect that I was at the most remote part of Renaurd Island when a stray palm frond veered into my eyes, and through several more fronds, I saw a patch of land that was littered with strange objects. Painted fish heads. Colorful beads. Sticks carved into unknown shapes. My eyes wove through them. Who recently had been here? Who had traveled deliberately into a place fraught with sombrous half-light? What I saw disturbed me so much that I stopped, and it was then that I found myself face to face with Zaccheas Bird, his painted body resembling the rigidity of a totem pole while a crowd of flies symbiotically, I suspect, buzzed silvery lips that repeatedly smacked like cymbals. Startled by the sight of him, my intention was quickly to get away, but instead, I stepped forward then backward before his eyes steered me to a halt. And then he opened the palm of his hand to reveal a mottled piece of granite, and I had remembered Allison talking about voodoo thunderstones, pieces of large rock fragmented by lightening and believed to hold magical powers.

He bolted toward me. "Kou le!" he shouted, the stone levitating above his fingers. "Kou le!"

There was finality to his clamor—the language unintelligible, but its energy meaningful—and in anticipation that Zaccheas Bird would cast a spell over me, and as if to create a boundary, I covered my face with my hands! "Stop it!" I screamed.

"Kou le! Kou le!" he said, his voice vibrating.

I waited; he said nothing more. He turned and like a deer trotted swiftly toward the east.

My heart began the monotony of a slow funeral drum. For several minutes I didn't know where I was, and then as if someone had opened the windows of a long sealed room into a bright sunlight, there appeared a rectangular building on stilts, one as old as the towering live oaks around it, one probably built during the 1800's to withstand the tidal surge from hurricanes that sometimes suffocated the outer islands. *Had I been running? How did I get there?*

There was nothing unconventional about the plantation porch that wrapped entirely around the house. It was abundant with well-worn rattan chairs straddling over bright new timbers that shored up gaping cracks which allowed a peek at what must have been hundreds of empty milk jugs and Coke cans stored beneath.

But before I reached the top step, I became riveted on someone peering from a window. A stark figure, large and robust, with hair like a white poodle and dark oval eyes that had the heavily veiled lids of a woman of eighty came clamoring swiftly across the threshold. She spewed tobacco juice as she spoke Gullah from receding gums and gaps between teeth that revealed poor hygiene. Finally in English, she asked, "Ere…you ain't lost or somethin'?"

"Or something," I said going up the steps. She moved aside. "I'm Kate Guesswine."

"Uh huh. I knows."

"Is this Coneras's place?" I asked.

"This is hisn's."

"Is he here?"

"Somewheres 'round," she said opening the screen door with hands as big as a large man's. "Sit a 'pell."

An old partly blind beagle lumbered in front of me. When I sat down, I pitied his hammock-like back…until his arthritic paws wrapped around my ankle and his nose shot toward my crotch.

"Son-a-bitchin' mutt!" the woman shouted. "Ain't never too old to have an itchin' for it!" Then she kicked him out the door.

"You're Tapest?" I asked.

"Yep. Wan' some wooter?"

"That would be fine."

"'Ere's a well o't back. I'll git you some."

"Thank you."

"I'll see if Coneras's workin' in the shed," she said as she wiped tobacco juice from her chin.

I nodded and she disappeared quickly. My eyes took in the strange, unfashionable shabbiness of the room, the chairs, couch and tables candidates for the junk yard. Shredded shears covered windows that hadn't been washed for a long time. Light diffusing from tattered lampshades, spread across objects that the rest of us might find appalling: a doll with a large pin in its chest, a stuffed alligator's head and small boxes with carvings of demons as their clasps.

Suddenly I was absorbed by the portraits across one wall. After awhile their wretchedness itched like an unwanted rash, for I had seen paintings like these in Goya's Nightmare series, the figures grotesque and disturbing, the reflection of an artist whose unconventional personal life had strayed into his art. I found it curious that there appeared to be strange similarities between these paintings and the landscapes in the Renaurd library, and I assumed immediately that perhaps Jennifer Renaurd must have been the artist.

"You lik' 'em?" Tapest asked when she returned with water.

"I can't say that I do," I said.

But wasn't there a hidden intention about the paintings that drew you to them? An unexpected splash of color? A veiled line that curved inexplicably in the half-light?

Tapest sat opposite me, her elbows resting on a large stomach while her breast swayed from a too tight midriff as she inhaled and exhaled, "Coneras's comin' in a minit'!"

"Mmm hmm. Well, I look forward to seeing him."

"Washin' up," she said.

After awhile, I felt the burden of conversation was lifted when Coneras entered the room, shook my hand and sat in a nearby recliner, his boot heels pressing into the cracked leather of a separate footrest. "Don't get many visitors out here," he said, a cold straining his voice.

I smiled and sipped water. "Not your user friendly tourist destination…" I said, blinking at the table lamp that Tapest had turned on and that was now flooding the paintings.

He frowned. "You're wonderin', 'Now why would anyone want to paint people dyin' in such a bad way?' But we gotta die one way another, don't we? Same for most folk. End up under all that dirt, dirt and more dirt. No use frettin' about it, now is there?"

"Oh, but I'm not so sure that I see your point!" I stood up and perused the canvasses again. "Strangling, disembowelment, burning? Women and animals? Perhaps Jennifer was severely disturbed."

"I wouldn't know. You either," he said, the way someone does when he wants to be finished with a conversation.

"Thar's more of 'em at Gabe's and in his attic," Tapest said. "Coneras says that eve' he can't put his eyes on 'em."

"Don't concern you none, Tapest," he said angrily. "Get your pills. Take a rest like the doctor told you!"

Her face flushed like a scolded child. Then as if for balance, she wedged the palms of her hands against the wall, shuffling down the hall like someone who had drunk one too many martinis.

"Every last one of those damn paintings oughta be burned," Coneras said vehemently.

"But why do you display them?" I asked.

He uncrossed his legs and looked at me suspiciously. He abruptly got up and held the screen door open. "Better get back to cutting wood," he said, his expression grave. I felt the reproach of his eyes telling me to leave.

"Thank you for your time," I said politely.

"A rail fence turns northeast," he said. "Follow it to the end. Take the left path. It's the safest way back to the inn."

Immediately, I wanted to mention that I had seen Zaccheas Bird, but it was as if any thought of him had strangled my vocal cords, and I was constrained not to speak. I knew that was nonsense, so I sucked air and turned before Coneras was out of earshot.

"What does *Kou le* mean?" I shouted.

He reeled around. His body went rigid. As he ran his fingers along the side of his face, his eyes tightened. "Where'd you hear that?"

For an instant I almost told him. "Oh, I don't know. From one of the guests at the inn, I suppose."

"It's associated with black magic," he said, "and power that snakes the air! Can cause you to be sick! Or worse! Now don't mess 'round here! Get back to the inn!"

"Can't say that I believe it," I said making light of it. I dragged my hand into a salute and picked up my pace.

"She's a stupid fool," I heard Coneras mutter. "Keeps messin' where she shouldn't and she'll get herself killed!"

CHAPTER 17

It seemed as though Coneras lived in about as desolate part of Renaurd Island that he could. Still, I didn't regret that I had gone there, although his clamming up to any discussion about the paintings only piqued my curiosity about Jennifer Renaurd's artistic talent. But I knew that this was neither the time nor place to dwell on it. Humidity was simmering like warm tea in the crevices of my body. With Coneras's warning still etched in my mind, I followed the old wooden rail fence that closed the symmetry of a narrow ridge by the mud banks where the coastal tides laced the black needle rush with brine. I stopped long enough to realize that something had disturbed the dark layers of muck, the air pockets in the banks of the marsh collapsing into a soft thud under the gentle pressure of the incoming tide. But then all at once the path looked untrammeled, and I knew I was lost.

As I was about to turn around, something caught my eye, an undetermined shadow among a phalanx of salt myrtle near where sea currents had drowned pines to line them like broken tombstones in an old cemetery. I resisted a compulsion to turn around; I paused again—I did so deliberately—instead going forward, crossing several narrow estuarine creeks until the last one ran between barricades of reddish boulders, their only purpose I thought, to divert the northern slap of the heavy sea away from the island.

Off to my left was the trail again, which abruptly dismounted onto a stone breakwater that snaked among hammocks—jungle-like islands with evergreens and palmetto scrub that was long ago sculpted by the harsh winds which often rattle the headwaters near the island, headwaters that present a dangerous forbidden barrier to boats passing too close to the coast.

Beyond the seawall that ran perpendicular to several submerged concrete jetties similar to the ones off Dragon's Point, there was moored a boat, its hull long and narrow, its call numbers indiscernible. Churning in the surf like some ghastly beetle, it stayed in my mind's eye for a long time. I found the path again. I knew too well that I should immediately turn back, my eyes prodding sharply through the rough foliage all around me, the tide line no longer visible.

And then I saw settled in among old abandoned ship's ballasts, a small shack with its wood weathered like a very old man's skin. I drew closer. My heart jumped when from a tiny window, light speared shadows across a small porch. Who was here?

I steadied myself against a large cylindrical propane tank under the window pane. Inside, voices became stronger, and then slacked off, and although there was an ear of familiarity, I simply couldn't place tone with face. Then I heard the dragging of heels. For fear that I might be seen, I crept away, perhaps ten yards or so, where I saw two corrugated metal structures supported by rectangular stones to hold the marsh tide beneath it. I crouched beside one. Out of sheer ambivalence, I remained for an unknown time. Then someone came onto the porch and urinated before returning to the building. He left the door ajar, and although I could discern part of the conversation, voices were still unfamiliar.

"So she was at Coneras's place, heh? I'm not concerned."

"Hullo? Things ain't going good!"

"I told you, I'm not concerned! But notify the suppliers. There won't be any *transactions* for a while. Then you head for the Bahamas. Stay put! And lay off the booze, you hear? Your piss is so soused it's coming through the fucking wall! Now I've got to go. And you get your ass moving, too!"

For a long time I heard only the collective voices of cicadas and tree frogs circuitously about me, but I continued to crouch in the quietude for what must have been ten more agonizing minutes until I was sure that the two men had gone out a back entrance. Then I returned to the trail.

To my left and partially hidden under a tarp, was a boulder-like object, the size of it hitting me at midriff. I yanked back the cover, and the smell of recently burned incense was sharp. Only a fool would be doing this, I thought referring to my sleuthing, and when I examined what appeared to be a long slab that leaned unevenly forward, I saw rust colored flecks across the mottled top. Was it dried blood? At each corner I saw stones, shells, feathers and similar items like the ones I had seen on the trail and at Coneras's. Within seconds—it seemed longer—I knew what it was that I was looking at; there was no other logical explanation for it being there, but my thinking that it was an altar upon which sacrifices were made was almost unconscionable. Someone actually believed that while shrouded in secrecy and under various phases of the moon, voodoo ritual could procure a doorway to the innermost chambers of both the physical and spiritual realms of human nature for some unfortunate victim!

Then I heard a noise behind me. Unexpectedly, someone exited the building. *So they both hadn't gone after all!* I dropped and groveled upon the ground, my eyes pawing the man's back, neck and head. From where I was, I didn't know him. Yet, there was something unsettling about his gait, as if he had suffered a debilitating assault upon a foot which forced him to move in excruciating pain. Before long he disappeared.

Although I was shaken with fear for my safety, I stood to leave and was about to step back onto the path which was separated from the altar and shack by a thin stand of pine trees, about to round the curve near the stone breakwater when the grayish, distorted face of Stacks Sandover stopped me cold! It was as if he had jumped from an uncovered grave, the crown of his head shaved and the thick hair on his upper lip matted with drippings from his nose.

His voice rocked like a squeaking old chair, "Hey you! Hey! Hey! Hey!"

I tried to go around him, but he threw a block. His knuckles showed white around my left wrist at the same time that my other hand fanned his heinous face.

"Get away!" I shouted.

"Bitch!"

"Let go!" The soulless blackness of his eyes emboldened me! My knee found his crotch. He rolled.

"Fucking bitch!" he groaned. I saw that he had a walking cast up to his knee.

He wouldn't be able to keep up, but still I bolted away from him, pausing only where the path changed by the seawall and then sprinting onto the wooden planks again, my feet treading on an inch or more of the tide that had come in with a shift of wind. I kept thinking of my Beretta and how foolish I had been to go into treacherous territory without it! Suddenly, I stopped. I was at once nauseous. My legs felt invisible. Slowly, I leaned forward, crashed to my knees and tumbled into the muck. Then I was palpably cool and falling swiftly into a place of bright light.

It seemed to me that I was with my mother, Catherine Ashley Guesswine, her beauty simmering in the arms of the young men who had broken her boredom at the Ashley estate during the many celebrated parties there. Black caretakers roamed about with sweet tea and jars of strawberry jam, and Courtney was a pink-faced tyke who cried too much when I tweaked her cheek for taking my toys. A safe and virtuous place it was there with my mother, and that I might only have imagined it and dreamed it the way a child dreams the long dream, the innocent dream, the safe dream, was unbearable when I thought that someone was shaking me, arousing me, and lifting me into firm arms. It was then that I knew that I was convulsing into the curvature of someone's shoulder as I was being carried. And then I went into a long dark sleep.

*   *   *

I didn't expect to wake up in a strange bedroom while a violent storm raged outside, clad only a man's pajama top. There was a smell of a wood burning in the nearby corner fireplace, the drone of Bach from another room. To my right I didn't expect to see Gabe Coneras sloshing a washrag in a basin; but there he was. There's awkwardness to having a shamefully attractive man come uninvited to the edge of a bed and sit next to your thigh, even if his face is doleful.

"Welcome back," he whispered. He folded the cool washrag onto my forehead. "How do you feel?"

His presence was comforting. "What happened?"

"You still look pretty out of it," he said.

"That's absurd," I said trying to sit up only to be thwarted backward by a spinning head.

"You slipped on the trail. About thirty yards from my place."

"Mmm hmm. No broken bones?"

"Were you running from someone?" he asked.

"I got lost when I left Coneras's," I said sheepishly.

"And we didn't run into each other? I was at my grandfather's only minutes before I found you."

"No? Well, it was much earlier. On the way back to the inn, I took a wrong turn." I wasn't ready to tell Gabe what or whom I had seen at the north end. I wanted Justin to run a computer check on Stacks Sandover first.

His eyes tightened. "I see. It can be very dangerous out here," he said in a voice that seemed full of meaning. "Didn't I warn you?"

I managed a smile. "Not to stroll without the nickel tour? Are you going to gloat?"

Gabe stood up. "Would I do that?"

"I feel like I should get up, too," I said, "put my jeans and tank back on."

"Oh that," he said pointing at the bathroom door. "I'm sorry. I didn't want you to get pneumonia. They'll be dry in the morning."

"But I can't possibly stay here! I'll call someone."

He rolled his tongue around his lips. "Phones seldom work out here when it's bad weather. While you were sleeping, I went to the inn and told Allison that you were okay. It's a mean night! By now the storm has flooded the boardwalk."

I glanced at my watch. "Nine o'clock!"

"You've been asleep for hours," he said. His eyes dragged over my body like an old anchor. "I didn't wash you. You and the sheets are covered with mud. Perhaps you'd like a shower?" he asked.

"Mmm hmm. Thank you. It would be nice."

"Some broiled flounder afterward?" he offered.

"With lemon?"

"A woman after my heart," he said lightly.

"Just the flounder, I think," I said back.

He stood in the doorway. "Careful now when you get up," he said. "I laid out towels for you. An extra toothbrush. Oh, and the cold and hot are reversed."

"Fair warning," I said.

"Here's a clean robe," he said after going to his closet. Then from a plastic storage basket, his hands filtered out blue socks from a cache of various colors. "The floor's not always the cleanest."

"Are we going to eat off it?" I joked.

"Never know, now do you?" He laughed easily, and suddenly I was laughing, too. "See you in a bit," he said over his shoulder as he left the room.

I suppose that it showed something about the man—the way he kept house—the way he kept his shower and toilet, the way he kept himself. Gabe was well-kept in every way, clean in his own person and manners, the same as his place. But later when I went into the living room, a large but cozy area with fine leather furniture and hand-carved wooden tables and simple lamps—the kind that give off subdued lighting, I realized what Tapest had meant about the portraits. They were like sores on a splintered finger, collectively adding a kind of unwanted chaos to an otherwise orderly wall. Fortunately, the aroma of dinner and the pop of wine being uncorked tempered the atmosphere. I was hungry and eager for a glass of Coastal.

"You don't care for them, do you?" Gabe said when he saw me scanning the canvasses.

"Do you display Jennifer's paintings as a memorial to her?" I asked.

He frowned. "They simply reflect the lives of people. And geniuses have a way of culling out what's extraneous, now don't they?"

"A bit gruesome for my taste, I think."

Gabe sucked his breath and cleared his throat. "Everyone wears a mask," he said. "Hides dissatisfaction with life. Doesn't reveal fantasies for fear of reprisal from a hypocritical society that suffers from some of the same hang-ups. But the poets, writers, musicians, artists…they stick their thumb in the air and say, 'Who gives a rat's ass.'"

"Oh, but they're just as vulnerable!"

"In an egotistical way, I suppose."

"Mmm hmm, but you must agree that there is a kind of sadistic violence in what she painted," I said. "A worrisome violence!"

"I don't agree at all," he said in an indignant tone. "There's a heart beat in every brush stroke! I wouldn't part with any of them."

It was time to cut him some slack. He was scowling. I laughed and asked, "Are you a closet 'angerer?'" I wrapped my forefinger around his.

He eased his finger to the top of my wrist, and then swept my hair back from my forehead. "I'm not a closet anything," he said smiling. "But I am a fair cook. So let's eat."

I thought of how cleanly handsome he was in his knit shirt, the top two buttons opening to fine hair that matched a day's facial stubble. When he returned to a small corner table with fish that were surrounded by fresh green beans and two red potatoes on a blue plate obviously thrown by an adept potter, I wasn't surprised.

"Ah…the perfect spinach salad," I said, putting some on each of our plates.

"Taste my dressing first," he said, and I thought immediately of David whose homemade vinaigrette would put Paul Newman's to shame.

"Gabe, I need to talk about Jennifer. You knew her better than anyone."

He held a smile, his eyes following as I sipped wine. "We were kids together," he said finally. "That was some time ago."

"Were you close?" I asked. "I mean, would it embarrass you if I asked how well you knew her?"

He slumped back and stabbed his fork into the flesh of the fish. "Oh, you do trespass easily, don't you? And didn't we have this conversation when we were sailing?"

"It was interrupted by Stacks Sandover," I said quickly. I watched for a response. There was none. I could have mentioned the Pope for all he knew.

"You couldn't help but be fond of her," he said, his voice firm. "Now do you mind? I really did try to make you a nice dinner."

"Egg on my face, huh?" I asked, collecting a fork of potatoes.

"A little scrambled," he said. "But it's a face that I still want to kiss."

He could easily make me blush and he knew it. "I told you…that talk makes me uncomfortable."

"All right then, I take it back," he offered. "How's your fish?"

"Perfect." But I had no intention of letting the subject of Jennifer drop. Better to maneuver the conversation back to the paintings. "You're an artist, too," I said, "so what do you really think of her work?"

He swirled his wine before taking a sip. "Do I think of it at all?"

"She was so young to have painted so intensely," I said.

"Age isn't a barrier to enlightenment, is it?"

"I gather a matter of interpretation," I said. "She was damn mad at something or someone!"

He shook his head again. "You don't get it, do you?"

"That's what I'm trying to do, Gabe," I said, leaning forward.

He poured more wine. "Look, she was lonely. Painting was a way for her to express that. I taught her technique. And geniuses have a way of culling out what's extraneous."

"The point is," I said, "it's rare at such a young age, isn't it?"

"And if you're not loved…"

"But she was! Adored by Allison and the Renaurds!"

"A lost child!" he retorted.

I settled back in my chair and embedded my wrists on the table. "You can't be serious!"

"Now she's free of them," he insisted. He picked up his fork. "I really believe that our tongues should focus on the flounder."

But I still needed to make a point. "And you went away after she disappeared."

"What was done was done. Why stay around?" he asked slowly.

"Why not?"

He was agitated, grinding his teeth, obviously withholding a full-blown outburst. "Are you interrogating me?" he asked forcefully.

"But wouldn't you expect me to ask about her? Her running away? You're leaving so soon?"

"Mind you," he said—I could tell that he was weighing his words—"the island wasn't the same. Her damn laughter…and well, the hours of conversations. I missed that."

"Mmm hmm. And did she confide in you? Did you know her friends? Who she saw when she went to the mainland? I want to get her killer!"

He folded his hands and sat silently before saying, "Look Kate, I believe I have grounds to complain here. I feel like this evening has turned into a coroner's inquest."

The attention he had given to dinner had touched me, and to my dismay I was going to have to spend the night. "Well, anyone who makes balsamic dressing the way you do, deserves a break, I suppose. I'm sorry. Really I am. I forget…"

"…that you have needs?" He said under his breath, "and so do I." He stared at me.

The thought had to be faced sooner or later, and the invented anxiety waning with the glow from the wine soon caused me to forget the paintings. He was easy to be with. Everything he said or did was contagious. He smiled. I did. He laughed. So did I. He took me in his arms and danced with me. I wanted to. He kissed me. I kissed back. There was the strange sensation that I had known him all of my life. On and on he went, saying the same about me, until there was no more evening or very little night, and near the dawn, he gestured that we should go to sleep.

"I meant to change the sheets," he said, following me into the bedroom. "Your backside was covered with mud when I brought you here. It reminded me of when I used to go skinny-dipping in the tidal creeks."

"I can picture it."

He took fresh sheets from the bottom drawer of a chest. I got on one side of the bed and he on the other. "It was at Piker's Creek, a short distance from here. One dry summer there was a fire. Then there was only mud. I'd jump in and hope I didn't meet a water moccasin. The mud would creep around my ankles. Damn sight trying to walk. It was like the quicksand you see in the Tarzan movies. It's gone now. This whole island is in danger of being gone, I suppose."

"Why walk in mud at all?" I mumbled into a case that was between my teeth as I stuffed in the pillow.

"It was fun for one thing. But it was the only way to get to the salt-water pools where the creek passed by. And the water was so deep that I'd float there, too, my body as naked as plastic cork."

"That I don't want to imagine," I said laughing.

"When the tide went out, I'd throw a cast net. I'd get enough shrimp for my family. My grandmother was alive then."

"Do you still do that thing with the mud? Go there and do that?"

"No,"—he hesitated—"I'm all grown up now!"

My face flushed and my eyes moved away from his. "Yes, yes you are, aren't you," I said.

After he had put the soiled sheets in the hamper in the bathroom, I wished there had been a warning, a signal of sorts before he drifted over to me. I stood very still, thinking desperately how I might make a graceful exit.

"*Very* grown up," he said slowly.

He stared at me and then took me in his arms, rubbing his chin against my cheek, never breaking his eyes from mine as he removed his shirt. Everything about him smelled good. His face, chest, arms. "I'm suffocating," I whispered into the nape of his neck.

He raised my chin and kissed me deep. "God, you are delicious."

"You take away the air," I said.

"Yes," he said, "and you…mine."

"I really can't," I said. "There's no air."

"There doesn't need to be."

"It's a mistake, you know," I said, my heart pounding wildly.

"I took you in my mind the first time I laid eyes on you," he whispered. "And now I want to take you in my body."

His tongue flooded my mouth. "Mmm hmm. But I'm not ready for this," I said as I considered rolling out of his grasp.

"Oh yes you are."

"This isn't a good idea," I whispered into the corner of his lip.

"I can give you something," he said, "something you haven't had in a long time. And I'm not talking only about sex."

He lifted me off the floor, my robe slipping down, his lips wildly inquisitive and awaking orifices that long hadn't been touched, and then in an awkward shuffle he removed the rest of his clothes and transferred me from his arms to the bed, his palms flattening against mine until we lay perfectly together.

"I need you to stop," I said, his tongue like a magnet on my breasts.

"Stay with me, please," he whispered.

It had been a long time since I had been with anyone, a long time since I had been absorbed in anything but crime, family trauma and self-pity. It had been a long time since anyone had said 'please' to me for anything. It felt good.

"Stay…"

I wanted to, and yet a deepening darkness suffocated my feelings until I felt nothing but a subtle numbness. He was so absorbed in me that he didn't hear me plead, "This is a mistake, Gabe! Now, please let me up!"

"Stay with me, Kate. The rest of the night. The rest of tomorrow. And after that, because you want to!" he whispered.

"No!" I said, knowing that there would be insurmountable consequences for us both. He attempted to pull me further into him, but I retracted abruptly, and only after I turned my head away and put my hands sharply across his mouth did he collapse, the hair of his chest and legs wet with sweat, his eyes anchored to mine in disbelief. "I just *can't*, Gabe!" I pushed against his strength and slid out from under his body.

"Then I won't force you," he said. There was sad disappointment in his turned-down jowls, but hadn't he forged his way a little too fast into my life? Hadn't he caught me like some half-starved animal with my defenses down and fired round after round into my body so that I lay wounded and perhaps unable to recover? This was unneeded trouble, I thought as I watched him lying there with the calm and resolve of a hunter about to come after its prey again in the brush. Then he was peculiarly silent while I was shivering and suddenly aware that I was naked. He rose, handed me a robe and opened the window, pulling cool air into his lungs. His eyes in a frenzy, he shook his head and sighed, "I can wait."

"Mmm hmm, I'm sorry, but please don't," I said. I broke into tears. "My life has too many *ifs*!"

"Ifs? Well, I don't think so," he said with disbelief. "Even now I want to have you. And I will."

"It won't happen, I tell you!"

There he was, putting on his clothes and looking doubtfully at me, as if anything I might say were to be taken lightly or not be considered at all. "I'm a patient man, Kate." He tightened the belt to his jeans, came back and kissed my forehead. "Well, the tide will go out in about an hour. When you leave, take the left trail to the inn so you don't get lost again."

After he left the room, I came to rest on top of the sheets, sobbing away months of anger, and finally dozing until the sun washed my face like a warm cloth. I wanted to smell flowers, there were none. I wanted to hear birds, there was no sound. In an almost unbearable ritual, one that I had done all my life, I struggled to put on each piece of clothing. As I went out the door, I took notice that Gabe hadn't left my mind. But on the walk back to the Renaurd Inn, I also was aware that David had never left my heart. The old cliché, 'Better to have loved and lost than never to have loved at all?' Forget it!

CHAPTER 18

After crossing the Cassawatchi Bridge, I drove to North Street and pulled under Dahlia Tarteton's scalloped overhang that was partially covered with the sleeping vines of winter. Across the street and beyond the tall brick wall was St. Helena's Church, established by an Act of the Assembly in 1712. A brass sign stated that its first rector frequented settler's homes before the parish was decimated during an uprising by the Yemassee Indians. It was well known that St. Helena's once stabled British horses during the American Revolution and harbored the sick during the Civil War, but I wondered what it was like for Mrs. Tarteton to look beyond the wall at the burial ground for British and American officers, ministers and citizens of the area. I gripped the steering wheel, sighed and got out, imagining breathing from graves whose headstones and above-ground sarcophaguses—some cracked and tilted—bore names like Wheeler Calderwood and Augustus Croft. I settled by the car, the earth around me seemingly barren when it wasn't, a place where tree branches twisted to the ground from years of coastal rain and wind.

Ten minutes later Sara Baird slid from the leather seats of a silver-gray Cougar, what teens call a 'hot' car and chop shops call a moneymaker. Recently hired as a police reporter for the *Hilton Head Tracker*, a tourist rag owned by her father, a prominent New York businessman who had retired to Shipyard Plantation, it was well known that she had worked as a reporter in several cities, eventually gravitating to *The National Inquirer* where after a disagreement about editorial rights, she was fired and moved to England. There she wrote several pieces about Princess Diana's death and the dalliances of other Royals. In fact, those who knew her said that she had files tucked away with information on the affluent and wealthy—both in the United States and Europe—that would make the FBI blush.

Her reputation solid within the Beaufort County Sheriff's Office, I suspected that Sara Baird had carte blanche to police press releases, frequently went on ride-a-longs and knew details about the bone cases that never should have been 'off the record.' I kept thinking that this wasn't the best of days for Sheriff Sparkman to have asked me to take her under my wing as a PR favor to him—I hadn't slept again and had a slight sinus infection—but little did I know that I would immediately regret that I was about to be saddled with holding Sara Baird's leash.

"Hello Ms. Baird." I waved.

She descended on me quickly. Mid-thirties, I would guess. Noticeably straight and curvaceous like a bottle of designer perfume on a fine glass shelf in an upscale store. Champagne hair. Silky skin. Expensive packaging.

"Where's Justin, Katie," she said with uninvited familiarity as if she already knew me.

Her voice was nasal-ish. I politely shook her hand. "Mmm hmm. Detective McCreary is getting paper work, Ms. Baird," I said. "He'll be along later."

"I've seen you all over the TV and papers. You're famous! Justin's got your picture in his office, too. But, say, did I tell you that I'm used to first names? How 'bout you call me Sara? There's no 'h'."

"Fine," I said with a straight face. "There's no 'i' in Kate."

"So's this case special to you or something?"

I stopped in the middle of the brick walk and placed my fingertips on her shoulders. "Ms. Baird, let's get something straight. *All* my cases are special. You need to…"

"Oh golly, I've done it again," she interrupted. "Sometimes I yak too much. But say now, if this old gal can put a finger on that scarf that was in the paper, well, who knows? Case solved!"

"Let's wait and see," I said unconvincingly as we climbed the steps.

"I've never interviewed the relative of a murder victim," she said.

I stopped. "Rule number one," I cautioned, "Don't refer to the deceased in the past. We aren't positively sure if Anastasia is this woman's niece."

"If it *is* Mary Elizabeth Tarteton, golly, Justin said it's a done deal."

Sometimes my Ex had an indefinable ability to irritate me even in his absence, and I was positive that he would somehow manage to do it from his grave someday. "Your job is to observe," I said, taking her by the arm and pulling her up onto the porch. "This is an investigation. I'll ask the questions. Do you understand?"

"H'mph! Thank you *mom*," she said with a deliberately saccharine voice.

"No bell," I said. I knocked on double oak doors.

She flaked rust off a brass plate with her thumbnail. "333 North Street. Say! This place looks like the termites got it!"

"I know this area well. Pre-Civil War," I said. We waited for Mrs. Tarteton to answer the door. "Circa mid-eighteen hundreds, once grand and part of Beaufort's historic neighborhoods! A favorite of the tourists!"

"The snowbirds?"

"Well some, I suppose. They like to stroll under the giant live oaks, and…"

"Golly, imagine the chattering of slaves and the rocking of grand coaches. Their wheels stirring tornados of dust from the dirt streets. You know, before their owners, dressed in their finery, disembarked and strolled through the iron gates of the stone walls that surrounded the mansions?"

"A very pretty verbal exhibition, Sara. An original?"

"Well, wasn't Mrs. Tarteton's old blighted mansion once like the stately ones you read about in Southern romance novels?"

In a way, I suppose she was right. Up close the Tarteton place showed the hardship of age and disrepair. Supported by tall columns, the splintering boards of the double verandahs looked like tattered ribbons of gray across the front. It hadn't seen paint in years and there was little color anywhere else. Three brown wicker rockers in poor shape were beside petunias languishing near death, their clay pots too long in the blistering afternoon sun. I wondered why nobody had taken in the yellowed newspapers that were stacked like sewage pipes in the corner. All this prescribed an unhealthy display of poverty that was unlike many of the other mansions which had been restored to their original opulence on both sides of the street.

I knocked again. Eventually a frail woman peeked from behind a blind. She cracked the door and came out. "Please," she said, waving two fingers that gripped a cigarette as if it were a wand, "sit down, won't you?" Her hair was piled up like mashed potatoes, but mostly I was taken by her good-hearted brown eyes.

Sara whispered to me. "Golly, she's got *two* hearing aides!"

I frowned. This was not going to be a pleasant experience, I thought.

Introductions were brief: reporter, attorney general and Anastasia's— I hoped, anyhow—Aunt Dahlia Tarteton.

"Did Detective McCreary explain why we wanted to see you?" I asked. "He'll be here later."

"Yes, but it makes not a bit of sense," Mrs. Tarteton began. Her smile was stifled because of a jaw that she told us had recently been wired because of an accident. Near her waist, I recognized a morphine pump. "My niece was admired by important people. And unfortunately she liked the men, you know, maybe a little too much."

"What did Mary Elizabeth tell you exactly?" I asked.

"My niece traveled," she explained.

"Did she ever stay around Tybee Island?" Sara Baird interrupted. She was about to scribble notes onto a pad, but then she seized a package from a large leather tote. Like a deck of cards, she fanned pictures of the Dolphin Motel and of the clothes that had been left there. Immediately, I was furious. How did she get those? I had to bite my tongue to keep from asking. Then she put them down and ceremoniously balanced her pad and pencil again in the center of her lap.

Mrs. Tarteton coughed. "She lived a lot of places," she said. "Probably there, too."

"How might you know that?" I asked.

"Well, she…"

"Why didn't she use her own name?" Sara Baird interrupted.

"Will you let her answer my questions, please?" I said.

"I told you, she knew people!" Mrs. Tarteton said, tears welling up. "She liked to play games. She put ads in the *Personals* of newspapers. She liked to be other people."

"Golly, she's not going to bawl, I hope," Sara Baird muttered under her breath.

I glared. "Excuse me Mrs. Tarteton! What did you mean, 'she liked to be other people?'"

"Oh yes. Pretend she was rich," she said. She flicked ashes into a large yellow dish. "Anyone would think that she was a lady from one of those big beach mansions on Hilton Head Island. I saw ads she put in *The Packet* newspaper there and other papers, too."

Sara Baird clumsily tapped her pencil on my wrist. "I have a question," she said.

"Mmm hmm. Go ahead, but be careful," I cautioned.

"Whenever she stayed with you, did she have visitors?" she asked. "Did any stay overnight? Did she go to bars?"

"Easy Sara! I mean it!" I said sternly.

She sighed. "Golly, Katie…uh Kate? What the heck am I doing here then? Get her to the point!"

"Excuse us Mrs. Tarteton!" I said. Then I dragged Sara Baird to the edge of the steps. "Now here's what I'm telling you," I said, pulling her eyes into mine. "I can kick you off this porch and you won't work with anyone in the Beaufort Police Department again or the state of South Carolina for that matter. So I'd advise you to keep a lid on that mouth of yours. She's an elderly lady who is worried about her niece! Be respectful! Do you understand me?"

All expression drained from her face. "But your questions sound like you're a politician running for office."

"Oh? And you're being insensitive and impertinent. I don't like it." Our eyes squared off again. I didn't expect tears from her blues, and I don't know what I would have done had she plummeted into a full sob. I backed off.

"You don't like me for some reason," she growled with the tone of a spoiled child.

"That's nonsense. You're here with me, aren't you?" I reminded her. "Look, you've obviously got what it takes to be a good crime reporter. You visit morgues, do the 'ride along' with cops. Put yourself in harm's way. And writing about blood soaking into the concrete or some poor guy's guts hanging out because of a shotgun blast takes skill. But then there's a gift that every crime reporter must have. It's called empathy. Searching for justice. Not only for the victim, but for those left behind. And timing? You have to know *when* to ask the tough questions."

"Are you telling me that I don't know how to do my job?"

"Maybe for those half-assed rags you once worked for, you did a great job. But here in this state, we don't run things like they do. And it's obvious to me that you haven't learned how to decipher the bereaved."

Her cheeks were wet. She moved back like someone who had been struck. "Golly, are you finished?"

"Not quite," I said more softly. "One more thing. When I was your age, I thought I had the skin of Goliath. I was a tough young prosecutor who never slept. Caffeine and liquor revved up my engine. My marriage suffered. Friends stopped calling. I thought I was invincible!"

I could tell that she wasn't about to be lectured. But I went on. "A minute more, please," I said. "In spite of my downward personal spin, my career soared. I thought I *had* to know it all. Yet I almost crashed and burned trying to. Then I met a lawyer who was running for office. Judge Allison Thomason. You've probably heard of her."

"Who hasn't? I suppose you think that she's the Martin Luther King of women," she said with a subtle contempt.

"Mmm hmm. She's certainly close. She took me into her campaign. And then she gave me something no one else had. She gave me 'time'. And she bothered—I say bothered in a revering way—to give me honesty. She cautioned me above all to listen to those who had experience."

"Oh, and I imagine you did just that, didn't you, each and every day of your life?" she said sarcastically.

"I'll tell you what," I said, not wanting to get into it any further, "you ask me that over dinner sometime and we'll discuss it. And for now you may ask Mrs. Tarteton questions, but I am warning you to be courteous. Pay attention to her humanity!"

She took a deep breath. "I suppose you expect me to thank you?"

"Not at all. In fact, I suspect that you would rather kill the messenger?" I said grinning at her.

Sara Baird tried to smile. "Golly, that wouldn't be a good career move, would it?"

"No it wouldn't," I said, touching her hand. "All right then, let's clean this up and get out of here."

After we returned to our chairs, Mrs. Tarteton looked hard at the pictures again. "Oh my, oh yes. That looks like her scarf," she said pointing. And then she was quiet.

The air moved unexpectedly. Sara and I shared a glance. Mrs. Tarteton struggled up and told us she would make tea. We followed her into a large foyer, and even though the windows were ajar, there was a peculiar odor, much like the mustiness of shirts and jeans left too long damp in a clothes drier on a hot summer's day. In the living room to my left the furniture was sparse. A couch, two chairs and a side table with a crocheted doily symmetrically hugged the ornate wainscoting that ran the perimeter of the oblong room.

Abutting the bottom part of the stair railing to the second floor was an old Victrola like one that my Grandmother Ashley once owned. If you wound it up, would the music still flow from it? Then we walked through a narrow archway into the circulation of a ceiling fan and fresher air, into a kitchen that was sparse, too, with little behind the glass fronted cabinets or near a Formica table with vinyl-backed chairs, and all the while, Mrs. Tarteton continued silently to work her lips as though her tongue were a large sucker.

When she opened a vintage refrigerator that had a motor on top, there was a draft of sour wet air underlining more sparseness. An opened can of moldy peaches. A bottle of catsup. She shut the door and my eyes fell upon a teakettle on a 1930's cast iron stove. "There was a gas leak," she said. "It was strange. Strange things have been happening here lately. I was almost asphyxiated. And sometimes I hear sounds like someone walking, especially during the day when I'm a napping. Or mumbling-like voices. But then I am getting up there in years. Can't hear as well. Can't afford to fix that stove either, so I can't cook anything. Can't even afford one of those new microwaves, though Elizabeth told me she was going to buy me one."

"Golly, I once knew a guy who cooked exclusively with charcoal when he got behind in his bills," Sara Baird offered.

After a couple of minutes, Mrs. Tarteton filled three salt glaze mugs with hot water from the faucet. She added sugar.

"Thank you," I said.

"My pension is small. But Mary Elizabeth helped sometimes," she said, her voice suddenly lighting up so that the sadness in her eyes fell away. "She bought me four boxes of tea bags. Why, they came all the way from Ceylon!"

"Where are her parents?" I asked.

"My poor sister passed on when she was five. There was no father around. Least none that I ever met. I'm all she has left," she said. Her mind seemed to drift, and then she asked, "But are you sure that's her scarf?"

Someone from the Sheriff's Department will bring it for you to decide," I said.

"There's something else…" Mrs. Tarteton said. Then she left the room.

For the longest time there was no sound…until Sara Baird dumped her tea into the sink. "The way some people live! Can you believe it? The old gal should be put in a home."

"You're unrelenting, aren't you?"

"Huh?"

"She's going on with her life, isn't she? I admire her for that," I said. "That tea was her act of social kindness. It's more than you've shown her today!"

We sat in silence, her face upturned and away from me, her fingers like little batons around each other. I was sure that she had no idea at the inappropriateness of her behavior. I needed another problem in my life?

Then Mrs. Tarteton returned to the room with a shoebox. It could have been significant, so I used my pen to remove the lid. I singled out a red journal. "How long have you had this Mrs. Tarteton?" I needed Justin's warrant and a criminalist to bag it and check in all the other items as evidence, so I quickly closed the lid.

"Mary Elizabeth left it here a few days before she disappeared," she said.

She began to sob. I jumped up and pulled her face against my chest. "I'm sorry! I'm afraid that we've upset you!"

"What kind of work did she do?" Sara Baird asked.

Mrs. Tarteton dabbed her cheek and said, "I'm not sure. She was a waitress once. But lately? Well, she told me that she was making good money, that's all. And listen, I don't want to make trouble. I don't want any more trouble in my life. I've got neighbors, you see. And my minister wouldn't like it if I had anymore trouble!"

Sara Baird stood up and paced the kitchen, her hand on her hip. "Did she sleep around a lot?"

Would I last much longer before I dragged Ms. Sara with no 'h' outside and beat the brains out of her? "What she means is," I said quickly, "did your niece have boyfriends? Who she dated for awhile?"

"Golly, that isn't what I meant!"

"Oh yes it is!" I said, my voice losing control.

Mrs. Tarteton knotted her fingers together, and I could see that her nails were bitten to the quick. "Oh yes. She told me I'd like him, too. That he was handsome and special to a lot of people!"

"Did you ever meet him?" I asked.

"He came here once. He waited in the car. A dark car with dark windows."

"When was that?"

"Maybe a couple of weeks ago. Maybe a month. I'm not sure."

Sara continued to look sullen, so she sat down, kept her head lowered, her mouth shut, and her pen moving again like a stenographer taking notes.

"Would you like to search my niece's room?" Mrs. Tarteton asked.

"And perhaps some other parts of the house, too," I said. "Detective McCreary will be here soon with some other officers. Would you mind?"

"Well, I suppose not."

"He'll have a piece of paper that makes it legal," I said.

"Okay," she said, "but what should I do with this shoebox?"

"Please put it back where it was," I instructed. "And now, Ms. Baird and I would like to thank you for seeing us. We really must leave."

Mrs. Tarteton folded her arms. "So tell me, is the body at Dragon's Point my niece?"

It was the sort of question that I dreaded. However the outcome might be, the uncertainty of not knowing for sure one way or another was like having an undiagnosed illness. "We aren't positive," I said, trying not to avoid her worried eyes. "We may have to get a blood sample from you to compare DNA. Then we'll know for sure." I got up. "I'm sorry if we've tired you out Mrs. Tarteton."

"You're very kind, Attorney General Guesswine."

"Perhaps I could come back in the morning to clear up a few points?" I asked. "Would that be all right?"

"Just you?"

"Yes," I said glancing at Sara Baird, who then said a quick goodbye and made a dash through the door. I followed down the steps, while wondering how soon Justin would arrive.

"Golly, I can think of a dozen unanswered questions," Sara said. "You know that I have a right to interview her on my own? When you're not around?"

I pulled my canvass bag over my shoulder. "Of course you do. And I can place yellow tape around this place and make it part of the crime scene. Then you can't set foot on the premises. Do I need to do that?"

"H'mph! What ever happened to freedom of the press?"

I ignored her. "I'll be right back." I went back into the kitchen. "Mrs. Tarteton you've been very kind," I said, putting several twenties into her hand. "Suppose you buy some groceries."

She stood quietly fingering the money, and then she burst into tears. "This will get a couple of month's worth," she said.

"In the meantime, I'll send someone to have your gas fixed and take care of that, too. Would that be all right?"

"You'll never know…"

"I think I might," I said remembering the early stages of my career and marriage to Justin when we lived on kidney beans and hamburger, and occasionally the checkbook would get as low as $10.00 with several days still left in the month. I squeezed Mrs. Tarteton's arm, smiled and left the kitchen, my feet tapping the wood floors of the next room as I headed for the front door. In the unfathomable stillness, I heard the ceiling joists expand, the way they do when the humidity stretches the fibers of old dried wood—the opposite in the winter when the wood shrinks. I paused, about to go up the stairwell, but Mrs. Tarteton must have heard the cracking, too, for she came from the kitchen, looked up at the ceiling, smiled and said good naturedly, "Lucifer's a good mouser, isn't he? Now goodbye, Attorney General!"

Unconvinced, I went onto the porch, down the steps and got into my car. Sara Baird drove up beside me. "Eventually, I *will* write Dahlia Tarteton's story, Kate," she sputtered through an open window. "One way or another!" Neither of us said anything. Then. I watched her lips turn to a haughty triumph as she floored her Cougar and sped away leaving a veiled exhaust of dust in front of my windshield.

Sara Baird was a 'piece of work' that I wanted to pummel with darts, and yet, there was something pleasantly irritating about her…a kind of energy and charisma that was hard to dismiss in young women. Somehow I knew that eventually we were going to get along just fine.

CHAPTER 19

Courtney had a bad cold so I was glad that my birthday dinner at The Old Oyster Factory was cancelled, as the service call at Gary's Garage on Hilton Head Island to fix a broken fuel pump on my Explorer took three hours. It was nearly nine. There was little traffic along 278, and I tried not to focus on the possibility that I was coming down with a thunderous migraine that would require a preemptive strike of Imitrex if a couple of glasses of wine didn't knock it all to hell. Besides, I wasn't looking forward to dying of pain in my bed at the motorhome.

After going through the gate at Anchor Resorts, mushrooming sea fog obliterated the lighting around the clubhouse and pool. My street was pretty deserted; most motor-homers had gone to Florida for the cooler months. I slid from beneath my steering wheel, slung my laptop over my shoulder and snatched up my purse and overnight bag with my left hand, telling myself that I was glad that I had left the sewer, water and electricity hooked up.

Once inside, the atmosphere was quiet and cozy. Without question nothing could tempt me from my nightgown. I smothered my pores in a ton of facial cream, knowing that a semi-truck full of it probably would be of no help either. After pulling my legs under and hugging the corner of the sofa, I then dawdled over a glass of chardonnay, a Stouffers chicken and half a Sara Lee cheesecake. Frustration food…and my headache began to wane.

A second glass of Coastal was within reach of my TV table. I flipped on my computer and began scrolling my e-mail. A neon E-card from Dr. Bree Packer flickered a glittering 'Happy 46', and I shuddered that I was beginning to skid from my forties toward the big 'five O'. Suddenly an incoming message appeared.

It was officially from FBI agent Drew Greer:

Happy birthday old friend! I mean old! I'll bring you a garish present when I return from my in-service. And now down to business. If you haven't already done so, take a look at this blog that has been posted on several web sights around the world. Only hours ago it came to our attention. As we speak, our internet division is checking to see if it's authentic or if whoever posted it is playing a very bad joke. What alerted us, was that the blogger has sent you text and a pictorial attachment…and sent us copies, as well. It's pretty gruesome, so Kate, we're monitoring your in-box short term. We'll be in touch. Drew Greer.

I knew that blogs were becoming more and more popular forums for discourse. They were free internet sites where would-be authors could publish any narrative, in most cases, with little regard to voice, style or grammar, and on any subject and without restrictions. In spite of my annoyance with Drew for invading my e-mail, which I already knew could be breeched by almost anyone—even those with minimum hacking skills—I opened the text.

The message:

"Mirror, mirror on the wall, who's the fairest birthday girl of all?"
Surprised, Attorney General? E-mail's great, ain't it? I send to many people. Even in South America and Germany. A slimy old broad there wants to marry me. Crazy bitch. Even though I've killed nine women! Or were there eleven? Maybe fifteen? I can't imagine when my trial will begin. Can you? My lawyer says that he will use the 'nut plea'. It always works. Especially if you hang your tongue down your chin and act like your brain has been breaded and fried to the size of an oyster.

The jury? I'll tell them what they like to hear. Oh, it's true, ain't it? When I was a kid, I had fantasies. But don't we all? In my mind I made up worlds. Heard voices. Wife and children. Beautiful women, their paper faces torn from magazines and glued onto mannequins, their lips real, their wooden bodies real. Ooh, I got more than one splinter up my ass. Practice makes perfect!

They'll want to know how I scammed my victims, I suppose. Me…Tarzan. They…Jane. I cruised the highways. Was one of the dudes at the truck stop counter eatin' the Blue Plate Special and lookin' for hitchhikers hangin' around. Ain't one of them bitches had their antenna out!

No, no attorney general! You're thinkin' now that you wanna flick the flap on your 'lappy' and call one of your crony cops? You got one of those laptops, I suppose. Not one of those big shits that crowd a desk? Say…do you go in seedy chat rooms? Nah, why would you? Your life's a chat room. Oh shit, I've got all the time in the world. But it's almost ten. Lights out baby! See you soon! Cole Barnett

I tried not to tremble, caught my breath and stood up. I wasn't going to let him be the anticlimax to my day. He didn't have access to a computer, but in my mind, I kept thinking over and over that it was possible that he was smuggling information out of prison to someone who was writing his blog and that perhaps this was a foretaste of his intention to continue to torment me for putting him on death row.

I sat down. I was starting to get an ache across my shoulders and forehead so I poured a third glass of wine and pondered whether or not to open the e-mail attachment which Drew said would contain graphic pictures. As the attorney general, shouldn't I want to understand why some men live and lurk undetected in communities while torturing and killing again and again? I thought of the BTK killer—married with children, a vicious man who stalked and murdered women over several years.

But then as if I had been in a semi-conscious state, my wine glass almost slid from my fingers, and I suddenly realized that Cole Barnett had swept uninvited back into my life for the third time. And after many years, his yellowish eyes could still linger like streetlights that dimmed before the dusk and dawn, the memory of his swarthy body, too, turning my head toward a shadow whether I was in a mall or frolicking in the surf. But thinking too hard about Cole Barnett had absorbed all of my energy, I knew, so I gulped more wine, put the computer in suspended mode, made a mental note to call Warden Denise Duffy and have Barnett's cell searched, and headed to bed. Simultaneously I doused the light just as a familiar voice and tapping at the door startled me. I threw the dead bolt and Justin McCreary followed a yellow lab puppy up the steps and into the motorhome. For once I was half glad to see him.

"Oh, don't tell me," I said touching the dog's head. "Yours?"

"Damn it Katie, don't start!"

"Mmm hmm. Well, you can barely take care of yourself," I replied. "I don't quite see you as a papa."

"Didn't I always want a shot at it?"

I gathered the lab into my arms. "Does this little guy have a name?"

"His handle is 'Craps'. Uh, it seemed the right thing since he's always doing it on the carpet."

I frowned. "Mmm hmm. Well, look here Dad, you take the baby and I'll pour you some wine."

"Jack Daniels?"

"I suppose," I said reaching into the cupboard above the small sink next to the sofa.

"I always said you'd make a good mom, Katie. We needed kids, you and me."

"We were kids ourselves. *We* couldn't even take care of each other, Justin."

"After the miscarriage, I begged for a second round. No dice, remember?"

"Oh, of course," I droned. "I was the one who was insensitive and career obsessed. That it? Well, it's the past. I refuse to live there. So change the subject."

"Did I ever blame you?" he asked softly.

"A gratuitous attitude doesn't quite cut it!" I said again. "Besides, your sperm count had bottomed out, and you know it!"

Justin went white. He seemed surprised and looked me hard in the eyes. Then he laughed. "I never knew you saw the medical report. But the truth of it is, Katie, that…nah, it was those colored jockey shorts you liked to see me in. Way too tight."

"Is this your soap opera version?"

He leaned against the recliner. "The Old and the Restless," he said. "Anyhow, I only stopped by to show you the new puppy and wish you happy birthday. Not to get my ass chain-sawed."

"Nor mine," I said, shoving the whiskey onto the table, "and I can't imagine why we always have to plow through old times when there's never going to be a damn resolution about whom did what to whom and why! So why don't you take Craps here and go home and let me go to bed!"

Justin raised both hands. "Shit. I give up."

"Good."

"But I'm not ready to leave."

"Then tell me what happened when you saw Mrs. Tarteton today."

"Well, I got there with the search warrant," he said. "She's hiding something."

"I found her cooperative," I said defiantly.

He fell to the floor and began rough housing Craps. The dog yelped with delight. "Every time one of the detectives came near…well did she cry for you?" he asked.

"I don't understand. I told her that you would ask questions."

"Nah. She acted like she didn't speak the English language."

"Look, I'll see her again in the morning," I said.

"Be my guest."

"Did you look at the journal before you checked the shoebox into lock up?"

Justin scraped Craps into his arms and stood up. "You joking?"

Sometimes I found it impossible to carry on a conversation with him. As if he were reading a different paragraph and I needed to wait for him to catch up, I threw up my hands and slipped into the small bathroom in the middle of the motorhome and pulled my French braid apart. "*Did you look at the journal?* I repeated slowly.

"Come again?" he said. "Nothing in that box except some letters and a red cloth pad. Like that thing that my grandmother used to hook and my mom would hang next to the stove."

"A pot holder," I said.

"Yeah. And that's probably what you saw, too."

My eyes drifted down the hall. "Damn it Justin. I know the difference between a book and a rag! Mrs. Tarteton *told* me that I was holding her niece's journal. I skimmed the pages with my pen."

The idea of sleep was overwhelming me; the wine had kicked in, so I was annoyed with Justin who had stretched onto the sofa and Craps who had sprawled across my bed pillows as if he owned them. All this business with Cole Barnett had left me drained, too, so I opened the window to an aerosol of damp sea mist. "Come get your dog, Justin!"

"Katie, you're positive about what you saw?"

I faced the bathroom mirror again and brushed my teeth, saying between swishes, "Didn't I tell you that your protégé saw it too? Sara Baird? Ask her." I didn't give him a chance to answer. "Now please! I have to get up early."

He came down the short hall. I leaned into the faint scent of his cologne, and when I noticed that his eyes were paying too much attention to my gown, I closed my robe. He grinned. "Still got the best set of knockers this side of the Mississippi!" he said.

Set? He might just as well have been talking about golf clubs. He picked up Craps and followed me to the door. "Out!"

"I meant that as a compliment."

"Thank you, but go home," I said, "and there is one more thing…"

"Yeah?"

"That horrific odor on your shirt?"

"Oh shit…"

"I don't think so! But I think Craps expelled his anal glands!"

Thankfully, the wind began to siphon off the ghastly odor after Justin and his lab disappeared into the darkness. I dragged myself to bed. With legal papers piled next to me, I wondered why sometimes there was something about Detective Justin McCreary that still made me want to crawl into his arms and something, thank goodness, that kept me from doing it.

CHAPTER 20

On this bright winter day, Mrs. Dahlia Tarteton never answered the front door. Through the etched glass panels, I could see that the space inside seemed eerily undisturbed. It was unsettling. Had I known, of course, what was beyond that door, I would have smashed the glass and gone in.

Instead, I threaded a side path made of claim shells that lead to the rear gardens. The back porch sloped perilously like the bow of an old schooner, and as I looked up, I saw that I had disturbed South Carolina wrens that flew from their nest to the safety of nearby magnolia trees. Near splintered railings that had become lost in gnarled vines long abandoned, I climbed the steps into more dark shadows that reflected shards of light from a rear transom into the kitchen beyond the open screen door. My eyes fell upon a table chair on its side. Something was wrong. Terribly wrong! I unsnapped my Beretta and went in.

Whenever a cloud rode across the sun, the counter was foreboding with the strange paucity of silhouettes—of spiders and snakes, and lizards, too, shape-shifting across the cast iron sink. Suddenly, the stark silence itself compelled me to call out, "Mrs. Tarteton?" I didn't hear the faintest sound, and I knew that if I had any worth at all as the attorney general, I needed to draw upon my courage. Instead, I drew my gun.

At first I had a desire to crawl along the floor like a soldier on a mission. Instead, I bent slightly, while a fly—an errant airman—tailed me past the stairwell that seemed boarded up with the shadows of two by twos cast from the wide railing. It was early. *Should I go up and into the bedrooms first?* I called out again, "Mrs. Tarteton? Are you here?"

A quick check of the recessed alcove by the front door revealed nothing, and then I went into the living room, expecting to see her sitting on the sofa or in a chair, asleep or reading a magazine, the scent of lemon wafting from a tall glass of sweet tea.

The room was undisturbed; yet, I was beguiled by a ghostly sense, as if the all the people who had once lived there—all of them—even those from the seventeen hundreds were waiting within the walls to conjure Mrs. Tarteton into their presence. And upon her recall there would be subdued conversation with others about the threat to slavery from the 'New Republican' government. And later, their shoulders would heave with wild laughter as the hospitality of food, the promise of social discourse and the regaling of fine music radiated within the mansion.

However, presently, the disturbed air churned a muffled sound directly from a closet behind me, but once I concluded that there were only boxes of old National Geographic magazines stacked to the ceiling there, I continued cautiously into the hall before finally arriving at the bathroom door from which water trickled and vanished into old cracks in the solid oak floor. I stared in disbelief. I grasped my Beretta so hard that I could feel the sweat between my fingers. I called, "Mrs. Tarteton?" I took a deep breath and realized that I had no more voice. My knees and hands shaking so hard caused me to give into an impulse and shove my foot against the bottom panel. The hinges screamed like fighting cats.

Surely there was something unusual about Mrs. Tarteton lying against the overflowing tub, her face fiercely contorted as if it had been trapped between panes of vaccuumous glass, the resolve of hope lost in an implied confrontation with her attacker who probably had impaled her in suspended flight until her inability to speak or move was no longer an illusion.

I bent down. Except for her forehead, which was as cold as a jar from a refrigerator, her body was warm and clammy to touch. She hadn't been dead long. Her face was ashen. Her blue eyes clouded over. As soon as the medical examiner arrived, he would insert a chemical thermometer in Mrs. Tarteton's rectum, and with an assumed initial temperature of around seventy-three, he would calculate that she would cool one and a half degrees each hour for the first dozen hours. He would also check the liver and for rigor mortis, rigidity of the body. All this would help him to determine the time of death. Later, much later, and after photography and the collection of evidence, Daliah Tarteton would be transported to the morgue in a vinyl body bag, and an autopsy would violate her privacy one last time.

As if I were caught in a cobweb, I stared at her for a while. Then I heard the back screen door snap. Footsteps rattled a shortcut through underbrush beneath the bathroom window, avoiding the more exposed garden path, I was sure, so I bolted out the front door and raked across adjoining lawns but saw no one except two toddlers adrift in play. Whoever had been at the Tarteton home, knew his escape route.

Back at my car I took a moment and then called Justin McCreary. Immediately, I had a mental image of him chomping on his cigar, his siren blaring as he and the other cruisers barreled at dangerous speeds down Route 170 toward Beaufort.

*   *   *

Within an hour a criminalist and medical examiner took over the crime scene, and after walking toward me, Justin was soon in earshot. "Shit, I'm starting to feel like I'm one of those big city Centurions who bags a body a day! And my mug's been showing up on the news too damn often! All those shit-head psychos out there will be sending me fan mail like they do you, Katie."

I thought I was looking at a clone of the old days. He needed a hair cut, a shave and his civvies pressed, and I was glad that he explained that he had been up all night working on a hostage situation involving a jealous husband near the Hilton Head outlet malls and instead not 'tying one on.' He pulled his gray wind-slicker off and threw it to his partner, Detective Marinchino, who went outside to throw up. It was her first case with a cadaver. I knew the feeling.

In my twenties I had spent a week in New York, doing 'ride a longs' with the NYPD, which included picking up corpses in stairwells and on street grates, interviewing drunks in holding tanks, touring morgues, scouring drug bins and feeling fear every time the radio blared that we needed to chase some burglar who might be carrying a sawed-off shotgun. I remembered vomiting my guts because of the horrific odor from a victim who had been three days in a trash bin with her head looking like it had been through a meat grinder.

"Check out those pressure spots on her neck," I said.

Justin shook his head. "I bet the goddamn hyoid bone cracked when the son-of-a-bitch strangled her. So what the hell happened when you got here today?" He opened his murder book again, smoothing the spine and preparing to take my testimony.

"I suppose I should start with yesterday," I said. "I've gone over and over it in my mind, and I suspect the killer was here while Sara and I interviewed Mrs. Tarteton. In fact, I'm positive someone was upstairs and heard us talking about the journal. Thinking back, I suppose I should have taken a look."

"No you shouldn't. That's what I get paid to do. That's what the big boys are for!"

"Mmm hmm. Well, I thought you Neanderthals died out long ago," I said tartly.

"Look, if the son-of-a-bitch took the journal," Justin noted, "would that have been reason enough to kill her?"

"He probably intended to," I said pulling him into the living room. "I think he was waiting for us to leave, but then you arrived, and not having time, he thought a warning was enough for her not to tell. Last night you told me that she seemed frightened?"

"Yeah. Closed up like a cocoon!"

"Later he undoubtedly had second thoughts and came back to…"

"Scan her ticket one way," Justin interrupted. We went out onto the back porch. "You're lucky he didn't tweak your pretty ass, too!"

I laughed. "*That* would make the evening news, now wouldn't it?" I said. We went down the steps. "Do you think you'll find any prints?"

"Nah," Justin said as he gestured with his index finger. "He probably wore gloves. This guy's fuckin' with us."

"Not entirely," I said, not knowing why I believed that. It started to rain, and I pulled my keys from my pocket. He followed me to my car.

"Where you headed?" he asked.

"The contractors are putting the finishing touches on the cottage," I said. "Time for me to check on them."

He reached through the window and pressed his fingers into my shoulder. "I don't know why you let Allison Thomason think you're taking comp' time. If you're not going to use it, why have vacation time at all? After court the other day, she told me that you said you'd go to the inn on weekends. Then you seldom do. You give her goddamn excuses. You miss the ferry. Get a headache. Have an appointment. Shit! You can't sit on your ass more than five minutes, can you? Never could."

He watched me open a bottle of water. "Mmm hmm. You either," I said, "and a hard day's work is the best therapy, so don't lecture me! And Justin?"

His back to me, he swept around. "Yes?"

"I want you to run a check on Senator Holden Renaurd's finances."

"How soon?"

"In the morning?" I said, thinking of something Bina had told me. "Oh, and will you come to the cottage for dinner tomorrow night? Drew will be there, too."

As he sprinted the stairs, he looked over his shoulder and flashed a big grin before disappearing inside Dahlia Tarteton's house. *It was time for the big boy to finish his job!*

CHAPTER 21

At the cottage on Mudbar Lane the painters hadn't finished the living room, and there still were drop cloths on the floor. I punched wood in the fireplace with a black andiron, and a comforting fire flared, back-lighting unpacked boxes that were stacked nearby. Many with old and worn memories of good times—I had chosen not to dispose of those—made the room feel hospitable enough, although I thought that perhaps it was Drew's baked steak with wine and mushrooms and my decadent mashed potatoes with a half pint of real cream that charmed our appetites.

Justin refused the spinach salad and made a point of repeating, "My teeth don't like whacking weeds." And then he asked, "You crashing here for awhile, Drew?"

"Kate and I have some papers to go over," she sniveled, tracing the crease of a crescent roll with her fingers. "Our killer is about to get his wings clipped. And don't get riled, Justin, but I'm going to be your official FBI sidekick for awhile, too."

"Oh yeah? Not if I have anything to do with it," he said.

With all that had passed between them over the years, there seemed to be unconscious contentiousness when they spent more than a few minutes in the same space, and my frustration with the two of them was at the boiling point. "Spoil a perfectly scrumptious chocolate mousse with your bickering, and I'll toss you both out the door!" I said, although I had already decided that if the hour got too late that I would put him on the sofa for the night and drag her up the stairs to bed.

"Screw the mousse, Katie," he said. "You know that the FBI stays in business because of big cases like ours. Next it'll be the CIA helping. Then MI 6. Isn't that the truth Drew?"

"About as true as your brain, honey," she said.

"No shit…"

"She's only doing her job," I added quickly.

Drew examined the 'A' on the knife handle. It was Ashley silver and needed a good polishing. "Don't defend me, Kate," she said, dragging the words.

"Was I?" I retorted.

"What about doing an aerial of Renaurd Island in my Cessna?" she asked.

Justin's eyes boomeranged the room. "What the hell for?"

"Call it a hunch," Drew said. This was her Mensa mind working overtime. One of Drew Greer's hunches was as reliable as the swallows returning to Capistrano.

"Shit, I can tell you right now it's a waste of time," Justin said, puckering his lips. "There's nothing strange there except an old medicine man."

"Oh? And when were you at the north end?" I asked.

"Say Katie, you don't know everything my office investigates! Detective McClenahan and I went over with the Coast Guard last week. But I'll give you this. You were right about the newly made inlet and dock on that northwest section. But Senator Renaurd told me that he had it built a couple of years ago."

"You talked to him? When was that?"

"Yeah. Right after we arrived, his boat was about to pull out. He was with some dudes. Businessmen, I guess. They had been touring the inn," Justin said. "And he took them out for a boat ride. He said he stopped to show them the wildlife."

"Mmm hmm. I'm James Audubon if you believe that! They are probably investors who are interested in buying part of Renaurd Island for development," I said. "Bina may have been right."

"Don't know about that, but that stone you saw, Katie?"

Drew popped a black olive into her mouth and grinned at me. "The so-called altar?"

"Well, it was covered with fish scales. That's all. Big nada else," Justin said, pushing mushrooms to the side of his plate after taking a bite of steak. I wish he didn't talk with food in his mouth. "A fish cleaning table, that's all."

I poured a glass of water. I was getting a sore throat. "Well, you're wrong," I said. "I was there. There were no scales. And there was blood. And items used in a ritual!"

He looked at me and pointed his finger. "Damn it, Katie, I talked to Gabe Coneras. He says it's a fish cleaning table, too! He uses it himself."

I piled the dishes into the sink. "Oh?" I glared at him. "And what were the two of you doing discussing this investigation?"

"That's not the point!" Justin said.

I waited for Drew to interrupt.

Justin took a swig of wine out of the bottle.

"Don't do that!" I yelled.

"What?"

"When we were married, you did that with milk and Coke bottles, too. I hate it even more now!"

"Well, we're not married now," he said, his lips drifting to the rim again. "And by the way, Gabe told me that Stacks Sandover phoned him from the Bahamas at the very time you claimed to have seen him at the shack. The phone records check it out."

My temper went into overdrive. "You talked about *that,* too?"

Drew folded her arms and raised her brows. "Shit's hitting the fan!"

"Oh be quiet," I warned her.

"Look Katie, there was a lot of stuff going on when you got lost out there. You were…ah, disoriented. Afraid, so you told me yourself. Maybe it was someone who looked like Stacks. Maybe one of the islanders who helps at the inn? There's about a half dozen of them. Maybe the old medicine man, is that it? Spooked you, that's all."

With vehemence I snapped the dishtowel onto the counter. "I did see Zaccheas Bird earlier. I'm not wrong about Stacks Sandover!"

Drew's mouth curled. "You two are like bulls locking horns."

"Don't get in this," I said glaring at her. Then I took a deep breath and put away perishable items and was glad that our meal was finished. From the first forkful, this charade of a friendly little dinner that was supposed to be like old times was wrought with tension, and I wished I *had* gone to the inn. Suddenly, I was possessed with a stalwart resolve. I would return to Renaurd Island as soon as possible and go back to that shack. "Talking about what I saw is a waste of time," I said, as I sprayed water over the plates in the sink.

Drew propped her feet on the chair, resting her elbows on her knees. She seemed insensible, distant, and unable to get her bearings, her colorless cheeks collapsing under an expressionless gaze. She sagged and almost fell off her chair. I sprang to her. It was times like this that I feared that her illness was winning the battle.

Justin stood up and then shied away from the table. "She soused?"

Firewood repositioning in the dying flames, snapped and fell away. Then without any help Drew pulled her self upright again. She shrugged her shoulders and said, "It's nothing. I'm all right."

"Damn it, you need to be in a hospital," I whispered into her ear. I pressed my fingers into the upper part of her arms to keep her steady, but she begged me with her eyes not to make a scene. My stomach sank. The message was deafening: the idea that the day would arrive when she involuntarily would stretch out on white, cold sheets with IV's streaming medicines into her veins, while at the bottom of the bed, her chart with its medical jargon would fail to reveal who Drew Greer really was. This vibrant woman whom I had known most of my adult life. Dark and bright. Someone who could enter a room where everybody spoke in whispers and later leave them roaring with incontrollable laughter because of her stories about the agency. Kate Guesswine's dear friend! "All right then. I'll shut up," is all I could say as I kissed her cheek. Then I felt a sudden violent contempt for the man who had told her that he loved her while he see-sawed a vile serpent into her beautiful body on some other kind of cold, white sheets.

She grinned. "I guess I shouldn't mix wine and pills, huh?"

"I'll never understand," I said, referring to her carefree disregard for herself. Didn't she owe it to those who loved her to do everything in her power to keep alive? Must she consciously hasten her death the way that she consciously hastened her life?

"Oh, you worry too much," she said. Her eyes looked hard at me for reassurance.

Justin looked relieved. "The monthly thing?"

"Oh dry up," I groaned.

Drew stood up and straddled her arms over Justin's shoulders. The softness returned to her face and her eyes were bright again. Thankfully, she had recovered. "This is what I think, you two," she said, "If Kate saw an altar, then it was an altar! If she saw Stacks Sandover, then it was Stacks."

Justin couldn't have looked more disagreeable. But he knew that he was outnumbered so he defiantly scooped another helping of mousse and slid it into his mouth to cover his anger. "All right then, don't piss around!" he mumbled. "Do the goddamn fly over. We'll all go."

I thought about it for a minute. "You throw-up every time you're more than twenty feet off the ground. Drew and I will go. What else will we be looking for?"

"I don't know, but you can't hide a change in landscape," she said. "Not completely anyhow. I can't tell you how many times we've found cocaine factories and gun runners in Columbia by looking at so-called hidden terra from the air!"

I said, "Definitely need a trained eye then. But I'm still going back to that shack. You missed something Justin!"

Whether I was feeling drowsy or simply closed my eyes a moment, I don't know, but when I opened them, and from where I stood, I thought I caught a glimpse of movement outside the window, something other than the intermittent moonlight across the small square panes. In a perilous state had someone with a sinister motive traversed the long narrow lane through the dark marsh? Should I trust my feelings? Say something? I looked again and saw no one. Then I returned to wipe around the burners on the stove, my mind in a half conscious state of sold furniture, of laughter long forgotten, of old friends coming and going like fine wine and good bread. *Hadn't I gotten rid of practically everything?* Yet, if only David would come strolling across the Mexican tile floor the way he used to, his after shave wafting through the air as if from a simple aerosol of spring room freshener. My longing for the strength of his arms around me, brought such a terrible sadness that I thought I would never find any pleasure in the rest of the evening.

Drew and Justin were discussing the art of fingerprinting when my peripheral vision gathered in movement at the window again. It could have been a thief or scoundrel or the likes of both of them, the outline of his face and neck a blur as he peered intrusively through the panes. And like prey in a spider's web, I made a conscious effort to frame his features.

This time I bounded to the window and flung it up with such force that the sash twanged like a hundred tuning forks. One of my hands was against the screen while the other cupped across the bridge of my eyes in time to see the wisp of a figure, dark and in full stride vanish into a curved part of the path near the smokehouse. I put my hand over my mouth and stumbled back.

Drew quickly flanked me. "What is it, Kate? What's wrong?"

"Someone's outside!"

Like a rabbit flushed from weeds, Justin sprang to his jacket and yanked out his Smith & Wesson while Drew got her Glock—standard FBI issue. I yanked my Beretta from my purse and got a kettle of water to douse the fireplace embers, their sizzling matching my nerves while Drew jumped from light switch to light switch, plunging the cottage into darkness.

"Get back! Get down!" she yelled.

"I don't see the son-of-a-bitch!" Justin said as he shrank to the side each window after studying the space beyond. "No wheels out there by ours either! Where'd he come from?"

"Probably parked at the end of the lane," I said behind him.

"Do you have any flashlights?" Justin asked.

"Packed. But I think I know where."

"Get them!" he said.

My fingers ripped off masking tape from an old sea chest that had been paint stripped. I prodded through candles and flares before pulling two Workhorse lights and a lantern from the bottom. There was little doubt that I knew what was about to happen, or thought I did, inasmuch as we were three of the best shots in law enforcement—our having spent many Sundays together firing at a large bull's-eye in front of sheaves of cereal grass that David had rigged for us near the dock. Wouldn't we stick together like a pack of wolves? But Justin had other ideas. We crouched low and followed him out the front door of the cottage into an eerily bronze haze created by clouds hanging like an old fishing net over a yellow moon above the horizon. Then it disappeared behind a stand of pines and without warning we were gathered into the shadows.

"What happened to the pole light?" Justin asked.

I swallowed hard, knowing that it was one of the many times that I shouldn't have procrastinated in having something repaired. "That storm two weeks ago," I said meekly.

"Shit Katie, see, you need me after all to fix…"

"Look, Justin, you head around the back, circle and flank us at the dock," Drew interrupted. "We'll scour the front."

As we moved further down the path, I could barely make out the cottage. A grave forbearance overwhelmed me, and the image of our straddling against the cedar siding of the smokehouse soon came true. The door was ajar. With my elbow I pushed it open, my Beretta in one hand, the halogen light in the other, illuminating an area that held a big hopper used to smoke fish, a broken bench, corded magazines and old clothes that I hadn't taken to the Salvation Army yet. Stacked wood for the fireplace was across one side. We saw no one. I pulled the door and secured the hinge.

"Let's go," Drew said. "Lights off!"

The moon that seemed to have dissolved completely before, blinked now and then, providing a glimpse of the nearest marsh plants as if they were a ghastly army of tanks and rifles, and I rubbed my eyes to rid them of this illusion. There was a stir of wind, a stir of blood in my neck veins as we descended further along the stone path. We stopped every three or four feet, and I expected a cry to break the repose, as if whoever had been at the window would stumble from behind the palmetto scrub and show himself!

What really was a short distance seemed to take forever, and I was aware of everything—the dank smell of old water, of grasses grabbing my ankles when I veered away from the path. Every stone, every shell crunching underfoot seemed like a blast of dynamite in my ear, but I knew that I must stealthily go forward or lose my nerve. Call it intuition, call it folly, but something damnable was going to happen. The hard pulsing in my veins was incessant now, and I was about to speak about it when Drew came to a halt and stumbled back against me.

"Damn it!" she said.

I flipped on the light. We were standing in a stream of blood that looped across the path and through the grass and disappeared off to my left. In the quiet surrealism of the scene, Renty was lying still as an old log, his throat hollowed into a gaping crevice. Drew must have sensed that I was about to scream. She cupped her hand over my mouth. A shot blasted the silence.

"Down. Down!" she yelled.

But suddenly my legs were steel, while she, already crouching—her arm like a fulcrum—yanked my ankle so hard that I crashed to the ground, and we rolled into a pyramid of flagstones that were to be used eventually to set a more stable path. I winced with pain and came to my senses.

"That came from the back of the cottage," I said, frantically trying to get up. "Justin!"

"No! Stay down!" she ordered. She compressed the small of my back with her elbow, and after I calmed a little, she released it. We started to zigzag through the grass, the bramble nicking my skin through my light slacks and sweater. Skin flaked from the pads of my fingers.

Finally, we reached the front of the cottage and stood up. Our weapons were perpendicular to our faces, and as we edged around the side, I could almost make out the lines of the new screened in porch that protruded like a proboscis.

"Stay close Kate!" she whispered. "Do exactly as I tell you!" She reached back and patted my knee. "I'm going to run like hell to that tree next to the edge of the porch. Cover me! If it looks clear, I'll signal for you come on. And if you should have to shoot at someone, just don't get me in the ass!" she said.

"Right"—my voice broke—"or left cheek?"

"Look, for Christ's sake, you've had as much training with weapons as I have. I'm not worried. On the count of three I'm going!" She didn't hesitate. "One. Two. Three!"

And after she skidded on her knees behind the tree, she gave a short whistle. My fear was ebbing. Sifting the darkness with my eyes, I ran first to the right, then left and right until I dropped to my stomach again in the middle of dead plants where I felt the brittle stems against my cheek. I raised my head and with both hands brought my gun in front of my nose. I got to my knees. To my right Justin's body was like a coiled water hose across part of the spouting. He wasn't moving.

In an instant, Drew was next to me. Then her hips spun like the hands of a clock while she perused the area one last time. "Whoever it was has split," she said. "Quick! Put the light on Justin!"

I cradled his head in my lap. His mouth sagged, closed completely and finally opened. His eyes fluttered. He was coming to. I saw no bullet wounds. "Talk to me!" I told him softly.

"Geeish, who cold-cocked me?"

I trapped a wisp of hair from his forehead between my fingers and saw a large abrasion. "I think you fell over that big cement crock by the new spouting. Your shoe's there."

"Hell, you mean I tripped?"

"Mmm hmm."

He struggled up. His voice broke. "Listen, we don't need to write it in the police report, do we? Say…where's my gun?"

"Here," I said retrieving it from under his foot. "I don't know what I would have done if you had shot yourself Justin McCreary!"

"You still love me then, Katie?" he asked.

"Only in your dreams," I said frowning.

He grinned. "So was this a false alarm?"

"Come with us," Drew said.

As often happened when the tide came in, the wind rose and carried a light mist of brine across the marsh. My nose shrank from it, but I welcomed it with deep breaths that seemed to cleanse my lungs and sharpen my mind. The yellow moonlight came out again, lifting the somber scene of Renty's mutilated body to our eyes. With absolute dread on her face, Drew dragged the flash light to the water by the dock, and there was little doubt what I thought when I blurted out, "The dinghy! David's dinghy is gone!"

CHAPTER 22

For two days, detectives from the Beaufort County Sheriff's office combed the area around the cottage and found no forensic evidence except that the killer, who had abandoned the dingy near Route 170, wore sneakers that probably were caked in mud, the tide having destroyed the only possible clear prints. There were no tire marks either, and Sheriff Glennie Sparkman theorized that the killer might have had an accomplice who picked him up at the marsh's edge.

The bigger question was why kill Renty? And who was the face in the window? It all added up to a fat question mark. Still, I had an uneasy feeling that all boats led to Renaurd Island. The sheriff seemed to think that, too. At his office the next morning he grilled Bina, Gabe, and Barclay, all—who in his words—had pulled the wagons into a circle and appeared to be hiding something. It was possible, and Glennie's investigations were generally predisposed to an old fashion interrogation that could fan any burning embers into a raging fire. But Allison and Holden would not be intimidated and threatened to file charges for harassment until I intervened and calmed everyone down. After a couple of hours, nothing came from the questioning and everyone returned to the island. Glennie ranted that it still was 'who you are' and 'who you know' that kept him from doing his job, but I disagreed with his premise, knowing that he had contempt for the rich and powerful.

After a few days of break-necking it back and forth to my office in Columbia and 'doing official business while doing official vacation', Allison called and invited me to return to the inn. She sounded depressed. On Friday I caught the ferry.

Before, during and after dinner I noticed that none of the Renaurds spoke of Renty's murder…in what appeared to be the same extraordinary restraint which they had shown while dealing with Jennifer's death, and I considered it strange that Allison herself hadn't asked if I had any new information. Instead, without any further words to me, she excused herself around nine and disappeared into a nearby corridor—to bed, I assumed—after Holden joined the guests for bridge, and Barclay parked at a small game table to play solitaire. I kept my eyes upon a few pages of a new Cornwell mystery, but I didn't retain one word, went off to bed myself, sleeping fitfully until 'nature' awakened me from a pleasant dream, a dream which dissipated into a waterfall as I opened my eyes. So much for symbolism.

But once in awhile I know that I have to cut to the chase. It wasn't quite time for breakfast when I threw on my robe and went down the hall to Allison's private quarters. She answered my knock with a polite, "Do come in, Kate."

Logs had recently been ignited in the fireplace, and on the nightstand were tea and two fine vitreous cups. *So she was expecting me.*

She showed no inclination to get out of bed, so at her direction, I poured, and her hand swept the air for me to straddle the edge of her large down comforter. For the longest time, her eyes were spent on me before she said anything more.

"The deaths of those women, the deaths of Elizabeth Tarteton and the others, and now Renty," she mumbled over the rim of the cup when it reached her lips, "I could understand, but there's no way…not Jennifer's death!" She paused. "Barclay wouldn't harm his own sister!"

The very stillness of the room made me aware of an unexplained disturbance in her voice, and when I could no longer bear it, I intentionally looked away and then back to her demeanor which pled for nothing less than honesty from me. "Oh, perhaps not intentionally, dear Allison," I said, waving my hand. "But you've heard of somnambulistic homicide?"

She sat straight up and placed her cup on the nightstand. "Yes. People who sleepwalk, and while doing so kill someone. But it's rare, isn't it?"

"There are many cases in the literature," I said.

"I see," she replied simply. Her leg shot out from under the comforter, and I watched her forefinger flick a piece of lint from her big toe. "I know that sometimes Barclay's behavior is rather, well unconventional. But murder?"

"Recently I had a chat with a friend from Interpol who once worked on similar case with London's Metropolitan Police a few years ago. He's retired now, but he told me about a man who stayed a few days with his sister who lived in Hounslow, a sprawling area near Heathrow Airport. From the time he arrived, his behavior was very unsettling, although I guess he had no animosity toward his sister or brother-in-law. However, one particular evening, they had drinks after dinner, all very jovial-like. In fact, they shared a hockey game and more drinks later. Then everyone went to bed."

"I'm afraid I don't know the case," she said impatiently. "And you certainly must be wrong about Barclay," she said, struggling to constrain her voice. "Yes, he may sleepwalk, *but that's all he does!* He's done so since he was a child!"

"Just hear me out," I said. "His name was Roy Trimmer. At his trial he explained that while sleeping, he dreamed that he needed to go to his car. In his dream it was snowing. So he put on his coat and boots and grabbed an ice scraper. A plastic one with a serrated edge. He told the jury that when he walked into the garage, a stranger suddenly appeared…his arm raised as if he were going to attack. Trimmer said that he fell against the doorframe, causing great pain to his spine. Then the figure came hard and fast at him."

Allison jumped from the bed, and I followed her. She looked regretfully at me and repeatedly patted a plume of hair at the crown of her head. "Kate, you're my dearest friend. But you are crossing the line here!"

"For heaven's sake, Allison, there's an investigation going on!" I said. "But for the moment I'm forgetting that I'm the attorney general. Can't you see that I'm trying to help this family?"

"But if you persist," she said closing her eyes, "if you persist, well, I can tell you that Barclay Renaurd is innocent!"

"Just listen! Please!" I begged. She didn't move. "In his dream Trimmer explained that as the attacker lunged, he saw himself reach up and grate the man's carotid artery with the scraper as if it were thick ice on a windshield! Blood spurted into the air! He ran back into the house. But his very own screaming had already awakened his sister who found him in the kitchen. It was completely dark. She fumbled for the light switch and..."

"Why must you tell me this?" she moaned.

I took her by the shoulders. "Listen to me! Her brother was lying in a fetal position and covered with blood. He *appeared asleep*. His eyes were closed, but when she touched him, he resumed screaming as if he were in the pits of hell! Then he fell asleep again. And immediately she rushed into the garage where she found her husband covered with his own blood. He later died!"

Allison paced in front of French doors that opened onto a balcony, and when I saw how distraught she had become, I went quickly and wrapped my arms around her.

"Well, now, my friend, that's a frightening story," she said into my eyes. "But do you have evidence? I mean, what evidence could you possibly have that involves Barclay?" She crossed the room, and suddenly the air seemed cold and drafty, as if some ominous specter might materialize from the dying embers and suffocate us both with his darkest breath. I riddled the ashes with the andiron and threw on a couple of logs.

"I'm sorry," I whispered wearily, "but I think he needs to be examined by a doctor. Perhaps he walks out of his night terrors into the real world. He takes the images with him, whatever horrors they may be, and he acts them out!"

Allison poured more tea. Her marquise cut diamond tapped the edge of the pot and gave a harsh ping. It startled us both. "So what happened to Trimmer?" she asked without looking at me.

"No premeditation. No motive," I explained. "Several psychiatrists testified that there was no criminal intent. In fact, they testified that

Trimmer's deep hypnotic state was identical to the period between sleep and waking."

In her face was a pitiful blank dejection, as if she hadn't heard a word I had said, but even though I could feel the rumblings of anxiety in my stomach, I was committed to making sure that she understood the seriousness of Barclay's illness. And because she was my friend, better that there might be a viable defense in court should the worst prove to be true. But then what was I thinking? Even though they didn't know about Barclay's suspected somnambulism yet, was I trumping the hand of the investigators? Was I involving myself in a conflict-of-interest case? Jeopardizing my job?

"When Barclay was a little boy, he always slept deeply," Allison said with a noticeable trill of laughter, "but sometimes after he had been asleep a short time, he would bolt down the hall and stairs, you know, like a horse spooked out of his stall. Whinnying, too, like one that was spooked. And Holden would usually follow him outside and carry him back to bed. Always afterward he slept so soundly that we had trouble getting him up to go to school. He didn't remember…"

"And he probably doesn't now," I replied.

"Yes, well, so tell me, what happened to Roy Trimmer?"

"He was found not guilty."

"By reason of insanity?"

"No. He was acquitted."

"How is that possible?"

"When someone commits a murder while in a somnambulistic state, it is an involuntary action and often referred to as 'automatism' or something that happens without the mind having any control. In a way it's similar to an epileptic seizure. The muscles complete the act without the person knowing."

"So what you are saying is that sleepwalking is an unconscious state? The acts that a person does in that state carry no criminal intent?"

I had an idea where she was leading me. "Don't misunderstand me. Violence in sleep is abnormal," I said. In fact, it's estimated that only one in ten will carry out the terror of the dream, but yes, when it happens, then I suppose that's what I'm partly suggesting."

"Then Barclay isn't mentally ill?"

"Not in the legal sense," I conceded. "He probably doesn't have a disease of the mind; there's no underlying impairment caused by psychosis or delusions, for example. In fact, even though a good prosecutor would 'try' a somnambulistic murder case as premeditated and accept a plea bargain for an insanity plea, in most cases, a good defense lawyer would use 'automatism' as a defense and go for an acquittal. But for those who are acquitted, usually, there is a term of hospitalization, testing and follow up."

And then Allison thrust her hands in the air and said, "All right Kate, lay your cards on the table!"

"I've told you all I can tell you. You know that."

"But why this much?"

"I'm sure that he'll be called to Glennie Sparkman's office again. I'm your friend. I'm a friend of your family's. I've seen Barclay with my own eyes. And you can't feign sleepwalking," I said with conviction. "If he has committed these hideous crimes, then I must be honest with you and say that if he were my brother, I would have him detained in a sanitarium, possibly for his protection and the protection of others. And there are tests to find out if he is prone to any kind of violence while he is sleeping."

"Barclay would never agree…"

"Then I want you to keep an eye on him! If he leaves his room at night, you need to know. You must tell Coneras to confide in you when Barclay goes to the Mainland. And if you see any other aberrant behavior, you must call me immediately!"

"I've got to shower," she said heading toward the bathroom. She turned. "There's no real evidence connecting him to the bone cases or you'd have him in jail. Isn't that right?"

"Look Allison, although the chance of a sleepwalker killing anyone…even in an altered state is infinitesimal, in Barclay's case—in light of what's been going on—we need to be vigilant!"

"…if he indeed committed any of these murders," she said sharply. "I'm afraid that I believe that Barclay's sleep habits and their similarity to this Roy Trimmer's behavior is simply a bunch of nonsense!"

Had she gone into denial? There was a knock at the door, and with her fingers glued to the handle for a very long time, I wondered if her reasoning had been captured by the dull tapping. She gave it a yank. From where I stood, I could see Barclay, his thumbs thrust in his pant pockets, his face crimson and his lips cornering left when his eyes caught mine.

"Good morning dear," she told him.

"I thought you two ladies might need something from the mainland," he said, smoothing his hair back.

Allison turned to me. Her eyebrows arched with surprise, and then she stepped aside and took Barclay by the arm. "Why, my dear, you deserve the psychic of the year award!" she told him. "How on earth did you know that I needed to get papers from my office? Why, I'll go right along with you as soon as I shower and dress. Now give me a half an hour! And Kate, we will continue our conversation at another time. Will you be a love and please excuse me?"

Near exhaustion, I returned to my room and made an effort to put Allison out of my mind. After Barclay had come to her door, it was as though she had betrayed herself to me. The message was clear. Family was family. There was a connection between Allison Thomason and the Renaurds that ran as deep as any river of bluebloods whose generations were irrevocably connected through the purity of their genes. For her I suspected that it was the same as an adopted child, embracing an endearing sense of familial history as her own, of knowing Jennifer, Barclay and Holden in bad and good times the way someone knows her siblings. But there was one thing for sure. I had the feeling that my welcome at Renaurd Inn was questionable and that my friendship with Judge Allison Thomason might be irreparably damaged, even though I suspected that she might be going to the mainland with Barclay so that he wouldn't be alone. Honesty can be brutal.

CHAPTER 23

At the cottage on Thanksgiving eve I was miserably in bed with a raspy throat and dripping nasal, something that seemed to be reoccurring in spite of another round of antibiotics. Courtney stopped by and bombarded me with Watkins salve, her guaranteed cure-all, while Justin insisted that a double Jack Daniels with organic honey would overcome any imminent biological threat to my life. Both remedies helped, although I disliked thinking about the unsolved Dragon's Point cases, intrusive thoughts that seemed to mock the intermittent breeze that wafted through my window. Suddenly in a burst of energy, I was better, needing to go to Renaurd Inn, needing to see Allison, needing to get out of bed and needing to drive like hell to catch the ferry.

By late afternoon I was sure that the Jack Daniels toddy had put the infection in my body on hold, although Coneras had a different view, and after we backed away from the dock, his hinting that I looked pale and gaunt made me feel worse. I stayed on deck. He was friendlier than I had remembered—his rare, talkative mood a surprise.

"You any closer to finding Renty's killer?" he asked. "Doesn't pay to open your mouth, now does it?"

His comment startled me, and I reflected that Coneras at times was like a wild animal, cautious and skittish, yet with the control and strength of a great lion who if hurt would only be more determined to stalk and kill its attacker. Allison loved that old man though, and in spite of her constant reprimanding, there was a tie that transcended employer-employee relationships.

I gave a throaty groan. "Mmm? 'Not pay to open your mouth?' What do you mean?"

His face bent upward, and then he looked abstractly and said, "The Judge never should have hired Renty in the first place." He walked to the bow of the boat, leaving me to reflect on his nagging dismissal until my ears focused on the dull steadiness of the engine and my eyes on the dark line that separated the sky from the water. Coneras remained silent. After we came into the channel to Renaurd Island, he seemed morose and said nothing when I pointed out that both Holden's and Gabe's boats were gone.

Later, during supper, Mrs. Trample-St. Synge stumped back and forth to the buffet, each time rummaging the containers of stuffed chicken breast, roast pork, mushrooms and green beans, and casseroles of red potatoes and yellow rice. With her mouth full and with the singsong of her voice, she told us that she had thoroughly studied the newspaper pictures and copy related to the Dragon's Point victims, mentioning to my dismay, that she had already expounded her theory to Stephen Atchinson and Trudie Peabody that the murders were committed by 'an irrational man' who had a 'thing' against hitchhikers, and when he saw one, he picked her up, and after 'doin' the unspeakable' ta' her private parts', he sacrificed her body ta' the fish' in hopes that she would become a mermaid.

Unlike Barclay, Allison, who looked preoccupied, paid little attention to Mrs. Trample-St. Synge's theory and excused herself—Barclay did, as well, then—and I didn't see them the rest of the evening. Near eleven, I wrenched back the comforter and collapsed into bed and was reading when I dropped into a deep sleep from which Allison, tweaking my arm as she turned off my light, roused me only slightly before I slept all through the night without ever knowing why she had come into my room. I slept until flakes of sun flooded a glorious morning through my eyelids. But unaware of the early hour, I crept down the stairs to visit the sauna and meet Renaurd Inn's masseur.

At the far end of the hall, near a plant stand with a huge ligustrum, there was a small sign perched on what looked to be a converted cigarette stand like the kind you find in old movie houses that haven't yet been torn down, ones renovated and used by communities hoping to keep alive the performing arts. It was thick with paint. As if I were some-how trespassing, I opened the door to a nearby room. I saw and heard no one. I wondered if a massage were such a good idea after all, and immediately felt anxious and turned to leave.

Then I saw Mack behind a huge oak roll-top desk, his over six feet frame unraveling from his knees as he got to his feet. No doubt in his early twenties, with saddle colored hair and piercing eyes, he was a per-fect specimen of a body builder who not only flexed his barbell biceps and abs for his own well-being but especially for the women who came to Renaurd Inn. He was holding up a black pen.

"I'm afraid I might be lost," I said.

He grinned. "Search and rescue?"

"My confession is this, Mack," I said lightly. "I am on the edge of a stress breakdown. I understand that you have the power to fix such things?"

"No skulking allowed at Renaurd Inn," he said with a roaring laugh. "I'll make you a new woman!"

At some point during my visits, would there be stone therapy, facials and perhaps shots of B-6? The entire health package? It was a lucrative moneymaker for the inn and cost guests several hundred dollars, and although Allison had offered me a generous discount, I insisted on pay-ing full price, deciding that my well-being was worth every penny of it.

There was excitement in Mack's blue eyes as he boisterously took my arm. There was lingering tobacco on his body, reminiscent of the many young ambitious attorneys who with their negligible eating and sleeping habits often worked to the point of exhaustion to impress me at my Columbia and Charleston offices.

We didn't venture far into the narrow room. Filling one entire end was a hot tub that had been sculpted from large boulders and which gave the room a contemporary look. Near another door, a lacquered tri-fold wicker screen provided privacy for changing. There was a lingering musty odor—the hum of a dehumidifier—and although I was sure that Allison had attempted to create a soothing atmosphere, the cool, blue-gray slate tile floors and low ceiling gave the impression that the area had not been visited by anyone for centuries!

After Mack shut the door, he rolled up his sleeves. "I'm to go easy on you. That's what Allison told me. Only the Effleurage part of the massage the first time. The Petrissage another. A vigorous application when you're completely relaxed. Then all three at one sitting."

"Mmm hmm. So how long will I be? I mean, will I be long?"

"Normally ninety minutes. Today thirty max. You'll need to strip," he said handing me two large towels. His entire shirt was hanging out, and it seemed frivolous when he intentionally tucked it under his belt.

"Oh my!" I said grinning. "The moment of truth has arrived."

"Are you nervous?"

"My first massage by a professional! I suppose I am a little."

Mack gave a sheepish grin. "Some say that my touching them the first time is very sensual. Especially if they're shy. A couple of ladies told me they were as nervous as on their wedding night."

Wedding night. He must be kidding, I thought. There hadn't been any shyness with Justin McCreary. There never was. And I thought of how ambiguous men could be when it came to sex. Some, cold and harsh, like a winter gale, and others like a soft breeze on a warm summer night.

I thought that perhaps Mack had misunderstood me. "I was referring to your hands tenderizing the flab on my thighs and abdomen—like one does a good flank steak."

He went on grinning. "Never heard it put that way. I'll be easy. Gentle."

Minutes later I realized that he had opened bottles, and I was still standing there fully dressed. He moved one in front of my nose. "Oh, I am dreadfully sorry," I said sniffing the air. I went behind a small screen, removed my clothes and covered myself with warm towels before I jumped up on the heavily padded table.

"On your stomach, please, Mrs. G."

"Mmm hmm," I said, rolling over. One towel slid to the side and a blast of cold air grabbed my buttocks. I shivered.

"You've seen one, you've seem 'em all," he said repositioning the towels while swathing my back and neck in several more. "Buns, I mean."

"That's a bit of information that I really didn't need to know, Mack." I moved my arms in the same position that I had when taking a mammogram, with my elbows high and at right angles and my thumbs resting on my head.

"Sorry," he said quickly. "Allison said you have an analytical mind. So you probably want to know the lingo for what I'm doing. Don't you?"

"Do I?"—I paused—"Why not give me the massage and be done with it. I have some briefs to read this morning."

"I made up your formula yesterday," he explained. Then I heard him mumble something about how he couldn't understand why there was so much excess substance on two of the bottles. "I mixed five teaspoons of avocado oil. What we call carrier oil or base oil. It dilutes the essential oils. I put in beeswax and borax to make a nice cream."

I laughed. "So you've heard the rumors," I said. "Fat gut? Unstable mind? Then you've picked the right oils for me, haven't you Mack!" I was beginning to like this. I dropped my arms along my waist and the right side of my head sank into the tiny pillow.

"Three kinds. Seven drops each. For you I chose vetiver, a hormone balancing oil. Jasmine gives you an emotional kick. And rosemary reduces fluid retention."

I giggled. "Finally, no pouches under the eyes!"

"You've got it, Mrs. G'. Now here we go," he said, pivoting from one side of the table to the other. "Take a nice slow breath!"

A small vaporizer began spewing a light fragrance of lavender into air that was warm and filtered by soft background music. Mack shook his wrists and put a tiny amount of substance on his hands. The tips of his fingers gently formed warm medallions on the small of my back—as if he had lighted flares over my body—and my muscles flexed.

"Oh, am I in heaven, Mack?" I moaned, spittle drooling deliciously from the corner of my mouth.

"Whatever turns you on," he whispered.

"Please scrape the cellulite away!"

"In situ. But you don't have much. Actually pretty firm. In better shape than you let on," he said wiping perspiration from his forehead with the back of his hand. "Soft skin, too. You work out?"

"I jog every morning when I'm at my cottage," I said, remembering several weeks before when the scales blared that I was five pounds too heavy, and in a moment of disgust I immediately went into a fitness tirade and ate no refined sugar or white flour.

"Feels a little strange," he said suddenly.

"What does?"

He pulled the towel down to my tailbone where he flicked drops of oil, his fingers stroking softly along the sides of my breast until they returned to the middle of my back as if he were kneading bread. Strong, out of body experience. Was I being levitated from the table? When he began effleurage on my leg, his fingers touching my foot first, his hands gliding to the top of my thigh and down the back of my knee, it was so sensual that I had to concentrate on not becoming embarrassingly orgasmic by focusing on new anti-terrorist data that the attorney general of Florida, Tricia Sankorski had shared with me. Thank God I recovered quickly.

"Has my overwrought state disappeared?" I asked.

I saw him glance at his watch and grin. "*Oh yea…h,*" he said hanging onto the 'h'. But then I saw his cheekbones arch and his mouth flatten into a grimace. He stepped back. Terror fixed his eyes. Something had changed! He stumbled away from me and dropped onto one of the red chairs.

From over my shoulder, I had the odd sensation of having gone somewhere else, of losing time, uncertain what was happening, as though I were in a trance, my skin being seared by a giant flame, the horror of burning in such a way that the rattle in my throat presented the illusion of death, both near and far—tortuously plunging or thrusting forward and being suspended in the fabric of space. Whiteness? Blackness? Hollowness? Nothingness? Yet, might the abyss of death be liberating?

Suddenly, there was the presence of others, their muffled voices sliding into shouting. I strained to hear. Was I eavesdropping on a dialogue of army commands? Then someone was lifting me. Several were lifting me, their faces not unlike theatrical masks, dark and grim while plunging a dagger of fear into my pounding heart.

At the same time that I was bombarded by these rumbling thoughts, my body seemed to be merging with several lingering hands. I gave a lurch before they settled me into a large area of warm water, and then my half opened eyes attempted to follow Allison Thomason who was in the water, too. Her fingers were locked around my neck to keep my head from falling forward, and I was gasping for breath while someone else was carefully sponging my body. It was Bina.

"Easy, Kate. You've got to remain quiet until we're sure you're decontaminated," Allison said with a quavering smile. She began to force water from a bottle into my mouth. "You need fluids!"

"I know," I whispered, when I really didn't. I sipped as much as I could and then vomited.

There was a long silence. My eyes became transfixed on Mack's hands. They were swollen and red. Then glancing under his arm, he told Allison, "I've added baking soda, Epson salt and sea salt to the water. That should help ease the burning."

I slid backward with Allison still holding my head. At once I thought of how immodest you become in a crisis. In front of Barclay, Holden, and Mack, the privacy of my body was no longer my own. Their quick glances extracted my nudity like hummingbirds at a feeder.

Finally, I found my voice and asked, "Could you cover me please?"

Allison dragged two large Turkish towels into the water and they floated over me like a canopy. "The oil chafed your skin, but you'll be all right," she said reassuringly. "We've gotten you in water quickly enough to dilute whatever burned you!"

I sighed. "Mmm hmm. That's one hell-uv-a massage, you give here, my friend!" I said breaking into a smile. "I can't say that I would recommend it!"

She shook her head. "Neither would I. C'mon now, Kate." Then she carefully helped me out of the water and wrapped me in a terry cloth robe.

Holden Renaurd picked up the ringing wall phone. "Your father is coming over to the island to have a look at you, Kate. Just to be sure," he said.

Everyone drew near. "I wish you hadn't done that!" I told them. Dr. Clifton Guesswine was the last person I wanted to deal with.

*   *   *

Barclay and Mack couldn't have been a better pair of crutches, getting me up the stairs and to my room. I was in pain and dreading the visit with my father, a man whose career recently had been scrutinized by a medical board of inquiry, a man who had escaped permanent loss of his license because he could afford a high powered team of lawyers to absolve as benign—in my father's mind, anyhow—his role in matters dealing with my mother's estate and other horrible events from months before. I no longer had feelings for him, deliberately avoiding him these past months when in his arrogance he called to invite me to dinner, and I made no excuses except to say that I simply was too busy.

So when he came through the door, it was his dull green eyes that I first noticed, for as usual they were furled with annoyance, but that wasn't all. Unlike everyone who knew him, his success had never impressed me, nor did his impeccable good looks. I expected him to lecture me—his favorite line had always been—'what have you gotten your self into now, Caitland?' But he said nothing. Neither did I. Instead, he took off his pin-striped suit jacket and folded it methodically across a nearby chair and then rolled the cuffs of his shirt. He sat on the side of the bed and patronizingly patted my head. The tension was premium, perfect for the boxing ring. He pinched the top of my hand and the skin retracted slowly when he released it.

"Dehydrated, huh, Dad?"

"Not too bad." He opened his bag and pulled out a needle, which he inserted into the back of my hand before connecting it to an IV line that hung from a bag that he secured with tape to the top of one of the four posters of my headboard. A saline solution began to drip into my vein.

Allison entered the room, hugged my father and stood at the foot of the bed. She was still disturbed, wiping her forehead with her sleeve and looking as if she had aged ten years. Holden didn't come, but Barclay and Mack came then and simultaneously their hands went out. It had always been interesting to me, this shaking of hands, an unconscious ritual between men immediately upon meeting, yet, generally, as a woman, I had to extend my hand first or our hands would never touch. Equal respect still had a long way to go.

With obvious professional confidence, my father's fingers began to peruse my body. "Caitland, it's beginning to welt up a bit. What was it?"

Mack said, "I'd tell you that it was an allergic reaction, but it burned my hands. You see?" He rotated them. "Why, I mixed the oils myself last night. I was careful! A million times I've been careful!"

Allison was unconvinced. "You must have made a mistake, Mack!"

"Here. Here's the rest of that particular jar," he said, reaching into his pocket.

I sat up. My father quickly pressed his fingers into my shoulders. "Worse than any damn sunburn I've ever seen." I thought he seemed perversely amused. "You'll probably have a few blisters on that pretty backside of yours."

There was a strange look on Allison's face. Why was she turning the bottle to a forty-five degree angle? Putting a sample to her lips? Why was she lunging for the nightstand and gulping the rest of my water? She laid her arm on my hand. "I can't believe it! It's *bitter almond!*"

"Cyanide!" I yelled. Immediately I knew of the possible consequences and sat straight up.

Barclay winced. "It couldn't be!"

Mack, who had been looking out the window, spun around. "Holden okays all the supplies. Gabe usually picks them up over in Savannah!" he said defensively. "I personally check them when they arrive. Put them in the cabinet. No way that bitter almond could have gotten in there!"

"A case for good ole' Sherlock McCreary," I said, causing everyone to stare at me. "Attempted murder and mayhem at Renaurd Inn."

Allison wrung her hands. "That isn't funny, Kate!"

We both looked down. "No, no it isn't," I said sorrowfully.

My father reached in his pocket and pulled out his cell phone. "How long was the oil on her?" he asked.

"No more than a few seconds," Mack pointed out.

"Hopefully not long enough to get deeply into her system," my father said. "But to be sure I want blood tests. I'll call Nurse Cool. You remember her, don't you Caitland? My old assistant?"

I did. A battleship to say the least. I had heard they were seeing each other. I didn't answer.

"She'll come here, Clifton?" Allison asked.

"Yes. Take blood and return immediately with it to the lab. I'll make all the arrangements. Can Coneras make the extra run?"

"He will," Allison said, drumming her fingers against the air.

My father took my hands again. "But not to worry, I think. Her nails are still pink!"

Cyanide would have presented dark streaks down them. That little vision in my head, with me writhing in pain and losing my ability to talk and walk, forced me to drop back into the feather bed like a boulder. Cyanide poisoning isn't pretty.

"Mack, bring me all the essential oils that you used," Allison said. "I want Dr. Guesswine to take them to the mainland and have them tested."

"I'll go, too," Barclay offered.

"And get a bag to put this jar in!" she ordered.

They quickly left the room. Allison was putting the top back on the container of bitter almond just as Gabe came in. His underarms and neck were wet with sweat, and I wondered where he had gotten the dirt on his jeans and shirt. I was glad to see him. I smiled.

He poured a glass of water and put it to my lips. "Holden told me about this. You're okay, then, Kate," he asked softly.

"Perfectly okay," my father said, as he took my pulse again. "I've got her stabilized."

Gabe folded his arms and stood beside me, his eyes locking mine with reassurance.

When Allison reminded him that he had work to do, he turned and glared at her with chilling indifference, and I wondered about her abrupt dismissal of him when usually the two of them played farcify off each other like the bow and strings of a squeaky violin. Now I was wondering about a lot of things at Renaurd Inn.

Ten minutes later Mack, coming off of a full sprint and out of breath returned without Barclay. He wouldn't look at me. He stepped between Allison and my father and leaned forward, glancing side to side as if he were afraid someone who didn't belong might be eavesdropping. He looked baffled.

"I keep everything locked up," he said excitedly. "You know that!" He raised his hands to his temples. "But when I opened the small glass doors…"

"Well, out with it!" Allison demanded.

"The cabinet…why they're gone," he said. "All of the other oils are gone!"

CHAPTER 24

So much for the therapeutic hullabaloo about a massage, I said to myself the next morning as I plowed through scones and tea. Nurse Cool had left spray that was soothing on my back and legs, and Drew Greer arrived with the toxicology report which she had gotten from my father. I was glad to see her, glad to feel a lingering hug.

"Let's see," Drew said. "Pull up your gown."

"A well done lobster, I've been told."

"Only medium. Hurt?"

"I'll manage," I said bravely.

"Judge Thomason cornered me in the hall and told me you were moaning about David when you were coming to."

"Oh hog wash," I said during a sip of water. "He's a damn hangnail that I cut off and comes right back. One of these days…"

"You need to fucking grieve, that's all."

"Last I checked, you do that for dead people," I said.

"He might as well be."

"Was I too needy?"

Drew took my hand. "Hell, how do you judge a thing like that? Who knows? A cow needs to be milked. She doesn't give a rat's ass about the farmer. A baby wants a bottle. That has nothing to do with loving a mother. And at the end of the day, it's the vibes you get from your partner that counts. The way he pours you a glass of wine and rubs your back when your muscles ache. His smile when you're miserable. Or how he holds you when the rest of the world looks like it might end because of all the injustice. And don't forget his belching and farting. In spite of that, at the end of the day did you *feel* a rush of contentment when he was there? If that's being needy, then 'a plague on all our houses!'"

"I think you're talking about soul mates," I said sadly.

Drew frowned. "Only if he holds your head when you're throwing up at two in the morning. And after you have damn good sex, he somehow lets you know that when you're so old that the wrinkles from your face practically fall into the Coco Puffs, he still believes that you're the only woman who can spark his fire. Can you honestly say that was David Smithe?"

"Maybe the question should be, was that me? You know, I can't tell you whether he brushed his teeth up and down or horizontally. I should know that! I bet he knows that about me!"

"God, get a life! Get over him! Get rid of this convoluted, guilt ridden shit. The son-of-a-bitch walked out on *you!*"

Yes he did, I thought sullenly. Many times he only gave pieces of himself, saying that it was all that anyone should do because pieces given weren't pieces taken. And if we were lucky, we might be with someone who understood the privilege of not taking. "I think his leaving me was his way of surviving," I said, pointing to my watch. "So where's the toxicology report?"

"The bastard lied to you several times!"

I took several slow breaths to curtail my anger. "*Where's the toxicology report?*"

"You never like to own up to the truth," she said.

"That's bullshit and you know it," I said adamantly. "I mean it when I say shut up about it."

Drew jabbed her hand against her head. "Shit!" Then she grabbed a yellow file from her briefcase and clutched it to her chest. "All right then. The only reason the aromatherapy oil didn't kill you was because the main ingredient was *not* bitter almond and arsenic as Allison thought. It was narcissus," she explained.

"A benign flower!"

"Yes, but one is often mistaken for the other. It can be dangerous," Drew said. She stretched out on the bed beside me. "I'll tell you about it."

"I'm perfectly capable of reading the report myself. The oil didn't burn my eyeballs!"

"Save your strength. I'm taking you for a stroll after bit."

"I don't want to."

"You'll get stiff."

"Walking will hurt."

"Don't be such a baby," she said punching me lightly in the arm.

"Oh yeah? Remember that flat by the beach in Hilton Head right after college? When we were first practicing law? You sprained your ankle? You acted as if had been amputated. *That's* being a baby!"

"You expected too much!"

"Mmm hmm. And you used it as an excuse to pine over that Marine who dumped you," I said. "Sit around and cry. But I made you hobble to the beach."

"Where you took one look at the bulge in Justin McCreary's speedo and said, damn it Drew, I want *that!* And you two were married five months later."

"There isn't the faintest truth to it! I believe he was wearing green boxer trunks, and I never saw his package until our fifth date. Now give me the damn report, please."

She shook her head. "Narcissus comes from the Greek, *narkao*, which means 'to be numb'," she began.

"Mmm hmm. Go ahead and show off then," I said, sighing.

"A long time ago, the white flowers were used as an antispasmodic and aphrodisiac. Some have noted its emetic and sedative abilities, although I once heard of a woman who sucked the sword-shaped leaves as a narcotic."

"That doesn't sound so dangerous," I said almost in a whisper.

"Ah, that's just it. There's one strand…the bulbs of N. poeticus, one of the main family of amaryllidaceae. If you extract it, it becomes a solvent. Can be blended undetected with jasmine, rose, and other fragrances. Screw up the nervous system. Too much can cause paralysis and death."

"What about the burning of my skin? Remember, Allison could taste bitter almond."

"Something else had been added. *Tonka.* Mostly comes from the Netherlands. It's a solvent extraction, too, and is often sold as 'taquin butter'. Kills bugs, but the oil extract is used for coughs. Too much can scorch the skin. In your case, lavender was added to mask any odors the solutions might have."

"But there wasn't enough to do me in?"

"Uh-huh. At first I didn't think that was the intent either. The oils have compounds—hydrocarbons and oxygenated compounds, most of which are harmless. But the phenols can be skin irritants. The right amount and we'd been visiting you in the morgue!"

I was perplexed. "I don't believe a word of it. Anyone here at the inn could have gotten aromatherapy at that particular time, although I might have mentioned my intention to do so at dinner."

"Oh for god's sake, Kate, someone did a real number on you," Drew said with all the drama of a TV detective. "That particular mix was meant for you. Mack said so. I don't know what happened, but I'm going to find out!"

We both sat up. "Mmm hmm, I'm sure you will! Meanwhile, let's get on with the bone cases," I said with great irritability.

Drew had an earnest look on her face. "Look, you've stumbled onto something, and you don't even know what it is. Don't you give a fuck that someone tried to broil you?"

I smirked. "Oh you do have a way of cheering me up," I mumbled to myself.

"Yeah, well, open your parachute and get grounded here. Let Justin and me do our jobs! Go to Columbia and sit your ass in your office where you belong! I'm sure you've got enough cases to keep you busy there!"

I jumped out of bed. I wasn't surprised that she said that, but I was surprised that she said that while knowing what my answer would be. Anyhow getting out of the investigation would break her heart, I thought, if she were to admit it. Our history of solving cases together went back to when we were roommates in college, and we investigated the disappearance of the floor monitor's hamster.

"Well, now that you're on your feet, are you ready?" Drew asked.

"What on earth for?"

She slipped around the other side of the bed. With my robe hanging from her hands, she grinned. "We're going to get the jangle out of your joints!"

"You love it, don't you? Making me suffer!"

"It's pay back time."

We both laughed. Then we went into the hall. I thought that she was supporting me, when, in fact, we were supporting each other. I had a sudden pain in my stomach when I envisioned how empty my life would be when Drew Greer was no longer in it.

CHAPTER 25

Allison seemed compelled to look after me, but after a couple of days, I returned to my office in Columbia via busy 95 to 26 where I had to slow to a crawl because of black ice that the six a.m. weather report had failed to mention. Several cars and a semi were in ditches, so I stopped for breakfast and hoped that by the time I was through with assaulting myself with gravy and grits that the sun would have melted the ice, but then again, the way the jet stream was hanging to the south, I suspected that I might see rare snow flurries.

An hour later I pulled into my assigned parking place and changed from my tennis shoes to Sidonie Larizzi 1970's pumps that Courtney had given me for my birthday and headed to the front entrance of my office building. After the 911 disaster in New York, we posted security through-out the building and added a metal detector to the main lobby. Even though he knew me, Wally, a robust, retired police officer turned security guard, who was very much into his family, insisted that I surrender my Beretta and walk through the 'arbor' as we all called it. Overkill? Then he pulled out the picture of his latest grandchild.

The recently installed high-speed elevator was a welcomed addition. I was soon in my suite of offices when I heard staunch good mornings from the assistant attorneys, interns and Fran Dunlap who had returned from her medical leave. I was grateful that her old habit of taking my leather trench while presenting my schedule and then pouring a cup of cinnamon tea was hard for her to break.

Soon I was squinting at my e-mail when Paul Hanes, my assistant attorney general, bolted across deep maroon carpet. It was no surprise that despite his upbringing in foster homes, he later worked three jobs and graduated Cum Laude from Yale Law School and had become one of the best attorneys in the nation.

"That new?" he asked referring to my black pique rayon suit with u-neck.

I nodded. "So's the blouse. Courtney dragged me shopping and I maxed my Visa. No more recycling the old duds."

He regarded me with warm eyes and a perpetual grin that had frozen the corner of his lip upward when, as an amateur boxer, he had taken a very bad punch. Known as a fitness nut who worked out in the building weight room, I was curious as to why he had put on a few pounds around the middle. The corner of his blue coat brushed my sleeve as he laid a stapled packet on my keyboard.

"Of course, you know that the FBI keeps certain dossiers on…let's say—they keep tabs on public figures," he said.

"Oh, oh. I don't know if I want to hear this," I said wearily.

"For example, your friend, Judge Allison Thomason?"

I must have had a blank look. He tapped the unmarked packet with his finger. My wrist bone brushed his hand as I picked up the papers. "Is that what this is?" I asked before removing the clip. It was hard to look at him then. I sipped tea.

He moved to the front of my desk and sat in one of two olive leather chairs. "According to this investigation, the judge has been keeping company with questionable radicals who practice voodoo," he said. "This is about the participants."

I stared at him in disbelief. In as much as I didn't have time to read the report before my appointment with the governor, I perused it quickly. A sentence here, a sentence there was somewhat disturbing, but I didn't intend to make heavy weather about it at this time. I slumped in my chair and said, "Oh, for goodness sake, Paul, you can't be serious about this! Allison believes more than anyone in following the rules. Would she do anything to screw up her principles? Would she?" I turned the report over. "In fact, I think it's probably bullshit!"

"What she's doing could be dangerous!" he said nervously.

"Now *that* is exaggerating, isn't it?" I reminded him. "Dangerous? Hardly! All those misconceptions—zombies, black magic and sacrificial rituals? Why it's right out of the Hollywood 'B' flicks of yesteryear! Even my father told me once that my own Grandmother Ashley practiced a little voodoo herself, something she learned from two old Gullah servants with whom she would have trusted her life. And as a Black man, you should understand that Allison's roots go back to Africa and…"

"…so do mine," he interrupted, "but I would never practice voodoo or…"

I interrupted, too, "…and you're forgetting that Allison's extremely bright and curious. If only from a historical perspective, wouldn't such a rich religion and culture interest her? Especially if it were to reveal some linkage to her own past?"

"Read it carefully, Kate," he said cryptically. "She's attended several meetings! Chickens sacrificed! Spirits invoked! People put into trances!"

I stood, the palms of my hands firmly planted on the packet. "What's in here—in these notes—can't possibly be a realistic portrayal of modern voodoo," I said dismayed. "What you speak of is sinister. It has its roots in ancient practices! It's not done today. It simply isn't! How did you come by this information?"

"They've been keeping an eye on the judge's group for about two years now."

They've? "But this data points to an FBI investigation!" I said quickly.

"I thought you should know."

Who else knew about this, I wondered. Justin? Drew? Glennie Sparkman. Before I had a chance to mention anything to them, I wanted to read the whole report. I hoped it to be of little importance. "Is there anything else?" I asked.

He folded his arms and leaned on the corner of my desk. "I don't know. I was told that there's another file as thick as a law book."

"I see," I said. "And because of my friendship with Allison, I'm not in the loop? We've got some over-zealous idiots making assumptions. That it?"

He headed for the door. "It's your call now."

"By the way, I suppose that you know that bringing me this information could get you in a lot of trouble. And you know that I'm grateful, but I won't tolerate your breaking the law for me or anyone else."

Turning around, he adjusted his blue tie and grinned. "The fact is that it simply appeared on my desk one morning."

We both knew better. My eyes told him that I was worried about the report's source. It was true that a friend here, a colleague there, a friend of a friend—whoever had an 'in'—as well as 'off the record' statements or networking, often moved data in a way that would put a computer to shame.

Finally, he said with an edge to his voice, "Look, I didn't want the judge's practice of voodoo to come back and haunt you someday."

"Mmm hmm. Well, if I believed it had any validity, I'd be the first to look in to it," I said as he continued out the door. "But thank you!"

My hand shook as I shuffled through the file again, and then I went around my desk while Mrs. Dunlap came into the room and mouthed silently that the governor had arrived.

"In a sec," I told her. I partially closed the door. I buttoned my suit jacket, and my thoughts focused on a previous discussion with Allison about pre-Civil war slave owners, who after kidnapping her ancestors from Africa and taking them to the New World, beat them into submission and separated them from their families and communities so that they couldn't rise up. To the dismay of those plantation owners, many of their forced Christian religious beliefs intermingled with the slave's tribal voodoo rituals which they continued to secretly practice.

Uneasiness came over me as the governor came into my office, but I heard little of what he was saying to Mrs. Dunlap because I was remembering that Allison had also told me that some day white folks would pay horribly for what they did to the slaves!

CHAPTER 26

Dr. Roberta Coffey's Sea Pines therapy room looked like an abandoned green house crammed with too many plants in water-stained pots, their terra cotta décor spilling out onto a large deck beyond the ceiling to floor windows across the west wall. To my right, the double glass doors dripped with the unrelenting salt spray from the Atlantic that lapped hard at a nearby terraced seawall.

Scattered about the floor were several large pillows with dark tassels, all in earth tones. No furniture. No sofa or chairs or ottomans, except that in the corner was a farmer's table adorned with several hand carved florets. I wondered about the motivations of avid collectors, myself having once searched every antique and rare book store in the southeast for first edition classics until David pointed out that I had become obsessive about it, and he wasn't about to put up with the smelly, mite-ridden books, insisting instead that they stay behind glass enclosed shelves at my office. Still, there's something about holding an old book...

The door hinges clicked eventually, and a tiny, flat-chested woman with reddish wavy hair and a nose that had a small bump at the tip, motioned for me to join her in lotus style in the middle of a thick striped rug. At once she stretched arms and legs. Her references to news and magazine articles indicated that she had followed my career, and we chatted about that and my family history for a short time. In as much as she seemed immediately interested in me, I found her affability hard to resist.

"Hell, with all that's happened to you in the last year, you oughta be a damn wreck!" Dr. Coffey said, her back and neck perfectly straight. "I would be. What's *your* take on it?"

The economy of her point astounded me. I cleared my throat. "My take?"

She hesitated and then retrieved a yellow pad from the floor. "Sweet Jesus, I've got an idea. See what you think. You game?"

I didn't know how to answer. For one thing, I didn't want to be there, but lately I was given to crying jags, the kind that stomps on you when you are in the most ungodly places. I made the appointment with Dr. Coffey only after I made scribbles inside of my monthly planner: Binge eating. Sobbing while driving. Night sweats. Bursting into tears while doing the dishes. I suppose it wasn't like me to give in to those crying jags, was it? But I wasn't taking any chances because I remember my grandmother telling me that if you held in your crying, your stomach would fill up and you'd burst wide open and the water would drain out of your toes and eyes, too, and you'd drown! It was awful enough then. Scarier than hell now. And something else? For all I knew about psychology, it simply didn't occur to me that I was in the ravages of a midlife crisis. I thought that only happened to men. Dr. Coffey would show me otherwise.

"I'm not sure I know what you mean," I said.

"How about I'll throw out a subject," she said enthusiastically. "You react to it."

"Mmm hmm, intriguing," I said, nervously picking at my cuticle. *Where was that damn hangnail?*

"All right then. But first, relax your shoulders. I can see that they're as rigid as the pin I've got in my hip."

"Oh? Replacement?"

"Ski accident."

That she didn't look a day over fifty was impressive, I thought, even though I knew that there had been talk of retirement.

"Okay that's better," she said while I mimicked her stretches and rotated my arms until I looked like a rag doll. "So here's the first subject. Remember, don't think! Say what *first* comes to your mind!"

I would have a hard time at this. "I'll try," I said squeamishly.

Long pause. "*Sleep!*"

Something stopped me. I didn't trust the damn game. I didn't know why.

"Kate? You with me?"

I took a deep breath that was almost a gasp. "Oh well, sometimes I can't sleep," I said finally. "But then that's true of a lot of high energy people, isn't it? So I listen to the radio or get up and work."

She sloped forward and twined her fingers. I caught the scent of Elizabeth Taylor's *Passion*. "My husband's snoring keeps me awake. Damn irritating," she said laughing. "Thinking about getting up early makes it worse, too, doesn't it? I mean, I worry that I won't get back to sleep. Worry that my ass will be a chunk of concrete the rest of the day! You too?"

"Mmm hmm."

"*Dream?*"

"I think so," I said, "but I don't usually remember."

"Not uncommon," she said. "Do you recall any of your dreams?"

"Oh I don't know. I guess about my relatives," I said. "My mother, Catherine Ashley Guesswine. And all the Ashleys before them."

"Go on…"

"Around me like sea fog sometimes. As if they're dead and alive at once, their sleeves black, the rest of their clothes like large white flags in the wind. Sound crazy? Mmm?"

"As hell. But isn't that why you're here? To separate the corn from the stalk?"

She had a point.

"What are you feeling right now?" she asked quickly.

I coughed with both hands over my mouth. "Anxious!"

"Well, write a *word* in the air with your forefinger," she said. "The first that comes to mind."

"I don't know."

She was still. I was still. Then she said, "Kate, that old ploy of 'wait out the shrink?' C'mon. Write the *word* that you are feeling this very moment in the air, please."

I exaggerated my eye contact. "I can't think of any," I insisted. "My mind's blank."

"By the way, where did you hear about me?" she asked.

"My sister," I said. "She's in one of your self-awareness groups. Courtney St. James?"

There seemed to be no recognition of her until Dr. Coffey raised her eyebrows and laughed. She leaned over and tapped me on the knee. "Yes, of course. She's a delight. In fact, I told her group that when I was in high school, I was socially years behind my friends. Didn't they bring home guys while I brought home stray dogs? Guess I caught up with them later on by having several delightful husbands,"—she laughed heartily—"at different times, of course! And your sister wanted to know if all of my spouses were into Monday night football? I told her only if they had gotten the 'Saturday night special.'"

"What do you mean?"

"Recreational sex."

"Well, Court didn't exactly go into that," I said.

Her eyes locked on mine. "And how was all that for you?" she asked in a monotone and with no discretion. "You and David have your *Saturday night special?*"

"Good heavens," I said blushing. But then therapy was all about breaking down barriers, wasn't it? Embarrassing as they may be. Dr. Coffey remained still and silent, her eyes searching for some response in mine. I sat there with my hands folded. Had she really asked? Was it any of her business? Quickly I decided that I didn't want any pretenses, but had I been Catholic, I would have crossed myself several times before I spoke and then headed to confession afterward. With my face averted, I tried to be tactful, "We didn't only have the Saturday night special. There were other nights…"

She flipped back the cover of her notebook. "Do you think that this was the bond that held you together?"

"I don't know," I said. "No, I don't think so."

"Who broke up with whom?"

"He left me," I said quickly.

"How do you feel about that?"

Now we were back to 'feeling' statements. I was tired. Time to wrap. I didn't answer.

"Kate?"

"Mmm hmm."

"Do you want to tell me today?"

"I don't think so," I whispered.

"Uh huh. Too painful. We'll try that one later. I'll give you another word then," she said. "*Work.*"

Outside the window, the shadow of a pelican passed by, the light inside the room wavering and then turning bright again. I caught my breath and said, "Sometimes I feel like one of the bone case victims. Sometimes I feel like Anastasia."

"The woman in the newspapers? The one found at Dragon's Point?"

"Her real name is Mary Elizabeth Tarteton," I said. "Anastasia is what Dr. Bree Packard called her before we identified her. You know the case?"

Dr. Coffey swallowed hard. "Of course. I'm as interested as the next woman. It's a small island for so many murders. I know Bree, too."

"It's a cold case that's suddenly turned hot," I said. "Finding a body and not just bones gave us a lead."

Her pen drifted to the side of the yellow paper. "Are you saying that you sometimes feel physically dead like this Anastasia?"

My leg muscles tightened and I pulled my knees up to my chin. Dr. Coffey remained in the lotus position. Should I go on, I wondered? Would she call upon me to tell her more? And more? At some point would she own parts of my mind, parts where there are fantasies and fleeting thoughts so uncharacteristic of what everyone believes you to be that you'd be skewered alive if they knew. Parts that are 'not for sale' under any circumstances? "Not physically dead," I said finally.

"Emotionally then."

"Mmm hmm. Sometimes."

Dr. Coffey looked stern. "Are you comfortable?" she asked.

She waited for an answer. I studied the room. I stared at her. "Yes, of course."

"No. I mean are you comfortable talking with me?"

Something else was happening. I was getting a migraine, feeling lethargic, too, and like a child, I had a sudden compulsion to lie to her. Instead, I sat perfectly still and straight. Outside the window it had begun to sprinkle. Beyond the seawall I could see that the wind was coaxing whitecaps from waves that appeared to vacuum the beach. I looked down. "Mmm hmm. Why yes. Yes I am."

"Uh huh. But you're feeling really screwed up right now. Part of you is angry with me, too."

My throat seemed to be closing off. I could feel my eyes welling. But this was one of those times when silence was dreaded, when not speaking could cause my whole face to dissolve into a handful of tissues.

"It's okay to feel screwed up," she said gently. Her hand on mine was comforting. "We all are at one time or another."

I could hear wood creaking in other parts of the condo. I could hear footsteps shuffling, but Dr. Coffey never took her eyes from me. She sat perfectly still.

"I've got it under control," I said finally.

"I suspect you do," she said. "But what is the 'it' that you have under control?"

I shrugged, desperately trying to think of a way to leave, and glancing at my watch couldn't have had a more blatant meaning. Could I have told her that the 'it' was my work? My strength? My nectar? That the rest of my life was in the crash mode?

"We're almost done for today," she said. "Forgive me, but there's one other thing…I remember hearing about that business with serial killer, Cole Barnett," she said, "your sister and the rest of your family."

"I'm afraid that it made me a media star," I groaned. "And Barnett hasn't come to trial yet."

"Do you want to talk about that?"

"Not today," I said quickly.

"Then tell me about your father, Clifton Guesswine?"

"You know him, I suppose?"

"I have privileges at the Hilton Head Medical Center. We've consulted about cases. But what we say here is confidential."

"I realize that," I said sighing. "My father can be difficult." I moved my watch back and forth.

"His professional ego is intact," she said laughing. "That's for sure!" Finally, she put her hand on my wrist and winked, unraveled her legs and without effort we both stood. We wandered into the foyer and from a small desk, she took a calendar and penciled in another Tuesday date. "You'll come again then? I think I can help." Dr. Coffey then opened the door and followed me onto the porch.

"Thank you for your time," I said simply. But as I hurried down the brick walkway, I decided that I would break the appointment. It was settled. I would put up with myself and get over it.

CHAPTER 27

On the way to the National Center for the Analysis of Crime in Washington, DC, Justin attempted to program the address book of his new cell phone while our Italian taxi driver spouted a recipe for cheese toast, which included one-half can anchovy fillets and a tablespoon of capers, neither of which I knew anything about since my cooking expertise was all about stirring Healthy Choice soup.

Before we arrived, I warned Justin not to bring up our earlier visit to Dr. Bernadine Tynbrock. Profiler and psychic were like vinegar and oil. Once inside the building, we took the stairs to the second floor—the elevators were not working for some reason—and after catching our breath, we went through two double doors into profiler Bryce Jordan's office. I noted that there are never many offices that don't have at least one engraved bronze nameplate, letter opener, pen or marble paperweight. I lost count of Bryce's. I had forgotten that he had a fetish for monograms, and after he had swept through the door, I watched him finger the big maroon BTJ on his tie.

Admirably, he had worked in the investigative support unit of the FBI for as long as I could remember, and like his father who had served directly with J. Edgar Hoover in the seventies, he was the lead agent or coordinator who met with local police departments and other profilers. He focused mostly on cold cases.

"Long time no see," he said with a deep voice.

"At Drew's fortieth?" I said.

"Yeah, where is Miss off-the-wall IQ?" he asked.

"Had a pressing case," I said.

As he shook Bryce's hand, Justin couldn't resist, "The 'pressing part' was probably some dude with an attaché *case*."

"Not true," I said sternly, "and you can bet she's got a darn good reason for not being here."

We sat around a large oval table in the corner, one that would make for a great poker game. Agents are known to play cards when things are slow—but only after they've spread their cases across the table, examined pictures, and made graphic analysis of the evidence.

"You're going to drop that paper weight, Justin," I said sucking in a breath.

"Don't pick, Katie!"

"Tough investigation detective?" Bryce asked. His features were animated, even more so from the deep bronze that I knew his body had gotten from one of those home tanning booths. He had recently had a manicure and haircut, too.

"You've read the file about the Dragon's Point bone cases. What's your take?" I asked.

Bryce cleared his throat, something he did frequently while crunching one menthol lozenge after another. "Well, first I look at where the body is dumped. Uh, it usually reflects the age of the killer. Sherlock Holmes came up with the theory on this, you know."

Justin groaned a yawn. "Hell, you base your murderer on something a dead gumshoe said?"

"Of course not," Bryce said. "Uh, we computerize data of past killers and come up with a profile. You know that. I have other ways, too. C'mon," he said taking us into a large room next to his office. On a long metal table someone had constructed a miniature town with cars, people, animals, even a church and gas station. It seemed strange seeing Hilton Head and Beaufort, too, but anyone not knowing the location of Renaurd Island would have thought it no more than a rich man's private enclave. At the flick of a switch, Dragon's Point came alive with wave action and plastic loggerhead turtles.

"How'd you do that?" Justin asked hanging under the doorframe while folding his arms and planting his feet apart. "Say, you in to Barbie dolls, too?"

Bryce sneered. "I like to use the miniatures to act out crimes here. It makes it more 3-D in my mind."

"Like when I was a kid and had those tiny metal tanks and artillery. You know? Those military guys were metal, too," Justin said.

Bryce continued. He took a small plastic man and a boat and planted them in the water off the beach. "It's a given that our killer has access to a boat."

"Not a revelation since we found our ladies off Dragon's Point," Justin said in an unkind tone. "Hell, the whole Atlantic coast can cop a boat, anytime, anywhere."

"But something disturbs me," Bryce said. He fumbled with several of the figures, moving them around the board. "The *way* that someone kills is different when he grows older. But I can't pin point this guy's age."

"In his fifties? Sixties?" I asked. "Do you think he's at least that old?"

"That's just it," he said, planting his knuckle on Dragon's Point. "I sense an ambiguity in the age. And what really strikes me is that Jennifer Renaurd was probably killed with the same knife that was used to kill the other women. Do you know how remote that is? All these years later?"

I opened the spigot from one of those water coolers at the end of the room, filling the small V-shaped cup a couple of times. "About the same odds as getting hit by an asteroid?"

Justin fumbled with a wad of gum between his fingers and then flipped it into the paper basket beside the door. "Maybe he used one of those collectibles knives that a guy buys from one of those on-line army catalogues. Expensive and hand carved. So a guy might keep it all those years? I'll be checking that out."

"It's the one time I can't find a connection," Bryce said as he flipped through the files again. "One victim eighteen years ago. And now these women all these years later! I'll need to think on it more."

Justin finally came completely into the room and shut the door. "How about we're dealing with a *bunch* of wacko killers…"

"Only if he wants us to think so," Bryce said.

I leaned over the simulated town. I could almost see the seagrass shimmering near the coast line and hear the surf prying around the tree roots, while all the time the ghosts of Jennifer, Anastasia and the other victims crept about the beach and rested in the rivulets carved by the tidal pools. I kept thinking of what their lives might have been like, and I wondered what bastard had opened the door to their deaths and simply said, 'I have the right!'

"Using a knife indicates that our killer probably got to know his victims. They felt comfortable around him," Bryce stressed. "Unfortunately, he's a killer who can commit murder dispassionately and go about his business."

"We know that this last victim may have been a little naïve," I said.

Justin opened and closed the doors on a miniature fire station. "A prostitute by any other name may smell as sweet."

"I didn't mean that," I snapped. "A few one night stands—we have no proof Elizabeth Tarteton ever took money."

"Look, my intuition tells me there is something unique about this guy," Bryce said. "I think he knows a lot of people. Yet, they don't know him well. But I've got a hunch that he'll show his cards soon. Uh, he may have already done so and we don't realize it. Killers like this often want to know what the police know. He'll ask questions about the case. He may call the newspaper." Bryce pointed to the Dragon's Point. "He may even go back to the crime scene."

"He'll get his ass caught if he walks into my territory again," Justin blurted out.

I ignored his comment. "But won't he want to protect himself at all costs?" I asked. "Won't he be even more careful?"

"Perhaps. But I can guarantee that he's going to make mistakes! They all do when they're this close to getting caught."

Somehow I'd have to put together what Dr. Tynbrock had to say with what I was hearing from Bryce Jordan. "Do you think that he plans the killings right down to the final detail?" I asked.

"No I don't. He's much too confident. Doesn't think he needs to."

"But he messed up on Elizabeth Tarteton," Justin said walking in front of me. "That's why we got her DNA."

I looked at my watch and ventured toward the door, remembering that Drew wanted me to meet with a VIP friend of hers back at the hotel. "I've got to go," I said. "I have another appointment. Justin can you finish up here?"

"I won't be much longer," Bryce said. "Look, I heard about the switching of the oils at Renaurd Inn. Watch your back, okay?"

"I intend to," I replied.

Justin puckered his lips. "I'll take you and Drew to supper. Where we can get a rack of ribs and a beer?"

"We'll see," I said, thinking that his credit cards were probably maxed. I'd pay.

After I got into the cab, this time with an Hispanic driver with whom I could speak the language, I watched the sun slide behind buildings that quickly looked dark and empty. Beneath the cool streetlights, the city seemed paralyzed with traffic. It would be awhile before we got back to the hotel, so I let my head fall back against the seat and closed my eyes. Was it really David's chateaubriand with artichoke béarnaise that came into my mind? Come to think of it, when I got back to my room, I would pass up dinner with Drew and Justin and call room service. A club sandwich and a martini—maybe several would do.

CHAPTER 28

The forecast of a terrible evening storm, even the rare possibility of a tornado, was the last thing I heard on the taxi radio before I told driver, Jose, 'hasta la vista'—which I didn't really mean because I had no intention of 'seeing him later'—and then I checked for messages at the desk and returned to my room to find Drew Greer leaning against my door, her arms folded over a big briefcase she cradled against her abdomen. Her face looked even more drawn and pale.

"You're late!" she snipped.

When I noticed that she was alone, I suppressed a desire to be snide. "Mmm hmm. Sorry. Couldn't help it. There are a lot of conventions in town. Your VIP friend isn't coming?"

"He's here."

"Well, I feel like a tank has run over me," I said. "Can't we postpone this until tomorrow? I want to assault a tub of water and crawl into bed. And will you do me a favor? Will you take Justin to dinner? I'll treat," I said. I opened my billfold and then stuffed a hundred dollar bill inside her jeans pocket. "No matter what he says, take him to some nice place where he can get fish and a green salad. His blood is probably pure lard."

"He's on Lipitor."

"When he takes it," I said. "And he should drink only one beer, do you hear?"

"Hell, he likes to put the hair on the dog!"

"Yes. Unfortunately full beard," I said laughing. "So where's this mysterious friend of yours?"

"In a minute. Let's wait in your room," she suggested with a sliver of irritation.

I unlocked the door and flicked on the light. Drew jumped in front of me. I couldn't see beyond her head. "What *are* you doing?" I asked.

"Prepare yourself, Kate," she said soberly.

"Don't be ridiculous."

When I stepped to the side of her, I almost sank to the floor. The man sitting in the chair didn't speak, his hand out as if paying tribute. He stood and moved toward me. Drew left the room, and I had the suspicion that she was lingering outside the door, half expecting to catch me if I should bolt from where I was standing. Could I imagine it true? Or was I lost in the luminescence of a dream? Shouldn't I know if I were?

To my surprise I regained my balance and sucked in all the air I could. Finally, I shifted into the man's chest, looked up and watched his lips articulate sounds that appeared to my eyes more like ethereal hiero-glyphics on an old cave wall. I said nothing. I looked away, aware that my head was cradled hard against the hollow of his shoulder, and when I reached for the long black curls that once brushed the nape of his neck, I couldn't imagine that they had given way to a close cropped haircut.

"Be still, Kate," he said, pressing his hand to the back of my head. At that moment I backed away from David Smithe.

My lips were trembling. "You son-of-a-bitch!" I whispered. And then I did something that I had never done to anyone. While watching his eyes, I reared back and tattooed his cheek with the palm of my hand.

He didn't flinch. "You been practicing that?" he asked, undaunted that I had struck him.

"Only about every minute on the hour," I said.

Wasn't he going to beg for forgiveness? Offer an explanation? I came fully to my senses when I heard the clatter of the dead bolt. Like a timid boy he stood by the door.

"Whew, isn't it warm in here?" he asked lightly. His eyes were locked in mine in hope for some civil reparation between us. He unsnapped the top buttons of his blue denim shirt and turned toward the wall, his fingers finding the down arrow on the temperature control gage. Slowly he passed me. I noticed that his jeans stretched tightly over firm buttocks, but the rest of his body seemed emaciated. He went to a round table where roast beef sandwiches, fruit and Coastal Mondovi chardonnay looked inappropriately opulent. Drew had thought of everything. I didn't know whether to hug her or rip off her nails.

"What are you doing here, David?" I asked.

"No questions, Kate," he warned.

"You can't be serious!"

"Damn it. I don't want to spend our hours together bickering."

"*Hours?*" I laid my purse down on the dresser and hung my suede jacket over a chair.

"I have 'til seven," he said in a low monotone. He poured wine and put the glass to my lips. "Relax."

I stepped away. "No thank you," I said. "All these months. Not a word. I want my mind to be perfectly clear!"

Was he about to cop an insanity plea? Instead, he smiled, set the glasses down and reached for my hands. "I told you a long time ago that people..." he faltered, "don't own each other! You won't make me feel guilty. No matter how much you rant and rave. And even that won't change my feelings for you."

"Feelings? You mean you still have some?"

"I'm not letting you cut off your nose in spite of yourself."

"It's my damn nose!"

"I've always loved it," he said smiling.

Ridiculous? Unimpeachable? Stubborn? He still had control over me. I knew better than to dwell on it. He looked exhausted. I felt that way, too, and all the strength that I had, all the anger, the will, was like an ill wind that had suddenly gotten trapped in some far away canyon. There was little fight left in me. "Well, all right then," I said simply.

He sighed, and the sparkle swirled in the brownness of his eyes once more. Without any hesitation he stretched out on the bed, arms loosely clasped across his chest. I watched him study me, and admittedly, I understood how much of my life was a famine without him.

"Come here," he said clearly.

"Actually, I have one more question," I said.

"I wouldn't," he said.

I needed to understand. "The Special Forces," I said, "it has you lock, stock and barrel then?"

He jerked his head up. "Don't be stupid."

"You forget. I'm a damn good attorney general," I said with a more conciliatory tone. "Your files crawled with clues. Did you do that on purpose? Leave your files at your office?"

He frowned and pulled at his ear. "Dr. Briggs was to forward them to an address in Germany."

"Well, he gave them to me instead," I said, "to give to you."

He sighed. "Remarkable, isn't it? A Ph.D. who can't follow a simple request?"

"You're a Ph.D. and seldom did."

"Do you need to do this? Act like an ass?"

"Tell you what," I said. "So there's no confusion, I want to tell you that you nearly destroyed me by leaving the way you did."

His smile faded, and the serious, resolute expression that I had so often experienced during a disagreement appeared. "Nah. Not the woman I know. Strong, unflappable Kate Guesswine? I knew it wouldn't happen."

"We'll you were wrong! I've been hiding from professional and social obligations. Booze often drags me into bed and I sneak far too many cigarettes!"

His eyes pledged understanding. "Lie down," he said swiftly. He had always been able to do that—transform his demeanor—softer voice, egalitarian eyes—which I thought was an act of blatant manipulation, I might add, but no matter how equal he thought the turf was, I never believed it. I was helpless. My shoes fell to the floor.

"I'd like you to understand," he said. He pulled back my blouse and his facial stubble chafed my breast, an act of deliberate subterfuge, I thought.

"Oh? After all this time? I'm to understand? This is totally unfair of you."

"If anyone knew I was here, I could get thrown out of the Force. Drew could be fired for arranging this."

"You both would deserve it," I said. "I may squeal on you myself!"

We turned on our sides and clutched each other. He pulled my chin up, my will neutralized by his tongue in my mouth. He rolled over me.

Later I would remember that his impatience sprang in subtle ways, a frown, a tightening of his biceps and leg muscles. And then there was only talk. "What I do is very dangerous," he continued, "and where I'm going next…well, there's a strong possibility…, and anyhow, I can't be a question mark in your life, that's all. Do you understand?"

"Then why in the hell didn't you stay away?"

"Drew thought you were having a bad go of it. I didn't believe it. I still don't."

"And you both think that my being with you for a few hours is going to make my life any easier?" I asked. Wasn't it uncanny? That Drew Greer whose own life nearly always had been in shambles should spend energy arranging for me to get on with mine?

"It's your call."

"A more pleasant goodbye than the one on Mudbar Lane?"

"You always overreact!"

This was the usual backlash—his powerful ego intimidating me. I slipped out from under him, around the bottom of the bed and into the bathroom. There was something disturbing about looking at myself in the mirror, and I thought that 'killing' can come in many ways. As I released a small black bow and my hair fell onto my shoulders, I saw flashes of Elizabeth Tarteton, and I wondered if she, too, had studied herself while the killer waited for her. And after the storm off Dragon's Point freed her body could her spirit feel her skin and blood mixing with the mud and sand on shore? After this man in the other room was no longer there, would my skin feel dead and discarded, too?

I shut the commode lid and almost knocked over a large artificial bamboo tree outside the bathroom door. David was eating a sandwich. The thought of putting anything into my stomach made me almost ill, except that this time, I gulped down a glass of wine to sooth my nerves.

"I've missed you," he said simply.

I didn't answer. The atmosphere was strained, like small talk after a violent argument. Like empty chit chat before obligatory sex. "I'm renovating the cottage," I said, and I didn't know why I said it, except that letting him know that I was at least trying to get him out of my life seemed suddenly important.

"Do what you want with it," he said dispassionately. Then he said no more about it, and although my eyes dared him to say something, I knew that he would outwait me. He always could. Stand there stiff and arrogant, as he had done so many times before. Was he waiting to steal what dignity that I had left? Someone across the hall slammed his door, and I imagined footsteps on the hall carpet disappearing into the elevator. My confidence was waning. I stared at him with disgust! "David, what a mess!" I broke into sobs. "If you aren't coming back to me—why I won't believe it! You can't do this to me again!"

"Poor Kate," he said gently. "You can be so full of passion! When we are together, and I mean with no distractions from murders and robberies and briefs that have to be read into the early morning hours, well, hell, you are the most exciting woman I've ever known! Every day of my life I find refuge in that. Pig-headed, too, that you are. But we don't always have choices!"

It was a long while before I took the wad of tissues away from my nose. Slowly he raised his fingers and slid the palm of his hands under my bra.

"You've been in a lot of danger, haven't you?" I asked. "You're in Iraq now? When I try to sleep, I want to think of you in a...*place*," I said, following him over to the bed, where I pulled back the chenille bedspread. "Couldn't I get a short wave radio and play it? Couldn't I hear the voices of wherever you are and know that you're there, too?"

He laughed. "Very well. Afghanistan, then," he said quickly. "But I won't be there much longer. The least you know from here on out, the safer you are."

"There must be something," I said desperately, "What about now? Give me something to help me!" I kissed his forehead. "What was it like there?"

He pulled me onto the bed, and we were on our sides again facing each other. His hand supported his cheek. "I swear Kate, you're masochistic! All right. I'll tell you that the terrain there is like that area near Blowing Rock, North Carolina where we climbed," he said. "Remember? All craggy and remote as hell."

"What else?" I asked, my eyes taking every pore, every line of his face.

"What else? Well, at first I was traveling alone. You know, I had to wait until the last light to move. Then I was always crawling. Got scrapes all over my knees. Cuts on my hands. Convoys of Americans would pass me, their lights illuminating the rocks. You know? I thought they might see me. Shit, maybe mistake me for the enemy. Shoot me. I was always one boulder away from being shot."

"Poor darling!"

He put his hand across my lips. "And I've killed people. I know it's hard for you to hear that. One time I met up with some other Special Forces guys. We came upon an Afghan villager. An old man. I was sure that he had run guns to Al Quaida. I disarmed him. I spoke Arabic to him and his family. And then all the other guys and me ate some of his grub. I took him off to a cave. I shook his hand. It was the hardest thing I've ever done."

My eyes dropped. "You did that when you were in South America, too?"

"In the beginning when you moved into the cottage, you knew that I had been in the Special Forces."

"But I thought that you had retired!"

"You know that I never talked about my past," he said defensively.

I helped him take off his shirt, and I pulled him as close as I could so that my cheeks rested on his warm chest. There were fresh scars across the corner of his shoulder. I massaged them with my lips. "I can't stand to think of you in any pain," I mumbled.

His scowling made me sullen. "This isn't a conventional war, Kate. With my Greek heritage—my dark looks—I can pass for Middle-Eastern and sniff out those son-of-bitches in hell holes where other soldiers can't." He rocked back on his hips and his jeans hit the floor again. "Now come closer. Let me hold you."

He wasn't smiling, but I pictured him so. He needed a shave, but I pretended he didn't. It seemed unbearable that he would go away again, that there would be no exchange of telephone numbers, no place to send a Christmas or birthday card. No, he would be gone without a trace like one of those characters in a missing persons TV movie who disappears from a jogging path in an isolated part of a park. But I decided that no longer would self-pity be the barrier between us.

My watch said a little after ten o'clock. Somewhere in the steam and neon of the city, Drew and Justin were finishing drinking and eating along with the evening crowd, and before they returned to the hotel, their taxi would streak respectfully past the Lincoln Memorial, and if they were drunk enough, they might stop and climb the steps to salute the man who freed the slaves, even though none of us—black or white—is ever really free from the tyranny of our emotions. We are tethered as surely as if they were our master.

I was seething with exhaustion, overwrought with sadness, and even though I had a wretched sense of loneliness as David edged closer, the fact that we might never be together again was no longer a concern. Mechanically, and with little cooperation from me—for it seemed to give him great pleasure—his hands tore at my light wool skirt, silk blouse, slip, bra and panties as if they were of no consequence. There was simplicity in his tongue stroking my breast, his hands groping to untangle the rest of my body from disheveled sheets. Then I lay still and without a word watched with some urgency as he pitched over me and wedged his knees against my inner thighs, his eyes tracking every gesture that I made as I responded frantically to his arousal.

His lips were unbearably sensual, rocking my skin like an eager adolescent for the first time, and when he was more restrained and steadied himself, our flesh resonated again and again, singularly surpassing anytime that we before had shared. Then unquestionably our breathing drained, we lay asleep until we awakened looking at each other, or so it seemed, for his eyes were veiled with a transparency that I had only seen in the dying.

Suddenly he shifted from my arms to his back, his right hand doing a u-turn across my fingers. "Kate? Kate? It's time, I think," he said, his voice cracking.

If I answered, I knew that I would scream like a fitful child.

I laid my hand upon his abdomen, and then my fingers vanished among the strands of thick hair above his navel. Outside the rain was relentless and the world still the same mess that it was in the hours before. Somewhere a person was being murdered, raped or robbed every minute. Yet in more peaceful homes, wives and husbands and children were sleeping in. But waitresses, taxi drivers, mothers with newborns who needed feeding—they were awake. It was Saturday, after all. And then I couldn't help but wonder, if I had to be a woman, did I have to love so stupidly like one?

"Seven A.M. then? That it?" I said.

"Kate? I'll never regret the years we've been together," he answered with finality. He touched my cheek with the back of his hand and then got up.

"Mmm hmm. No ring on my finger, but one in my nose," I said hurtfully. "I'll only hope..."

"No. No you won't!" he said averting his eyes. "Always remember, my dear Kate that you can't have one foot in the past and one foot in the future or you'll never have any way to walk in the present!"

I studied his face. "It's no use asking," I whispered into the canal of his ear. "Is it?" There was no answer. I rolled onto my stomach and sobbed. Then I was alone. And when I got up, I stumbled to the door and opened it, my eyes straining to take in the intolerable emptiness of the hall. At first my body was numb with suffering; yet, after a long while upon my knees, I could feel the cessation of a gnawing semi-consciousness that had gone on for months. I dragged myself up, drew a long breath, felt one last trickle of grief in my stomach and sprang back into the room.

"Damn you, Kate Guesswine! He'll never do this to you again," I said, a wave of adrenaline raising my hand to make an obscene gesture in the mirror. As I walked away, suddenly I was energized. For the first time in my life, I really believed that something was irrevocably over and it didn't matter. I felt free.

CHAPTER 29

The Saturday morning flight from Washington was bumpy. Justin threw up several times, and we were late getting into Savannah because we had to go around storms. At the last moment I was glad that Drew had gone on to New York to meet with another agent and couldn't come back to Beaufort with me as she had intended. Admittedly, I was still agitated because of her so-called surprise. Hell…it was an all out 'operation shock!'

As we got off the plane, Justin remarked that I looked like a drunken bag lady…eyes like prunes, French roll straggling down my neck, and I hadn't opened my makeup kit. My suit needed a good press, and while I was oblivious to Justin's babble about the Dragon's Point cases and his preaching that I needed to see my gynecologist and get hormones because of my moodiness, in retrospect, I was happy that he didn't know that I had been with David; it would have meant a lecture—or worse, a pout on his part. The airport shuttle dropped us at the cottage on Mudbar Lane. I got the Explorer and took him to his office on Hilton Head Island, and then I planned to spend the rest of the weekend at my motorhome, relieved that feeling like shit was beginning to take on a lighter color.

Dinner was a carry-in from Publix and a Coastal from my wine rack. I read what seemed like hours of fax reports from Paul Hanes about the Dragon's Point investigation, information that state investigators had dredged from every corner of South Carolina, and I suppose from other pockets of the country, too. Yet, as I freshened the linens with a swish of Chanel, I was sure that I was missing something, and like a VCR, I ran every detail of the investigation backward and forward until it was impossible to sleep.

I flipped on my laptop and immediately recognized that Drew had forwarded more e-mail from Cole Barnett's blog. I knew immediately that once again he had broken through my newly installed PGP—pretty good privacy or personal e-mail encryption. It was the very last thing I needed. My pulse raced.

Say, there's one slick attorney general out there who gave meanin' to my life by not dying when she was supposed to. Think of it like this. I've already been to hell. Taken people with me. You'll want to know that because all of us have fears that crawl on us like maggots. I killed women to dump those fears. Ain't no bull, attorney general, no bull. When you receive my very last e-mail, you'll know how a serial killer is wired. There ain't gonna be no ground wire!

You're thinkin' that this is a job for a shrink? Been there, done that. Oh, I want you to know that I hate the term serial killer. 'Serial' means that somethin' is arranged…one after another in a kind of order. To make a plan. I ain't never planned to kill no one.

No, I tell you what. The truth is that you can be pissed at somethin' and still like it. When I was a kid, I had this baby chick that my mother got me for Easter. It pooped on my bed. I broke its neck. I loved that yellow bastard, but it didn't have no right to poop on my clean white sheet.

Oh listen, I met this broad once. After two months she split. I found her. But before I killed her at that motel in Charleston, I yanked her halter up, crisscrossed her arms and tied them behind her. Then I pulled her shorts to her ankles. I never spoke a word to her. I smiled. Straddled her, the way a cowboy does his horse when he's ropin' a steer, my arms flayin' as if I had a hat in my hand and a rope in the other. I stuffed her mouth with my fist.

Do you know the difference between fuck and rape my dear attorney general? We were equals when we fucked. But I was superman when I raped her. Power! I yanked her by her hair. I remember lickin' the tears from her cheeks. You know, I don't even know the color of her eyes. Even though they stared at me. Now that pissed me off. I beat her until she bled from her nose and ears.

You are thinkin' what a deranged son-of-a-bitch I am right now. You are thinkin' how I could do this to a person. But I strangled the bitch and took a long shower. You know what I wanted to do? I ain't gonna lie to you. I wanted to skin her and bleed her. I wanted to tie her to my roof the way hunters do a deer. But I had my job as parkin' attendant over in Savannah to go to. Couldn't be late. Ooops. Lights out attorney general. Sleep well! Cole Barnett

I stared at the computer. Every word was like an eye in the darkness, jumping and cursing, the letters alive and ready to kindle my laptop into a thousand flames. Cole Barnett didn't have access to a computer in prison, the warden had told me, but I believed that in his overwhelming arrogance, that he could easily arrange for a cyber assault against me. But if Barnett weren't responsible for the blog, it was possible that the hacker was a 'Black Hat', a pain in the ass who generally makes up his own rules, someone who has a vendetta against a corporation or individual. We all knew that a modem in the next block or as far away as China could break into any computer, the perpetrator no doubt using encryption—codes—to hide his crime. I saved the blog, pushed the off button and slid back into bed where I wrapped my arms and legs around pillows and soon scraped sleep from a long night filled with images of strangers throwing lemon meringue pies and a dog licking my face. So much for sleep symbolism.

＊　　　　　＊　　　　　＊

Daybreak came mercifully. I gulped two aspirins and peered at the light fog filtering through the surrounding pines, but I didn't know if the motorhome was unusually still because it was dreary or because it was Sunday, the time when people slept late or quietly read newspapers on their decks as the sun came up. The phone rang. A simple conversation. Meet Drew at the Hilton Head airport at noon. Off to the Bahamas to learn about a prostitution ring that she hinted might be the missing link to the bone cases.

Flying with Drew in and out of clouds was like sitting in the front car of a roller coaster with no tracks beneath you. My stomach was as knotted as rope. We needed headsets to talk over the loud noise of her single engine four seat Cessna 172, a basic training aircraft that she had purchased as used for just under $40,000 a few years before. She had been hoping to give lessons when she retired (I reminded myself that with her illness she shouldn't have been flying at all), but I watched as she worked the rudders, glad when the flaps went down so that we could land at New Providence Island airport in Nassau, even though we bounced on the tarmac like a badly chipped golf ball.

We stopped at the terminal bar, and I had a Caesar salad while against my protestations, Drew ate very little of hers and downed a shot of tequila. She admitted that the FBI was still monitoring my e-mail, and I was dismayed to learn that the Barnett incident had been turned over *completely* to the agency's internet crime division, which made the e-mails much more threatening than I had originally thought.

"We've traced the Barnett blog—I mean if that's what's going down here—to an internet service provider in Taiwan," she said. "We looked at their logs on their e-mail server, but the IP address that was on your computer belonged to some poor priest there who was totally innocent, of course. Whoever this asshole is, well, we think that he's simply re-routing his e-mail from somewhere here in the US through Taiwan so he doesn't get caught. Now we've temporarily run into a dead end. This guy's been sending similar shit to the prosecution witnesses who may testify at Barnett's trial!"

"I bet that sends them to the phone!" I said.

Drew sucked on a breadstick. "Look, when does his trial begin?"

"It could be several more months. You know how these things work!"

"Well, although we know that it could be Barnett who is responsible for the blogs, we believe that it's more likely some Cyberpunk whose been following the case," Drew explained. "And Kate, even though you don't like it, we're going to keep monitoring your e-mail."

"I've already cancelled my on-line banking," I said lightly, and then felt a compulsion to add with a grin, "Oh yes, and I promise that I will no longer take advantage of the female Viagra ads that flood my screen!"

"Get a life!"

Soon we were in a rental, an older Jeep Cherokee that should have seen the junkyard. Although I hadn't been to the island in years, it hadn't changed much. At Prince George's Wharf my eyes gathered in large cruise ships, yachts and a fleet of fishing boats. Nearby, fire walkers and snake charmers still mesmerized the tourists before they headed to downtown Bay Street where long ago Blackbeard, rum-runners and others of the most unsavory of characters terrorized the locals while spending their bounty in run down hotel rooms. Prostitution had always been the run of the day there, too. But I supposed that everyone knew that for centuries, the world's oldest profession was a tune that had hummed in every corner of the world.

After dodging potholes that could swallow half a car, we sped away from all that and wound through a collection of dilapidated shanties. Even through the closed windows, I could hear the rain clattering on their tin roofs.

"Did you know that in the 1700's South Carolina Governor William Sayle established settlements throughout the Bahamas? Both Whites and African slaves lived here," she said. "Haitian immigrants, too."

"But not many Whites now?"

"Only twelve percent. Very small percentage. And three, I believe, of Hispanics. And by the way, ironically after William Sayle, there was Don Antonio, the Spanish governor."

"Mmm hmm. But what does a history lesson have to do with why we're driving down this damn road?" I asked. I tried to adjust the air conditioning. It had one temperature. Broken. We lowered windows slightly and used our hands to clear swaths of humidity from the windshield.

Drew brushed wind driven coils of hair from her forehead and said, "According to the Immigration Act of 1996, there are strict penalties if illegal immigrants land here in the Bahamas without a visa."

"Doesn't the penal code ban prostitution?" I noted.

"Who's going to enforce it," she said matter of factly.

"So Paul Hanes was right," I said. "For years, these islands have been a stop off for smuggling women. Mostly from places like the Czech Republic, Rumania, Panama and Sierra Leone. Many eventually heading to the US."

"That's right. So close to the mainland," she said, "and don't forget, prostitution is the perfect cover for sanitizing illegal monies."

"This is big shipment area then," I said. Drew ran over a large two-by-two construction board and our heads buffed the ceiling. "Will you please slow down!" I added.

"For other stuff than women, too."

"Huh? Like what? And what about New York?" I asked, suddenly remembering our phone conversation. "What did you find out there?"

I could hear a distinct wheeze in her breath. I was concerned.

"In due time," she said. "Follow the yellow brick road."

"For all I know this *is* the yellow brick road," I said. "Now what other *stuff?*"

"You remember that case I worked on last year? The eight drug dealers from the Dominican Republic who suffocated off the coast of Maryland?"

"Mmm hmm. They were in a shipping container for days, I remembered you telling me, along with cartons of an illegal supply of human growth hormone. It must have been a dreadful way for them to die, too, the air going out of their lungs like the slow leak in a tire."

"All these tributaries—drugs, prostitution and even the sale of body parts—lead to that same river."

I laughed. "My! You are metaphorical today," I said.

"Get your life jacket on," she said. "We're about to take the plunge!"

I sensed that Drew was in a state of euphoria. We both loved the intrigue that goes with being involved deeply in a case, but she 'James

Bonded' the process far more than I, who was prone to follow procedure. Instantly, I was worried that her 'river' might be a 'river of no
return!'

The last shanty, one with a half dozen kids playing with broken toys
in grassless dirt fronted the road at a corner, our tires crunching gravel.
Then we passed the skin of a vacant lot, blemished by abandoned cars
and a burned out garage before Drew slammed on the brakes in front a
two-story house, which close up, had too many layers of pink paint,
some of which were mottled with mildew and rot. Rusted iron posts
held up storm shutters. Downspouts were broken, and water spewing
over garbage straddling the sides of abutting outbuildings flailed rancid
in spite of the purifying effects of the rain. The scene presented something other than five-for-a-dollar post cards portraying Bahamian
beauty. No grand hotels. No opulent homes. No stellar cottages clois-
tered in scrubbed suburbs. The sanctity of manicured paths meandering
through prisms of flowers and vines had long been lost in this area of
the island. Yet, didn't every country have its slums?

"This place advertises as a massage parlor," Drew said. "A clever way
to disguise their real business."

"Yes. Well, what's the connection to the States?"

Drew finished off a bottle of water. "C'mon, let's get this over with,"
she said ignoring my question. We got out of the car. I dragged up steps
where too many untamed palm fronds smothered the railing, but it
hadn't obscured a scruffy man with long white cascading hair who was
rocking in a wicker chair. I was relieved when a voluptuous woman in a
light blue pinafore straightened up and bounded inside the house when
she saw us. The man toiled with his zipper, sighed, closed his eyes and
continued rocking. It was an unprecedented sight. I thought I had seen
everything in my career when I realized that I had seen very little.

The wooden screen door was unlocked and obviously opened to
'clients.' We went inside, and I was immediately distressed by the odor of
cat feces that had permeated the flowered sarong worn by the woman who
was suddenly beside us. Slender and sixtyish, Phoebe Longa nervously led
us to the discarded carcasses of two oddly shaped sofas...similar to the

ones that litter town dumps, and because there was no excuse for rudeness, we chose a long sleek one with a gaudy leopard throw that was tucked into the creases of spongy cushions. We had trouble finding an area that wasn't stained. My lungs sucked in the stifling heat and my first visit to a brothel.

After we showed our credentials, it took only a couple of minutes for Drew to explain the reason for our visit. I was dumbfounded when she mentioned Elizabeth Tarteton's journal. What else was FBI Agent Drew Greer keeping from me? Who was in possession of that journal? How did they get it? Why wasn't I aware of it? "What else have you forgotten to tell me?" I whispered.

"I didn't forget," she replied.

"I've had it with you," I said firmly.

Drew's eyes rolled. "You know that Elizabeth was murdered," she said looking over at Phoebe Longa. "And there's a reference to you on page fourteen of her journal. How'd you know her?"

"I had nothing to do with it," she answered with a very English accent, her relatives no doubt going back to pre-WWII when the Bahamas was a British outpost. Then she wiped away dribble from the corners of her eyes.

"Did she work for you?" Drew asked.

"I suppose if I don't answer, I'll get into a lot of trouble," she said to the rattle of a 'gris-gris' amulet on her wrist, all too familiar pieces of animal skulls, cuttlebone, and shells used for conjuring spirits and protecting against evil.

Drew frowned. "That's putting it mildly," she said. She promptly pointed to the door. "In fact, we can go to the Deputy Commissioner of Police right now. Over at the Detention Center off Carmichael Road. You know, where the authorities detain illegal immigrants? I'm sure some of your girls know the place. I'll get you all busted!"

Drew was bluffing. She would never turn in these poor, wretched women. She had worked at shelters for the poor and abused. Wasn't she a champion of the underdog? In fact, I was sure that the locals would more likely frown at *our* unauthorized interrogation of Phoebe Longa.

I cautioned Drew to be quiet. Like Elizabeth's Aunt Dahlia, this madam needed a spoonful of honey instead of a bowl of shaved iced, so I spoke up. "Ms. Longa, do you know anything that might help to solve Elizabeth's murder? We need your help!"

Phoebe Longa took out a cigarette. She studied us both and then drew several puffs. "Elizabeth told me that she had gone to a college in the States," she said. "In New York. Yes, she told me that. She'd hop a plane down here on her spring break. She was a tourist then. At first hanging out at one of the cheaper hotels. Later, I kept telling her that this place...this life wasn't for her!"

"I don't understand," I said. "Didn't she work for you?"

She studied us. "Not in the beginning."

"Then how did Elizabeth come to you?" Drew asked.

"He sent her here."

"Who?" I asked.

"Trainer," Phoebe Longa said.

Drew bristled and caught my eyes. "That's not his real name, of course. These big fucks are body brokers, Kate. And sometimes the pie looks so good that they take a slice for themselves."

Irrationally, I was thinking, don't tell me they're also part of the South American drug cartel or Italian mafia or I'll probably sprint to the nearest pay phone and S.O.S. the Attorney General of the United States. But I knew better. The speculation in my office was that we were dealing strictly with a Southeastern prostitution operation.

"Is that what happened Ms. Longa?" I asked. "Your boss had a relationship with Elizabeth?"

"That's right."

"What about the other women?" Drew asked.

"Most often the girls are my girls," Phoebe Longa said, her proudness like a board across her shoulders. "I recruit them and they get their 'technique' here. Usually Trainer arranges for their jobs in the states. Usually he doesn't have anything personal to do with them."

"...and that protects his anonymity," Drew added.

"But how long were he and Elizabeth together," I asked.

Mrs. Longa leveled her eyes at me and frowned. She needed to know that she could speak frankly and in confidence. I leaned forward and touched her hand. It was a trick that Justin had taught me to disarm anxiety. "Please, it's important," I coaxed.

"She met him at one of the hotels," she said "But didn't she go and quit school when he got tired of her? She couldn't get a job. Came back here again. It was then that I got the call from him with an order to take her in. I do what I'm told."

"*Can you describe Trainer?*" Drew asked.

"No. He never came here. It was all taken care of by phone. But there is something else," Phoebe Longa continued. "I heard Elizabeth tell one of the other girls that she couldn't live without him! Shortly after, she moved to the mainland."

Drew looked at me. "By any chance to Tybee Island?" she asked.

"Maybe," she answered. "One of the girls here got a postcard from there."

"To the best of your knowledge, did Elizabeth ever see Trainer after she left here?" I asked.

"I wouldn't know," she answered.

Selective memory, I thought.

"Your girls take human growth hormone, don't they?" Drew asked.

Phoebe Longa receded as far as she could in her chair. Her forearm swabbed perspiration from above thin brows. "Ahhh…" she sneered, "you ask too much. What would I know about that?"

Drew gazed unbelievingly at her. Then she lost it. "Listen lady, this whorehouse is nothing more than a sanitizing station for women. Most are here illegally. An embarkation point before their asses are carted off to the states for who knows what! I believe that some of your ladies have ended up as fish food!"

Phoebe Longa's jaw tightened. She stood up and pointed to the door. Our interview was over. We should have hurried, but Drew lingered, and as I began turning the handle, I couldn't hear what she was saying. It was then that I was aware of a rattle from above. At some point my eye noticed a metal ceiling register just as feathers and scorched bone fragments funneled onto my face and shoulders. When it stopped, Phoebe Longa's face was mottled both white and red. Her palms shot into the air.

Drew yanked me outside and down the stairs, and even after we were in the car, she was still distraught. "What was that about?" I asked. "And don't lie to me!"

She gripped the wheel and sped away. "Black magic! Spirit possession that lasts only a second or two."

"Mmm hmm. Have we been zapped?"

"Someone's trying to jerk our chain," she said. "Not to worry." She patted my knee and smiled, her usual way of reassuring me.

"Oh? But I've never seen you so concerned," I said. "And another thing! For starters how did you get Elizabeth's journal?"

"I don't have a clue where that journal is."

"Page fourteen? Mrs. Longa's name?"

"Just call it saccharinely inaccurate," she said.

"You lied?"

"Well, it worked, didn't it?" The car hit a pothole and jerked to an abrupt stop. It was then that I noticed a small cloth pouch on the floor by my foot.

"What's this?" I said, dangling burlap from between my fingers.

Drew's eyes froze on my hand. "Don't!" she shouted.

"But what is it?"

"Give it to me!"

She yanked the pouch away. She pulled the strings as if she were testing the doneness of two hot strands of spaghetti. When the top opening fell back, a rank odor wafted into the air. She peered inside. I sat very still. "Whew! Probably suffocated," she said. In the excitement, she was wheezing again. "That was close!"

"Cut it out! You're really scaring me!"

She kept staring at the pouch. "Yes, well it's a bouga toad! And it's native to Haiti and poisonous as hell! You get some of that baby in a cut and you'd be very sick! Had it bitten you...well, screw that! You wouldn't have had time to get sick."

"Mmm hmm. Another warning like the oils and the old medicine man? And Phoebe Longa?"

She turned her head toward the window and sat very still. I had seen Drew Greer like this many times before. At any second her mind would begin to work like a computer, loading start-up data, figuring out what to do next, doing a little mental traveling into the past and future. She put the pouch on the floor near the lever that moved the seat front or back. There was a little gurgle in her throat as the Jeep wound around the potholes again, the blinding rain obscuring our approach to the airport. Her silence led me to believe that she still would be trying to put it all together in her mind.

I was already wondering if the Cessna would be able to take off or if we would have to spend the night in the Bahamas. As we scrambled into the cockpit, I kept thinking about Elizabeth Tarteton and Jennifer Renaurd and the disarming fear they must have felt at the moment of their deaths, and I was even more determined to give them justice. Drew was steadfast with seriousness as she tested our headphones and mouth pieces. As the engine turned over, she shook her head, all the while her mind working and working, and then as if she had recovered from mental drain, she sat straight up, and said, "Kate, someone really wants you dead! And I'm not going to let that happen!"

"Mmm hmm. Well, at least my life insurance is paid up!" I said, trying to smile. Then I settled back and secured my seatbelt. I pulled it a little tighter than usual, fully aware that there were no parachutes in Drew Greer's plane.

CHAPTER 30

After a grueling week at my office in Columbia, I was happy at last to be back at my completely renovated cottage. Drifting in and out of rooms, I still faced the daunting task of unpacking boxes and reorganizing my life without stumbling across any remnant of David having lived there, for unfortunately, memories have a way of being real, as if their sound and movement in your mind have substance. So I was glad when slightly after four, Allison called with a litany of reasons why I should spend Saturday and Sunday at the Renaurd Inn to enjoy the guest-less atmosphere. It fascinated me that she seemed determined to tell me that Coneras had taken Mrs. Trample-St. Synge, (who had stayed a week later than the others because of the flu) to the mainland while Holden abruptly had left early Friday in his own boat for Charleston before returning to Washington. I alerted Allison that Drew Greer would join me Sunday afternoon because of an important development in the Dragon's Point cases, to which she only said, 'Well, then, the more the merrier!'

Coneras was waiting for me at the dock. He seemed quite happy to see me, but when I asked about the welfare of Gabe, his answer was strained, his saying only that his grandson had been gone a lot lately and had not been well.

The journey across the sound seemed shorter than usual, perhaps because I stayed inside the cabin with my nose buried in a case about alligator poaching in the southern part of the county. When we arrived at the dock, no one was there to greet me, but after I went into the inn, Bina promptly took me to the small family dining room where Allison rose unexpectedly from the shadows of an eighteenth-century tea table, laughing heartedly while explaining that she had been searching for a lost button. Barclay joined us for dinner. We chatted about how delighted we were that according to the forecasters, the December weather looked promisingly warm, although presently it was raining, cool and overcast, the weather having the same depressing affect on all of us.

The next morning, we had a light Sunday brunch in the same room, with Barclay apologizing for Allison's absence because of some personal business she had to attend to. She didn't join us until early afternoon. At that time Barclay fretted over the menu for the 'newbies', as he called them, who would arrive midweek. The new cook went about restocking the Chippendale mahogany china breakfront with culinary snacks while referring to the guests as 'The vegans. The no cholesterols. The salt frees. The sugar frees. The low carbs.' Humorously, given that I had little will power, I was glad that I was none of those, although I heard that I was called 'the bottled water in the VIP suite.'

Finally, in hopes of heading off an impending migraine, I went back to my room for a brief nap. A little after two, I joined Allison for tea in her office, a rectangular room about the size of a walk in closet just off the kitchen. She became busy with the details of judicial briefs while I studied a bill legalizing birth control pills for teenagers—and without parental approval—that was about to be introduced to the state legislature. As the attorney general, I had already decided not to enforce whatever the outcome. It wasn't a personal stand. It was a matter of law. Ultimately, it was an issue best left to the US Supreme Court.

Soon it was three o'clock. I couldn't think of any other reason for Drew Greer not to have arrived except that the impending bad weather may have kept her plane grounded in Washington or she might have missed Coneras's final crossing of the day. Eventually Allison left the room to check our dinner menu, and I put my papers back in my briefcase and called Justin on my cell phone. He sounded as if he were dragging on one of his cigars. When we were married, I nagged him about it. Now his lungs were his own business.

"Is Drew with you?" I asked.

"No. She there?" he asked, static beginning to interfere in our conversation.

"Would I be asking you if she were?" I said, thinking that he sometimes made me want to enroll in anger management classes. "Have you talked with her today?"

"Last night."

"Then she was with you?" I bit my tongue. A bad question deserves a bad answer. It was coming.

"You know, Katie, it's asinine comments like that which put us in divorce court," he growled, "Is it your goddamn business if she stayed here last night?"—he thought it over—"which she didn't, in case you'd like to know. I said that I *talked to her last night.* She told me that she was gonna take the shuttle directly from the Savannah airport today so she'd make the ferry to Renaurd Island."

"Mmm hmm. Well, she's not here," I said with much concern.

"So don't pop a pimple! If she missed the goddamn boat, she'll call," he said confidently.

"I'm worried…"

"Look, page her!" he said. I wasn't surprised at his flippant tone. He seemed more and more disagreeable since buying Craps.

"With what? Smoke signals?" I said. "I've tried. You know she always forgets her battery charger for her cell phone! And would you speak up? I can barely make out what you're saying. There's terrible static."

"Well, I'm on top of the motorhome. Maybe that's why. The goddamn fan in my bathroom won't stay closed. If I don't fix it, I'll be taking a shit with the rain on me. I'm getting soaked out here now."

At the moment the woes of his motorhome or his bathroom habits weren't on my agenda. I pressed him. "What about those faxes Drew was going to send me? I never got them. Did she tell you about them?" I asked.

He covered a slow burp. "Come to think of it…she said they were too sensitive to send over to the inn's machine. She wanted to specifically speak to Allison. She sent me copies. Though I haven't seen them. Tell you what. As soon as I'm through here, I'll go to my office. Call you from there. In the meantime, if you hear from her, let me know, will you? So I don't have to make the trip?"

"Look, will you hurry?"

"Aggravating woman," I heard him mumble, and more boldly: "I'll throw a tarp over this damn roof and go now. You always get your way!" Then there was a click.

His belligerence hadn't changed and could still put a wince on my nerves, so I went down the hall and onto the front porch for a breath of fresh air. The landscape kept deserting the fog, pieces of it coming back again and again, finally disappearing completely until I could see very little and only hear the boats grinding against the docks, but I was sure that the most dangerous part of the Ghost Rain hadn't reached Renaurd Island yet. Storms seemed to have a mind of their own, the land, too, as if that land nearest the sea knew it was about to do battle, as if the animals that had been bred on the land knew the battle was coming and moved to higher ground because of some innate knowing.

A short time later Allison joined me, but the chill finally sent us inside, leaving me to wonder if perhaps the dampness invited a fire in the fireplace; instead she poured brandy into large snifters. That did the job.

"Barclay's nowhere to be found," she said lightly. "The storm is supposed to produce heavy coastal flooding, so I want him to get Tapest and Gabe and bring them here to the inn—away from the low lying areas."

"Perhaps he's already gone after them," I said.

"Well, he'd better hurry," she said as if there had been a startling revelation. "The latest weather report says there may be as much as a half foot of rain by tonight. Gabe's place is at the highest elevation on the island, but you never know, now do you? It's flooded out before."

"Mmm hmm. Then it may take a good while to come from his cottage, won't it," and I said that because it occurred to me that the tides had been high all day and the inlets might have already run over the trails.

She looked at her watch and cupped her palms together to make a telescope against the window, peering for a long time before going to the intercom near the door. "Bina, see if Coneras is still at the ferry," she said in to it. "Bring him up to the inn, please."

Without saying anything, Allison drifted by me and disappeared. At the window I watched the walkway leading to the canal where the fog lifted and fell like an elevator. I thought of how often the weather played a part in our lives, how many times life had been put on hold, sidetracked or stopped because of it. Ferocious storms grounded airplanes. Snowdrifts blocked roads and stranded people for days. The sea clawed at cruise ships. And Renaurd Island had been brought to its knees before, too. In fact, although there had been many destructive hurricanes to hit the southeast coast, including the Great Sea Island Hurricane of 1893 in which 2000 people perished, I had mostly heard about Hugo, a storm that in 1989 brought a 20 foot storm surge and 135 mile hour winds that put six feet of water around the inn and covered the beaches for weeks with coastal debris.

I was feeling anxious again. Bina came around the porch and was quickly out of sight. Soon at the top of the stairs, I could hear Coneras stomping his feet. He turned the door handle, leaned in and looked around, his eyes widening as they fell on Allison who had returned to the room. A stiff wind caught the door. Startled, Coneras darted in front of me. Once inside, he was oblivious to his parka dripping on the oak floorboards and the water coursing off his massive hands, and so with his forefinger he tapped the brim of his hat and stove it against his underarm.

I placed my hands on his shoulders and they shriveled down. He seemed to know the answer before I asked. The words rolled off his tongue. "I dropped Miss Drew at the dock. Not more than half hour ago!" he told me.

"Then she did come on the ferry!" I said taking a step back, a sudden dread overwhelming me.

"Well…where on earth did she go?" asked Allison.

Coneras hacked yellow phlegm into an already soiled handkerchief. "I wish to god I had seen! I was back by the motor."

Allison reigned in his eyes as if she were his queen. In fact, he knew that he was in her realm—I really believe so—when she commanded him to, "Think Coneras! I want to know everything Drew Greer said!"

His eyes dropped. He hacked again. "Don't know. She and Barclay talked on the steps," he said. "Don't know after that."

"You must tell us everything!" Allison persisted.

"How long ago did you see them?" I interrupted.

"I suppose right before Gabe came," he said.

Had he misstated? A look passed between us, and he lowered his head. "What was he doing at the boat?" I asked.

"Got a box," Coneras said. "Mack came down, too, and talked to him about it. He took it. I didn't see where Gabe went."

"And he didn't come up here to the inn?" Allison asked. She looked perplexingly at me. "Why, he always stops by."

"Said he was sick. Said he ate some bad fish. I told him there ain't no bad fish in the waters 'round here, least not if they're cooked right," Coneras said. "Said he was going back to his place. Said he was going to bed."

Overhead the wind had begun to rattle through the rafters. I glanced up. So did Allison. After all, there was no curfew on wind like that. It put an edge on everyone's nerves, especially Coneras who pulled at the lapels on his shirt, and I could see that his fragility was beginning to wear thin. The process of our grilling him had exhausted him so much that I wasn't surprised when he sloped against the wall.

"All right then, Coneras," Allison finally said with a detached look. "You finish securing the boats. Then come back here. Get those wet things off! Tell Bina to give you one of Holden's robes. I don't want you going to your place with that dreadful cold. Now hurry!"

Outside the thunder broke hard, raising the anxiety that had come over all of us, and I could see it more so in Allison, whose hands were shaking, as she crossed the room to answer the phone.

"Wait! Coneras, don't go just yet," she demanded after he had thrown open the door. He closed it, keeping his fingers on the handle while he stood very still. She handed me the receiver.

"Katie, that you?"

Static.

"Justin?"

"I tried your cell phone." His baritone voice disintegrated into more static. "Dead, I think. Can you......the faxes. You'll…"

Static.

"I can't hear you!"

"Drew…" Static. "…New York."

"Speak up!"

Static. "…coastguard." Static. "She's coming to arrest someone!"

"What?"

Static. "Holden…and no…" Static. "…you get out!"

More static. Then the signal was irretrievably lost. No cell phones. No line phones. Renaurd Island was isolated from the rest of the world.

Allison stiffened. The sideward movement of her eyes directed Coneras to go on down to the dock, but he didn't move, holding his place like a man frozen in ice.

"Wait," I said anyhow. "We may need help."

Her jaw became hard-set, but what concerned me the most were her eyes—eyes that looked oddly dispassionate, so much so that I didn't expect her to say what she did, to speak at all. "You know, Kate, it is funny, isn't it? I mean, isn't it peculiar that Barclay is nowhere to be found? Now, frankly I will understand if you are upset with me, but I suppose I should have told you that he might have gone off somewhere. You know? Like an alcoholic does to sleep it off?"

But he's not an alcoholic! He might be a dangerous somnambulistic!

"Why, I should have told you," she continued, "but sometimes he sleepwalks all the way to that little shack at the north end. We've had to go and get him numerous times! But I'm sure that Ms. Greer is okay."

"No she isn't! She would have 'checked' in with me as soon as she arrived! If she went with Barclay, it was against her will." I said, wavering. And then I thought, steady your hands! Don't knee jerk! Think! Drew's life might depend on it! "Allison, I'm getting a jacket! I'm going for her!"

She pointed to the hall closet. "My dear girl, you are over reacting, but I'll go with you. Get mine, too," she said.

"I know that Detective McCreary will try to find a way over here," I said over my shoulder to Coneras. "Wait for him at the dock! Tell him we've gone to Gabe's for help!"

He nodded with a heavy sigh.

When I returned, Allison said, "Oh I do wish Holden were here right now, Kate. He'd know exactly what to do! In fact, I half expected him to show up today. I called that nice young secretary of his. She said he wasn't due back in Washington until Monday. Why the scoundrel! I do wonder where he has gone! Do you suppose he has a woman stashed in one of those filing cabinets of his?"

I didn't answer. I thought only of Drew and whether she would survive Barclay's captivity, if indeed she had gone off with him while he was in his demented state. In a strange unobtrusive way, the inn itself seemed deathly disturbed, fragmented, too, like my thoughts, and I felt sick, as if I were about to eat something that once had disagreed with me and I had been forewarned not to do it again. I knew that I needed to be careful that I didn't plunge into anything I couldn't handle. Yet, inside I was driven like the force of a hurricane to find my friend.

Coneras pulled at his ear as we went onto the porch. "Hell, Judge, if you're thinking about taking the trails...why soon they're gonna be under water! Sure as anything you'll drown! Why don't I hug the coast with the trawler? Take the boardwalk from the beach. You can reach my place and go on to Gabe's from there!"

"That's much too risky," Allison answered. "They'll be ten footers out on the Sound, and you could easily scuttle the boat. I've traveled through that marsh a hundred times. Why I could swim every inch of this island with my eyes closed if I had to. We'll take the path!"

We went onto the porch. For the first time I was startled by the wind and rain swatting the boughs of trees, the thunder slow and tinny like the tumbling of pins at a bowling alley. I wanted to get going. But before I started down the steps, Coneras maneuvered in front of me and broke for the path to the canal. I turned right. My strides on the stone walk around the side and to the back of the inn were long. Then Allison set the pace. It was her watch now. I suspected she wanted it that way, and I was surprised how quickly I relinquished control. This was the real nickel and dime tour. I was following a Thomason on Thomason territory. Instantly, my slacks and shoes were soaked, and I trembled not from damp clothes but from a slow, squeezing fear while imagining what could have happened to Drew.

"Barclay has her, doesn't he?" I asked.

Allison slowed. "I don't know!" she answered, her voice trailing off into the wind.

"Has he threatened or hurt anyone before?" I yelled. "Has he? Have you told me everything?"

She stopped, turned and gathered her collar around her neck. She didn't answer. I had never meant to raise my voice to her, and out of loyalty never wanted to because I respected her so much. I took her arms. "Damn it! This may be Drew's life that we're gambling with! Answer me Allison! What are you afraid of?"

She was frowning, but then the frown unfolded like an accordion. "Last year in one of his 'states', Barclay held Bina at gunpoint. I got there a few minutes after it happened. Oh, she was all right, mind you. But a couple of months ago he drugged me and took me in a wheelbarrow to the shack! Holden found him asleep beside me. I tell you, he has never *really* harmed anyone!"

It would have been futile to have told her how angry I was that she had sprung this on me. "Mmm hmm. And you don't know that for sure!" I said with dread. "Two percent of somnambulistics turn violent! He might have killed Bina or you! He might have killed those women at Dragon's Point!"

She staggered. "It's absurd! I tell you that he wouldn't! He takes Clinasopane. It reduces deep sleep where most of the violence occurs! I'm telling you that he won't harm Ms. Greer!"

So he was on medication. So she did know about somnambulism all along! "Let's keep going," I said. "I don't want to take that chance. Do you?"

"I'm warning you, Kate, you must not interfere with things that don't concern you!" she said, her voice hardily threatening. I had heard the intimidating tone before; my father's voice could bring me to my knees. I had always been aware of the hierarchy of parent-child, of doctor-patient, of man-woman, and yet I had unmistakably fought against authority all my life. Odd that I should think so strongly about it when Allison stopped again, turned and blocked the path, her hands on her hips, her legs as if she were riding the statue of a great stone horse. "And something else. While you were talking with Justin, you were noticeably upset! Tell me what else you know, or think you know about my family!"

The rain came hard again. Meanwhile, tiny pieces of debris boomeranged in the wind while brackish water lapped the sides of the planks. Rancid muck seemed to boil around hidden predators, snakes and gators who were waiting for us to pass so that they could crawl upon the wooden planks to escape slow flooding. I told her that I wanted her to know everything, but there wasn't time. "We'll talk as we go!"

She saw the gravity of the weather. We pressed forward. "All right then," she agreed. "But spare nothing! Do you have evidence that Barclay killed Renty?"

"I think that he may have been coming to my cottage to tell me something crucial," I said. "And I suppose you knew that Coneras took both Renty and Barclay to the mainland and Barclay didn't return here the night that Renty was killed!"

"Coneras told you that!"

"Justin's an excellent detective," I said without further explanation.

The water crept over our toes, but we paid little attention and sloshed along swiftly, the planks becoming more and more obscure, the rain running in rivulets down every crease in my face, but my instinct told me that we had been on the trail for quite awhile and should be at least as far as Coneras's cottage.

"There's something else bothering you, isn't there Kate?" she said, the notes of her voice breaking.

"Mmm hmm. I believe that it's also possible that Barclay is illegally using human growth hormone at Renaurd Inn," I said.

Allison's hands were taut, and then she slipped them into her pockets. "Nonsense! Wouldn't I know?"

I thought about the shots of the so-called 'B-12' that the guests had been receiving. "Millions of dollars worth of HGH is being smuggled from South America to the states," I told her. "Much of it is funneled through the Bahamas. In some places women will pay as much as a thousand dollars per month for these anti-aging shots. Men will, too. And the FBI has been investigating a connection to prostitution and perhaps the sale of body parts. Drew was coming here today to make an arrest!"

"Not because of a few shots!"

"Of course not!" I said. "That's only part of it! Should I suspect that you already know that?"

She paused at a bend in the trail and took notice of the boards that weren't under water by emptying her shoes. She looked distraught, as if she had resolved to take some sort of action, but then suddenly her eyes had the oblivious stare of a blind man. Without warning the rain stopped. I could only hope that the weather had turned northeast. The sudden stillness brought swarms of no seeums. Mosquitoes droned, too, but we took no notice of them and pressed forward.

"Ah Kate, I suppose that you believe that all evil has its root in power and money, my friend," she said with passion. "But there is such a thing as loyalty to one's family heritage now isn't there…"

It seemed a bizarre statement, as if she were speaking about a premonition that possibly could come to fruition, or one that needed to be said out loud. I would like to have told her 'no, I didn't think that about *all* evil, but instead I said, "It's brought down the best of us, hasn't it? Right now, Allison, my concern is for Drew!"

A look of quiet resignation swept across her face. She took the lead again. As if on cue, the rain came relentlessly, foraging the trail and the underbrush until I could no longer discern between them. My sinuses were so clogged that I could hardly breathe, and I knew that we were no doubt in the middle of a vicious storm that was barreling like a train across the island. Just when I was thinking that we might be in real trouble, I saw the top of a roof, and instantly, my mind became stranded in its safety.

"We'll have to wait it out there!" Allison stammered, as if against her will. "It's far too dangerous to go on to Gabe's."

We struggled the rest of the way through water-covered St. Augustine grass, water that lapped at the skirting around the building, and when we climbed the steps and reached the porch and I looked back, I had a peculiar sensation in my throat, as if someone were tightening a noose around it. I gulped. Across the first step, a four foot gator swam by with a small mammal in its jaws, its neck hanging like the snapped wishbone of a Thanksgiving turkey. We turned and went inside Allendro Coneras's cottage.

CHAPTER 31

Inside the cottage, we found the air cool, the dampness mopping around us like the ragged hem of an old monk in a Tibetan monastery, and I was sure that she, too, had the same feeling of isolation, of remoteness, as if no one else had been present for years. We took off our shoes, socks and jackets, but could do nothing much about the rest of our soaked clothing.

Allison stood perfectly still in the middle of the room, her eyes sweeping the mound of unread newspapers and unopened mail. I stepped to the side of her, walked forward and thought I heard something. At once I opened the door to the bedroom and was met with the sourness of mildew. Through the seaward window I could hear water lashing the fence behind the cabin, and I expected it to creep through the floorboards at any time. It's why these island houses are buttressed high on tabby stilts; yet, David's cottage—our cottage wasn't, and I wondered if the marsh had flooded the screened in porch there that was lower than the rest of the rooms.

When I returned to the living room, spider webs festooning the door-jamb caught my face, and I swept them away. Allison was giving serious attention to the paintings that I had seen on my first visit, and with an irreverent subtleness, she ran her fingers over the brush strokes as if she were reading brail.

"I understand that Jennifer came here a lot," I said. "That she went to Gabe's too?"

"Why yes, she loved Coneras…she loved them both, I suppose."

I took one of the paintings from the wall. The body was that of a vivacious young woman, one whose nostril cavities were grotesquely exaggerated and dripping with blood. I cringed. "It harbors such horror," I said.

Allison laughed. "Why it's nothing! Nothing at all. Meant to be embellished only in your mind the way you do without ever actually eating photographs of gourmet food in a good cookbook!"

The shadow from the frame slit like a razor through the table light, and I returned the painting to the wall. "But why would Jennifer have painted these?" I asked.

Allison swung around, her dark eyes bright with amusement, her lips bending into a broad smile. She coughed. "Why I have no idea! I never knew her to paint anything but landscapes! Like the ones in the study at Renaurd Inn!"

It seemed to me that she was in denial. Denial was one of the vertebras that held together the human psyche, kept us from collapsing into a pile of worthless flesh in times of stress, I had long ago learned. I had seen people go into near hysteria when a murderer or rapist who lived down the street and wore the respectability suit of society got arrested. *Not my neighbor! Why he was so nice!* I imagined that Allison Thomason was like the rest of us. Denial and truth? Weren't they one in the same? No sense in committing to an argument I wouldn't win, so I simply didn't say anything else.

She was still studying the pictures when, in spite of the weather and to her dismay, I insisted that I should go on to Gabe's, and with an obligatory nod she agreed to remain in case Justin showed up. Minutes later I was near the door when the old beagle shot out from behind the sofa, disappeared and returned immediately with his paws a bright red. He turned and licked the floor behind him, wagging his tail before he sprawled on his belly. At first I didn't know what to make of it.

But when you see blood that you don't expect, there is at once a dullness in your thinking, and in that few seconds that you must acknowledge what you suspect, you feel your spine tingle while legs and arms become incapacitated, and out of nowhere comes an adrenaline rush that floods your pelvis and puts your reflexes into overdrive.

In an instant I jumped over the dog and sprinted down the hall. Stepping slowly through the kitchen, I saw nothing but clutter. I made no attempt to look in cupboards or a small utility closet. No attempt to examine the cups and saucers on the counter or look carefully at the blood soaked wad in the sink. Instead, I peered through a partially propped-open screen door that led to an enclosed back porch and a splintered wooden floor. It took a minute for my nose to register that the blood, which was dripping from the bottom of a large metal storage cabinet, was already presenting an odor that rose up like freshly cut limburger cheese.

"Oh god, Allison, come here!" I heard myself yell from a cavern of melancholy, a place where I had explored often before but thought now to be inescapable! Desperately my feet stumbled and froze at the same time. Was it Drew? It was odd, but I don't remember at what moment my senses returned so acutely that I propelled my body over the blood at such a sharp angle that I lost my balance, only to steady myself by splaying my fingers against the door. I gritted my teeth and hesitated. I needed to find the will to slide my right hand downward and to wrench the L shaped handle of the gray metal. Even today I have no memory of having done so, and my only recollection is of the door springing at me like the fangs of a rattlesnake.

It would not have been irrational for me to lift Tapest from the hook—like taking from the limb of a live oak the pathetic, naked body of a wild animal left to bleed in the cold, its tongue the last ember in a gaping pit that reaches from ear to ear so that it is practically decapitated. And even after her final breath, it appeared that Tapest had suffered, for the conjunctiva of her eyes, although dry and marble-like, didn't have the usual gray of someone who had long been dead. I stepped back and desperately tried to stay in one place so as not to contaminate any more of the crime scene.

Then I heard the slap of Allison's bare feet as she crossed the linoleum. Without a word she came onto the porch, stared dispassionately at Tapest and then firmly propelled me back into the kitchen.

"You probably wiped out a half dozen prints, Kate," she said, emotion having shriveled her voice.

My lips quivered. "I suppose you think that I shouldn't have looked inside! But I had to see! I had to know! I had to know if it was Drew!"

Allison stared hard at me, as if she had seen *into and then beyond* me and then had seen nothing. It was such a fixed look, that to my surprise, I spontaneously swiped my hand a couple of inches from her face to get her attention, but she had scarcely noticed. We returned to the living room, and she slumped in the chair next to the front door as if for hours she had worn a sign on her body that said, 'vacancy', with eyes that were colorless, empty, and cold, a contradiction between daydreaming and death.

"Oh! How I'd like to talk to that Barclay Renaurd right now," she finally said with a light voice—she even half smiled—as if Tapest were of no consequence. "Why, you see, he trusts me. I'm not the least afraid of him. And there's something you ought to know. He didn't kill anybody! I *know* he didn't!" she said with more authority. She crossed her heart. "No matter what happens, you'll remember that, won't you? I've been given many honors in my career. As a judge, I can do what I damn well have to in order to protect my family. You'll remember that, too, won't you, Kate?"

At that moment I knew that she would do everything in her power to cop a sanity plea for Barclay…that she had the resolve of someone who could not be persuaded to think otherwise. Yet, why did I feel that there seemed to rise from each of her breaths an indefinable suffering and a consciousness of guilt that can assimilate into an act of contrition to save one's own soul while hoping to save another's? But she couldn't walk on water. Neither could I. I could not help her. She began to stiffen from the cold…and maybe her nerves. I got a blanket from the bedroom and covered her, her fingers drawing two corners of it around her neck, where I had the feeling that if it had been a hangman's noose, Judge Allison Thomason wouldn't have given a damn.

It had occurred to me that the wind had died down and it had stopped raining. "You rest. I'll bring Gabe back here, Allison. We'll decide what to do then," I said as I slipped on my shoes. "Promise me that you won't go back into the room where Tapest is?"

I leaned over and patted the top of her head. Surprising me, her arms drew a hug, enveloping me in a sense of urgency, and I thought that she would never let go. But she yanked free and buried herself again under the blanket, tightening her lips and focusing on the paintings once again, as if they were a barrier between us, like those yellow barricades that warn 'no trespassing,' at a construction sight. "I've always been fond of you, Kate. You've been a good friend," she said. "I'm sorry about all this."

"It has little to do with you, Allison," I said reassuring her. "Now don't fret! Gabe will help us!"

She never responded to my 'goodbye'. Outside my feet and ankles were instantly alert to the half-foot of water around them. As I sloshed along the path to Gabe's cottage, I felt great compassion because I had the strong premonition that the Renaurd family was about to be rocked with scandal. Little did I know how much!

CHAPTER 32

Although it was no longer true of most places in the United States, locked doors on Renaurd Island were still unheard of. I knocked on Gabe's door. There was no answer, and thinking that he might be more ill than his grandfather had suggested, I slipped quietly into the interior. The air was heavy with dampness, and except for wind and rain, brought the same chill as being outside. I didn't hesitate but headed to the bedroom. The door was ajar, and I could see that a light from a floor lamp penetrated the room, so I went in and found Gabe lying on his side clad in deep blue briefs and a sleeveless tee. His face glistened with perspiration. When I moved closer, I saw that he had a somewhat haggard look, his unshaved cheeks, chin and upper neck presenting the appearance of someone who had been on a two day binge. Suddenly, his eyes opened and the darkness in them struck with the cunningness of a fox.

"I knew you would come," he said in a detached tone.

He beckoned to me. I didn't move. He got up, slipped on his jeans and shirt and bolted toward me. Instinctively, I put my hands in front of my face, a warning that caused him to step back. He looked startled.

I sucked in my breath. "Tapest! She's been murdered!"

"You came alone, then..." he asked, as if he already knew the answer.

His statement caused me some uneasiness. Still, I wasn't afraid of him in the conventional sense, but I was surprised that my physical abilities were trailing behind my mental so that I finally collapsed into a nearby spindle rocker, my knees and hand shaking. "I left Allison at your grand-father's," I said. "And during his sleepwalking Barclay may have taken Drew to that shack near here!"

Pulling me up into his arms, he whispered, "You're soaking wet! Now try to calm yourself! I'll take care of everything!" His fingers brushed my Beretta through my suit jacket but he said nothing.

"Don't you have a short-wave radio?" I asked. "By now Justin McCreary should be on the island! We've got to call the inn!"

To my surprise his arms dropped away, and with his back to me, he went to the top drawer of a nightstand and pulled out a pack of cigarettes. He turned, staring wide eyed into the flame of a match. "Why no, I don't have a shortwave. But let me bring Allison here," he said, his words exhaling with a drag, "where she'll be safe."

I began to pace. "Mmm hmm. Yes, but won't you hurry? I don't like her being alone."

He slid the cigarette to the edge of the nightstand, took my arm and led me to the bed, looking down on me while his hands coaxed my shoulders flat upon an old quilt. He removed my shoes. "I always seem to be helping you out of wet things, don't I?" he asked. He covered me with a plaid throw. "I'll go now…I won't be long."

As he walked away, for some unexplained reason I had nothing but fear in my mind. Once more he came back and stood very rigidly beside the bed. He picked up the cigarette and stuck it between his lips. The ashes hung for a moment and then tumbled down the front of his chest as if they had come from a great volcano. Slowly he shook his head and sighed. "For Christ's sake, you have no idea…do you?" He gave a little smirk. "Not a fucking clue!"

My heart pounded with terror as the tip of his forefinger crawled across my forehead, along the side of my temple, over my cheek to my nose and then down my chin to the nape of my neck, his eyes pulling at mine like a suction cup. With the cigarette still hanging from his lips, he slowly kneaded his palms upon my breasts. Sensing the whip of his strength, I did not move, afraid that if I did, he might begin a passage of no return, that there would be no way to fight him off. I muffled a gasp and gently pressed my hands against his chest. I waited, my ears adjusting to the sound of his labored breathing. His face came close to mine, but then he took two steps back and on the nightstand drummed the cigarette to a stub with his thumb, his knuckles finally scraping it onto the floor. Then as if bowing to an impulse, he strode across the room again—away from me—and without looking back said metallically, "I won't be long."

The closing of the front door was a welcomed sound. I sat up, trying not to tremble. I assumed that Gabe was thoroughly aware that the darkness would soon be settling, even perhaps before he reached Allison, but then with mixed feelings I worried that he might not return and I would be left alone to search for Drew. Nervously I went into the bathroom and pulled a ceiling chain, the bulb flooding yellow streaks of light across the dark paneling. One of those sanitizers had changed the toilet water to blue. I slipped off my suit jacket and unbuttoned the second and third buttons of my white cotton blouse, bent over the antique galvanized sink, and with my cupped hands, vaulted water from the basin to my cheeks and forehead. Nearby was an empty towel rack. By the shower, a door to a recessed wall cupboard was partially open. I suspected towels were there. I was wrong.

When I scanned the three shelves inside, I was confused; yet, I shouldn't have been. '*Why no, I don't have a shortwave!*' Gabe had told me. My pulse raced. The scene was surreal. I imagined myself sprinting on top of the water at breakneck speed to get help at the inn. I imagined Justin McCreary arriving at any time. I imagined Drew standing over me and smiling. It was after all of this 'imagining' that I saw several wigs. Gray ones. Black and brown, too. Long ones. Curly ones. Separately they were perched on Styrofoam heads, each leaving me with the caricature of a phantom face that could be sculpted from the many jars of clay and paint stacked on the bottom two shelves. It wasn't unusual to find evidence where you would least expect it. What was mind wrenching was to find that it belonged to someone whom you had trusted.

It was with that thought that I attempted to work the radio, but I received nothing more than garbled chatter. I re-buttoned my blouse, put on my jacket and went into the living room. With some reservation I threw open the door and huddled against the doorjamb while watching the rain intermittently sheet through the bright beam from a pole light the way the spray does when you go through a carwash. Instantly, the wind ratcheted up my instincts. My immediate concern now was for Allison, but darkness had fallen, so I decided to stay put and hope that Justin would arrive with the authorities. I shut the door, and my eyes quickly fixed on the pull-down attic door that Tapest had mentioned a few weeks before. It took all the muscles in my arms to unfold the stairs.

While clinging to railings, I ascended the narrow steps, got astride a small landing and was immediately blasted by a musty, down-drag of cool air. The attic was dark. Soon my eyes adjusted to thin splits in the roofing that allowed outdoor light to hang from the sloping rafters. It was then that I swung my leg over a joist, and my knee collapsed dead center onto a flashlight wedged between two boards that crossed a panel of insulation. I retrieved it and flipped the switch. A quick search revealed that there was no other light source in the attic.

From a hole in the roof, water spurted like a clipped artery, pooling beside two frameless pictures, which were about five feet away and to my right. Immediately to the left of those there must have been ten more, the silhouettes of others too far away to discern. At once I was compelled to stare, convinced that I had stumbled upon something revealing…something horrifying. Realizing that there wasn't much time, I scooted across a six-by-eight piece of plywood, my buttocks soaking up the moisture, my palms pummeling through dust webs that seemed to have imprisoned the remaining portraits.

My next conscious thought was one of startled recognition! It was like traversing an unfamiliar curve before passing down a long, steep hill into a known landscape. I hoisted myself across another four-by-four and braced my knees against the wall for balance. There in front of me was a canvass of Dragon's Point! It kept tumbling over and over in my mind, and it was only when I maneuvered the light to fall upon the likeness of Jennifer Renaurd ensconced within its colors, that I lost my breath! Every feature of her face was in disorder and exaggerated gray, the way someone might be if her corpse had lain under a shroud too long before burial.

I scanned more canvasses, the terror of the other victims of Dragon's Point there, too, and I could only think that finally forensics would be able to match faces to bones—faces painted by an artist who at his pleasure had controlled the tortured final moments of these women, portraying them in the worse possible perversion while they gave up their souls in the night houses of the Southeast. One by one, I scrutinized them—pausing as if I were an eager art critic in a gallery. And then to my left and framed between the castaway spindles of an old table, I saw a thing so grotesque that it was all that I could do to stifle a cry. Beneath the creaking rafters, the light had waned, and I strained to understand the grim self-portrait of a man whom I had come to trust, my eyes extracting the horror of his self-mutilation, as if the bad in his mind had somehow come to fruition upon the canvas. I put my head in my hands and fell back, and with a dull thud smacked my elbow against a sidewall joist. It seemed to jolt my mind and without any caution and at breakneck speed, I scraped across the floor boards and clattered down the rungs of the stairs onto my knees.

There in the dull half-light of the room, Gabe's presence reigned terror over me. He saw it, I was sure, and with a heavy sigh grasped my wrists and yanked me up. I dropped the flashlight. Then he let go and with an unusual coarseness to his voice said, "Well, Kate, I've come to a fork in the road. Which one should I take?"

"At the moment a lose literary allusion to Frost doesn't become you," I said. I looked behind him. The door was wide open, the air hammering in as if it were from one of those loud industrial fans, and I was tempted to take my chances with the weather, but Gabe moved quickly to close the door. As if I were in a half-conscious state—when thought and fear get all mixed up and provide a barrier to rational action—I closed my eyes, swept toward him anyhow, the movement of my own feet finally giving me renewed strength and a clear mind.

"Just stay put," he said.

"What have you done with Allison?" I asked, thinking the worst might have happened in the short time Gabe had been with her.

"I told her I hadn't seen you."

"Mmm hmm. Why…would you do that?" I said slowly, while moving away from him.

He pointed both arms toward the attic. "I suppose that you think that they are pretty gruesome paintings?"

Under my jacket my fingers climbed to my Beretta. Would I find out where Drew was if I pulled it? It was then that I believed that Gabe didn't know that I was armed. I lowered my hand. "Jennifer didn't paint them, did she?"

"Only the landscapes. Can't you tell?" he asked as he caught the door with his foot. It slammed hard. "She had a wonderful sense of color. Extraordinary depth! But she never quite mastered people's faces." He looked over at me. "You know, like some writers write fiction? Other nonfiction? Some chefs are best at French cooking? Italian? Take you, for instance; you're not a common cop, are you?"

He shuffled into the shadow of an old cupboard. I could barely see his face, but it no longer mattered. All at once he was repulsive to me, someone who had committed hideous and unforgivable crimes, and I wondered how I could have been so deceived by the artificiality of his boyish playfulness and perceived sensibility, when instead, he was more like a rough-hewn laborer disguised in a tuxedo!

I had to ask…

"Except for Jennifer, the women in the other portraits were prostitutes then," I said, "warehoused out of the Bahamas?"

He seemed amused. A subtle arrogance bent his lips. "One could argue that they were simply whores."

"Rid the world of vermin, is that it?"

"Heaven's no!" he said. "Although they frolicked through a decadent life, I must admit that they provided a morally disgusting service. And a higher power than me saved their souls from dishonor!"

I swallowed hard. Giving in to an impulse, I asked, "Would you care to explain the items in your bathroom closet?"

"Boy, you were busy while I was gone," he said, dragging his hand to his forehead. "It's why I'm so damn attracted to you, Kate Guesswine. It's your nature to be ice and fire! An indomitable spirit! Ah, but I suspect you've already figured out what you want to know, haven't you?"

"Not all of it," I said coolly. "The disguises explain in part why we had two different profiles on you. A psychic put you older. An FBI profiler put you younger. Because that's the way you dressed, isn't it? With wigs? Blue or brown contact lenses?"

"What I learned off Broadway in New York about bent old gentlemen and the demeanor of young studs could win me a Toni, my dear!"

New York. That's why Drew had gone there. That's what Justin was going to tell me!

"I'm not your *dear*," I snapped.

His dark eyes teemed with animation, "Oh but you will be," he said quickly. "You'll go with me willingly just like the others!"

He spoke with such raw assurance that I moved back. "Are you going to drug me, too? Sacrifice me on that altar near the shack?"

He shook his head. "I won't need to do that," he said with conviction.

I was losing my confidence. I wanted to get out of there. "Tell me what you've done with Drew Greer!"

"She's no longer your concern," he replied with a venomous tongue. Then a strange expression consumed his face.

Did he mean that she was dead? I was barely able to breathe. If he had lost his mind, if he had planned this all along, then there would be no reasoning with him. It was as if I were in the middle of *his* nightmare, and my only power of escaping was under my jacket. Without hesitation, I yanked my Beretta from its holster. It was warm from body heat. I pointed it at his chest. It took both hands to hold it steady.

Startled, he stepped back and folded his arms. His face went pale, and for the moment as I read him his rights, he had no expression. He shrugged and then stood quietly. My fingers trembled. I lowered the gun slightly.

"Well? Now what?" he asked, his tone almost cheerful, as if he had done nothing wrong.

I made a gesture for him to sit down, but he didn't, and with some uncertainty my eyes trailed about the room as I tried to figure out what to do next. It was a matter of time before Justin would bring help. And within hours, just like Coneras' place, Gabe's cottage would be part of a crime scene, too. There would be detectives and forensics personnel jostling to secure boxes and boxes of evidence. Sofa and chairs would be ripped apart. Dry wall demolished. Ceiling tiles removed. The attic itself would take on a bizarre life of its own, and the portrait of each victim would be treated like an exhumed grave.

Outside, after the water had receded, detectives would gouge the surrounding property in search of victims' belongings. Dragon's Point, too, would be dragged again for bones that might still be sleeping in the shifting sands. The media would descend, and because of the increased foot traffic across the wooden paths of Renaurd Island, the creatures of the marshes—both the day and night inhabitants, would themselves become the voyeurs of unwanted intruders.

"I prefer that you sit down," I said.

His cold eyes never left mine. "You must despise me!" he said.

I didn't answer him, my opinion of him no longer important. But in a way, I suppose I had a perverse need to find closure. In my mind I wrote out a list of questions. Yet, fear of what he had done to Drew kept me still. At least for the time being. Instead, I said, "Jennifer Thomason wasn't a prostitute. So why…"

"With her artistic talent, she wanted to study in Paris. But it wasn't going to happen. She drank too much and used bad judgment." He patted his stomach.

I stared. "Self righteous son-of-a-bitch! Don't tell me it was because you were the father?"

He pointed his finger. "You're right on it, aren't you?"

"No, it adds up, that's all," I said. "Renty told me that Jennifer was like a leech when it came to you! She'd sneak away from her room at night. He'd have to drag her in a drunken stupor from your cottage the next morning to the inn before Allison and the Renaurds awakened."

"You know what? The sad part is that she couldn't help it!" he said. "Creative people have a missing gene, don't they? But they have a kind of delectable madness so that their genius can punch through all the damn social shit."

I scowled. "An imaginary, egotistical gene," I said. "Should I try to understand you?"

He clenched his fists. "*Understand me?* Now that does not become you! Don't fucking toy with me!"

I didn't reply, and I knew that my silence probably enraged him even more. Yet, his reaction was no longer of concern to me, and suddenly, I was overwhelmed with contempt for this man who had kissed me more than once, and under the pretense of affection had laid his hands upon my skin.

And then he became more subdued, his grave expression bending into a half-smile. "You should know that after Jennifer learned about the baby, she went to Allison," he explained. "Isn't she one damn tough lady? Do you know, she was going to bring statutory charges?"

"So you raped Jennifer?"

"Of course not, but the bookmakers wouldn't have taken the odds," he said. "She was, after all, underage. You know what that means in South Carolina. I'd been buried with some lowlife in one of those medium security prisons for most of my youth."

"Then she consented…"

"Don't they all at first?" He folded his arms, grinned and then added, "She begged me to paint her nude. I was startled at how her beauty leaped from my brushes. Like a chrysalis unfolding. So during our break, you know what? She came on to me. Like nothing I'd ever experienced. For over an hour. No complaints then, mind you. One minute I was a lover. Two months later I was a rapist. Her word against mine, she told me. Do you know, it would have destroyed my grandfather?"

I steadied my hands. "What about Renty? Why was he coming to my cottage?"

"I suspect you tweaked his conscious when you were chatting with him in the kitchen that day and he was about to tell you all he knew—or thought he did. Stacks picked me up in his boat. He dropped me off before the ferry arrived, and I got my car and followed Renty out to your place."

"And Barclay?"

"How in the hell would I know? He hangs out near Shelter Cove. That gentlemen's club."

"Then I cut Renty off before he turned onto your lane," Gabe continued. "I didn't mean to cause his car to go down into the marsh. I tried to persuade him that he was putting himself and you in great danger!"

"After you killed him, you looked in my window, didn't you?"

"Call it an adolescent moment of curiosity," he drawled defiantly. "I wanted to see who you were with. But Renty was very much alive when I left him standing down by that old smokehouse of yours."

"I suppose that you didn't use the dingy as a diversion then? So that we would think that you escaped into the marsh?"

"You're hunting the wrong fox in the chicken coop, Kate. And that's all I'm obligated to tell you!"

I was gripping the Beretta so tightly that sweat began to drip from between my fingers. "I don't believe you," I said. "And I suppose you didn't kill Elizabeth Tarteton's aunt either?"

"I have something for you," he said, pointing to a small desk in the corner. "May I?"

I relaxed my fingers and with the gun motioned for him to continue. I followed a couple of feet away, and rammed the nozzle into his side as he opened a small drawer.

"So that's what happened to the journal!" I said, knowing that I had mistakenly believed that Sara Baird had 'borrowed' it for her article and then was afraid to return it. I really did owe her an apology.

Gabe stuck his hands in his pocket. He seldom looked anywhere but at me. "Okay. The truth is that when Elizabeth was going to school in New York, she didn't give a damn about anybody except me," he said with an unusual spring in his voice. "Didn't she have a sense of freedom in knowing that? It's the power a woman has over a man. Makes her dig up all that love. Plant it in his soul so that nothing will ever grow again but what she planted in him in the first place."

"Oh, but you must have cared for her!"

"I suppose a little love means as much as a lot when you've never had any at all," he said. "Responsible. That's what I finally felt. After I returned to Renaurd Island, I got involved with Phoebe Longa's operation. She gave Elizabeth a job."

"So you're the infamous *Trainer*?" I noted with surprise. "But oh, Gabe! Why *did* you have to kill her? Why *did you have to kill anyone*?" I was caught in a sense of both pity for myself and relief that I had spoken with such fervor. It was like expelling all the annoyances in my brain.

He frowned. "Protect their family at all costs! That's what the Renaurds always said. Anyhow, she shacked up with Holden for a while. The old bastard likes them fast and temporary," he explained. "No drags. Didn't she put the screws to him in the end? Her last entry in that journal was very incriminating. She had dates and times."

"So Holden was at Tybee! Mrs. Trample-St. Synge did see him!"

"That's right! But I detest victimization, don't you? Poor parentless girl. Traumatic childhood! Taken advantage of. She would have been on all of the talk shows with her revenge! Imagine Elizabeth's satisfaction in bringing down a US senator? He needed my help."

Then did Holden know about Elizabeth's death? I kept my composure. "So it was a matter of time before Dahlia Tarteton identified him," I said. "You were upstairs when Sara Baird and I arrived in Beaufort, weren't you?"

"That's right," he said. "After you left? I got the journal and was about to get the hell out of there. But didn't that meddling reporter come back? The bitch hung around, so I split."

Sara Baird returned to look at that journal after all! Screw the apology!

"And you frightened Mrs. Tarteton so badly that she wouldn't talk to police officers when they came later!"

"You *are* a good attorney general!"

"That doesn't take a rocket scientist, Gabe," I said. "Tell me…when I found Mrs. Tarteton's body…"

He interrupted, "Lady luck was with you that day, Kate!"

"Or you would have slit my throat like the others?"

I thought it peculiar that his eyes didn't even show a sliver of remorse, the look that often comes about during a long interrogation in which one avoids admitting guilt but feels guilty. But he had no intention of revealing any details. No, I would have to dig them out, the way someone digs at an ingrown toenail. Suddenly he smiled.

"To me those women were commodities," he said. "After Phoebe trained them, I arranged for them to move to the states. I simply provided the goods when they were needed. Stacks Sandover got them jobs."

"Goods? I don't understand."

No answer.

"So each time it was an easy theatrical makeover?" I asked. "To protect your anonymity, you crawled into your get-ups and lured those poor women to a motel and drugged them?"

His eyes brightened with satisfaction. "Rather fun to think that I could pull it off. In fact, Justin McCreary himself told me that his investigation was leading to more than one killer!"

My knees were shaking, but I didn't want him to know. As if my mind were a rope, I willed them tightly together. Although I was afraid that there might be too many more surprises, I decided to probe further, no matter how bizarre. "You switched the oils when I had my massage?"

"Actually, that didn't seem to chase you away from Renaurd Island, did it?"

I paused and then stepped closer. "The teeth of the victims were missing," I said.

"You know the answer to that…"

"I suppose I do. Even prostitutes go to the dentist. Leave records."

"That's right."

"That doesn't account for the striations on the bones."

He began to move toward me. I waved my gun. He stopped. "The sharks and other fish near Dragon's Point cleaned the bones," he said. "No tissue. Harder to identify."

"No, there's something else you're not telling me," I said. "During one of our bad storms, Elizabeth broke free of whatever you had tethered her to. She washed up on the shore. She was still pretty intact. But organs were missing from her body. Dr. Bree Packer suggested that her death might have been part of a ritual. What do you know about that?"

He guffawed deliriously. It was then that I felt a wrenching jab between my shoulder blades. Paralyzed, I sank to my knees, rolled and sprawled onto the floor, my arms and legs splayed as if I were making angels in a snow drift. The pain seared my neck and rib cage. I had no sense of where I was until I realized that I wasn't holding my Beretta. Then for a long time I lay perfectly still, footsteps all around me making the floor boards vibrate under my cheek. In agony I raised my head and was astonished to see that my Beretta had tumbled under the footstool and that nobody had retrieved it. My eyes must have warned Gabe—at least I thought so—for he dragged me to my feet so that we were both facing Stacks Sandover who was holding a rare metal sawed-off shotgun with a silver black handle, known among law enforcement as a Snake Charmer. There was some rust on it, too, and I hoped that it didn't have some quirk in it that might cause it to fire the 410 gage six-shot which could tear my lungs out.

"You better let me kill this bitch!" Stacks said.

"I'll handle this!" Gabe said. He had little expression on his face, but his eyes seemed to say that he was not going to hurt me. "Did you drug Drew Greer?"

"Didn't take much!" Stacks said.

I was terrified. "Please don't hurt her!"

That's when Gabe cupped his hands over mine. Then he said to Stacks, "Leave the agent alone. I'll take care of her. You get the boat ready. There won't be time to do the *other*."

Stacks knitted his brows. "Not even the kidneys and liver? We can get seventy-five thou' for 'em."

I gasped. So that was it. They were body brokers. They brought prostitutes from Phoebe Longa's to work throughout the Southeast. When they needed kidneys, hearts, eyes or whatever, they harvested the organs from these disenfranchised women. It was about to get uglier, I thought. Seldom did I think of myself as a victim, but now the impulse to go down fighting was so strong that after a brief struggle, Gabe's powerful biceps twisting my arms to my back was his only statement to me. I couldn't move.

"Damn it, Stacks, you'll do just what I tell you!" he ordered. "That load of human growth hormone that my grandfather brought over today? We'll need to run it up to the coast before we head south. That will be the last of those big bucks. Now get your ass moving! I'll be there in ten minutes."

Stacks drew his belt tighter. "Can't wait, huh? You want some of her booty right now, heh? Well, then I gotta right to fuck the other one."

My stomach turned over. "No! She's ill. She's got aids, I tell you!"

Gabe's eyes opened widely. "Get the supplies on board like I told you! Leave the gun! And don't touch the agent! That's an order!"

"We'll see about that!" Stacks Sandover said, his voice hanging like the screech of an animal being eaten alive as he slammed the door.

"Punishment or proposition, Kate?" Gabe whispered into my ear.

I said nothing.

"Your organs would bring a tremendous price," he continued, "but frankly I don't want anyone to destroy that beautiful body. Even being near you right now makes me crazy. It has since day one!"

The grip of his left hand tightened on my wrist. I winced and let out a moan. He relaxed his fingers, letting go because he sensed that I had no strength left. I turned around. Our faces were no more than a few inches apart. "Behave yourself now," he cautioned. His forefinger outlined my upper lip.

"Proposition?" I asked. "What do you mean?"

"You'll come willingly with me. And I'll spare Drew Greer's life," he said. "I'll leave her tied up. She'll be found. Stacks' boat can have you and me in Cuba by early tomorrow. I've got cousins and an uncle. He's loyal to Castro, but who gives a damn? There won't be a problem with our being there. I have lots of money. Money will buy us an incredible life there! You'll live like a queen! My queen!"

I took a deep breath. Slowly I moved back a few inches, wondering what to do, what to say next, my body shivering as if I had been caught in a thirty below wind chill. "How do I know that you'll keep your word?" I asked.

"If we're to live together the rest of our lives," he said almost apologetically, "then I sure as hell don't want you royally pissed at me!" He grinned. He was paying close attention to me.

I stepped back another couple of inches and unfolded my arms. "May I sit down?" I asked. "I feel faint."

"Go ahead," he said, relaxing the gun to his side.

The room was completely still. Outside there was no more storm. No more rain. No more wind. Help would be coming soon. Yet there might not be time! I was inches from my Beretta!

"At some point if I decide to leave you?" I said.

"I'll kill you."

No stranger's face had ever looked more inscrutable. I could see that there was absolutely nothing about him that I cared for. Not a line in his face or the color of his skin, the texture of brows and lashes or the way his nervous eyes rode across every unexpected sound in the cottage. "So it's as simple as that, then?"

"Killing you would not be simple," he explained. "Don't ever misunderstand that about me. There's a bond between you and me. I know there is, but I guarantee that you'll die if you don't come with me. Breaking the bond would cause that. That's what's simple."

He looked bewildered. I didn't move. I watched his eyes partially close. His lips tighten. He casually wiped under his nose, and I could see sweat had darkened the blue of his collar and underarms. He was growing impatient. So was I. I dropped my hands between my knees. It would take no more than a couple of seconds to fall to the floor, reach under the stool and grab my Beretta. Or would he be on top of me before I even got my hand on the gun? Once I had possession, would I have time to warn him before I fired? I had never killed anyone in my life, and all the hours of training at gun school hadn't prepared me for the possibility. I felt dizzy. Saliva came from the corner of my mouth. It tasted like pure salt. I hadn't bargained on vomiting! If I passed out, there would be no hope!

"Make up your mind right now!" he said. "Stacks is waiting!"

"One more thing…" I said. "Are you the mysterious priest then that I've been hearing about? Are you the one who hides his face during the voodoo ceremony?"

"I won't betray the trust of others!" he said defiantly.

I needed time, and while I believed that he was growing weary of my questions, I needed to outsmart the enemy and keep him talking. "Tapest? Did she have to die, too?"

The silence rose up around him like a dark fence. He stared at the ceiling, gritted his teeth and finally said with much anxiety, "Listen to me! My grandfather told me that the brain cancer was already making her a burden to him. Don't you put dogs out of their misery?"

Was I beginning to hallucinate? Had I heard him right? Disgusting and vile, he was. I lowered my head. I really was going to be sick. I bent and dropped my hands to my ankles. It was time for our tryst to be over!

"I think I'm going to faint, Gabe!"

The inches to the floor seemed as long as a football field! I crashed to my knees. He reached out. By then I was in a fetal position and rolling to the right, and I never hesitated to shove the footstool with my elbow. I rammed my hand against the Beretta so hard that I broke a thumbnail back to the quick. With absolute dread, I flipped on my back and grasped the trigger as I brought it to waist level. Gabe raised the Snake Charmer.

"Stop!" I shouted.

I don't remember the loud *ba…rrroom!* But I remember when the hammer of my Beretta moved and the bullet exploded from the firing chamber. I remember the Snake Charmer gliding through the air in front of me as if it had wings. I remember Gabe moaning, *'but I never wanted to kill anyone…'* and then there was his not breathing in the unforgettable silence of the cottage—as if a fire had gone out and brought all the shadows together to make the room dark and still. I remember my eyes pacing the room, my mobility frozen under Gabe's weight. I remember the warm blood from his chest turning cold under my blouse, the taste of it between my lips, of wiping it away with the back of my wrist.

I had only to look at his face to see that he was dead. Slowly with my arms, I pushed his shoulders up. With all my strength—with every part of me, I heaved him into the air. It seemed that he hung there briefly, his mouth a wide yawn and his eyes still open, as if all that they had ever seen was lost forever. And then he hit the floor with a dull thud.

I grabbed the flashlight and left the room. I did not look back. I was suddenly incapable of feeling anything, and before I knew it, I was tumbling down the porch steps into cold water.

CHAPTER 33

With much discouragement and extreme remorse for having taken a life, I followed the path to the north end and soon came out of the darkness to see Stacks Sandover beneath the rigging lights of his cigar boat that was moored at the end of the dock. It looked as if he were loading supplies, so while staying low to the ground, I moved along side the palmetto, aware that it was good cover from the revealing spray of several pole lights. No matter what happened, I knew that I must be cautious and not panic.

It seemed that I had not gone far, when off to my right, my plight suddenly overwhelmed me, for I stood recklessly amid a pitiless carpet of flickering candles surrounding the altar I had seen before! Except for a large white sheet folded and draped across the bottom of the stone slab, nothing else I suspected was there, for I believed that no living animal would dare cross the earth, the leaf covered silt of human blood and bones rendering it inhabitable like those dump sights across America, the land too contaminated there to even set foot upon. I maneuvered around it and climbed the steps to the shack.

How much more remote it seemed, the night conjuring up a new image of the porch, as if it the boards themselves had doubled in size to make it appear larger in the diffused light from the windows. I peered through the panes, and my eyes fell first on Barclay Renaurd lying very still in the far corner. He seemed asleep—I was sure he was—I could see his chest going up and down, the way someone sighs when he is on his back in bed in the middle of the night. I stepped to my left, and strained to look near the door. There was the very still, full-body profile of Drew Greer, the bill of her FBI cap across her eyes like a blindfold, but I wasn't certain whether she was alive or dead. Her hands and feet were bound. My pulse pounded.

My fingers crept to the door handle and hung rigidly there like stalagmites. I stopped cold. Without warning someone was at my side, *someone in a long white robe,* someone staring into my eyes, the dim pallor of recognition growing as something hit my other hand and my Beretta disappeared into the nearby palmetto scrub.

"Allison!"

The barrel of cold metal stunned my ribs. "Please go inside, Kate."

I knew then.

The room was like the inside of a meat freezer, the side wall having been cut to accommodate an air conditioning unit. It was grinding full blast, having many times before cooled the dead, I expect, who had stopped there before their final desecration.

I barely found my voice. "Damn it Allison!"

She arched her brows "I see from the blood on your clothes that you got the upper hand? Poor Gabe. I've never seen him so smitten over anyone! Why he actually loved you, I believe. It made him careless. Stacks will have to do it all now, I suppose," she said. "He'll have to bring those wretched women to me!"

Her voice was strained, and all that Allison Thomason had led me to believe about life, all goodness and kindness and loyalty, seemed impossible to comprehend now, and as if she had stapled her betrayal to my body, I could not hide that I was in pain and grief-stricken. She saw it in my eyes, and for a moment I saw it in hers. Then she knotted her fist.

"This is the very last thing I ever wanted, Kate!" she exclaimed, her eyes drawn to a large serrated knife in a white leather sheath on her belt, and when she shifted her weight from one foot to another, a rattle and pouch spun on her waist like a child's mobile.

I swallowed hard. "You're the priest!"

The rain had returned to shoot at the tin roof like a B.B. gun. She looked up. Even in the gravity of the situation, she gave a slight smile. "I prefer to be addressed as a priestess."

Paul Hanes had been right about Glennie Sparkman's investigation into Allison's activities. How could I have been so far off base? A doctor must never treat his own family member lest he miss the symptoms, my father used to say. Love, friendship and loyalty could be walls to the truth! Lesson well learned, I thought, but maybe I'd never live to test it again! "My god, then Gabe didn't actually kill those poor women, did he?"

"He drugged them and brought them to me. He was my Initiate to the priesthood. He would have taken over some day."

"But to murder them the way you did!"

"Hardly," she said with indifference. "I've saved their souls!" And think of how many good people have lived because of their organs...organs which I have harvested. Think!"

"You didn't have a right!"

"Oh yes I did," she said quickly. "They came before me in my court. I gave them a lecture and then sentenced them to thirty days. But did they learn? A few weeks later the police would haul them in on another prostitution charge. They're the ones I saved! The repeats! But now you and Ms. Greer have forced me to take a different path."

"Damn it, Allison, you and I are like sisters!"

"Yes. Believe me, Kate, none of this bodes well with me either. In fact, when I thought you might die because of those oils that I mixed, I was actually upset about it! All I intended was to warn you away."

A wave of nausea swept my stomach.

"I wasn't positive that Renty saw me in the aromatherapy room," she continued, "until I found out from Bina that he was going to your cottage. Two and two do make four! Of course, Renty only thought that I was going to my office to pick up some papers."

"*You* were at the cottage, too!"

"And at Mrs. Tarteton's the day you returned!" she said. "I was afraid that you might notice my perfume..."

"All these years you've blackmailed Gabe into doing what you wanted him to. All because you believed that he killed Jennifer!"

"Believed? Oh no, my friend, for what it's worth, it was an accident. That whole mess. It would have been bad publicity for the Renaurd family—you know about that, Kate, what with all you've gone through with your own relatives."

"Accident? I don't understand!"

"Gabe and Jennifer got into a shoving match and Jennifer struck her head. Fortunately, Gabe always believed that she died later that night of an embolism. Actually, it wasn't anything like that at all. She took an overdose of Barclay's sleeping pills and went into a coma! I thought it best not to involve the police. Gabe agreed."

It was difficult to look at Allison, her mouth turning over and over, her robe mockingly reminding me of the stranger I was seeing whenever she moved even slightly to the right or left.

"Allison, listen to me…"

"Then Gabe dumped her body off Dragon's Point!" she interrupted. "It was better for everyone to think that she simply had run away, wasn't it? So we had an agreement. He left the island. I kept him out of prison. But I was surprised when eventually he came back. Begged for forgiveness. Wanted a home. Wanted power. I gave all three to him."

"How could you let him live under the horror that he had killed her! How could you!"

Allison seemed not to be paying attention. "It's all very tiresome," she said. "So very long ago. And he didn't live under the horror. He painted his depression and paranoia away…very much like Walter Sickert, a well known artist in the late 1800's who was thought to be Jack the Ripper and had a penchant for painting prostitutes in the nude."

"And what did you do with all of the money that you got from the procurement and sale of the body parts?" I asked.

"You know, it's so easy to get a hidden account in Switzerland," she said. "Soon I hope to own Renaurd Island in my family's name again."

"And you think Holden and Barclay will allow that?"

"But wouldn't Holden be surprised if he knew that it was my dummy corporation that is interested in developing the north end? Something I set up all by myself?"

"You will do that?"

"Oh yes, and I also plan to ruin Careco Industries by linking him to the sale of human growth hormone. His career as a United States senator will be over!"

I heard Drew Greer moan. I prayed that she wouldn't come around, and then her voice died like an old car engine.

Without warning Barclay Renaurd sat up. His eyes flew open. His elbow hit the wall. Allison turned. He grabbed her ankles, yanked hard and like a falling elevator her buttocks hit the floor. Whether Barclay was awake or asleep I couldn't tell, but I understood that I had only moments to make a move. My leg came up. My toe caught Allison's wrist. The Glock landed on the floor. Barclay grabbed it. As I took the knife from her belt, she looked at me in disbelief. And then we couldn't look at each other at all. Barclay had aimlessly fired a bullet into her chest. And then his eyes closed and he sat very still with the Glock dangling from his finger, his head off to one side and his breathing as calm as a sleeping baby.

Outside I could hear the distinct whirl of the Coast Guard siren. Drew raised her head. The color had come back to her face.

I untied her. "We'll get you to a hospital," I said softly when I saw that her jeans were ripped from her waist to her crotch.

"Where's that piss ant Sandover?" she asked, tears filling her eyes. "I want to tell his sorry ass about his goddamn Lilliputian dick." Simply no one was going to steal what little dignity Drew Greer had left.

CHAPTER 34

Friends mean a lot in times of crisis. I didn't even mind Justin McCreary snapping the morning newspaper on top of a palmetto bug that had invaded the kitchen tile at the cottage. "Shit Katie, you're in the rags again!" he said, highly amused.

I glanced at the headline and cringed.

Attorney General Guesswine Slays Serial Killer Accomplice!

My stomach churned. All night Gabe's face had ridden into my sleep like one of the Four Horseman of the Apocalypse...*Death,* proud and triumphant, and yet pathetic and wasted. Poor, poor Gabe! With a kind of revulsion, I was convinced more than ever that he had been misled! And when I thought of Allison, her face was a void, as if it never had existed, her voice a void, too, and I wondered if I ever again would remember the character of her eyes, nose and lips or the tone of her words.

"It mentions Barclay, too," Justin said reading below the byline with Sara Baird's name on it.

I shifted a big plate of donuts to the side of the table but I couldn't eat any of them. Nothing pleased me. "What's Sara say about him?" I asked, politely interested.

Drew brought bacon and eggs to the table. "Yeah. The Bark's my new best buddy," she said. "He's gonna take me on his Harley!"

Justin slurped coffee. "Goddamn it, his shrink says Barclay was in one of his somnambulistic states at the shack. Woke up long enough to attack the nearest thing to him. Says he sure as hell didn't know that it was Allison! I heard he'll get off. That right?"

GHOST RAIN

My knees almost buckled at the mention of her name. I breathed deeply. "Possibly," I said. "A good defense lawyer can do wonders."

"It's a goddamn hoot that Holden was never involved in any of this. I would have laid money that the sleazy son-of-a-bitch was," Justin said. He ran his tongue around the center of the donut and then ate it in three bites. "So it was the tap on the Renaud phones that gave us the last nail in the coffin! Bina helped us get that tap set up, you know. My idea, huh Drew?"

The tap was a surprise to me. It must have shown on my face. So I didn't say anything more and simply waited for an explanation.

"I was going to the island to fill you in, Kate," Drew said finally, toying with the spoon in her coffee. "There had been very revealing conversations between Stacks Sandover and Allison. On the morning that you were at the inn for the last time, she made two other calls. One to a bank in Switzerland where she had been stuffing big bucks, and another, to a teller in charge of a numbered account that she set up and which would have eventually falsely implicated Holden. And by the way, surprisingly, every penny of the Renaud Careco Company is clean."

"Yeah, but our tap revealed that Stacks was bringing in the human growth hormone from South America," Justin said, as he let out a slow belch, "and stashing it at the shack. He and Gabe sold it to a bunch of unscrupulous clinics throughout the East."

"And sometimes used it at Renaud Inn, too…" I surmised. "I suspect that Mrs. Trample-St.Synge paid big bucks for it."

"She'd need a semi of it to inflate that puss of her," Justin said.

Drew laughed. "She bought it innocently, of course."

"The other guests, too," I said.

"And later we weren't too surprised when we actually could confirm that Stacks was selling the harvested body parts from the women who Allison carved up during those voodoo rituals that she and Gabe were holding," Drew said.

"Well, I'm still angry with you for not stopping at the inn before heading to the shack on your own!" I said. "You might have been killed!"

Justin looked hostile. "And carved up like a Sunday chicken and packaged!"

"How could I know?" Drew said though her napkin. "Gabe was at the dock. He lied when he said that he saw you leave the inn and head down the trail. He said he would help me find you, but when we got there, Stacks Sandover tied me up. I figured my life was history!"

"Nonsense," I said. "I'm not letting you go anywhere!"

Justin peered over his half glasses. "Shit, am I reading Sara Baird's feature to you or not? Give a guy a little respect here!"

Drew got up and straddled his lap. His arms circled her, and he read more. "So within minutes, the Coast Guard pulled up and Detective Justin McCreary bravely took Stacks Sandover into custody."

I went over and patted his head. "Bravely? Mmm hmm. Our hero, heh?"

Drew laughed. "As Paul Harvey says, 'And now you know the rest of the story'."

We all looked at each other. No, we didn't know the rest of the story. Nobody did. I went out to the front of the cottage and picked up small hand trimmers that I had left in the middle of an antique wheelbarrow. Suddenly the sky got as dark as mud. The wind had a strange pitch and the air had cooled. Near the tabby path that David and I had built on our knees and with our hands, I walked into a patch of dead flowers that would remain asleep until they received a message to awaken after the last frost and with the warm coming of spring. Behind me the door closed, but then I saw the green of Drew's sleeves as she hung her arms around the porch post.

"Where'd this shitty weather come from?" she asked. "It's going to storm!"

"Mmm hmm. I suspect it's the Ghost Rain. It'll whip the grasses in these marshes flat as hay and then be gone in a flash. And then the sun will be back. But until we get that first drop, I really must cut back these perennials so they'll have a fair chance in the spring. Do you want to help?"

"Remember me? All thumbs?" she said, bounding over beside me. "But here I am!"

We were quiet as our knees reached the ground and the ghosts of old mariners struck up a hard rain that quickly soaked our clothes. We caught each other's eyes as the water clung to the furls in our faces and soaked our clothes.

"You okay, old roomy?" I asked. "Want to go in?"

"Nah!" she said relaxing back. "What's a little bad weather now and then?" And then she looked up. The rain stopped. Drew folded her arms and rocked back. Her eyes held the smile of a child.

978-0-595-37245-4
0-595-37245-7

Printed in the United States
47172LVS00005B/2